CLIVILIUS
WHERE CREATION MEETS INFINITY

© 2024 Nathan Cowdrey. All rights reserved.
First Edition, 13 March 2024
ISBN 978-1-4461-1340-0
Imprint: Lulu.com

Step into Clivilius, where creation meets infinity, and the essence of reality is yours to redefine. Here, existence weaves into a narrative where every decision has consequences, every action has an impact, and every moment counts. In this realm, shaped by the visionary AI CLIVE, inhabitants are not mere spectators but pivotal characters in an evolving drama where the lines between worlds blur.

Guardians traverse the realms of Clivilius and Earth, their journeys igniting events that challenge the balance between these interconnected universes. The quest for resources and the enigma of unexplained disappearances on Earth mirror the deeper conflicts and intricacies that define Clivilius—a world where reality responds to the collective will and individual choices of its Clivilians, revealing a complex interplay of creation, control, and consequence.

In the grand tapestry of Clivilius, the struggle for harmony and the dance of dichotomies play out across a cosmic stage. Here, every soul's journey contributes to the narrative, where the lines between utopia and dystopia, creator and observer, become increasingly fluid. Clivilius is not just a realm to be explored but a reality to be shaped.

Open your eyes. Expand your mind. Experience your new reality. Welcome to Clivilius, where the journey of discovery is not just about seeing a new world but about seeing your world anew.

Also in the Clivilius Series

Paul Smith (1338.209.1 - 1338.211.3)

Paul is a tale of survival, leadership, and the enduring power of family ties in the face of overwhelming odds. It's a story about finding light in the darkness, hope in despair, and the unyielding strength of the human spirit in the most challenging of environments. Join Paul and his family as they navigate the treacherous and transformative landscape of Clivilius, where every decision could mean the difference between survival and obliteration.

Luke Smith (1338.204.1 - 1338.209.2)

Charismatic and thoughtful, yet sporadic and often random. When Luke discovers a mysterious device, he must quickly learn to accept that every action has an impact, and every decision has consequences.

Jamie Greyson (1338.204.1 - 1338.209.3)

Withdrawn and bitter from a troubled youth, Jamie's fractured relationship with Luke faces greater challenges when he finds himself fighting for survival in an unfamiliar world.

Glenda De Bruyn (1338.206.1 - 1338.209.1)

A reputable doctor, aiding an identity known only as "The Fox" to uncover the truth about a deadly government conspiracy, finds herself more determined than ever to resume the search for her father who went missing when she was a child.

Kain Jeffries (1338.207.1 - 1338.211.2)

    Kain Jeffries, of well-known Tasmanian convict heritage, is a young trainee construction worker awaiting the arrival of his first child with fiancee Brianne, when his life is turned upside down. Now, he must throw himself into helping a struggling settlement survive before its too late, and the nightmare consumes him.

Beatrix Cramer (1338.205.1 - 1338.211.6)

    Independent and strong-willed, Beatrix' obsession with stealing and passion for antiques and wild animals make her both a valuable asset and a dangerous liability.

4338.204.1 – 4338.209.3

PAUL SMITH

CLIVILIUS
WHERE CREATION MEETS INFINITY

"When life throws you into a parallel world, don't just stand there. Build something."

\- Paul Smith

4338.204

(23 July 2018)

SERIOUS

4338.204.1

"What the hell did you...?" Claire's voice, sharp and filled with an icy rage, cut through the tense atmosphere of our small, cluttered kitchen. Her words, like daggers, seemed to hang momentarily in the stale air, which was heavy with the scent of last night's unwashed dishes and the lingering aroma of burnt coffee. As her voice trailed off, my phone erupted into a jingle, its cheerful tune striking a surreal contrast against the backdrop of our escalating argument. It was a bizarre juxtaposition that almost seemed out of place, yet there it was, a lifeline thrown amidst the storm of our discontent.

I couldn't help but seize the moment to escape, even if just temporarily, from the relentless barrage of conflict that had become the soundtrack of our lives. Claire's accusations and questions, each one dripping with contempt and laced with derision, seemed to bounce off me as I reached for the phone. It was as though each word she uttered was a reminder of how far we had drifted apart, of how the simple, loving conversations we once shared had morphed into this endless loop of blame and bitterness.

Picking up the phone, I felt a fleeting sense of relief wash over me. It was an escape hatch, a brief respite from the verbal onslaught. Without a word, I turned my back on the kitchen - on Claire and the suffocating atmosphere of our failing relationship - and made my way towards the sanctuary of the bedroom. Each step felt heavy, laden with the weight of unspoken words and unresolved issues that lay between us like a chasm.

As I moved away, I could feel Claire's gaze burning into my back, her harsh words still echoing off the walls, but I chose to ignore them. It wasn't indifference that propelled me forward but a desperate need for a moment of peace, a sliver of space where I could breathe without the oppressive weight of our troubles bearing down on me. The contrast between the cheerful ringtone and the bitter scene I was leaving behind wasn't lost on me; it was a stark reminder of the duality of our lives together, where moments of light were increasingly overshadowed by the encroaching darkness of our discontent.

In the solitude of the bedroom, with the door softly clicked shut behind me, I allowed myself a moment to reflect. The phone call, whatever it was about, had given me a temporary escape, but I knew it was just that - temporary. The issues with Claire, the growing divide between us, they wouldn't just disappear because I walked away. Yet, in that moment, I allowed myself the luxury of avoidance, clinging to the brief respite as a drowning man clings to a lifeline, fully aware that once the call ended, I would have to face the storm once more.

"Hey, stranger," Luke's voice crackled through the phone line, slicing through the lingering tension that clung to me like a second skin.

"Hey, you," I responded, a smile unwittingly curving my lips for the first time in what felt like an eternity. The sound of my brother's voice acted as an instant balm to my weary mind, momentarily clearing the fog of war that the recent conflict with Claire had left in its wake. "What's up?"

The casualness of his next question caught me off guard. "You feel like flying to Hobart tomorrow morning?" Luke asked, as if he was proposing a quick hop to the local café and not across states.

"I'd love to. But I have work and—" I began, the words trailing off. The reality of my situation, with its obligations and constraints, quickly seeped back in, dampening the brief flicker of excitement his question had sparked.

"You can do your work from here," Luke interjected, his voice carrying a note of persuasion that made me pause. It was a tempting offer, one that appealed to the part of me yearning for an escape from the current drudgery of my life.

"I suppose..." I found myself saying, a hint of surprise in my own voice at the realisation that I was actually considering it. "But I can't afford it, especially at this late notice. Besides, I don't have any annual leave left."

The conversation took a turn then, as Luke's voice softened, imbuing his next words with a heaviness that demanded my full attention. "Paul," he said, my name infused with an emotional weight, "I need you... I'm having a few... a few issues."

There was a brief silence, a moment suspended in time where the gravity of his words sank in. I quickly pulled the phone away from my ear, covering my mouth with my hand to muffle the involuntary snorts of laughter that bubbled up. Despite the seriousness of his tone, I could sense the playfulness beneath his words. Luke was good at many things, but his attempts at emotional manipulation, a tactic we had both tried and failed at with each other over the years, still needed work.

It was too much. Even in the midst of my own turmoil, the absurdity of the situation—the idea that after all these years, Luke thought he could still pull one over on me—struck me as hilariously improbable.

"Oh, shut up!" came Luke's laughter through the phone, a clear concession that his ruse had been nothing more than an attempt to persuade me into action.

Listening to Luke break, I couldn't help but erupt into a fit of laughter. My brother, with his easy-going nature and light-hearted approach to life, always crumbled so effortlessly under the weight of his own jokes. It was one of those endearing qualities that made him who he was, and I cherished that about him, even in moments like these.

But then, something unexpected happened. The line went silent, void of the usual banter and laughter we shared. It was an abrupt shift that caught me off guard, the sudden absence of sound feeling almost deafening. Luke's silence wasn't just a pause; it felt like a void, a stark contrast to the joviality that had just filled the air.

"So, what are the issues you're having then?" I managed to say, pushing myself to move past the laughter. I took a deep breath, trying to steady the residual chuckles that threatened to bubble up again. But my attempt at composure was fleeting at best. The laughter surged back with a vengeance, more intense than before, as if it were determined to undermine the seriousness of the moment.

"I've already bought you a plane ticket," Luke's voice cut through my laughter, clear and firm.

The words hit me like a splash of cold water, shocking me into silence. My laughter turned into helpless snorts, a physical reaction I couldn't control even if I wanted to.

"Paul, I'm serious," Luke insisted, his tone carrying an edge I rarely heard from him.

"You? Serious? Yeah, right!" I scoffed, unable to resist the temptation to poke fun at him. It was our way, always pushing and pulling in jest. But Luke wasn't having any of it this time.

"For fuck's sake, Paul, would you just focus, please!" His snap was a sharp contrast to the light-hearted brother I knew. It was a tone that demanded attention, a rarity from Luke that signalled the seriousness of whatever he was dealing with.

"Okay, okay," I relented, my laughter finally subsiding as I sensed the shift in his mood. The remnants of my argument with Claire had left me feeling emotionally sapped, a hollowed-out shell with little capacity for seriousness, especially when it came to Luke's often whimsical concerns.

"I've sent the e-ticket to your phone," he continued, a hint of exasperation in his voice.

"Oh. I'll... I'll check," I said, still struggling to wrap my head around the idea. *Luke, the eternal penny-pincher, splurging on a plane ticket for me?* It was out of character, to say the least. Generous, yes, but in a way that always seemed to have limits.

As I checked my phone and saw the confirmation of the ticket, a wave of sobering reality washed over me. "Yeah. Got them," I said, my voice losing its earlier lightness. My forehead creased with concern as the implications of his actions began to dawn on me.

"What's going on?" The question came out more as a whisper, a mixture of confusion and concern. Luke's sudden seriousness, his uncharacteristic generosity, it all pointed to something deeper, something that went beyond our usual brotherly antics. The laughter had faded, replaced by a growing unease as I awaited his explanation, bracing myself for what was to come.

"It's serious, Paul. Jamie and I are having some major issues and I really need a bit of support right now. You know I don't really have anyone else here," Luke's voice came through, laden with a weight that immediately shifted the atmosphere of our conversation. The levity of moments ago seemed like a distant memory now, replaced by a tangible sense of urgency.

"I know you don't," I found myself saying, the reality of Luke's isolation hitting me with renewed clarity. The distance between us, usually bridged by light-hearted banter and the occasional visit, now felt more pronounced than ever. "But I really can't afford these tickets, or taking time off work." The words felt hollow even as they left my mouth, a feeble attempt to cling to practical concerns in the face of Luke's evident distress.

"You don't need to worry about any of it. I'll cover your expenses, and you don't need to worry about paying me back," he said, his voice firm and reassuring.

I found myself sitting on the edge of the bed, the phone pressed against my ear as I absorbed the gravity of his words. Luke's generosity wasn't a common occurrence. It was a gesture reserved for moments of genuine need, a testament to the depth of his current predicament. The last time he made such an offer was several years back, when he and Jamie had insisted on paying for my flight over for Christmas. I remembered how touched I'd been by the gesture, fully aware of the financial sacrifice it represented for them at the time. Despite their better financial situation, Luke and Jamie were not the type to throw money around without careful consideration.

The memory of that Christmas, filled with warmth and a sense of belonging, contrasted sharply with the current scenario. It wasn't just about the money or the flight; it was about what these gestures symbolised. Luke was in trouble, reaching out across the distance that separated us, asking for help in the most direct way he knew how.

"Are you sure we can't just talk about this over the phone?" I found myself asking, the words laced with a sense of desperation. The reality of my situation was pressing in on me from all sides. With only a handful of annual leave days tucked away, the thought of dipping into that precious reserve was daunting. My affection for Luke was boundless, yet the complexities of my own life, the intricate dance of family obligations and personal responsibilities, couldn't be ignored. The thought of the kids coming home from their grandparents' place in a few days, was a beacon of light in the chaos, a moment I was genuinely looking forward to in the midst of everything else.

"I'm sure," Luke's reply came, firm and unwavering. "It'll only be a couple of days. I promise." The certainty in his voice was a double-edged sword; it cut through my hesitations, yet the implications of his insistence cast a long shadow over my trepidations.

I took a deep breath, the air filling my lungs as I sought to find a semblance of peace in the decision I was about to make. The room around me felt suddenly too small, the walls echoing the tumultuous emotions that swirled within. "Fine," I said at last, the word heavy on my tongue. "I'll leave Broken Hill in an hour and drive to Adelaide."

"Thank you so much," Luke's gratitude came through the phone, imbued with a depth of sincerity that resonated within me. It was a rare tone for him, reserved for moments of true gratitude. "I'll see you tomorrow then," he added quickly, the finality in his voice leaving no room for further discussion.

He hung up before I could muster a response, leaving me with a silence that felt both oppressive and liberating. The decision was made, irrevocable in the wake of Luke's swift goodbye. It was a commitment now, one that would see me driving through the vast expanse that lay between Broken Hill and Adelaide, a journey that symbolised so much more than mere distance.

In the quiet that followed, a myriad of thoughts raced through my mind. The anticipation of seeing my kids clashed with the knowledge of the support Luke needed, a tumultuous mix of emotions that left me feeling both drained and determined. The prospect of reuniting with my brother under such strained circumstances was daunting, yet the underlying current of familial loyalty, the unspoken bond that tied us together, propelled me forward.

Knowing my mind was already frayed at the edges from the earlier confrontations with Claire, and not feeling up to enduring another verbal skirmish, I approached the bedroom door with a sense of trepidation. My intention was not to spy, but rather to gauge the atmosphere outside my temporary refuge before deciding whether to venture out. Slowly, with a cautious hand, I nudged the door open just a sliver, creating a narrow aperture through which the sounds of the house could reach me more clearly.

Claire's voice, sharp and unmistakable, filtered through the gap. "That bastard! I don't know why I'm still with him, really! He's so precious." The words struck me like a physical blow, each syllable laden with disdain and frustration. There was a brief pause, a momentary lull in her tirade, before she resumed. "In the bedroom. Sulking." The disdain in her voice was palpable, a verbal dagger meant to wound.

A wave of hurt washed over me as I stood there, hidden behind the partially opened door. It was not the first time Claire had vented to her sister about me, but hearing her words so directly felt like a fresh wound each time. My brow furrowed, a reflection of the inner turmoil her words evoked. It was a painful reminder of the chasm that had formed between us, a gap that seemed to widen with every passing day.

Taking a deep breath, I tried to steady my swirling thoughts. Claire and her sister had a way of amplifying each other's negativity, a toxic synergy that often left me feeling like the villain in my own home. This moment of eavesdropping, unintended as it was, served as a stark illustration of the environment I was living in. It underscored a truth I had been trying to ignore: my presence in the house had become just another thread in the fabric of our shared discontent.

The realisation that stepping away, even temporarily, might offer a reprieve from the constant tension was unexpectedly liberating. The prospect of visiting Luke, of exchanging this atmosphere of bitterness for one of brotherly camaraderie, even for a brief period, suddenly seemed like a lifeline. It was an opportunity to recharge, to find solace in the company of someone who knew me not as a "bastard" or a "sulker," but simply as Paul.

With a newfound resolve, I gently closed the bedroom door, the soft click of the latch marking my decision. Moving with purpose, I began to pack an overnight bag and my backpack, each item I selected a step towards reclaiming a sense of self amidst the gloom of my domestic life. The task was mechanical, yet each fold of clothing, each carefully chosen necessity, felt like an act of defiance—a declaration of my need for space, for understanding, for a respite from the relentless cycle of accusation and defence that had come to define my marriage.

As I zipped the bag closed, the finality of the act was not lost on me. This trip was not just a visit; it was a necessary escape, a chance to breathe, to recalibrate. The distance it would put between Claire and me, both physically and emotionally, was a necessary boundary, a space in which I could begin to sift through the tangled web of feelings and frustrations that had accumulated like so much debris in the aftermath of our storms.

With my bag in hand, I stepped away from the door, from Claire's words, and from the home that felt less and less like a sanctuary with each passing day. The journey ahead, fraught with its own uncertainties, nonetheless promised a reprieve from the turmoil. In that moment, the prospect of brotherly solace, of understanding and acceptance, felt like a beacon guiding me towards a much-needed haven.

Not wanting to confront Claire in her current state, or worse, escalate the situation with my departure, I opted for a quieter exit. The bedroom window, an unconventional route under normal circumstances, now presented itself as my best option for a discreet escape. With careful movements, I eased the window open, the cool evening air brushing against my face as I leaned out, surveying the drop. My bags, a silent testament to my resolve, landed with a soft thud on the grass below.

The ledge was not particularly high—our house was modest, a single-story structure that had always felt more cozy than cramped. However, the prospect of navigating the descent without landing in the thorny embrace of the rose bushes below presented a challenge. The bushes, more thorns than blooms at this time of year, seemed almost to bristle in anticipation of my misstep.

Closing my eyes for a moment, I gathered my courage. "Right, here we go," I murmured to myself, the words a whispered mantra in the quiet of the evening. My heart hammered in my chest, not from fear of the physical act of jumping, but from the symbolic weight of what this act represented—a leap away from confrontation, from the pain and misunderstanding that had become all too familiar.

As I perched there, legs dangling, poised between the safety of the known and the uncertainty of escape, the sudden intrusion of Claire's voice shattered the momentary calm. "Paul! What in the name of fuck are you doing hanging out the window?" Her screech, laden with disbelief and anger, cut through the silence, the phone still pressed to her ear as if she couldn't bear to put her current conversation on pause even for this absurd tableau.

As I awkwardly turned my body back towards the bedroom, my hands, slick with nervous perspiration, lost their precarious hold on the windowsill. The momentary shock that flashed across my face morphed into a grimace of disbelief and embarrassment as I felt my centre of gravity betray me. My body, trim yet disproportionately lanky, succumbed to the unforgiving pull of gravity. The fall, though brief, seemed to stretch into a slow-motion descent into ignominy.

The landing was anything but graceful. The sharp, biting sting of thorns tearing through fabric and flesh marked my unceremonious introduction to the rose bushes below. As I flailed, attempting to mitigate the damage, the sound of snapping stems punctuated my fall, a chorus to the cacophony of rustling leaves and my own suppressed curses. The ground met me with a thud that knocked the wind out of me, leaving me momentarily dazed amongst the floral wreckage.

Gritting my teeth, I pushed myself to my feet, a silent prayer of thanks escaping me for the small mercy of having worn jeans. The denim had borne the brunt of the assault, offering some protection to my legs. My arms, however, exposed and vulnerable, bore the brunt of my ill-fated escape attempt, marked by scratches and punctures where the thorns had made their claim.

"Paul!?" Claire's voice, tinged with a mix of anger and concern, reached me from the window above. But the reservoir of patience required to engage in another round of explanations was decidedly empty. With a single-minded determination, I grabbed my bags, the thorns and leaves that now adorned them a testament to my ordeal, and made a hasty retreat towards the car.

The vehicle became my sanctuary as I threw myself and my botanical passengers inside, the engine roaring to life under my urgent command. As I reversed down the driveway, the compulsion to avoid Claire's gaze warred with an inevitable curiosity. Succumbing to it, I caught sight of her head protruding from the window, her features contorted in what I could only assume was a barrage of insults aimed at my hastily retreating form.

"Holy shit," the words slipped from me, a whisper of disbelief at the surreal nature of my departure. A short distance from the house, I pulled over, the adrenaline beginning to ebb, leaving a cocktail of pain and relief in its wake. Taking a moment to assess the damage, I gingerly explored the minor injuries with my fingertips, the stinging reminders of my hasty exit.

Once my heartbeat had returned to something resembling normalcy, and the initial shock of the escape had dulled to a manageable throb of discomfort, I set off again. The road to Adelaide stretched out before me, a long journey that promised ample time for reflection.

OUTBACK HIGHWAY

4338.204.2

The rhythmic hum of the tires against the dark outback highway provided a monotonous soundtrack to my thoughts as I drove. The vast, unending stretch of road ahead, illuminated only by the headlights of my car, mirrored the tangled web of thoughts swirling in my mind. It was almost an hour into the drive when my thoughts, unbidden, circled back to the phone conversation I had with Luke earlier.

What is Luke up to? The question seemed to echo in the confines of the car, blending with the low hum of the engine. Luke's words had been laced with an uncharacteristic seriousness, hinting at depths of dissatisfaction and unrest within him that I hadn't fully appreciated before. Despite his tendency towards spontaneity and his somewhat outlandish life choices, there was an underlying current of isolation and longing that seemed to pervade his existence in Tasmania. The thought of him feeling unfulfilled in his relationship with Jamie, coupled with his self-imposed isolation from the rest of our family, weighed heavily on me. Yet, despite these concerns, a small smile found its way to my lips as I thought about my younger brother.

Luke, with his spontaneous antics and unpredictable nature, had always been a source of worry for me. The fear that one day I would receive a call informing me of some tragic fate befalling him was a constant, unwelcome guest in my thoughts. Yet, this fear was tempered by the memories of the bond we shared, a bond that, despite distance and differences, remained unbroken.

As I drove through the night, my smile broadened with the flood of memories from our past. Our differences, stark as they were, had never been enough to drive a wedge between us. Indeed, these differences often served as the foundation for the countless debates and disagreements that peppered our interactions. Yet, no matter how heated our discussions became, our anger was always short-lived. The resilience of our brotherly bond ensured that one of us would inevitably find humour in our disagreement, leading to laughter and reconciliation.

Sometimes, when the drama of my own marriage was too much to bear, I longed to go back to those simpler times, before the complexities of marriage and adulthood had ensnared me in their relentless grip. A time when Luke and I, free from the burdens that now weighed heavily upon us, lived our lives with a sense of invincibility that only youth can bestow.

But those days were long gone. Luke, my little brother, had grown into his own man, forging a life distinct and separate from the one we once shared. His decision to buy me plane tickets, no questions asked, signalled an urgency that I couldn't ignore. Something was amiss, something serious. Despite Luke's penchant for what others might call recklessness, I knew better. Beneath his wild exterior lay a mind that was always calculating, always a few steps ahead. Luke's craziness was never without purpose, his actions always cushioned by a meticulously crafted safety net.

Yet, as I reflected on our conversation, a sense of unease took root in my mind. Luke's voice had carried a weight, a tension that was unfamiliar to me. It was as if he was teetering on the brink of something, standing at the edge of a precipice from which there might be no return. The thought chilled me. Could it be that this time was different? Was Luke about to embark on a path that would lead him into real danger, the kind from which even his well-laid plans could not protect him?

I let out a heavy sigh, allowing my memories to drift back through the years. Visions of our shared past flitted across my mind's eye – the adventures, the misadventures, and the countless times Luke had been the one to pull me back from the edge. Despite the doubts that occasionally clouded my judgment, deep down, I knew my brother. His actions, however unconventional, were never without reason. Luke had a knack for navigating through life's chaos with an agility that I often envied. More often than not, it was he who came to my rescue, extricating me from the latest quagmire I had found myself in.

The memory of that chaotic morning brought a light laugh to my lips, a welcome distraction from the heaviness that had settled over me during the tedious drive. The situation had been absurd: there I was, clad only in my dressing gown, the cool morning air prickling against my skin, locked out of my own home. The dog, oblivious to the pandemonium it had unleashed, had somehow managed to disturb a wasp nest, turning our small, enclosed yard into a buzzing war zone. With the yard surrounded by impenetrable brick walls, my only hope of escape—or re-entry, rather—had seemed to lie through the laundry window.

In hindsight, the plan was doomed from the start. My attempt at breaking in was nothing short of disastrous. But in that moment of desperation, I hadn't seen any other choice. The ordeal had left me with a bloodied finger, hastily bandaged with the tie of my dressing gown, amidst the backdrop of a broken window and an air thick with the angry hum of wasps.

The silver lining, if it could be called that, was the presence of my phone, miraculously left in the pocket of my dressing gown. A quick, frantic call had summoned Luke to the scene. I remember the relief that washed over me at the sight of him, spare key in hand, ready to rescue me from my plight. His arrival had felt like a cavalry charge, cutting through the absurdity and danger of the situation with the promise of relief.

Luke's reaction upon finding me in such a state had been to laugh. Not a mocking laugh, but one of genuine amusement, the kind that acknowledged the ridiculousness of the situation without diminishing the distress it had caused me. And somehow, that laugh had been exactly what I needed. It had cut through the tension, the pain, and the embarrassment, reminding me that sometimes, life's most chaotic moments can also be its most memorable.

Smiling at the memory, the darkness of the outback road ahead seemed a little less daunting. The recollection of Luke's laughter and the lightness it had brought to a dire situation served as a reminder of the resilience of our bond.

As the distance continued to unfurl beneath the tires of my car, my thoughts delved deeper into the tapestry of memories that defined my relationship with Luke. Among the laughter and the shared escapades, there lay a foundational bedrock of mutual support and understanding that had been forged in the fires of our challenging upbringing. Our childhood, far from idyllic, was a patchwork of moments that tested our resilience, our strength, and ultimately, our bond as brothers.

Luke, with his unyielding optimism and indefatigable spirit, often bore the brunt of our circumstances. Observing him navigate through the trials we faced, I was perpetually in awe of his ability to remain undaunted, his light never dimmed by the shadows that sought to envelop us. It was this very resilience, this unwavering determination to rise above every setback, that became the beacon guiding me through my own moments of doubt and despair.

In the silent companionship of those long-gone days, a silent pact was formed between us. A vow, unspoken yet understood, that when the world sought to weigh us down, we would be each other's anchor, each other's north star. I resolved, with a conviction as deep as the bond we shared, that whenever Luke called out for me, I would answer. I would be there, steadfast and unyielding, a bulwark against whatever storms might rage against him. No matter what.

Perhaps, as I navigated the dark road that stretched before me, that time had indeed arrived. The undercurrent of urgency in Luke's voice, the subtle tremors of vulnerability beneath his usually unshakeable exterior, heralded a call to arms. It was a call I was prepared to answer, not out of obligation, but out of a deep-seated sense of loyalty and love for the brother who had stood by me through thick and thin.

The sudden appearance of movement in the periphery of my vision snapped me out of the deep well of thoughts I had been immersed in. "Shit!" The exclamation tore from my lips as my reflexes kicked in, hands gripping the steering wheel tighter as I jammed the brakes. The car shuddered beneath me, the ABS system pulsating through the pedal under my foot as it fought to maintain control and bring the vehicle to a stop without skidding on the lonely outback highway.

In the tense moments that followed, a dazed kangaroo, caught in the high beam lights of my car, bounded erratically across the road. Its movements were unpredictable, a dance of fear and confusion illuminated by the stark white of the headlights. My heart raced, pounding against my ribcage as I watched, helpless to do anything but hope it avoided a collision with my car, and make its way safely across. With a final, frantic hop, the kangaroo veered off, disappearing into the thick brush that bordered the road. A wave of relief washed over me, the tight knot of panic in my stomach unwinding as the immediate danger passed.

"Bloody 'roos!" I found myself yelling into the emptiness of the car, an attempt to dispel the residual adrenaline that coursed through my veins. Pulling off to the side of the road, I took a moment to collect myself, my breathing still ragged from the scare. It was in this moment of forced pause that I glanced at my phone, only to be greeted by the digital evidence of Claire's fury—a never-ending barrage of missed calls.

A feeling of relief, profound and enveloping, swept over me as I realised the wisdom in my earlier decision to switch the phone to 'do not disturb' mode for the drive. The thought of dealing with Claire's anger, especially now, felt like a weight too heavy to bear. Grateful for the temporary reprieve from the storm awaiting me at home, I pushed aside any lingering guilt about the ignored calls.

Determined not to let the incident—or the missed calls—derail my journey, I returned my attention to the road. With a renewed sense of caution, I resumed my drive at a slightly reduced speed, the darkness of the night enveloping the car once more. The encounter with the kangaroo served as a stark reminder of the unpredictability of the road ahead, both literally and metaphorically.

4338.205

(24 July 2018)

TAKEOFF

4338.205.1

The transition from the solid ground of the airport to the transient world of the airplane always felt like stepping through a portal to me. The young flight attendant, with her practiced smile and graceful efficiency, served as the gatekeeper to this other realm. As she took my boarding pass, her fingers tracing over the details as if to confirm my passage, I couldn't help but feel a mixture of anticipation and relief. Her smile, bright and unwavering, offered a momentary respite from the swirling thoughts that had accompanied me to the airport.

"Welcome, Mr. Smith. Your seat is just down on the left," she directed with a tone that managed to blend professionalism with warmth. Navigating the narrow aisle of the plane, my backpack felt like a cumbersome companion, its bulkiness a stark reminder of the physical and metaphorical baggage I was carrying.

The aisle of the airplane transformed into a microcosm of life itself, each passenger absorbed in their own little dramas and rituals. The young child, defiant in the face of order, his refusal to settle into his seat, mirrored my own internal resistance to the tumultuous events of my life. The plump woman, her sudden urge to retrieve a donut, a whimsical yet poignant reminder of the small comforts we seek in times of stress. And the elderly gentleman, his gratitude for a small act of assistance, a reminder of the enduring strength of human connection.

Each interaction, each pause in my journey to my seat, felt imbued with a deeper significance, a reflection of the myriad ways in which our lives intersect with those of others, often in the most unexpected of ways.

Finally reaching my seat, I manoeuvred myself into the window position, a preference born out of a desire to find solitude amidst the communal experience of flight. The window seat offered a buffer from the world, a small sanctuary where I could retreat into my thoughts without interruption.

The initial hum of the engines had always been a comforting prelude to takeoff for me, a signal of the start of a journey, an escape from the present into the realm of the skies. My smile, a rare moment of contentment amidst the turmoil of recent events, faded as quickly as it had appeared when the engines ceased their reassuring roar, replaced by an unsettling silence punctuated by the flicker of cabin lights. It was an unwelcome reminder that, no matter how far you fly, you're never truly free from the unexpected.

"Ladies and gentlemen," came the calm voice of a young woman through the sound system, her words slicing through the quiet unease that had begun to settle over the cabin. The announcement, while delivered with a professionalism meant to reassure, only served to anchor my spirits further to the ground. A minor mechanical fault, the captain's words relayed with a practiced calm that belied the disruption it caused to our plans. The promise of a short delay did little to ease the tension that began to thread its way through the passengers.

I sighed inwardly, a reflection of the resignation that settled over me. Flying, with its unique blend of anticipation and liberation, had always been an experience I cherished. Yet, here I was, confined not by the skies but by the tarmac beneath us, a prisoner of circumstance and machinery.

The abrupt clunk of the tray table beside me shattered the last vestiges of my daydream, a jarring intrusion into the quiet bubble I had cocooned myself in. My eyes, which had drifted closed in a futile attempt to retreat from the current reality, snapped open, drawn to the source of the disturbance.

"Sorry, mate," came the apologetic murmur from the man beside me. It was only then that I realised the seats next to me were now occupied. The presence of strangers in my immediate space, previously a buffer against the world, felt like an additional layer to the mild claustrophobia induced by the unexpected delay.

The situation, a minor inconvenience in the grand scheme of things, nonetheless felt emblematic of the larger disarray that seemed to permeate my life at the moment. Each plan, each expectation, no matter how carefully laid or eagerly anticipated, seemed subject to the whims of fate, leaving me perpetually off-balance, searching for solid ground in a world determined to keep me adrift.

Yet, in this moment of introspection, surrounded by fellow passengers each absorbed in their own reactions to the delay, I found a reluctant kinship. We were all, in our way, navigating the uncertainties of life, whether they played out in the confines of an airplane cabin or the wider world beyond. The realisation, while small comfort, offered a perspective that I clung to as we waited for the resolution of our collective pause, a reminder that sometimes, the journey is as much about the unexpected detours as it is about the destination.

The intermittent crackle before the young woman's voice filled the cabin once more served as a prelude to the news none of us wanted to hear. "Ladies and gentlemen. Your attention please..." Her words, though delivered with a professionalism and calm that was almost comforting, couldn't mask the frustration that bubbled up within me. The announcement of the engineer's delay, while understandable, added another layer of angst to an already trying journey. Her pleasant voice was a small consolation, a silver lining in the cloud of another delay that now hung over us.

Resigned to the extended wait, my thoughts turned to Luke. It was important to keep him informed, to manage expectations on both ends. The act of pulling out my phone and typing out the text was almost mechanical, a routine gesture in the modern playbook of delays and disappointments:

7:00AM Paul: *Flight delayed 45mins. Let you know if longer. See you soon.*

The minutes that followed, marked by the absence of a reply, saw my concern inching steadily upward. Each additional message I sent felt like a pebble thrown into a well, waiting in vain for the echo of a splash that never came:

7:05AM Paul: *Did you get my message??*
7:36AM Paul: *Luke!?*

The subsequent announcement that the aircraft had been cleared for departure was a relief, a beacon of progress in the stagnant pool of delay. Yet, my relief was tempered by the silence from Luke. The final message I sent before powering down my phone was a blend of anticipation and a trace of worry:

7:41AM Paul: *Taking off! See you soon lil bro*

As the plane finally began its rumble down the runway, accelerating towards the sky, I allowed myself a moment to sink back into my seat, the headrest a welcome cradle for my weariness. The weight of my eyelids became increasingly difficult to resist, the events of the morning—a microcosm of the broader chaos that seemed to define my life recently—taking their toll.

With the steady hum of the aircraft as my lullaby, I leaned into the promise of a brief escape from the whirlwind of emotions and concerns. My mind, however, remained partially anchored to the world below by thoughts of Luke and the uncertainty of what awaited at the end of this flight. The act of closing my eyes was not just a physical response to exhaustion but a conscious decision to find respite, however fleeting, in the midst of turbulence, both literal and metaphorical.

As the plane ascended, leaving the world's troubles behind, I drifted towards the edge of sleep, a precarious balance between the need for rest and the undercurrent of anticipation for the reunion with my brother. The journey ahead promised not just a change in geography but a step into a familiar yet unpredictable chapter in the ongoing saga of family, loyalty, and the ties that bind.

❖

As I stood by the arrival gate, scanning the crowd for familiar faces, the sight of Jamie waving caught my attention. My hand lifted almost automatically in response, but my eyes continued their search, looking for Luke. The absence of his presence in the bustling crowd left a hollow feeling, an expectation unmet.

"Where's Luke?" I asked Jamie, my voice laced with a hint of confusion and concern as I approached. Jamie's response, delivered with a sour expression that seemed out of place in the midst of our greeting, did little to ease the growing sense of unease.

"At home cooking eggs," Jamie said, the words stark in their simplicity yet heavy with an undercurrent of tension.

The casualness of the activity clashed with the gravity of my expectations, creating a dissonance that was hard to shake off.

"Oh," was all I could manage, the disappointment evident in my voice. Luke's aversion to driving was well-known to me, yet the fact that he hadn't made the effort to come to the airport felt like a slight. After all, it was his insistence, his urgency, that had prompted this trip in the first place. The thought that he would delegate the task of picking me up to Jamie, leaving us to navigate the awkwardness of our limited acquaintance alone, was frustrating.

The car ride home loomed ahead, a journey I anticipated with a sense of reluctance. My relationship with Jamie was cordial at best, defined more by our mutual connection to Luke than any direct bond between us. The thought of being confined in a car, trying to navigate a conversation without the buffer of Luke's presence, was not appealing.

More than that, the situation underscored the seriousness of the issues between Luke and Jamie. Luke's decision to fly me down, a gesture that spoke volumes about his state of mind, now felt even more significant in his absence. The implications of being thrust into the middle of their relationship troubles, without the immediate support of Luke, left me feeling out of my depth. It wasn't that I disliked Jamie, but the dynamic of our interaction, set against the backdrop of Luke's unspoken pleas for help, cast a shadow over the reunion.

"You ready then?" Jamie's question pulled me back from my thoughts, his tone a mix of readiness and a subtle hint of impatience as he turned towards the airport exit.

"Have to collect my suitcase," I responded, my voice trailing off slightly as I glanced toward the baggage claim area.

Jamie paused, a look of confusion briefly crossing his face. "Suitcase?" he echoed, his nose wrinkling in what seemed like a mixture of surprise and curiosity. It was a small gesture, but it underscored the awkwardness of our interaction, the gap in understanding between us. "How long are you here for again?"

"Only two nights," I added quickly, a hint of defensiveness creeping into my voice. The realisation hit me then—Luke hadn't sent me the return tickets yet. A pang of anxiety knotted in my stomach at the thought. *Had I assumed too much about the length of my stay?* The oversight seemed to loom larger in the space between Jamie's question and my attempt at a casual response.

"So, why the suitcase?" Jamie pressed on, the chuckle that followed his question lightening the momentary tension. It was a fair question, one that, under different circumstances, I might have found amusing myself.

"It's more of an overnight bag, really..." I offered, trying to downplay my over-preparedness. The distinction felt trivial, yet I clung to it, hoping to bridge the gap of misunderstanding with a semblance of humour.

"Fair enough," Jamie conceded, his demeanour shifting to one of acceptance. "I'll wait over there for you," he added, gesturing towards a sparse row of plastic chairs set against the backdrop of the airport's expansive windows. The view into the carpark beyond seemed a mundane detail, yet in that moment, it represented a brief respite from the undercurrent of tension that had marked our conversation.

Grateful for the momentary pause, I made my way to the carousel. Thankfully, it didn't leave me waiting long. The sight of my bag, more an oversized reminder of my hastily packed anxieties than an actual necessity for the trip, was a small relief. As I collected it, the weight of it in my hand was a tangible connection to the world I'd left behind, a world that seemed increasingly distant with each passing moment.

Returning to where Jamie waited, the bag in tow felt like more than just carrying a piece of luggage; it was a symbol of the complexities I was bringing with me, the unresolved tensions and unspoken expectations that hovered just beneath the surface of this trip. The walk back to Jamie, each step a mix of anticipation and uncertainty, was a small journey in itself, a prelude to the larger, more daunting task of navigating the days ahead with Luke and whatever challenges he had prepared for us.

Following Jamie through the parking lot felt like navigating an unfamiliar terrain, despite the mundane setting. When we reached the parking pay machine, and I attempted to contribute, Jamie's refusal of my coins was both a dismissal and a statement, a subtle reinforcement of the unspoken dynamics between us.

"Don't worry about it," he insisted, his voice carrying an edge of finality that left no room for argument. Yet, in a silent act of defiance or perhaps solidarity, I pushed the coins into his jeans pocket anyway. It was a small gesture, but it felt important—a tangible expression of my willingness to share the burden, however minor it might be in the grand scheme of things.

Standing back, I took the opportunity to really look at Jamie, to search for any sign that he was as entangled in the web of Luke's problems as I was. But there was nothing. He seemed entirely unflustered, a startling contrast to the turmoil that churned within me. If Jamie was aware of the storm brewing around Luke, he masked it with an expertise that left me feeling even more isolated with my concerns.

The act of climbing into the passenger seat of Jamie's white Mazda was like stepping into another chapter of this unfolding drama, one where I was both a participant and a spectator. The bitter taste of anxiety was a reminder of my own apprehensions about the visit, magnified by Luke's cryptic messages and now, Jamie's apparent nonchalance.

As Jamie started the car, the engine's vibration seemed to resonate with my own unease. The anticipation of the drive, coupled with the uncertainty of what awaited at its end, coiled tightly within me. *This is going to be a long drive*, I thought, a silent acknowledgment of the emotional and psychological distance we would need to traverse.

Opening the window, I sought solace in the cool, fresh Tasmanian air, a brief respite from the stifling atmosphere of apprehension that had enveloped me since my arrival. The air, crisp and invigorating, offered a momentary escape, a fleeting sense of freedom from the weight of the unknown that lay ahead.

INTEGRITY

4338.205.2

The moment the car halted in front of the imposing gates that barred further access to the property, I found myself reacting almost instinctively. My hand reached for the door, eager to escape the confines of the car and the weight of the silence that had settled between Jamie and me during the drive. The gates, marking the threshold to Luke's world, seemed more like barriers to a realm brimming with unspoken tensions and unresolved issues.

Drawing in a deep breath, I tried to steel myself for what lay ahead. Jamie had made an effort to engage in conversation during the trip, a task I could tell wasn't easy for him either. My responses, however, had been curt, limited to single-word answers. The fear of inadvertently stepping into a minefield of drama had kept me on edge, turning the forty-minute drive into what felt like an eternity.

When we arrived, my reluctance to let Jamie handle my bag stemmed from a deep-seated discomfort with anyone meddling with my personal belongings. It was a quirk, perhaps, but one that felt increasingly pronounced in moments of stress. Despite the tight knot of tension in my stomach, I forced myself to relinquish control, to allow Jamie to take the bag from the boot. It was a small concession, but one that felt significant in my current state of unease.

Stepping inside the house, the immediate buzz that greeted us—courtesy of Duke and Henri, the two Shih Tzus—offered a brief distraction from the apprehension that had been my constant companion. Jamie's swift action to shoo the dogs away from the door was a familiar scene, a slice of domesticity that brought a brief smile to my face.

"Hey, Paul!" Luke's cheerful greeting, a distinct contrast to the tension I had braced myself for, momentarily disarmed me as I stepped into the open-plan living space. The warmth of his voice did little to quell the mix of emotions swirling within me—relief, confusion, and a lingering sense of apprehension.

"Why didn't you come to the airport?" The question slipped out, tinted with a hint of disappointment I couldn't fully mask. Luke's presence at the airport had been an expectation, one that had gone unmet, adding a layer of distress to an already fraught situation.

"I was preparing myself for your arrival," Luke's response, delivered with a casualness that seemed at odds with the situation, prompted a nervous laugh from me. My gaze took in his appearance—bare-chested, adorned only in bright blue boardshorts that seemed too cheerful for the mood. His state of undress seemed a visual contradiction to the idea of preparation, and I couldn't help but comment, "You don't look terribly prepared."

Jamie's interjection about Luke's apparent disregard for the chill in the air only added to the surreal quality of the moment. Luke's nonchalant shrug in response, a simple "Meh," was so quintessentially him that it momentarily lifted the weight from my shoulders.

However, the physical reminder of my hunger, a loud gurgle from my stomach, pulled me back to the reality of why I was here. Crossing into the kitchen, I approached the stainless steel fridge with a single-minded focus on sustenance. "So, what's the big emergency that couldn't wait another day?" The question that had prompted my hurried journey here spilled out, unfiltered, as I rummaged for food. My actions, driven by the immediate need to quell my hunger, were also a subconscious attempt to inject normalcy into the situation, to find grounding in the familiar act of seeking nourishment.

Discovering a small plastic container of leftover spaghetti, I indulged in the simple pleasure of consuming the largest meatball. My question, hanging in the air alongside the smell of saucy pasta, was an attempt to bridge the gap between the reason for my visit and the calm I craved. Luke's kitchen, a place of warmth and familiarity, had become the stage for the unfolding drama, a place where the mundane act of eating intersected with the complex web of family dynamics and unspoken concerns.

"Emergency?" Jamie's question sliced through the air with a hint of incredulity, his disbelief evident. "What emergency?"

As I cringed from the unexpected collision with the shelf above me, the action felt emblematic of the larger situation—caught off guard, navigating unforeseen obstacles. Swallowing the last of the meatball, I hastily reached for a distraction in the form of grapes, a futile attempt to buy time as I processed Jamie's query. Pulling back from the refrigerator, I was met with Jamie's blank stare, an unspoken demand for clarification that bounced between him, Luke, and back to me like a silent game of accusation.

"Aren't you the one with the... family crisis?" The confusion on Jamie's face, underscored by his lightly stubbled expression, added an unexpected twist to the unfolding drama. His words felt like an accusation, a spotlight suddenly trained on me, suggesting a narrative I wasn't prepared to defend.

"Me?" The word escaped me, tinged with offence and a rising tide of panic. My gaze flicked to Luke, searching for some hint of explanation, some clue as to what narrative had been shared with Jamie. The silence from Luke, however, spoke volumes, leaving me to grapple with the realisation that my own family dramas might have been misrepresented or misunderstood.

Luke's continued silence only served to heighten the tension, a palpable presence in the room that seemed to suffocate any remaining pretence of normalcy.

"Well?" Jamie's demand, directed at Luke, was more than a question—it was a call for transparency, a breaking point that demanded the truth be laid bare. "What's going on, Luke?"

A knot of anxiety tightened in my stomach, the implications of Jamie's words and Luke's silence coalescing into a dreadful epiphany. The fear that I had been brought here under false pretences, or at least misunderstood ones, began to take root. Was I here not as a bystander but as a participant, recruited for moral support in a moment of personal crisis for Luke?

The thought of being unwittingly cast in the role of support for a potential breakup, or whatever storm was on the horizon, was overwhelming. Rubbing my temple, an attempt to soothe the throbbing pulse of stress-induced pain, I braced myself for the fallout. The sense of impending doom, the feeling that I was about to witness the derailment of Luke's relationship firsthand, was suffocating.

In that moment, the kitchen, a place of warmth and familiarity, had transformed into the stage for a confrontation that promised to alter the course of our relationships. The tension, the unanswered questions, and the fear of what was to come left me feeling like a spectator on the brink of witnessing a collision, powerless to do anything but watch as the events unfolded.

As Luke began to speak, the tension in the room seemed to coil tighter, like a spring wound up to its breaking point. My hand found the cool, solid reassurance of the stone bench top, gripping it as if to anchor myself against the wave of anxiety that threatened to sweep me away. The anticipation of Luke's next words had my heart racing, a silent mantra of preparation echoing in my mind: *Brace yourself, Paul.*

Luke's apology, delivered with an incongruous wide grin that stretched across his face, did nothing to ease the knot of apprehension tightening in my stomach. The smile, so at odds with the gravity of the moment, sent a jolt of confusion through me. *Shit!* The thought was a reflexive reaction, a mental bracing for impact. *What the hell has he done?*

"But there is something that I really need to show both of you," Luke continued, his tone shifting from apologetic to mysteriously inviting.

"Sounds ominous," I couldn't help but remark, the words slipping out tinged with a skepticism born of the moment's charged atmosphere. Despite Luke's seemingly light-hearted demeanour, I couldn't shake the feeling of impending revelation, the sense that we were on the cusp of a significant turning point.

"What is it?" Jamie's response, a huff laden with discomfort, mirrored my own trepidation.

"Come with me," Luke urged, his hand waving us forward with an encouragement that felt almost surreal given the context. His invitation, meant to be reassuring, instead felt like a summons into the unknown, a step into a narrative whose course was yet to be revealed.

As we navigated the familiar yet tension-filled pathway to the study, my mind churned with questions and speculations. Luke's penchant for mystery and theatrics, although not unusual, seemed particularly pronounced today. *Why did Luke insist on being so cryptic all the time?* The question echoed in my head, a silent refrain that matched the rhythm of our steps.

Entering the study, my gaze swept over the room in an automatic survey, a habit born from a need to understand, to find clues in my surroundings. Books neatly aligned on the bookshelf, a testament to Luke's eclectic interests. The computer sitting dormant by the window, bathed in the soft light that filtered through the curtains. And that was it. The realisation that the room, for all its familiarity, offered no answers or insights prompted a half-smile from me. The ordinariness of the space stood in stark contrast to the build-up of the moment.

A glance towards Jamie confirmed that I wasn't alone in my confusion. His expression mirrored my own—bemusement mixed with a growing curiosity about what Luke had deemed so important to reveal in such a dramatic fashion.

The moment Luke produced the small, rectangular object from his pocket, Jamie's immediate reaction brought a fleeting sense of camaraderie. "Ha, I was right! It *is* something on the computer!" His triumphant declaration, assuming that Luke's mysterious item was related to the computer, was both amusing and slightly off the mark.

"What?" Luke's feigned confusion, paired with a tilt of his head, only added to the theatrics of the moment. Jamie's certainty about the USB stick, met with Luke's playful denial, transformed the atmosphere from one of tension to one of deeper anticipation.

I couldn't help but suppress a grin, intrigued by the interplay between expectation and reality. Luke's object, clearly not a USB stick, symbolised something else, something yet to be unveiled.

"Okay. So, what is it?" My patience, finally worn thin by the buildup and the cryptic exchanges, broke through the veneer of amusement. The question was more than a request for information; it was a demand for clarity, a need to understand the purpose behind Luke's enigmatic behaviour.

Luke's grin, confident and teasing, served as a prelude to the revelation. The small, rectangular object in his hand, now the focal point of our collective attention, held the key to the mystery that had brought me here, under the guise of emergency and familial duty. The anticipation of the reveal, coupled with the intricate dance of questions and half-answers, underscored the complexity of our relationships—bound by love, frustration, and an enduring commitment to navigate whatever challenges lay ahead, together.

Luke's action, pressing the small button atop the device, seemed almost inconsequential compared to the spectacle that followed. My initial skepticism was immediately replaced by awe as a small ball of energy erupted from its end, unfurling into a buzzing, electrical field of colour that danced across the back wall. The display was unlike anything I'd encountered, a dazzling phenomenon that defied explanation.

"What the—" Jamie's voice trailed off, mirroring my own disbelief. The incomplete thought hung in the air between us, a testament to the shock and wonder that had momentarily rendered us speechless.

My eyes were riveted to the spectacle before us. The colours swirled and intertwined, occasionally colliding to send bursts of rainbow hues in our direction. It was mesmerising, a display of light and energy that seemed to tap into something primal, something deeply human—a sense of wonder at the universe's mysteries.

"What is that?" I found myself asking, my voice barely above a whisper, as if speaking too loudly might shatter the enchantment. The question was rhetorical, born of a need to express my astonishment rather than a genuine expectation of an answer.

"I'll show you," Luke's voice, calm and confident, cut through my reverie.

"I can see," I replied, still captivated by the visual symphony before us. "It's stunning!" My words felt inadequate, a feeble attempt to encapsulate the beauty and complexity of the phenomenon unfolding in Luke's study.

"Just follow me," Luke urged, stepping closer to the wall of vibrant colours. His invitation, delivered with a casualness that belied the extraordinary nature of the act, was both an offer and a challenge.

"Follow you where?" Jamie's question echoed my own thoughts. His tone, softer and smoother than before, hinted at a mix of curiosity and apprehension.

Luke's response was to simply step toward the brilliant display. And then, with an ease that suggested he was crossing a threshold rather than vanishing into thin air, he was enveloped by the colours. And just like that, he was gone.

The moment of his disappearance was surreal, a break in reality that left me questioning the very nature of the world around us. The study, once a familiar space defined by books and a computer, had transformed into the setting for an adventure that defied logic and reason.

❖

"What the hell?" My voice echoed in the room, a mix of fear and astonishment colouring the words as I stared at the spot where Luke had vanished. The disbelief coursing through me was palpable, a physical sensation that seemed to grip my chest tightly.

"What the hell indeed," Jamie's response, equally bewildered, mirrored my own shock. His gaze remained locked on the mesmerising display of colours, as if by sheer will he could unravel the mystery before us.

The silence that followed was heavy, laden with unspoken questions and the weight of the decision that loomed over us.

It was a moment suspended in time, a crossroads between the known and the unknowable.

"You go first," I found myself saying, my voice slow, almost hesitant. The suggestion was more of a nudge, an attempt to offload the burden of the unknown onto Jamie. My hands gestured towards the buzzing wall of colour, an encouragement wrapped in the guise of camaraderie.

"Fuck off!" Jamie's reaction was instant, a swift return to his usual blunt demeanour. "I'm not touching that shit. We don't know what it is." His words were laced with a rational fear, a grounding in reality that momentarily pierced the surreal nature of our situation.

Jamie's resistance, his steadfast refusal to engage with the unknown, forced me to confront my own apprehensions. Yet, the thought of Luke stepping into the unknown with such ease gnawed at me. *Luke wouldn't have ventured forward if there wasn't some measure of safety, would he?* The trust I had in my brother, tempered by years of shared experiences and unspoken bonds, nudged me towards a decision.

"Fine. I'll go first," I declared, my resolve solidifying with the words. Approaching the vibrant, swirling energies, I took a deep breath, steeling myself for what was to come. The trust I placed in Luke, in his judgment and his intentions, was my anchor in the face of the unknown.

With a step that felt as monumental as crossing a threshold between worlds, I moved forward and vanished from the familiar confines of the study.

The transition was disorienting, the kaleidoscope of colours giving way to the stark, brilliant blue of an open sky. The sun's rays, warm against my skin, were an inviting contrast to the cool uncertainty of the moment before. Squinting against the brightness, I was suddenly aware of a presence, not in the physical sense, but as a voice in my mind, a telepathic communication that bypassed the need for sound.

"Welcome to Clivilius, Paul Smith," the voice intoned, its words resonating within me with a clarity that left no room for doubt. The greeting, though devoid of a visible source, carried with it a sense of purpose, a hint of destiny that seemed to wrap around me like a cloak.

❖

Standing there, amidst the vast expanse of brown and orange dust that stretched endlessly before us, I felt a deep sense of dislocation. The voice, so clear and yet without source, had claimed my attention wholly, leaving me momentarily lost in the alien landscape that unfolded around me. The hills, devoid of life as I knew it, painted a daunting picture of isolation that was both eerie and awe-inspiring.

"Did you hear it?" Luke's voice, tinged with excitement, broke through my reverie, snapping me back to the present. The sight of Jamie, pale and visibly shaken by our sudden transition, only served to heighten the surreal nature of our circumstances. My nod, an acknowledgment of the voice, was a silent admission of the reality we now faced, a reality that seemed as improbable as it was undeniable.

"This is where life will begin anew," Luke's declaration, delivered with a certainty that bordered on zeal, sent an involuntary shiver through me. His words, meant to inspire, instead evoked a sense of foreboding, a glimpse into the depth of his conviction and perhaps the magnitude of the change he believed we were on the cusp of, a confident stance sending a cold shiver down my spine.

The prolonged silence that followed became a canvas for my growing unease. Instinctively, I began to wave my arms through the air, my hands moving in a futile attempt to grasp the familiar, to anchor myself to something tangible amidst the intangible. The absurdity of the gesture, a desperate search for the study walls, was a testament to my struggle to reconcile the reality of Clivilius with the safety of the known.

"What are you doing, Paul?" Luke's question momentarily paused my search.

"I'm trying to find the study walls," I admitted, the words feeling both ridiculous and necessary in the moment. My query about the nature of our surroundings—a desperate hope for an explanation that would render this experience a product of technology, a virtual reality or hologram—was a clutch at the straws of denial.

"I can assure you, Clivilius is very real," Luke's response, devoid of any hint of jest or doubt, was a definitive statement that brooked no argument. It was a declaration that this was no illusion, no trick of the mind or technology, but a reality as yet unfathomable.

I ceased my futile searching, the realisation dawning that there were no study walls to be found. Turning to face my brother, I was confronted with the truth of his words, the undeniable reality of Clivilius. The weight of the situation settled upon me with a clarity that was both terrifying and enlightening.

As Luke retrieved a familiar book from the alien dust at our feet, the surrealism of our situation intensified.

"I recognise this book," Jamie declared, the words slicing through the quiet like a knife. He snatched the book from Luke's grasp with an ease that spoke of familiarity, of shared histories untold. "This is one of your uni books that you've had sitting in the bookcase untouched since we met, isn't it?"

"Indeed, it is," Luke confirmed, his voice carrying a note of pride, or perhaps it was nostalgia—a subtle acknowledgment of paths once trodden.

"I don't understand," I found myself saying, as I turned to face Luke. My eyes searched his for answers, for any sign of recognition that would bridge the gap between what was and what could possibly be. The emptiness around us, save for the forgotten artefacts of a life once lived, echoed back my sentiments. "There's nothing here."

"Apart from a pile of large boxes," Jamie corrected, his gaze shifting to the right of us. He walked over to the small stack, a curiosity in his steps that belied his earlier skepticism. "Why are all these here?" he asked, his tone shifting from accusatory to genuinely puzzled.

"It's going to be the first shelter here in Clivilius," Luke stated, his voice imbued with a conviction that seemed almost out of place in the desolation that surrounded us.

"What the hell does Clivilius need a shelter for?" Jamie questioned, his incredulity mirrored in the furrow of his brow, a silent testament to the absurdity of the situation.

"And what even is Clivilius?" I chimed in, unable to contain the burgeoning curiosity that Luke's proclamation had sparked within me.

"This place is Clivilius," Luke said, his arms outstretched as if to embrace the very air around us. It was a grand gesture, one that aimed to imbue the desolate landscape with a sense of purpose, of destiny even. "And the shelter is for the start of our new civilisation."

Jamie and I exchanged glances, a silent conversation passing between us. In that moment, the weight of Luke's words settled upon us, heavy with implications yet to be understood.

"It has to start somewhere," Luke murmured, his voice a mix of resignation and quiet determination. His shoulders lifted in a shrug that seemed to carry the weight of a vision only he could fully see.

"What the hell do we need a new civilisation for?" Jamie's frustration echoed through the air, his words sharp, like the crack of a whip. "I'm quite happy with the current one, thank you very much!" His stance, confrontational yet laced with a hint of incredulity, painted a vivid picture of his dissent.

"You'll see in time," Luke responded, his calmness a stark contrast to Jamie's rising temper. "It will all make sense." There was a serenity to his tone, a confidence that spoke of unshakable belief in the face of skepticism.

"Fuck time," Jamie retorted, his voice escalating. "I'm going home. This place is shit. It's just dust for God's sake! There's enough of that in the outback." His words, laced with disdain, seemed to reverberate against the desolate backdrop of our surroundings.

As Jamie made his way to the wall of colours, the surreal gateway through which we had somehow arrived, I found myself grappling with a mixture of emotions. Doubt, curiosity, and a rising tide of anxiety clashed within me. *How was any of this even possible?* My mind struggled to reconcile the fantastical with the tangible, the ordinary with the extraordinary.

Jamie's approach to the mesmerising colours was tentative, his movements marked by a hesitation that seemed out of character. He took a step closer, then paused, as if the very air around the portal was charged with an invisible resistance.

"Well, off you go then," Luke's voice carried a note of disappointment, tinged with an underlying concern that was hard to miss.

"I'm trying," Jamie shot back, frustration boiling over as he threw his hands at the wall of colour in a gesture of defeat. The sight was surreal, his body language a mix of defiance and desperation.

"What do you mean you're trying?" My voice barely concealed the anxiety that was knotting my stomach. *Had I unwittingly stepped onto a path from which there was no return?* The realisation that this adventure might have deeper implications than I had initially thought sent a shiver down my spine.

"I mean I'm trying to leave, but the bloody thing won't let me," Jamie's exasperation was palpable, his every word punctuated by disbelief and a growing sense of entrapment. He made a shoving motion toward the portal, a futile attempt to demonstrate his plight.

The scene unfolded like a vivid tableau, the interplay of disbelief, frustration, and the underlying thread of something inexplicable weaving a complex tapestry of emotions and realities. Standing there, caught in the moment, I couldn't help but wonder about the nature of the journey we had embarked upon. The portal, with its swirling energies, stood as a testament to the unknown, challenging our perceptions and daring us to confront the possibilities of what lay beyond the confines of our understanding.

The moment unfolded with a startling abruptness that left my senses reeling. One second Jamie was a figure of frustration and defiance, the next, he was hurled backwards as if rejected by an unseen force emanating from the wall of colours. My heart leapt into my throat, panic clawing its way through my chest as I dashed towards him, the dusty ground beneath my feet barely registering. Luke was hot on my heels, concern etched deeply into his features.

"What the hell was that?" The words tore from my lips, a reflection of the fear and confusion swirling within me. My voice, usually steady, now trembled with the intensity of the situation.

Jamie lay sprawled, his back against the unforgiving ground. "Jamie! Jamie, are you okay?" Luke's voice was thick with worry as he reached for Jamie's hand, seeking signs of injury. The fabric of Jamie's shirt bore the brunt of his unexpected flight, torn and dishevelled, yet, miraculously, his hand seemed untouched by harm.

"This fucking place is trying to kill me!" Jamie's voice was a blend of anger and shock, his words cutting through the tension like a knife. He pulled away from Luke, a clear rejection of any comfort or explanations. "What the hell were you thinking bringing us here?!"

Luke's response was laced with desperation, a hint of guilt perhaps. "I didn't know that was going to happen!" he protested, his voice climbing as the gravity of our predicament became increasingly apparent.

I moved to Jamie's side, my own heart racing as if trying to outrun the fear. "Let me try," I offered, despite the obvious danger. The need to understand, to somehow navigate this bewildering situation, overrode the instinct to retreat.

"Are you insane? Didn't you see what just happened?" Jamie's disbelief was evident, his eyes wide with the recent memory of his violent repulsion from the portal.

"Maybe you did it wrong?" I suggested, half in hope, half in desperation. The logic of my proposal felt thin, even to my own ears, but the urgency of the moment demanded action, however flawed.

"Oh, fuck off, Paul." Jamie's retort was sharp, his patience frayed by pain and the surreal nightmare we found ourselves entangled in.

"Hey! Don't speak to him like that," Luke interjected, his protective streak surfacing in defence of my suggestion, however futile it might have seemed.

"Fuck you all," Jamie growled, the pain and frustration manifesting not just in his words but in the way he cradled his arm, a physical barrier against the insanity that enveloped us.

Standing there, amidst the dust and the surreal glow of the portal, the tension between us was palpable. The air seemed charged with unanswered questions and the heavy weight of decisions made under duress. My mind raced, trying to piece together a puzzle that seemed to grow more complex with each passing second. The unity of our trio was fracturing under the strain of the unknown, each of us grappling with the reality of our situation in our own way. Yet, beneath the surface turmoil, a resolve began to take shape within me

As I inched closer to the mesmerising dance of colours, a mantra of reassurance played on a loop in my mind: *It's going to be fine*. Yet, with each step, an invisible force seemed to thicken, making my advance increasingly difficult. The air around me hummed with an electric charge as I neared the threshold, a finger's reach away from the wall of light. The fizzing and crackling of the air halted me, a vivid reminder of Jamie's recent ordeal. "What's wrong with this thing?" My voice, tinged with a mix of curiosity and apprehension, broke the heavy silence, seeking answers I was not sure I wanted to hear.

"There's nothing wrong with it," Luke's voice cut through the tension as he brushed past me, his determination unshaken by the recent events. I watched, mouth agape, as he stepped into the swirling colours and vanished without a trace, leaving behind a wake of unanswered questions.

"Fuck!" The expletive tore from Jamie's lips as he launched himself towards the portal, only to be rebuffed once more, his efforts futile against the unseen barrier.

My heart thundered in my chest, fear and confusion swirling within me as I stood, legs trembling, on the brink of an unfathomable reality. "I don't understand," my voice quivered, a reflection of the panic gnawing at the edges of my composure. "Why can't we leave?"

Then, a voice, devoid of warmth, echoed in the confines of my mind: *Welcome to Clivilius, Paul Smith*. The words, impersonal and chilling, sent a shiver down my spine, grounding me to the spot. I collapsed to my knees, the soft dust beneath my fingers a stark contrast to the turmoil raging within me. The voice, relentless in its greeting, repeated the welcome, each syllable a hammer strike to my sanity.

Beside me, Jamie's frustration erupted in a visceral display of anger, his scream slicing through the stillness of the air, a potent release of the helplessness we both felt. "Fuck!" The word stretched, a testament to the depth of his despair, as he kicked up a cloud of red dust, painting our desperation against the backdrop of this alien landscape.

Overwhelmed, I lay back, the ground beneath me a cold comfort as I stared up into the clear, blue sky. My heart raced, a drumbeat of fear, betrayal, and incredulity. *What the hell have you done, Luke?* The question echoed in my mind, a haunting refrain to the surreal nightmare unfolding around me.

FUTILITY

4338.205.3

As Luke materialised from the void, rejoining our desolate surroundings, the air seemed to shift, charged with the tension of his return. His entrance was met with a volley of harsh words from Jamie, a raw expression of our collective frustration and disbelief. I watched Luke, my gaze sharp, searching for any hint of foreknowledge, any sign that he had led us into this predicament with eyes wide open.

"Did you know?" The accusation in my voice was unmistakable, a direct challenge to his intentions and honesty.

"Know what?" Luke's response was tinged with innocence, but the simplicity of his question did little to quell the rising storm of doubts in my mind.

"That we wouldn't be able to get back," I pressed on, needing to understand, to find a semblance of reason in the chaos that had ensnared us.

"How would I have known? I've been the only one here until now and I've been able to come and go as I please," Luke countered, his defensiveness painting him as a victim of circumstance rather than its architect. Yet, his words did little to ease the weight of uncertainty that pressed down upon us, leaving a bitter taste of betrayal in their wake.

"So, this is it then," Jamie's voice cut through the tension, resignation laced with a dark finality. "This is our fate. To die in this god-forsaken dust." His declaration, though despairing, seemed to echo the unspoken fears that lingered in the back of my mind, a grim acceptance of our predicament.

"Not fate. Destiny," Luke replied, his tone shifting dramatically. The enthusiasm and excitement that bubbled up in his voice were at odds with the stark, unforgiving landscape that stretched out before us. It was as if he saw something in this desolation that Jamie and I could not, a vision that transcended the immediate peril of our situation.

Jamie and I exchanged a look, a silent communication that conveyed our mutual incredulity. Luke's optimism, unfounded and bizarrely out of place, grated against the reality of our circumstances, sparking a frustration that I could no longer contain.

"You're so full of shit sometimes," I blurted out, the insult slipping from my lips with a casualness that belied the depth of my irritation. It was more than just a reaction to his current delusion; it was an accumulation of feelings, a response to the myriad ways his dreams and schemes had entangled us in situations we never asked for.

Again, silence enveloped us, a heavy, suffocating blanket that seemed to smother any semblance of hope. The barren landscape offered no comfort, no answers, just the endless expanse of dust and the weight of Luke's unfathomable destiny. In that moment, the gulf between us seemed wider than ever, a chasm deepened by unspoken fears, unanswered questions, and the realisation that our trust in one another—and in the future Luke imagined—was as fragile as the dust beneath our feet.

The standoff between Luke and me felt as charged as the air before a storm, our gazes locked in a silent battle of wills. The question that had been tormenting me finally burst forth, sharpened by a desperation I could no longer contain. "What about my children? Am I ever going to see them again?" With each word, my voice grew tighter, the fear of never holding my kids again constricting around my heart like a vice.

Luke's response, when it came, was so unexpected it took a moment for the full impact to hit me. "I can arrange to have them come here?" he suggested, as if he was offering a simple solution rather than a sentence to a life in exile.

"Are you fucking kidding me?" I exploded, my voice ricocheting off the barren landscape. I couldn't believe what I was hearing. Luke's grasp on reality, on the very essence of responsibility, seemed more tenuous than ever. "I know you don't have the first clue about parenting, Luke, but here's the number one, golden rule for how to be a dad. You ready?" My sarcasm was a thin veil over the growing despair. "Don't, under any circumstances, bring your children through a one-way interdimensional Portal to an alien wasteland where there is literally nothing but dust and a tent!" The absurdity of the situation, of even having to articulate such a thought, was overwhelming.

As the words spilled out, fuelled by a mix of incredulity and protective fury, I felt the last vestiges of hope evaporate into the arid air. The notion of dragging my children into this desolate, uncertain existence was unthinkable. The very suggestion laid bare the chasm between Luke's idealistic visions and the stark reality of our predicament. It underscored a fundamental disconnect, a divergence in our understanding of what it meant to protect and provide for those we loved.

In that heated exchange, a painful truth crystallised within me. The adventure, the leap into the unknown that had once seemed like a thrilling escape, had morphed into a nightmarish trap. The weight of my choices, of the trust I had placed in Luke's hands, pressed down on me with an unbearable heaviness. The realisation that I might never see my children again, never share in their lives or guide them through their trials, was a torment unlike any other. It was a loss that extended beyond the physical distance between worlds, reaching into the very core of my being, tearing at the bonds that defined me as a father, as a protector. In that moment, the desolate landscape that stretched out before us seemed a perfect mirror to the desolation within, a vast, unending expanse of regret and longing.

Jamie's exasperation echoed starkly against the backdrop of our desolate surroundings. "I can't believe you've gotten us stuck in this bloody place!" His voice cracked with the strain of anger and disbelief, a brief pause breaking the tension before he pressed on, seeking answers, "How long have you known about this?"

Luke's explanation seemed almost mundane in the face of our extraordinary circumstances. He recounted dozing off at his desk, the surreal simplicity of waking to find the so-called Portal Key slipping from his grasp. The casual mention of such an object, as if it were a common occurrence, struck me as both absurd and unsettling.

"Portal key?" The skepticism in my voice was palpable. I couldn't help but add, "You're aware that you are not, in fact, living in a sci-fi novel, right?" The words were out before I could temper them, my incredulity at our situation finding an outlet in dry humour.

"Well, that's what it is, isn't it? The key to open the Portal?" Luke's response was laced with sarcasm, a defence against the absurdity of our reality.

"Yeah, but... Portal?" I echoed, the word feeling alien on my tongue, as if by questioning its validity, I could somehow dispel the nightmare we found ourselves in.

"What else would you call it?" Luke countered, his gaze shifting to the large wall of dancing colours that held us captive.

"A piece of shit," Jamie interjected with a flatness that left no room for interpretation. "One giant piece of shit." His blunt assessment of our predicament was devoid of any pretence, a raw expression of frustration and resignation.

At that moment, an unexpected snort of laughter burst from me, a spontaneous reaction to the absurdity of our debate in the face of such dire circumstances. The sound was out of place, a jarring note in the sombre melody of our situation, yet it was uncontrollably genuine.

Luke and Jamie turned their gazes towards me, their expressions a mix of surprise and confusion. "Sorry," I managed to say, the back of my fist pressed to my mouth in a futile attempt to stifle the laughter. My efforts only served to amplify the sound, a second snort breaking free, louder and more unrestrained than the first. I turned away, my back to their uncomfortable stares, as a wave of laughter shook my body. For a fleeting moment, the absurdity of our argument, set against the backdrop of our surreal and hopeless situation, became overwhelmingly comical. My exhausted mind, teetering on the edge of despair, found respite in the release of laughter, a brief escape from the grim reality that loomed over us. The near silence that followed, punctuated only by my sporadic chuckles, was a testament to the complex tapestry of emotions we navigated—fear, frustration, disbelief, and the unexpected relief found in a moment of shared absurdity.

After the laughter had subsided, a sobering silence took its place, like the calm after a storm. I took a deep breath, feeling the heat of embarrassment fade from my cheeks as I turned back to face my companions. The vibrant spectacle that had captivated us was gone, replaced by a large, translucent screen that shimmered in the desolate landscape. Jamie stood alone, his figure a solitary testament to our shared confusion and growing apprehension.

"He's gone back for supplies," Jamie explained, his voice cutting through the silence with a matter-of-factness that belied the surreal nature of our situation.

"Oh," was all I could manage, my gaze drifting to the ground as I grappled with the reality of our predicament. "What now?" I asked, more to fill the silence than in any real hope of receiving a satisfactory answer.

Jamie's shrug was a visual echo of my own feelings of helplessness. "No idea," he admitted, and in his voice, I heard the same mixture of fear and resignation that churned in my own chest.

With a heavy sigh, I turned my attention to the pile of boxes that Luke had optimistically dubbed our first shelter. *Rudimentary at best*, I thought, a bleak acceptance settling over me as I began walking towards them. The prospect of 'roughing it' in this alien wasteland was daunting, to say the least, and yet, it seemed there was little choice in the matter.

"What are you doing?" Jamie's voice reached me, tinged with curiosity and perhaps a hint of concern.

I paused, turning to face him, the weight of our situation pressing down on me. "I don't really know," I admitted, my voice barely above a whisper. I rubbed at my brow. My mind was a whirlwind of thoughts, each more unsettling than the last. *How could Luke do this to us?* This question, more than any other, gnawed at the edges of my consciousness. I had trusted him implicitly, believed in him with a conviction that now seemed naïve at best. With my life, I had placed my faith in him, and now, that trust felt misplaced, leaving me to question not just Luke's intentions, but my own judgment.

The sense of betrayal was acute, a sharp contrast to the physical barrenness that surrounded us. It was not just the landscape that felt alien, but the very foundation of our brotherhood, now fractured by the weight of decisions made and actions taken. As I stood there, confronting the enormity of our situation, I couldn't help but feel lost, adrift in a sea of doubts and unanswered questions, with no clear path forward.

The weight of the box caught me off guard. It slipped through my grasp, the end hitting the ground with a thud that kicked up a cloud of dust around my feet. I couldn't help but cast a glance at Jamie, who had returned to the large screen that served as our unwanted gateway to this place. His back was to me, his posture one of determined futility as he attempted to coax the portal back to life. I didn't linger on the sight; a deep, sinking feeling told me it was a fruitless endeavour.

Dragging the box by the strip of blue plastic, I felt a wave of despondency wash over me. The landscape stretched out endlessly, a monotonous expanse of brown and dust that seemed even more desolate than the arid reaches of Broken Hill—a comparison I had never imagined I'd make. The lack of shade, the oppressive heat, and the sheer emptiness of it all weighed heavily on me, a physical manifestation of our isolation.

As I trudged up the second small rise, a flicker of something unexpected stirred within me. Sound—a noise so out of place in this barren wasteland that I doubted my own senses. *Water*. The notion was so absurd, so implausible, that for a moment, I hesitated, afraid to give in to the hope that fluttered in my chest. Yet, the unmistakable murmur grew louder with each step, urging me forward.

Reaching the crest of the rise, the sight that greeted me was so starkly at odds with the desolation behind me that I could only stare in disbelief. There, cutting through the dust and desolation, was a river—a wide, meandering ribbon of water that stretched as far as the eye could see. The view was jarring, a vibrant vein of life in the midst of so much barrenness.

For a moment, I was rooted to the spot, my mind grappling with the implications. Water meant life, possibility, a chance. Perhaps not all was lost. The sight injected a sliver of hope into the bleakness of our situation, a flicker of light in the overwhelming darkness. It was a reminder that even in the most unforgiving places, life finds a way to assert itself. With a renewed sense of purpose, I felt the weight of despair begin to lift, if only slightly. The presence of water in this desolate place was a sign, perhaps, that our situation was not as dire as it had seemed. In that moment, the river represented more than just a source of physical sustenance—it symbolised a lifeline, a reason to believe that survival, and maybe even a way home, could be within our reach.

❖

"Jamie!" My voice, filled with a newfound urgency, cut through the still air, but the response I hoped for didn't come. The realisation that I had wandered far beyond a simple shout's reach hit me with a mix of frustration and concern. The landscape, once seemingly endless in its barren expanse, now held a secret I was eager to share. Jamie was nowhere in sight, hidden by the undulating terrain that I had, until moments ago, cursed for its monotony. "At least, I think it's only one hill," I muttered to myself, the uncertainty of the terrain mirroring my initial despair turned cautious optimism. I raised my voice once more, hoping against hope that my call would bridge the distance between us.

Finally, Jamie's head bobbed into view as he crested the hill, a sight that sparked a brief flicker of relief in my chest. "Come over here!" I urged, my arms flailing in a bid to draw him away from the portal's fruitless allure. "Hurry up," I added, watching him navigate the dusty ground with a reluctance that spoke volumes of his exhaustion and dwindling hope.

"What is it?" Jamie's voice carried a hint of curiosity as he neared, his figure emerging more fully against the backdrop of the hill.

"There's a river," I announced, the words tinged with an enthusiasm I hadn't felt since before we found ourselves ensnared in this alien landscape. The revelation felt like a small victory, a beacon of hope in a sea of uncertainty.

As Jamie drew closer, I could see the change in his expression, a subtle shift that mirrored the spark of hope I felt within me. The light in his eyes, though faint, was a testament to the power of possibility, however slight it might be in our grim situation.

Turning on my heel, I led the way down the hill, my steps quickened by the prospect of what lay ahead. The dust, a constant companion, shifted treacherously underfoot, threatening to send me tumbling. Yet, the promise of water, of life, propelled me forward, each step a defiance of the despair that had threatened to consume me.

Racing towards the riverbank, my legs moved with a fervour I hadn't known I possessed, driven by the sight of the water's promising clarity. Kneeling, I couldn't help but marvel at the river's purity, its surface a mirror to the sky above, unblemished by the dust and desolation that defined our surroundings.

Jamie, arriving moments later, echoed my thoughts with a mix of awe and skepticism in his voice. "It's so clear," he remarked, his eyes scanning the surface as he pondered out loud about its safety for drinking. The question lingered between us, an unspoken concern against the backdrop of our thirst.

My response was noncommittal, a shrug that betrayed my own uncertainty. Back home, the water's clarity was never a guarantee of its safety, a reality of life in the outback that had taught me to be cautious. Yet, here, the rules we knew seemed irrelevant.

Impulsive as ever, Jamie reached out, his fingers breaking the water's surface. "It feels so cool and fresh," he said, a note of surprise in his voice that piqued my curiosity. Compelled by his reaction, I extended my hand, immersing it in the cool embrace of the river. The sensation was immediate and intense, a rush of cool that seemed to carry an undercurrent of warmth, a dichotomy that felt almost magical in its effect.

"I could totally jump in right now," I found myself saying, the words borne of a half-joking longing spurred by the river's inviting chill.

Jamie's laughter cut through the air, light and carefree. "Well, you'd have to do it skinny," he teased.

His jest took a moment to register, prompting a puzzled glance from me. "Huh?"

"Well, we don't have any towels or spare clothes," he elaborated. His words brought me back to reality, a chuckle escaping me at the absurdity of our situation and the brief escapism the river had offered.

"Oh, of course," I conceded, feeling a mix of amusement and resignation. Despite the brief interlude of levity, we continued to immerse our hands in the river's flow, finding solace in the simple pleasure of the water's cool touch. Each time our fingers broke the surface, it was as if we were reaching for a connection, a reminder of the world beyond our current confines, a world where rivers were just rivers, and not symbols of hope in a desolate landscape.

"Do you really think we're stuck here?" The words left my lips, a mixture of fear and hope mingling in the uncertainty of our situation. Jamie's response, though soft, carried the weight of our shared apprehension. "I don't know," he admitted, his voice a mirror to the vulnerability we both felt. "I hope not."

The possibility hung in the air, unspoken yet palpable. "But what if we are?" I couldn't help but push for an answer, for any semblance of a plan. Jamie's reaction was immediate. "If Luke can get out, I am sure we can too," he asserted, his voice laced with a determination that bordered on desperation.

I watched as Jamie's figure receded, his silhouette a distinct contrast against the backdrop of the hill as he made his way back towards the Portal. A part of me wanted to call out, to say something—anything—that might ease the tension. Instead, I let out a gentle sigh, a release of the myriad emotions that threatened to overwhelm me.

Of all the people to be stranded with in Clivilius, fate had chosen Jamie. The thought crossed my mind, unbidden yet persistent. It was a moment of frustration, a questioning of the cosmic forces that had led us to this point. Yet, as quickly as the thought appeared, I pushed it aside. Life with Claire had taught me the value of resilience, the importance of focusing on the positive rather than dwelling on what couldn't be changed.

Turning my gaze back to the river, I allowed myself a few minutes of quiet reflection. The water, clear and tranquil, offered a momentary escape. My reflection stared back at me, a reminder of the person I was beneath the fear and uncertainty. Gradually, the tension in my shoulders began to ease, the water's gentle flow a soothing balm to the turmoil within.

In that moment, by the river's edge, I found a semblance of peace. It was a reminder that, regardless of our circumstances, there was beauty to be found, moments of calm amidst the storm. And as I stared into the water, I realised that survival was as much about maintaining hope as it was about finding a way back home.

❖

The emptiness of my thoughts was as vast and desolate as the landscape around us, a stark contrast to the usual clutter of daily concerns and responsibilities. As I hoisted myself up from the dust, the weight of our situation settled on my shoulders with a newfound gravity. The box, left atop the hill in a moment of distraction, now seemed like a symbol of the tangible challenges we faced.

Dragging the box behind me, the trail it left in the dust was a testament to our presence here, a physical mark on a world that seemed indifferent to our struggles. The contents of the box, metal poles intended for the construction of what Luke had optimistically called our first shelter, rattled with each step.

I had chosen a spot near the riverbank for our camp, a decision driven by the primal lure of water and the semblance of life it represented. The distance from the Portal, while making our return more cumbersome, seemed a worthy trade-off for the comfort and psychological ease proximity to the river might afford us.

The frustration that had been simmering beneath the surface found its outlet as I struggled with the box's stubborn blue plastic strip. "Aargh!" The sound tore from my lips, a raw expression of the myriad emotions I'd been trying to keep at bay. The plastic, meant to secure the box's contents, now felt like yet another barrier between us and a semblance of stability in this unfamiliar world. Without tools, the task seemed insurmountable, a cruel joke in our already dire circumstances.

The thought of enlisting Jamie's help flickered through my mind, his physical strength a possible solution to the immediate problem. Yet, the very idea of asking for his assistance brought a surge of reluctance. The tension between us, though unspoken, was palpable, and my pride balked at the notion of showing vulnerability. It was a petty hesitation, perhaps, but in that moment, it felt significant, a line I wasn't ready to cross.

So, there I sat, caught between the practical need to access the contents of the box and the emotional barriers that made the simple act of asking for help feel like an admission of defeat. The situation was emblematic of the broader challenges we faced: the need to rely on each other for survival in a place that demanded more of us than we might be prepared to give.

The sudden shift from bending to standing sent a disorienting rush through my body, my head spinning as if caught in a whirlwind. For a moment, the world around me —a blur of dust and sky—faded into insignificance, replaced by vivid images of Mack and Rose. Mack, with his wide, curious eyes, had just celebrated his tenth birthday, a milestone I now felt worlds away from. Rose, ever the spirited soul, was nearing her seventh year, her laughter a distant echo in my heart. The realisation that days had slipped into an unknown number since I'd last seen them, held them, was a weight pressing down on my chest.

The memory of leaving them, safe and happy at their grandparents' house, stung with fresh pain. Those visits had become a cherished tradition, a special time for them to bond with Nana and Grandad, filled with stories and adventures in the backyard transformed into a 'campsite.' When I had left for Adelaide, I promised myself, albeit silently, that the trip to visit Luke would be brief and that I'd be back before their time with their grandparents was over. The irony of that promise now twisted inside me, a cruel reminder of the uncertainty that lay ahead.

As I steadied myself, gripping the dusty box for support, the weight of my fear and longing threatened to overwhelm me. The thought of not returning to Broken Hill in time, of missing the chance to welcome my children back from their holiday adventure, seemed a minor concern compared to the gnawing dread that I might never see them again. The vast distance between Clivilius and home stretched infinitely larger in my mind, a chasm not just of space but of time and lost moments.

Questions with no answers circled relentlessly in my head. *Will I ever get to hold my kids in my arms again?* The possibility of a future devoid of their hugs, their laughter, and their boundless energy was a void too vast to contemplate.

The bleakness that had settled over me seemed to echo in the barren landscape of Clivilius, the dwindling hope of reuniting with my children mirrored by the frustration of not being able to open the box. Defeated, I trudged back to the pile of boxes, the task of relocating them near the river offering a semblance of purpose. It was a small, manageable goal in a situation that felt increasingly out of control.

Approaching Jamie, I found him engrossed with the Portal, his efforts yielding no progress. "Figured out how it works yet?" The question was as much an attempt to break his concentration as it was to engage in some form of conversation.

His reaction was immediate, the frustration palpable as he vented his anger on the inert dust of Clivilius. "This thing is fucking useless!" The despair in his voice was a mirror to my own feelings, a shared sentiment that transcended our current predicament.

Conflict was never my forte, the very notion often enough to set my nerves on edge. Yet, the pressing need to find distraction, to momentarily escape the grim reality of our situation, spurred me to action. "Why don't you give that a rest for a bit and help me move these boxes?" The suggestion was tentative, an olive branch extended in the hope of diverting Jamie's focus from the despair that threatened to consume him. "It might help you to keep your mind and hands busy with something else."

The silence that followed was heavy, charged with unspoken thoughts and emotions. I watched Jamie closely, the tension in my body mounting as I awaited his response. Every second stretched into eternity, each muscle in my body tensing in anticipation of his reaction.

"Sure," he finally acquiesced, the single word a balm to my frayed nerves. Relief washed over me, not just for the help with the boxes, but for the temporary truce it represented. In that moment, the simple act of moving boxes became more than just a physical task; it was a step towards maintaining my sanity, a distraction from the overwhelming sense of helplessness that loomed over me.

LOST CHILDREN

4338.205.4

Hearing Luke's voice was like a beacon in the dense fog of our frustration. "I've come bearing gifts," he announced, his tone injecting a rare note of levity into the heavy air that had settled around Jamie and me. Despite the gravity of our situation, Luke's attempt at humour was a welcome reprieve.

"There had better be a knife in that bag of yours," Jamie retorted, his voice laced with a frustration so palpable, it seemed to momentarily charge the air around us.

Luke, unfazed by Jamie's tone, reached into his bag with a magician's flair and pulled out a knife. "As a matter of fact, there is," he declared, his voice buoyant with triumph, as if he'd just pulled a rabbit out of a hat. The gleam in his eye was unmistakable, a spark of mischief that I knew too well.

"Thank God for that," I breathed out, the relief washing over me in an almost physical wave. I recounted our earlier folly, a mix of humour and self-derision in my tone. "We moved all these boxes ready to put the tent up and then realised we couldn't get that blue plastic crap off. I was about to start trying to bite my way through." The mental image of myself gnawing at the stubborn plastic wrapping must have painted a ridiculous picture, but the absurdity of the situation seemed fitting given the day we were having.

"You may find these useful too," Luke chimed in, his attention now on the small toolkit cradled in his left hand.

"Did you check that all the tools were actually in there?" Jamie couldn't resist adding a dose of skepticism, his condescension thinly veiled. It was his way, challenging every bit of good news as if bracing for the next disappointment.

"Of course, I did," Luke retorted, the snap in his voice revealing a flicker of annoyance. It was rare to see him anything but jovial, but even Luke had his limits. "And most of it is in there. Only a few random bits are missing. But I don't know what any of them were anyway so I doubt they would have been very useful." His admission, candid and slightly sheepish, drew a laugh from me.

"Now, why doesn't that surprise me?" I quipped, the laughter bubbling up from a place of genuine amusement.

"Well, it's not like you're any better," Jamie quickly jumped in, leaping to Luke's defence with a barb aimed my way. "I've seen the unfortunate state of your latest home construction project. Scrolling through your Facebook is like watching all the 'before' bits from DIY SOS back-to-back."

My face tightened, an involuntary reaction to Jamie's jab. My mouth, already parting to unleash a retort, snapped shut as vivid, embarrassing memories of a collapsed cubbyhouse—my handiwork—flashed before my eyes. The structure, meant to stand proud in my backyard, had instead become a monument to my overconfidence in my carpentry skills. A bitter chuckle escaped me, unbidden. I knew Jamie was right. This time, at least. It stung to admit, even silently, that my ambitious projects often turned out less than stellar.

"Anyway," Luke interjected, his voice cutting through the awkward silence that had settled between Jamie and me. He seemed unfazed by our sniping, his demeanour casual, almost nonchalant, as he shrugged off my failed attempt at a comeback. "The two of you had better get to work putting this tent together. We have no idea what the temperature or conditions are like here at night. We'd better be as prepared for the unexpected as possible," he said, his tone blunt, yet underscored by a seriousness that I couldn't ignore.

"We?" Jamie's skepticism was palpable as he gestured pointedly between the two of us, his eyebrow arching in challenge. "And what about you? Aren't you going to help us?" His tone was accusatory, as if Luke's leadership had suddenly placed him above the grunt work, a division that didn't sit well with Jamie's sense of fairness—or perhaps his reluctance to shoulder more of the burden.

"I'm going to see if I can get us a couple more tents. I know this one is huge, but I'm sure you'd both appreciate having your own space," Luke replied, his voice steady, revealing a thoughtfulness that contrasted sharply with the tension that had been building among us. His suggestion, meant to ease our discomfort, also hinted at a practical understanding of our situation. Being stuck in Clivilius, wherever that might be, pressed upon us the reality of our predicament. Space, privacy, and the semblance of normalcy would be scarce commodities here.

"Good point," I found myself saying, the words slipping out before I could weigh them. "He's not wrong." In truth, the prospect of sharing a tent with Jamie, given his current mood and my own fraying nerves, was less than appealing. His attitude, though perhaps justified by the day's frustrations, did little to calm the storm of anxieties whirling within me. The thought of a personal space, no matter how temporary or illusory, offered a sliver of comfort in the face of our uncertain future.

"Wait!" Jamie's voice, tinged with a mixture of hope and desperation, cut through the air just as Luke began to turn away, his intention to leave clear. Jamie's eyes met mine, seeking an ally in his sudden decision. "We may as well see if we can leave with you again," he said, his gaze imploring me for support.

"Sure! Good idea," I echoed, though my voice was hollow, lacking conviction. Deep down, a part of me knew the likelihood of our escape being that simple was slim. Yet, clinging to a sliver of hope, I followed, trailing behind Luke back to the Portal, the mysterious gateway that had brought us to this uncertain place.

As we approached the Portal, a tangible sense of tension enveloped us. I held my breath, my eyes fixed on Jamie as he stepped forward, his movements hesitant yet determined. He extended both hands towards the Portal, an air of expectation hanging heavily around us. But nothing happened. No flicker of light, no hum of energy—just the oppressive silence of our isolation. Watching Jamie's face lose its colour, the reality of our situation sank in deeper. *What the hell just happened?* The question echoed in my mind, a silent scream. I was too afraid to voice my fears, too afraid to acknowledge the possibility that we might truly be trapped.

Jamie turned to face me, a swift, almost frantic movement. He turned his back on the Portal, on the world we both yearned to return to. The look in his eyes—a raw, unfiltered expression of defeat—sent a chill down my spine. "You try," he said, his voice devoid of hope, as he gestured towards the Portal with a dismissive wave of his hand.

Taking an anxious step forward, I couldn't help but glance at Jamie. The sight of him, pale and shaken, looking as though he had indeed seen a ghost, filled me with dread. Something profound and unsettling had occurred in that failed attempt to connect with the Portal, and I wasn't sure I was ready to face the same. Yet, the weight of his expectation and the slim chance that my attempt might yield a different result propelled me forward.

"Go," Jamie urged, his voice a mixture of command and plea.

As I approached the Portal, a myriad of thoughts swirled through my mind, not least of which was my growing frustration with Jamie. *Why is Jamie always so rude?* The question echoed in the back of my head, a nagging reminder of the unnecessary tension between us. Here we were, stranded in an alien environment, facing unknown dangers and challenges, and yet, it seemed Jamie's harshness added an extra layer of adversity to our already daunting situation. I couldn't help but think that we had enough to contend with without turning on each other.

My eyes darted about, taking in the stark, unforgiving landscape of Clivilius. The harshness of our surroundings was palpable, a constant reminder of our vulnerability in this strange world. It was clear that any additional conflict amongst ourselves was not just unnecessary; it was detrimental.

Caught in these reflections, I was utterly unprepared for what came next. Without any warning, Jamie's impatience boiled over into a physical act. He shoved me firmly in the back, a jarring push that sent me stumbling forward. Instinct took over as I fell towards the Portal. My hands shot out in front of me, reaching for something, anything, to break my fall. But what I encountered was far from the solid support I had hoped for.

The Portal, with its swirling mass of colours, seemed alive, pulsating with an intense energy that repelled my hands as they neared its surface. In that moment, a blinding light erupted from the Portal, accompanied by a sound akin to thunder cracking directly overhead. The force of it was unimaginable, sending me hurtling backwards through the air.

I landed with a heavy thud in the soft dust. My clothes, singed by the encounter, emitted a soft, boiling sound. Lying there, dazed and confused, I struggled to make sense of what had just happened. Miraculously, I was unharmed, a fact that seemed almost impossible given the violence of the repulsion.

Then, as if to add a surreal quality to the already unbelievable situation, the same Clivilius voice that had greeted me upon my arrival once again filled my head. Its words, thunderous and inescapable, bore into me: *You will never leave Clivilius, Paul Smith.* The finality of that declaration, the utter hopelessness it conveyed, was overwhelming. Hot tears welled up in my eyes, a visceral response to the realisation of our predicament.

As I lay there in the dust, the aftermath of my encounter with the Portal still echoing through my body, Luke was at my side in an instant, concern etched across his face. "Are you hurt?" he asked, his voice laced with urgency.

Before I could muster a response, his attention whirled towards Jamie, his anger palpable. "What the fuck did you do that for?" he yelled, his voice a sharp rebuke in the quiet that surrounded us, furious at Jamie's reckless provocation.

Jamie, however, seemed unfazed by Luke's fury, his own turmoil bubbling to the surface. "So, you heard it too?" he asked, sidestepping the question, his eyes locking onto mine. His voice, a mix of defiance and a deeper, unspoken fear, hinted at the shared experience that had just unfolded.

I nodded, my response silent yet heavy with the weight of our grim reality.

"Heard what?" Luke's demand came softer this time, tinged with a growing fear that mirrored the unease clawing at my own heart.

The tears that I had been fighting back broke free, a silent testament to the despair that had taken hold. The words were lodged in my throat, a painful lump that refused to dissipate. The fear of voicing the truth made it all the more real, all the more terrifying.

"Fucking shit!" Jamie's frustration erupted in a physical outburst, his foot sending clouds of Clivilian dust into the air. The dust, like a tangible representation of our shattered hopes, swirled around him, prompting a coughing fit that seemed a fitting punishment for his earlier action. It was a moment of raw emotion, a release of the pent-up fear and frustration that we all felt but expressed in different ways.

"What did you hear?" Luke asked again.

The tears streaming down my face, I finally found my voice, though it was barely more than a whisper. "That we can never leave," I managed to say, the words tasting bitter on my tongue. "This is it. Forever. I'm going to die here." The admission felt like surrender, the final crumbling of any hope I had clung to.

Luke's reaction was subdued, a simple "Oh," that hung heavily in the air. His lack of surprise, the calm acceptance that seemed to underpin his response, caught me off guard. I eyed him suspiciously, the dampness of my tears doing little to obscure the sudden suspicion that flickered within me. *Why didn't he seem surprised? What did Luke know that I didn't?* His reaction, or lack thereof, added a new layer of mystery to our already confounding predicament. The implications of his nonchalance were chilling, leaving me to wonder about the true nature of Clivilius, and what it meant for our chances of ever finding a way back home.

The air crackled with tension, heavier and more charged than the swirling energies of the Portal itself. Jamie's anger, a tangible force, propelled him across the space that separated him from Luke. His strides were quick and determined, fuelled by a sense of betrayal that seemed to eclipse the fear and uncertainty that had governed us until now.

"You fucking arsehole!" Jamie's voice was a roar of fury, each word punctuated by his rapid approach. The distance between him and Luke disappeared in mere moments, culminating in a hard shove that sent Luke staggering back. "What in the name of holy fuck were you thinking? How the hell did you think this was going to go? Did you think we wouldn't find out? Is that it? Did you think you could literally kidnap us and no one would fucking notice?"

Luke's reaction was swift, a defensive move to swipe away Jamie's hands as they came at him again. It was a dance as old as time, aggression met with resistance, yet it solved nothing, only serving to deepen the rifts that had begun to form among us.

"Hey!" My own voice surprised me, breaking through the tension as I scrambled to my feet, driven by a desperate need to intervene. Grasping hold of Jamie's arm, I tried to anchor him, to prevent another blow that might irreparably fracture whatever fragile unity we still possessed. "Fighting isn't going to help any of us."

But Jamie was a storm, his anger uncontainable. He turned on me, his eyes blazing with a ferocity that matched his earlier charge. With a shrug and retort that sent a clear message of his disdain, "You're no better than your pathetic excuse for a brother," he cast me aside, his shove sending me stumbling backwards. The ground met me sooner than expected, the dust a soft but unwelcome landing that did nothing to cushion the shock of his betrayal.

As I sat there, the dust settling around me, a profound sense of disbelief washed over me. *Is this how he treats Luke?* The question echoed in my mind, a haunting thought that made me question the very foundation of our relationships. Fear mingled with the dust in my throat, a bitter taste that spoke of disillusionment and the dawning realisation of our precarious situation.

"Cut it out, Jamie!" Luke's scream sliced through the air, a desperate plea that seemed to hang, suspended, as if even the atmosphere of Clivilius itself awaited Jamie's response. The moment was a crossroads, the outcome of which would inevitably shape the days to come. *Would Jamie heed Luke's call, or had we already spiralled too far into chaos, driven apart by secrets and lies?* The uncertainty of it all was almost as daunting as the voice that claimed we could never leave. Amidst the alien dust, beneath a sky not our own, I realised that our greatest challenge might not come from Clivilius itself, but from within.

Jamie's abrupt halt was a physical manifestation of the turmoil churning within him. Luke's desperate cry, laden with fear and urgency, pierced through the red haze of Jamie's anger, reaching into the core of his being where the primal instinct to protect and preserve family still held sway. For a moment, Jamie stood frozen, a statue of rage gradually eroding under the torrent of Luke's emotional plea. His heavy, laboured breaths were the only sound in the tense air, each exhale a testament to the battle raging within him between fury and the remnants of familial bonds.

As Jamie turned away from my unwavering gaze, a palpable shift occurred. The immediate threat of violence dissipated, leaving behind an awkward silence that enveloped us like a thick fog, tangible and suffocating. This silence, stretching endlessly, felt like a chasm widening between us, an insurmountable gap that words could no longer bridge.

Luke, perhaps sensing the futility of further conversation, retraced his steps back through the Portal without another word. His departure, rather than offering solace, seemed to solidify our hopelessness. I watched, mesmerised yet hollow, as the Portal's beautiful, hypnotic colours faded into the surrounding air, a visual echo of our fading hopes. My head sank into my knees, a physical capitulation to the despair that had been gnawing at the edges of my consciousness. We were lost—utterly and irrevocably. Lost in a world from which there seemed no escape. Lost to my children, whose faces now seemed like distant memories, their laughter a melody I feared I would never hear again.

In that moment of profound despair, a desperate, almost instinctual act of defiance against the crushing weight of our reality, I did something I hadn't anticipated. With tears anew streaming down my face, I reached out with my heart, sending a silent message into the unknown expanses of the Clivilius universe. It was a message of hope, a plea cast into the vast, uncaring cosmos: that Mack and Rose, my beloved children, would one day find me again, somehow. It was a gesture perhaps futile, born not of reason but of the raw, unyielding love of a parent for their children. A love that refused to be extinguished, even in the face of overwhelming odds.

This act, though small and unseen, felt like a tiny beacon of light in the overwhelming darkness. It was a declaration, however silent, that even in the depths of despair, the human spirit could still reach for hope, still dream of reunion and redemption. And in the vast, mysterious universe of Clivilius, who could say what was truly impossible?

UNWANTED NECESSITY

4338.205.5

In the shadow of our recent confrontation and the heavy silence that followed, Jamie and I found a semblance of common ground in the task at hand. With words unspoken, we set about opening the tent boxes, the sound of cardboard tearing the only evidence of our cooperation. It was an awkward dance of necessity, each of us moving around the other, immersed in the confusing chore of assembling what would be our first shelter in this alien world of Clivilius.

As I unfolded the instructions, a glossy image plastered on the outside of one of the larger boxes caught my eye. The complexity of the ten-man tent laid out in front of me was daunting. *Bloody hell*, I couldn't help but think. The diagram, with its multitude of lines and arrows, seemed more like a puzzle designed to test one's patience than a guide to shelter. I let out a sigh, a mixture of resignation and determination, and allowed a gentle shrug of my shoulders as if to physically shake off the sense of overwhelm.

Glancing across at Jamie, I noticed, not without a hint of surprise, his methodical approach to the task. Despite the tension between us, it was clear he had a knack for this sort of thing. My nose scrunched up in a reluctant acknowledgment of his competence. *At least Jamie seems to know what he is doing*, I admitted to myself, a begrudging respect for his skills forming amidst the turmoil of my emotions.

❖

With my focus squarely on the task of erecting the tent, the world around me had narrowed to the immediate challenge of poles and fabric. Thus, I was taken aback when Luke materialised almost directly in front of me, breaking the bubble of concentration I had encased myself in. "What are you doing?" The question fell from my lips almost instinctively, as I observed him pulling out his mobile phone, an action so mundane yet so starkly out of place in the context of Clivilius' alien landscape.

Luke's attempt to make a call, the phone pressed against his ear in a gesture of hopeful communication, seemed almost anachronistic against the backdrop of our current predicament. After a brief pause, during which the silence of Clivilius seemed to press in on me with a weight I hadn't noticed until now, he turned his questioning back to me. "Did your phone ring?" he inquired, his tone suggesting a mix of curiosity and concern.

The question prompted me to fish out my own phone from the depths of my jeans pocket. The device felt odd in my hand, a relic of a life that felt increasingly distant with each passing moment. The silence of Clivilius enveloped us, a stark contrast to the constant barrage of notifications and calls that used to punctuate my days back home. Here, the absence of digital noise had become its own presence, a reminder of our isolation. "No," I responded slowly, the realisation dawning on me. "Should it have?"

Luke's reply, while expected, still carried the weight of finality. "Well, I just tried calling it," he said, confirming my growing suspicion. "I needed to check to be sure, but it seems like our mobile phones are useless here." His suggestion to hand over the phone, with the promise of it being useful on the other side, stirred a mix of emotions within me.

The realisation that I hadn't even considered using my phone to call for help until this moment struck me with a mix of confusion and disbelief. It seemed so obvious, yet in the whirlwind of our arrival and the subsequent challenges, the thought had eluded me entirely. With a burgeoning flicker of hope, I dialled Claire's number, pressing the phone to my ear with a nervous anticipation that made my heart race. But the silence that greeted me was profound, a void where I had expected—at the very least—the familiar sound of a ringing tone. There was nothing; not even the soft buzz of a connection being made. Just an emptiness that seemed to stretch into infinity.

Driven by a mix of desperation and the irrational hope that it might have been a fluke, I attempted the call twice more. Each attempt met with the same eerie silence, a non-response that felt like a physical blow. In a fit of frustration, born out of the futility of the gesture and the crushing realisation of our isolation, I hurled the phone towards Luke's feet. It landed with a muted thud, the soft Clivilius dust cushioning its fall.

Luke bent to retrieve the phone, his actions deliberate as he inspected it for any signs of damage. His next request was almost mundane in its practicality, yet it carried an undercurrent of finality that was hard to ignore. "You'd better write your passcode down for me," he said, his gaze lifting to meet mine. The simplicity of the request belied the complexity of the emotions it evoked within me.

I found myself staring at him, my bewilderment mirrored in my wide eyes. The rapid shift from attempting a lifeline to the outside world to relinquishing my phone entirely left me reeling. *Jamie and I have only been in Clivilius for a few hours and already Luke is trying to take my phone off me.* The thought circled in my head, a whirlpool of confusion and suspicion. *What does he think he's playing at?*

The instinctive search for a pen, a motion born out of habit and the need to comply, ended with my hands emerging empty from my pockets. The gesture was almost laughable in its futility—not only did I lack a connection to the outside world, but now I also lacked the means to even follow through on Luke's simple request. The absurdity of the situation did little to lighten the mood. As I stood there, penless and increasingly disconnected, the chasm between my expectations for this adventure and the silent reality of our situation in Clivilius widened, a gap filled with doubt, frustration, and an ever-deepening sense of unease.

Luke's readiness, evidenced by the bag of items he held out towards me—paper and pens—left me momentarily taken aback. It was as if he had anticipated every turn before it happened, a step ahead in a dance I hadn't realised we were performing. "So, you knew?" The accusation slipped out, laced with a mix of betrayal and desperation. The thought that he might have foreseen the uselessness of our phones in Clivilius, yet hadn't shared his suspicions earlier, gnawed at me.

"I didn't know," Luke countered quickly, his hands raised in a gesture of defence, his eyes seeking understanding in mine. "I only suspected they wouldn't work. It made sense. There's nothing to connect to here and, apparently, signals can't come through the Portal." His explanation, logical as it was, did little to quell the rising tide of frustration within me.

"You know what you're asking, don't you?" The weight of my words was heavy, charged with the implications of his request. I was asking him to confirm, to acknowledge the enormity of what he was suggesting. "You want us to give up. To allow ourselves to be completely cut off from... from everything." The idea of being utterly isolated, not just physically but in every conceivable way from the life we knew, was daunting.

"Did your phone ring?" Luke's challenge, simple yet effective, cut through the complexity of my emotions. Holding up the phone, he forced me to confront the reality of our situation.

"No, but—" My protest faltered, the realisation dawning on me that he was right. The phone, a symbol of connection to a world we could no longer reach, was just that—a symbol, and nothing more.

"So, what difference does it make then?"

With a heavy sigh, I accepted the inevitable. Luke's logic, stark and unyielding, left no room for argument. Whether the phone remained in my possession or was handed over to Luke, it would change nothing for me here. Taking the bag from him, I tore into the ream of paper with a sense of resignation, scribbling down the phone's passcode. In that moment, the act felt symbolic, a reluctant concession.

For now, at least, it seemed prudent to go along with my brother. The resignation that settled over me was not just about the phone but about our situation as a whole. *It's not like I've got anything left to lose anymore.* The thought, bleak as it was, carried with it a strange sense of liberation. In the vast, unknown expanse of Clivilius, devoid of any connection to the life we once knew, what more was there to hold onto but each other?

"Your turn, Jamie," I called out, the words slipping out before I remembered the silent wall that had been erected between us. But Jamie, as if encased in his own world, simply continued with his task, ignoring my voice as if it were no more than a whisper of the wind.

"Jamie!" Luke's voice, firmer and more authoritative, cut through the tension. Jamie paused, his hands momentarily stilling from the rhythmic motion of driving the tent peg into the soft earth. He glanced up, a mix of annoyance and defiance brewing in his gaze. "You're not having my fucking phone, Luke." His voice was a blend of irritation and a firm resolve, as he moved along to the next peg, dismissing Luke's request with a finality that left no room for argument.

"Why him?" I couldn't help but whisper to Luke, a mixture of frustration and resignation colouring my tone. The drama that seemed to cling to my heels, trailing me from a life I thought I had left behind, now manifested in this new world, refusing to be shaken off.

Luke merely shrugged, a gesture that spoke volumes of his acceptance of the situation. "I'll keep this safe," he said, his fingers gently encircling my phone, a silent promise of protection. "In the meantime, you should both consider what your immediate needs are," he continued, his gaze drifting to Jamie with a deliberate intent. "Write them down, and I'll get busy keeping you both alive, okay?"

"Sure," I replied, the word falling flat, my mind grappling with the scarcity of alternatives available to me. It was an acceptance of our dire situation, cloaked in the veneer of cooperation.

"Good. So, Paul wants to stay alive. Jamie?" Luke's inquiry was met with a curt and dismissive response from Jamie, a stark "Fuck off," that echoed with a blend of anger and stubborn resistance.

Luke simply shrugged off Jamie's outburst, his eyes rolling in a silent commentary on the futility of anger. "I have a few things to take care of back on Earth. I'll come back for your list soon," he said, his tone casual yet underscored with a sense of duty that could not be ignored.

"What things have you got to take care of?" Jamie's voice, laced with skepticism and a sneer that twisted his features, broke the brief silence that had fallen between us.

My stomach churned again, an uncomfortable knot forming as I observed the challenging stare Jamie directed towards Luke. It was a look laden with frustration and defiance, a silent battleground set against the backdrop of our grim situation. I felt a sense of foreboding, the weight of the coming days pressing heavily upon me. The uncertainty of our survival hung in the air, thick and unspoken, a spectre that whispered doubts about the possibility of a 'next few days.'

"Oh, you know. Just things that will keep you alive. I could not bother if you'd prefer?" Luke's response carried a hint of sarcasm, a coping mechanism perhaps, but under the circumstances, it felt misplaced. His attempt at levity clashed with the stark reality of our predicament. Stranded in what appeared to be a vast desert bisected by a lone stream, our only shelter a ten-man tent still packed away, and our food supplies non-existent, sarcasm seemed a luxury we could ill afford.

"Just fuck off already, Luke," Jamie snapped back, his voice harsh, cutting through the tense air. I found myself silently agreeing with him. Luke's sarcasm, usually a source of amusement, now grated on my nerves. Yet, I kept my thoughts to myself, wary of adding fuel to the already blazing fire of our discontent.

"Fine," Luke conceded, the word heavy with disappointment. I watched as his usual cheerful demeanour faded, replaced by a tight grimace. His brows knitted together in frustration. It was rare to see Luke without his signature grin, and the sight added a sombre note to the already dismal atmosphere.

Luke offered me a resigned shrug, a silent communication of his intent to retreat, before turning to ascend the small, dusty hill towards the Portal. His departure marked by a sense of abandonment, leaving Jamie and me to confront the reality of our isolation.

"And put some bloody clothes on while you're there," Jamie's voice rang out, a final jab at Luke's retreating figure.

Despite the distance, Luke's reaction—or lack thereof—spoke volumes. He continued on without so much as a backward glance, his posture rigid against the barrage of Jamie's words.

I remained silent, watching Luke's figure diminish against the horizon, feeling an unsettling mix of frustration, concern, and a deep-seated fear for what lay ahead. Our survival hinged on cooperation, yet here we were, fragmented by tempers and egos. The desert around us seemed to echo our isolation, a vast expanse of uncertainty that mirrored the turmoil within.

As the echoes of our confrontation faded into the oppressive silence of the desert, I felt an overwhelming sense of desolation take hold. My heart, heavy and sinking, seemed to retreat further into the recesses of my chest, as if trying to escape reality. A peculiar darkness, both foreign and unsettling, began to weave its way through my veins, filling the spaces left by my retreating spirit with a cold, creeping dread. This sensation was foreign to me, an unsettling contrast to the warmth and light I yearned for, yet the anger that bubbled up from within was all too familiar—a bitter companion in these trying times.

"Why do you have to be so bloody nasty all the time?" The words burst forth from me, propelled by a cocktail of frustration and desperation. As they tore through the tense air, I could see the small balls of saliva catching the light. A part of me recoiled at the rawness of my outburst, chastising myself for allowing emotions to override reason. Yet, amidst the storm of regret, there was a whisper of relief, a slight unburdening of the weight that had been crushing my shoulders. They relaxed, if only marginally, a testament to the complex tapestry of human emotion.

For a fleeting moment, time seemed to stand still. Jamie halted, his movements ceasing as if my words had rooted him to the spot. The air between us was charged, heavy with unspoken thoughts and the weight of our shared hardships. It was a moment of profound stillness, a pause in the relentless march of our survival struggle, where the world seemed to hold its breath.

Then, as quickly as it had arrived, the moment passed. Jamie returned to his task, moving on to the next peg with a deliberate focus that seemed to dismiss the exchange as nothing more than a brief disturbance in the vast, indifferent expanse of our desert prison. Yet, that brief moment of stillness lingered in my mind, a poignant reminder of the fragile human connections that persisted, even in the face of our overwhelming adversity.

❖

Needing some time away from the constant tension that Jamie, or as I'd mentally dubbed him, Negative Nancy, brought into our already strained situation, I sought refuge upstream. The distance wasn't vast, merely fifty meters or so from where the tent, our supposed sanctuary, was to be erected, but it felt like a necessary journey for a semblance of peace. The bank of the river, with its gentle murmur, seemed like an ideal spot to collect my thoughts and fulfil Luke's request. Armed with paper and pen, I was determined to draft a list of essentials that would, hopefully, steer us towards survival.

However, the task proved more daunting than anticipated. The tranquility of the river did little to unblock the dam of creativity within me. Minutes stretched into what felt like an eternity, the blank page before me an unfortunate reminder of my struggling thought process. Finally, the pen made contact, the word "Clothes" materialising on the paper. It was a simple start, far from groundbreaking, yet undeniably crucial given our dire need for proper attire in this unforgiving environment.

As I continued to stare at the paper, willing more words to follow, I became acutely aware of a growing restlessness within me. Ideas refused to flow, mirroring the stagnation that seemed to have gripped my ability to think clearly. The frustration was palpable, a physical itch that demanded attention.

Reluctantly, I placed the paper and pen aside, the tools of a task momentarily abandoned, as I stood up to stretch my limbs. The need to move, to wander even just a little, became overwhelming. I scanned the surroundings for a bush, a natural call compelling me to seek some privacy. Yet, the landscape offered no such solace. The absence of bushes, yet another reminder of our exposed and vulnerable state, left me feeling even more isolated.

Looking behind me, Jamie's figure was a distant silhouette against the massive tent, his attention wholly absorbed by the task at hand. My gaze then shifted to my left, where the ground gently rose into a small hill, offering a semblance of privacy in the vast, open expanse. "That'll have to do," I muttered under my breath, a mix of desperation and resignation in my voice as I sought a momentary escape.

As I neared the crest of the hill, the landscape unfolded before me in a breathtaking panorama. Dusty hillocks rolled gently into the horizon, the river snaking through the barren expanse, its course disappearing into the distance. The vastness of the scene, coupled with its profound silence, struck me with a sense of awe and stillness. It was a world so large, so empty, and so eerily quiet, contrasting sharply with the inner turmoil I felt.

Quickening my pace to the bottom of the hill, I cast a wary glance around, ensuring Jamie's absence. Then, with a sigh of relief mixed with urgency, I undid the zipper on my jeans.

The simple act of relieving my bladder, there in the open wilderness, brought an unexpected sense of liberation, albeit fleeting.

But the relief was short-lived. A sudden, unwelcome urgency took hold, leaving me no choice but to succumb to nature's call in a more humbling manner. With a heavy sigh of resignation and embarrassment, I squatted over the dust, lamenting the lack of foresight to even scrape out a shallow hole. The situation was far from dignified.

With the burst of wind that accompanied the bowel movement, I knew it wasn't pretty. A pressing concern emerged: *What on earth am I meant to wipe with?* My eyes scanned the desolate landscape in desperation, the discomfort growing as my thighs protested the unnatural position. Time was running out, and the practicalities of survival in such an environment became overwhelmingly clear.

The thought of calling out to Jamie for assistance crossed my mind, a fleeting consideration born of desperation. *But what good would that do?* It was unlikely he'd be prepared for such a predicament. The realisation that I was truly on my own in this moment, faced with a challenge as basic as this, was a sobering reflection on our situation. It underscored the harsh realities of survival and the need for self-reliance in an environment that offered no concessions to comfort or dignity.

"Fuck it," I mumbled to myself, the words barely audible, lost amidst the vast, empty landscape that stretched around me. The frustration that tinged my voice was palpable, a raw reflection of the inner turmoil that this situation had stirred within me. After a moment of hesitation, a moment that felt infinitely longer under the circumstances, I stood up. My hands trembled, not just from the physical awkwardness of the situation, but from the emotional vulnerability that it had exposed. As I pulled up my pants, a sharp sting pricked at my eyes, a physical manifestation of the emotions I struggled to contain.

There it was, a mess that seemed so out of place in the natural beauty that surrounded me, yet a stinky reminder of the primal, basic nature of our existence. I couldn't help but stare down at it, my own discomfort magnified by the embarrassment of the situation. From every angle, it seemed to mock me, an absurd symbol of our predicament. And yet, something about it felt oddly significant, as if even in this humbling moment, there was a lesson to be learned.

The urge to understand, to make sense of the oddity before me, was overwhelming. Yet, I knew some mysteries were better left unexplored, especially under such pressing circumstances. Crouching down, I scooped up handfuls of the soft, dusty earth, gently covering the evidence of my discomfort. It was a crude burial, an attempt to mask my presence in this vast, untouched wilderness, but it was the best I could manage.

Then, with nothing left to do, I walked away. Each step took me further from the physical location of my discomfort, but the emotional residue lingered, a reminder of the vulnerability and rawness of our human condition. This moment, as undignified and unsettling as it was, served as a poignant reminder of our fragile existence in the face of nature's vast and indifferent expanse.

❖

As I made my way back to our nascent camp, each step felt heavier than the last. The embarrassment of my recent ordeal clung to me, a cloak of discomfort I couldn't easily shed. Approaching Jamie, I couldn't help but brace myself, a storm of anxiety swirling within. *Would Jamie notice?* The thought repeated in my head like a mantra, a persistent echo of my insecurity.

Jamie's glance was quick, but it cut through the air between us with surgical precision. "You stink like shit," he remarked, his voice carrying the blunt force of his usual candour. The words hit me like a physical blow, confirming my fears. I gritted my teeth in response, a mixture of frustration and resignation tightening my jaw. Of course, Jamie would notice. *As if he wouldn't. But really, what else was I meant to do in such a situation?* The options available to me were as barren as the landscape that surrounded us.

As I weighed my response, a clarity emerged from the mire of my embarrassment. "I'm getting in the river. Don't come over," I stated, my voice flat, devoid of the emotion roiling inside me. It was a declaration of intent, a boundary set not just to preserve my dignity but also to carve out a moment of solitude

To my surprise, Jamie's face shifted from its usual irreverence to something resembling seriousness. He nodded, a silent acknowledgment of the gravity of the situation. It was a small gesture, but in that moment, it felt significant.

As I ventured further along the river's edge than I had dared before, the silence of the surrounding landscape enveloped me. It was a quiet that spoke volumes, punctuated only by the gentle murmur of the river as it wound its way through the barren expanse. Ensuring I was a considerable distance from Jamie, I began to undress, seeking the refuge the river afforded.

Holding my soiled underwear in front of me, I was overcome with a mix of emotions. Disgrace and embarrassment surged through me, tinged with a sharp pang of anger. In a moment of frustration, I threw them into the water, watching as they were quickly swept away by the current. A sigh escaped me, laced with regret, as I realised the impracticality of my action. I chastised myself silently. *What an idiot.* The thought that I could have washed them instead of discarding them crossed my mind too late. With no spare underwear to replace them, I had acted rashly.

Shaking my head at the futility of dwelling on my mistake, I resigned myself to the situation. *It's too late for that now,* I thought, a sense of resolve settling over me. The priority was to cleanse myself, to wash away not just the physical remnants of my earlier misadventure but perhaps also the emotional weight it carried.

As I cautiously stepped into the clear, flowing river, an unexpected exhilaration surged through me. The coldness of the water was a shock to my system, invigorating and intense. I ventured further, until the water barely reached my knees, the shallowness offering a sense of security amidst the unfamiliar. Looking down at my feet, I was captivated by the clarity of the water, the way it flowed seamlessly around me, a mesmerising dance of light and movement.

Lowering myself into the river, I allowed the gentle current to caress my skin, the coolness enveloping me in a soothing embrace. The sensation of the water swirling around me was both refreshing and humbling, a moment of connection with the natural world.

With my eyes closed, I allowed myself a moment of pure, unadulterated connection with the world around me. I inhaled deeply, the air filling my lungs felt cleaner, purer than any I could recall. There was a freshness to it that seemed to cleanse from within, and as I drew in each breath, I noticed a subtle vibration—a whisper of the river's song—filtering through my senses. It wasn't just air; it felt like life itself was entering me, revitalising every cell in my body. A smile, wide and genuine, spread across my face, a rare moment of unguarded joy in the midst of our ordeal.

Breathing deeply, I felt an unparalleled sense of peace wash over me. The tension that had knotted my muscles, the worries that had clouded my mind, began to dissipate, as if the river's currents were carrying them away. It was a cleansing, both physical and emotional, leaving me lighter, more present in the moment than I had been for what felt like an eternity.

As I navigated my way through the water, returning to my full stature, I became acutely aware of the tiny droplets cascading off my body. They sparkled in the sunlight, each one a miniature prism, reflecting a world of simplicity and beauty. For a fleeting second, perfection didn't seem like such an impossible concept. Everything around me, within me, felt right.

Stepping back onto the riverbank, the contrast was immediate. The soft, fine dust of the bank clung to my wet feet, grounding me once again. Looking down at the dust now covering my feet, a sudden warmth flushed through my body. My face grew hot, embarrassingly so, as I realised the extent to which my body had responded to the brief respite in the river. "Oh," was the only sound that escaped my lips, a simple utterance that somehow encapsulated the complexity of my feelings in that moment.

The absence of a towel to dry off had me sighing in resignation. This new life, with its continuous challenges and adjustments, was becoming more tangible with each passing moment. I shook my body, an attempt to shed as much water as possible, the droplets flying off in all directions, a physical manifestation of trying to shake off the discomfort and adapt once more to the unforgiving environment that was now our home.

Opting to forego a shirt, I carefully stepped into my jeans, taking extra care to tuck myself in a manner that would draw the least attention from Jamie. The absence of underwear made me hyper-aware of my own body, a sensation that was both freeing and slightly uncomfortable. With my t-shirt casually slung over my shoulder and carrying my shoes and socks in hand, I retraced my steps back to the spot where I had hastily left my writing materials prior to my urgent dash to the river.

To my mild surprise, the paper and pen lay undisturbed. It seemed almost miraculous that something as simple as a piece of paper could remain untouched, a small beacon of stability in the unpredictable whirlwind that had become my new life.

As I reclaimed my seat in the dust, the distant clang of tent poles echoed, a reminder of Jamie's continued struggle with the tent. It was a sound that, under different circumstances, might have been annoying, but now it served as a grounding reminder of our shared endeavour to survive. No longer enveloped in the cloak of self-pity that had weighed heavily on me before my impromptu bath, I found a renewed sense of purpose.

The list in front of me was embarrassingly short, a reflection of the overwhelmed state I had been in. Yet, feeling somewhat rejuvenated by the river's embrace, I felt a flicker of determination. I gripped the pen with a newfound resolve, the tool suddenly feeling more like a weapon against despair than a mere writing instrument. With deliberate strokes, I added a fourth item to the list: *toilet paper.*

❖

"What now?" Jamie's voice pierced the quiet that had settled over us, his tone a mix of curiosity and impatience. I looked up as Luke made his way towards us, his approach marked by a light-heartedness that seemed out of place.

"I've got clothes on," Luke announced with a touch of theatrics, performing a small twirl that kicked up clouds of the fine, alien dust beneath him. His jeans fluttered awkwardly around his bare feet.

"You're such a dork," I couldn't help but laugh.

Luke smiled in response, the easy acceptance in his gesture reminding me of the bond we shared. "I know," he shrugged, his nonchalance a balm to the undercurrent of stress we all felt. He then held up a roll of garbage bags, an offering that was both practical and strangely thoughtful. "I figured rather than dirty a beautiful, clean world, you can put all the rubbish in these and I can take them back to Earth."

Beautiful? The thought echoed skeptically in my mind. Luke's optimism, his ability to see beauty in this desolate place, felt jarring, yet there was a part of me that envied his perspective.

"But how is that possible? I thought we couldn't leave?" Jamie's question was a valid one, voicing my own confusion.

"You can't," Luke clarified, his tone sobering. "But it seems that items can. I took Paul's phone, remember?" His words offered a sliver of hope, a possibility of connection to the world we had been torn from.

I stared at Luke, the realisation dawning on me. *My phone has left Clivilius.*

"You might want to keep anything combustible," Luke continued, pulling us back to the immediate concerns of survival. "We don't know what the conditions are like here at night, remember." His caution was a stark reminder of the unknowns that lay ahead, the unpredictable nature of our new environment.

At night, the words repeated in my head, a chilling prospect. *Am I really spending a night here?* The reality of our situation settled heavily on me, the nightfall bringing with it unknown dangers and challenges. Yet, despite the apprehension that gnawed at me, I found myself nodding in agreement.

As we set about the task of filling the first garbage bag with the remnants of our day, I couldn't help but notice Luke's glances in my direction. His eyes seemed to linger a little too long on my bare chest, stirring a mix of discomfort and irritation within me. I know I've kept in shape, and under different circumstances, I might have taken pride in the attention. But from Luke? It just made my skin crawl slightly. I mean, admiration is one thing, but this felt uncomfortably close to gawking.

"So..." Luke's voice cut through the air, drawn out in a way that immediately put me on edge. Jamie shot me a look, a silent warning that seemed to brace us both for what might be another round of unnecessary tension.

"So, what?" Jamie's response was terse, his focus remaining on the task at hand, clearly not in the mood to entertain whatever Luke was hinting at.

"So..." Luke pressed on, undeterred by Jamie's tone. "Why is it that you made such a big deal about me, your boyfriend, having no shirt on, yet you seem to be perfectly comfortable with my brother flashing himself around?" The question hung in the air, loaded and awkward, turning my task with the garbage bag into a clumsy fumble. The bag slipped, spilling its contents back onto the Clivilius dust, mirroring the mess of emotions I felt inside. My face flushed with a heat that seemed to rival the sun's, embarrassment coursing through me like wildfire.

Jamie's next words came as a surprise, a sudden shift from confrontation to practicality. "I think you better bring us a couple of towels, a few rolls of toilet paper and a shovel," he said, his request cutting through the awkwardness with a clarity that was almost refreshing. It was a moment of unexpected focus, a pivot towards the essentials we so desperately needed.

Luke, too, seemed taken aback by the turn in conversation, his expression shifting from provocation to consideration. His surprise mirrored my own, a shared recognition of Jamie's constructive input breaking through the tension.

"Oh, and I really need my overnight bag of clothes, too," I chimed in, eager to latch onto this new thread of conversation, one that promised a semblance of normalcy, or at least as normal as could be under our strange new circumstances. Luke's nod, silent and understanding, offered a moment of truce, an unspoken agreement to move forward, focusing on the practical needs that would help us navigate the coming days in Clivilius.

❖

As the moment of truth approached, the air around us felt charged with a mix of anticipation and uncertainty. The three of us, united in purpose if nothing else, made the final adjustments before Luke's attempt to traverse the unknown with our refuse in tow. My thoughts momentarily drifted to the list I had compiled, a tangible representation of our hopes and needs. Retrieving it from my pocket, I noticed the damp patches that marred its surface—a reminder of the river's embrace. With a futile gesture, I blew on it, as if my breath could erase the marks of my ordeal. Handing it to Luke felt significant, like entrusting him with more than just a piece of paper; it was a piece of our collective hope.

Luke received the list with a solemnity that mirrored the gravity of the moment. His careful folding of the paper and the deliberate way he secured it in his pocket underscored his understanding of its importance. "I'll be sure to get everything you need," he assured us, his voice steady and resolute. The promise felt heavy, laden with the weight of our reliance on him.

As Luke prepared to step through the portal, Jamie and I stood by, a silent support network bracing for the outcome. The moment he walked through the mesmerising colours, disappearing along with the first two garbage bags, our collective breath caught in our throats. The sight was both awe-inspiring and surreal.

Jamie's reaction, turning to face me with a grin and a flicker of hope in his eyes, was contagious. "There may be hope for us yet," he declared, and I could hear the underlying belief in his words. It was a statement that carried more weight than a mere observation; it was a declaration of newfound optimism.

In the wake of Jamie's comment, I found myself caught in a whirlpool of thoughts. The successful departure of Luke, even if just to dispose of our garbage, opened a door to possibilities that had seemed firmly shut. *Could Jamie be right? Was there indeed hope for us in this bizarre twist of fate?* The very idea that items—and potentially, by extension, we—could leave this place ignited a spark of hope within me. It was a daunting prospect, riddled with unknowns, yet undeniably compelling.

THE POO QUEST

4338.205.6

"Shit!" The exclamation burst from my lips as the tent pole, slick with the sweat from my palms, escaped my grasp. The end of it struck me sharply on the side of the head, a brief flash of pain that was as surprising as it was sharp, before it clattered to the ground with a sound that seemed overly dramatic in the quiet of our surroundings.

"Hey!" Jamie's voice, tinged with concern and a hint of frustration, carried across the expanse of what was to be our first shelter. The structure itself seemed to share in our moment of disarray, wobbling precariously as the corner I had been responsible for gave way, yet again. The large tent, ambitious in its size given our limited experience, challenged our determination—or perhaps our naivety.

Despite the progress we had been making in Luke's absence, the incident left me questioning my own capabilities. The realm of manual labour, it appeared, was filled with nuances and difficulties that I hadn't fully appreciated until now. The irony was not lost on me; here I was, struggling to erect a basic shelter, a task that humans had mastered millennia ago, yet feeling utterly out of my depth.

"Sorry," My voice carried back to Jamie, an attempt to bridge the physical and metaphorical distance between us. As I rubbed the side of my head, probing for any signs of injury, a part of me expected to find a burgeoning lump, a physical manifestation of my ineptitude. Finding none, I let out a small sigh of relief, a momentary pause in the string of setbacks that seemed to characterise our attempt at setting up camp.

Bending down, I retrieved the pole from the dust, its surface gritty against my skin, as the fine particles clung to my hands. With a renewed sense of determination, or perhaps stubbornness, I grasped the pole firmly, ready to give it another try. The task at hand was clear, even if our success was anything but guaranteed.

The sight of Luke's returning figure was like a beacon in the vastness of Clivilius, momentarily eclipsing all other concerns. The pole, and with it the precarious stability of our tent, was forgotten as I rushed to meet him, the relief at his safe return momentarily lifting the weight of our situation. "Finally!" The word was a burst of emotion, a mixture of relief, anticipation, and a touch of desperation.

"I wasn't gone that long," Luke retorted, his voice carrying a lightness that contrasted sharply with the tension I had felt in his absence. The practical items he handed over—a shovel and several rolls of toilet paper—were symbols of the normalcy we were struggling to maintain.

"You were gone long enough," Jamie's voice cut through. His gesture towards the tent was a silent testament to the efforts and frustrations that had filled the interim.

Luke's optimism seemed undiminished by our clear struggle. "You've made great progress. You'll have it finished in no time," he said, his cheerfulness bordering on the unrealistic given the state of our construction efforts. His promise to return with clothes for me was a reminder of the basic necessities we were still scrambling to secure, the simple comforts of life on Earth that felt so distant here.

"Good idea," I responded, a touch self-consciously, the dust of Clivilius mingling uncomfortably with my sweat, creating a layer of grime that made me acutely aware of my current state of undress. Luke's hasty departure, with the promise of quick relief, left a void that was immediately filled by Jamie's pragmatic focus.

The look I shot Jamie, a silent plea for a momentary reprieve, went unappreciated. His directive to resume work on the tent, coupled with the moniker "clumsy," was a jarring call back to reality. I cringed, not just at the nickname but at the truth it carried. The tent, with all its challenges, did indeed feel like a 'bloody obstacle' in more ways than one.

Yet, Jamie's blunt encouragement sparked something within me—a determination, perhaps born of necessity or pride, or a mixture of both. With a renewed sense of purpose, I approached the task at hand. The tent pole, once a symbol of my frustrations, snapped into position with a satisfying click. It was a small victory, but in the vast uncertainty of Clivilius, even the smallest step forward felt like a monumental achievement.

❖

The tent, a beacon of our hard work against the backdrop of an unforgiving landscape, stood proudly as Luke's voice broke through the silence, vibrant and full of life. "The tent looks amazing!" he exclaimed, his excitement palpable in the cool air that surrounded us. "Is it finished now?" he inquired, his gaze eagerly sweeping over the structure that had absorbed so much of our time and dedication.

"Pretty much," Jamie replied, a note of satisfaction in his voice. He accepted the suitcase from Luke with a nod. Then, turning to me, Luke handed over my overnight bag and backpack, their familiar weight settling in my hands. "Thanks," I said, feeling a mix of gratitude and the impending sense of Luke's departure.

As Luke turned away, his next words lingered in the air, touching a soft spot in my heart. "Duke misses you," he said to Jamie, his tone laced with a gentle sadness. The statement, simple yet profound, echoed within me. I watched Luke's figure recede towards the pile of rubbish we had amassed. "He knew as soon as I got the suitcase out that you were going away," Luke's voice faded, trailing off into the distance.

In that moment, my mind conjured the image of Charlie, my dark grey Kelpie, her presence a vivid memory against the starkness of our surroundings. How I yearned for her companionship, her boundless energy and the unconditional love she offered. The thought of her brought a fleeting sense of comfort.

Yet, as I allowed myself another deep sigh, the reality of our situation settled heavily upon me. Observing the endless expanse of brown and yellow dust, a bleak canvas under the relentless sun, the truth became painfully clear. This environment, harsh and unforgiving, was no place for a dog as spirited and vibrant as Charlie. The realisation was a sombre one, underscoring the sacrifices and choices we were forced to make in our quest for survival.

"Take these back with you," I said, my voice more firm than I intended as I thrust several black garbage bags into Luke's arms. The bags, swollen with the detritus of our recent efforts, seemed almost comical in their bulkiness.

Luke's eyes widened slightly as he assessed the bulging sacks of rubbish. "I don't think the bin will fit both of those," he remarked, skepticism painting his features. His doubt was not unfounded; the bags were indeed a testament to our extensive cleanup.

"I'm sure you'll think of something," I encouraged, attempting to infuse a note of optimism into the situation. "We've also made a small pile of cardboard we can burn, over there," I added, gesturing vaguely to the site where a modest mound of cardboard lay as evidence of our attempt at tidiness.

A smile cracked across Luke's face, a silent acknowledgment of the challenge accepted. He hoisted the bags with a resigned determination and began his journey back to the Portal, the weight of our collective refuse in tow.

Turning back to our immediate surroundings, Jamie's voice broke the brief silence. "We may as well unpack these in the tent," he suggested, his tone pragmatic, carrying his suitcase with an ease that belied its apparent weight. His biceps flexed under the strain.

Dragging my own bag with considerably less grace, I followed Jamie into the tent, my enthusiasm waning with each step. "And put them away where?" I queried, my voice laced with a weariness that mirrored my physical state.

Jamie didn't miss a beat, placing his suitcase down in the right wing of our spacious tent. His movement was fluid, practiced, but the space did not welcome us as it should have. "For fuck's sake!" Jamie's frustration erupted.

I chose to ignore Jamie's outburst, though it echoed loudly within the canvas walls of our temporary abode. Inside, I felt a stir of agreement, a shared sentiment of frustration that I pushed aside. I took my bag to the left wing, seeking solitude in the act of rummaging through my belongings. Quietly, I found a blue singlet, a small comfort against the relentless dust that seemed to permeate everything.

Feeling the confines of the tent closing in, both physically and metaphorically, I made a decision. "I'm going for a walk," I announced to Jamie, the words barely escaping before I turned and left the tent behind.

❖

I collected the shovel from where I had left it lying on the ground alongside the two rolls of toilet paper. The items seemed almost out of place in the natural setting, a stark reminder of our human needs in the midst of this desert. Leaving the toilet paper behind, I ventured along the edge of the river upstream. The soft burbling of the water, a constant companion in this otherwise silent world, soothed my troubled mind. Its melody, both calming and relentless, hinted at the eternal cycle of nature, unbothered by human concerns. I could easily have stripped off my clothes and jumped back in, the cool embrace of the water promising a temporary escape from the heat and the dust. But I was on a mission—a mission that, in its absurdity, had become a focal point for my scattered thoughts. Somewhere, out there in the fine dust that seemed to coat every surface and fill every breath, a poo needed a proper burial.

Breaking from the river's comforting proximity, I turned due west. The transition was marked, from the soft, malleable banks of the river to the increasingly arid and unforgiving ground. I was nearing the spot, I was sure of it. My determination solidified with each step, even as the landscape offered no encouragement. My eyes locked in a constant stare on the ground around me, searching with a focus that felt oddly intense given the nature of my quest.

"Hmm," I wondered aloud, bringing myself to a halt. The large, round boulder protruding from the ground in front of me served as a landmark in this almost featureless expanse. *But where is my poo?* The question, absurd on its face, took on a gravity that felt disproportionate in the moment. My eyes opened wide with curiosity initially, then fear. The possibility that something—some creature of the desert—might have claimed my poo was unsettling. *Did something actually take my poo?* The thought was ludicrous, yet in the silence and isolation of this place, every possibility seemed magnified.

I raised the shovel, holding it in front of me more as a talisman than a weapon, ready for any fight. The gesture was more reflexive than rational, a symbol of my readiness to confront whatever this wild place might throw at me.

"Hello?" I called out, my voice breaking the silence with a note of defiance. Taking a few steps beyond the boulder, I peered into the expanse, half-expecting an answer. But the silence that greeted me was complete, a reminder of my isolation.

The absurdity of the situation wasn't lost on me. Here I was, armed with a shovel, on a mission to bury my own waste, confronting the vastness and indifference of nature with a mix of determination and unease.

A gentle breeze flirted with the edges of my fringe, offering a brief respite from the unyielding heat. I found myself rubbing at my arms, not entirely from the chill but more from a subconscious attempt to comfort myself amidst the vast emptiness. Lifting my gaze to the clear, blue sky, I noted its constant, unblemished canvas. Not a single cloud dared to mar its perfection, nor did any bird dare to slice through its expanse with a call. It was a silence so profound, it felt like a weight, pressing down with an almost tactile presence. I shivered again, not from cold, but from the realisation of my utter isolation. Another breeze whispered across my arms, as if nature itself was attempting to offer a semblance of companionship.

If I can't find the poo soon, I found myself thinking, a hint of resignation threading through the notion, *I'll just head back to the tent*. The thought of Jamie immediately surfaced, the possibility that he might be wondering about my whereabouts. But as quickly as it came, skepticism followed, snuffing out the fleeting concern. I shook my head, almost amused by my own naivety. *Or not*, I corrected myself, the reality of Jamie's indifference settling in. The absurdity of expecting any form of camaraderie or concern in this desolate landscape was laughable.

Motivated by a mix of determination and the need to conclude this bizarre quest, I took several more strides across the barren dust. The landscape seemed to stretch on endlessly, a sea of monotony. Then, suddenly, "Aha!" The exclamation burst from me, a small victory against the backdrop of desolation. There it was, the object of my singular focus—the dust-covered poo. It wasn't customary for me to fixate on such things. Yet, under the circumstances, this had become my mission, a peculiar but necessary task.

Crouching down, I found myself drawn into an inspection that felt oddly significant. *It's so strange*, I mused, the detective in me awakening. There were no ants marching towards it, no flies buzzing overhead, no signs of any critter that might consider this a feast. It was as if Clivilius was devoid of life, or at least, the kind of life that took interest in such organic offerings.

The realisation was eerie, unsettling even. Here I was, in a world that seemed to reject the very essence of what I had always known to be a natural cycle of life. The absence of life, or its apparent indifference to what should have been a natural attractant, underscored the alienness of this environment. It seemed Clivilius harboured no life that thrived on the remains of others, or if it did, it had no interest in what I had to offer.

The shovel sank into the soft ground with surprising ease, initially giving me a false sense of simplicity in the task at hand. But as I scooped away a couple of handfuls of dust, I quickly encountered the firm crust beneath—a hard contrast to the initial layer, almost as if the planet itself was challenging me, refusing to yield easily to my efforts. I crouched down to inspect this resistant layer more closely, its darker hue suggesting a compactness that the surface dust barely hinted at. Curiously, I touched the crust with the tip of my finger, pressing lightly. It left a small but visible indent, a minor victory against this unyielding barrier.

Standing again, I took a moment to steel myself for the next attempt. Gripping the shovel handle with renewed determination, I raised it high and drove it down with all the force I could muster. The crust gave way with a loud crack at the point of impact, a sound that echoed slightly in the silent expanse around me. Encouraged, I wriggled the shovel into the newfound crack, leveraging my weight with a heavy jump. To my satisfaction, the shovel sank beneath the dark crust, breaking through the barrier that had seemed so defiant moments before.

Much better, I thought with a small sense of triumph, as I tossed the last of the mixed dark soil and soft dust into the small hole where I had laid the poo to rest. *It's safe now*, I assured myself, a bizarre sentiment to have over such a task, yet there it was—a feeling of completion, of having done something necessary, however odd it might seem.

My gaze then shifted to the broader task of marking this spot. The thought of accidentally stumbling upon this toilet site in the future brought a grimace to my face. It would be most unpleasant, indeed. I scanned the desolate landscape for something—anything—that could serve as a marker. But the barrenness offered no aid; no tree, no bush, not even a stray branch to repurpose. My eyes fell back to the shovel in my hand, the only tool, the only companion, in this endeavour. *It'll have to do*, I resolved.

With that decision made, I gripped the shovel even tighter and raised it once more. This time, my action was not just about breaking through the crust but about leaving a lasting sign of my presence, of my intervention in this alien soil. I drove the shovel down into the firm crust with all the force I could summon, a final act of determination. The shovel stood there, upright and firm, a solitary marker in a vast, empty landscape, a testament to the oddity of the task I had completed and a guidepost for the memory of this moment, however strange it might be.

❖

The return to the tent felt surprisingly swift, the landscape having tricked my senses into thinking I'd ventured further than I actually had. The realisation struck me with a mix of relief and disorientation. *I haven't wandered so far after all,* I realised, the familiar silhouette of our makeshift home coming into view more quickly than anticipated.

Upon my arrival, Jamie's immediate concern cut through any lingering thoughts. "Where's the shovel?" he asked, his gaze scanning me, expecting to see it in my hands.

"Oh," I responded, slightly taken aback by the abrupt shift to practicalities. "I've left it in the ground to mark our toilet spot. We can use that as our guide. We may as well do our business in a single location." It seemed like a logical solution at the time, a way to bring some semblance of order to our barren living conditions.

Jamie's reaction was immediate, his face contorting in a mix of disgust and resignation. "I guess," he said, the idea clearly not appealing to him. His suggestion that followed was unexpected. "Maybe we should build a long drop."

"A long drop?" I echoed, the term sparking a vague memory of basic outdoor survival tips I'd heard long ago.

"Yeah," Jamie confirmed, his voice carrying a hint of enthusiasm now, mixed with a candid admission. "Although I'm not really sure how we do that," he confessed dryly, the optimism fading as quickly as it had appeared. His pause was heavy, laden with a grim acceptance before he added, "We're going to die here."

The weight of his words hung in the air, thick and undeniable. I found myself rubbing my forehead, a gesture of stress and deep thought. Jamie's blunt assessment of our situation was hard to dismiss. I hadn't been camping since I was a child. The skills, the knowledge required to survive in an environment as unforgiving as this, seemed beyond my grasp. *What hope do we have of surviving here?* The question loomed large, threatening to engulf the flickers of hope I tried to nurture.

But surrendering to despair wasn't an option. We needed to remain positive, to cling to any sliver of hope, no matter how slim. "We just need—" I began, my thoughts scrambling for a plan, for any course of action that might improve our odds.

Before I could gather my thoughts, the sound of Luke's voice cut across the distance, pulling our attention away from the bleak spiral of our conversation. The urgency in his tone was enough to shift the mood, to offer a distraction, however brief.

"The mattress!" Jamie exclaimed, the previous conversation momentarily forgotten as he set off into a gentle jog toward the Portal. His sudden movement, spurred by Luke's call, was a stark reminder of our situation—constantly reacting, constantly adapting.

Curiosity tugged at my thoughts as I followed Jamie, eager to discover what had unfolded between him and Luke during my absence. My initial step back into their company was met with a scene that stretched the boundaries of my imagination. Luke, with a display of both determination and weariness, was hauling a king-size mattress through the Portal. The sight was so out of place, so incredibly surreal, that my face instinctively broke into an expression of astonishment. The mattress seemed to wrestle with the confines of the Portal, a bulky invader from another realm making its grand entrance into ours.

Without a word being exchanged, Jamie and I instinctively knew to jump into action. We approached Luke, and together, we lifted the cumbersome mattress. It was a moment that seamlessly blended the absurd with the cooperative, transforming what could have been an arduous task for Luke alone into a manageable, almost light-hearted endeavour for the three of us. As we carried the mattress towards the tent, I couldn't help but feel a sense of unity, a camaraderie forged in the most unexpected of circumstances.

No sooner had we positioned the mattress inside the tent than Luke was off again, this time returning with an armful of sheets and blankets. The fabrics, caught by the wind, fluttered gently, adding a touch of grace to the ruggedness of our surroundings. As we spread the sheets over the mattress, transforming it from a mere object to a place of rest, the action felt deeply symbolic. It was as though we were staking a claim, marking this small piece of the unknown as ours, if only for the night.

Laying out the blankets, I was struck by the peculiar intimacy of the moment. Here we were, three individuals, united by circumstance, creating a semblance of home in the midst of nowhere. Every tug and fold of the fabric was a small declaration of our resilience, a testament to our ability to find a little comfort in the face of the unknown.

Luke's apologetic tone, "Sorry there's only one tent and mattress," was met with my instinctive shrug. "I can't believe we haven't even been here for twenty-four hours. It feels like a week already," I mused aloud, the sentiment echoing my internal disorientation and the skewed perception of time.

"I know," Jamie chimed in, a lightness to his tone that I hadn't heard since our arrival. "At least I might get a decent night's sleep without Duke and Henri," he joked.

Luke's chuckle, a low, self-amused sound, broke through my reverie. "And I forgive you for sleeping with my brother for a night." His words, meant in jest, seemed to bridge the gap between the tension of our situation and the semblance of normalcy we were all grappling to find.

Jamie and I both laughed in return, a spontaneous eruption of genuine amusement that caught me off guard. It was a pleasant surprise, a brief respite from the constant undercurrent of uncertainty. The laughter felt like a lifeline, pulling me back from the brink of despair to a moment of shared humanity. It was the first time either of us had laughed since entering this strange world, a world that seemed to demand so much of us yet offered these fleeting moments of connection in return.

"I've ordered a few more tents," Luke interrupted, his voice cutting through the lingering chuckles. "They should arrive tomorrow." His statement was a promise of improved conditions and perhaps a bit more privacy.

"I hope they're at least as big as this one," I found myself saying, the thought of space, of having a corner of this vast unknown to call my own, sparking a flicker of excitement within me. "I could get used to having that much space to myself."

"Yes. They're the same size," Luke confirmed, and I could feel my spirits lift at the prospect. The idea of enduring this adventure with just a bit of personal space made the challenges seem more bearable. I'd only have to spend one night sharing the tent with Jamie. We'd have to share the mattress, but the promise of our own private wing for dressing offered a sliver of dignity.

"Now," Jamie's voice pulled me back to the present, a note of practicality in his tone as he addressed Luke. "That wood you were going to get?"

I looked at Jamie. "Wood?" I asked, having clearly missed some vital information while I was... *preoccupied*... earlier.

Luke swallowed hard, his Adam's apple bobbing in a visible sign of his unease. "I'll get it right now." His words, simple yet laden with the weight of responsibility, reminded me of the precariousness of our situation. We were all leaning on each other, dependent on each other's strengths to navigate this unfamiliar terrain.

As Luke set off to fulfil his promise, I was left with a renewed sense of the delicate balance we had struck between camaraderie and survival. Each of us, in our own way, was trying to contribute, to make this strange world a little more hospitable, a little more like home. And in that moment, I understood that our laughter, our jokes, and even our shared discomfort were the threads weaving us together, creating a tapestry of resilience in the face of the unknown.

OVERWHELMING WATERS

4338.205.7

The thought nagged at the edges of my consciousness, an uninvited but increasingly irresistible guest. The river, with its clear, flowing water, seemed to sing a siren song just for me, its voice a soft, enchanting whisper that curled around my name. *Paul,* it seemed to sigh, a gentle caress against the turmoil of my thoughts. *Come bathe in me.*

I had been doing my best to ignore it, to focus on the myriad tasks and challenges that our strange new world presented. Yet, the call of the river was persistent, a reminder of simple pleasures and basic human needs amidst the upheaval of survival and discovery.

"Where are you off to?" Jamie's voice snapped, pulling me from the brink of my daydreams.

I paused, feeling the weight of the dust and sweat that clung to my skin. I looked down at my legs, brushing away the fine layer of dust that seemed to cover everything here, a tangible reminder of the distance between this world and home. "We've been sitting here for ages," I found myself saying, the words a mixture of explanation and justification for the longing that tugged at me.

"So?" Jamie's reply was curt.

"So, I'm going to go have a quick dip in the river." My response was more decisive than I felt, propelled by a need for the comfort of water, for the cleansing and renewal it promised. I didn't wait for a response, didn't pause to gauge Jamie's reaction. Instead, I hurried to the tent, driven by a sudden urgency.

Grabbing a towel, I felt a mix of anticipation and guilt. The luxury of a bath, of immersing myself in the cool embrace of the river, felt almost indulgent amidst our struggles for survival. Yet, it was a call I could no longer resist—a moment of respite I desperately needed.

Which way? The question echoed in my mind as I stood on the bank of the river behind our makeshift camp. The choice seemed significant, more than just a matter of direction. *Not upstream*, I reminded myself with a shudder. *That's poo territory!*

Deciding to go downstream, I allowed the river to guide my steps, following its path as it carved a serpentine trail through the Clivilius ground. The landscape here was alien yet familiar, a paradox that tugged at my sense of wonder and unease in equal measure. The river widened the further I ventured, its banks stretching out as if to embrace the horizon. It took a slow, meandering curve to the east, leading me away from the immediacy of our camp's concerns and into a tranquility I hadn't realised I was seeking.

After navigating a few small hills, an unexpected sight unfolded before me—a little lagoon, tucked away almost secretively at the end of the river's bend. It was fed by a small break in the main river, a gentle influx of water that kept it replenished. I approached with a mix of curiosity and caution, conscious of the newness of everything around me and the need to tread lightly.

Peering into the clear, calm water, I was struck by its transparency, the way it laid bare the lagoon's bed with a vulnerability that felt almost intimate. The bottom was a mosaic of small pebbles, their shapes and colours a hint to the river's long history, a story told in stone and sediment. Yet, for all its serene beauty, the lagoon was devoid of life. No fish darted in its depths, no mosquitoes or gnats skimmed its surface, and no signs of algae or plant life clouded its clarity.

This absence of life filled me with a profound sense of solitude. Here, in this secluded spot, the world seemed paused, held in a moment of silent contemplation. It was as if the lagoon existed out of time, a hidden corner of the Clivilius ground untouched by the unpredictability that marked the rest of our surroundings.

Kicking off my shoes, I took a moment to stand barefoot at the edge of the lagoon, the cool earth beneath my feet grounding me to this alien yet eerily serene environment. With a tentative motion, I dipped my toes into the water, feeling a cool tingle of excitement shoot up my leg—a sensation so vivid and refreshing it momentarily pushed away the lingering unease. There was a hesitation that followed, a brief battle within me. I knew it might happen again if I stepped in completely—the overwhelming sense of vulnerability, the stark reminder of my nakedness in this unknown world. Yet, the allure of the water, with its promise of a brief escape from the weight of our circumstances, whispered seductively, *But it's worth it.*

Yielding to the call, it took only a matter of seconds for my clothes to join my shoes, carelessly strewn along the bank. My naked body slid into the lagoon's embrace, the fresh water enveloping me in an intoxicating caress that sent ripples of sexual desire coursing through every inch of my skin. The sensation was almost too intense, a definitive contrast to the dusty heat and constant vigilance that had defined the day. Here, in the water, I found a momentary sanctuary, a place where the harsh realities of our camp seemed to dissolve, leaving behind a purity of sensation that was both exhilarating and deeply unsettling.

As I submerged further, allowing the water to cover me, to reach places parched by the sun and strained by the tension of constant alertness, I couldn't help but close my eyes and surrender to the experience. The coolness of the lagoon was a balm, a gentle yet powerful reminder of the life-affirming joy of water. It was as if the lagoon itself was alive, its waters whispering secrets of this strange world, secrets that danced tantalisingly just out of reach of my understanding.

The vulnerability of my nakedness in the water, far from the prying eyes of Jamie and Luke, allowed a rare introspection. It stripped away the layers of fear, responsibility, and the unspoken pressures of leadership, revealing a raw, unguarded version of myself. It was a version that I seldom acknowledged, one that craved not just physical but emotional release from the burdens I carried.

Floating there, suspended in the lagoon's gentle clasp, I felt a connection to the world around me that was both profound and profoundly disconcerting. It was a reminder that, despite the alienness of our surroundings, there were still elements of beauty, moments of respite that could be found. Yet, even as I basked in the sensation, the reality of our situation loomed at the back of my mind—a reminder that this escape, however intoxicating, was only temporary.

The water, with its clear, calm surface and hidden depths, became a metaphor for the journey we were on. It offered a reflection of the complexities and contradictions of our existence in this place: the surface calm belying the turmoil beneath, the tranquility of the moment a fragile barrier against the challenges that awaited us beyond the lagoon's secluded banks.

As the invigorating and pleasurable sensations coursed through me, a wild, unabashed grin took hold of my face. It was a physical manifestation of the pure, unadulterated joy that seemed to bubble up from somewhere deep within, a place I hadn't realised was parched for this kind of release. Laying on my back, buoyed by the gentle embrace of the lagoon, I could feel the tiny water particles, cooler than the air yet warmed by the sun's touch, mingling with my skin.

They seemed to seep into every pore, a delicate invasion that promised rejuvenation and a strange sort of communion with this strange world.

Be one with me, Paul, the soothing voice of Clivilius whispered in my ears, a figment of my imagination that felt as real as the water cradling me. It was a call to surrender, to let go of the barriers and walls I had erected around myself. I closed my eyes, not in fear, but in a willing embrace of this moment of connection. The feelings of joy and passion, so rare in my life, intensified, filling me with a warmth that seemed to radiate from my very core.

The lagoon, in this moment, became more than a body of water; it was a living entity, whispering secrets of Clivilius, secrets of life and existence so profound they defied words. I allowed these feelings to wash over me, to engulf my senses entirely, overwhelming yet oddly comforting. It was a surrender to the moment, to the sensation, to the undeniable truth that despite the strangeness of our surroundings, there were experiences here that touched on something universal, something deeply human.

This overwhelming sensory experience was not just about the physical pleasure of the water's touch, but about the deeper, almost spiritual connection it fostered. It was a reminder of the planet's raw beauty and mystery, a beauty that was both exhilarating and humbling. Floating there, I felt a part of something larger than myself, a tiny thread woven into the vast tapestry of this world.

Yet, even as I basked in this sensation, a part of me remained acutely aware of the surreal nature of the experience. This moment of unity, of almost transcendent joy, was a stark contrast to the challenges and uncertainties that lay beyond the lagoon's tranquil shores. It underscored the complexity of our situation—caught between moments of profound connection and the relentless reality of survival.

As the sensations reached their zenith, leaving me breathless and momentarily sated, I realised that this moment was a gift—an ephemeral taste of peace and belonging in a world that was still largely unknown and daunting. It was a powerful, if fleeting, affirmation of life's capacity to surprise, to offer moments of beauty and pleasure even in the most unexpected circumstances.

CAMPFIRE

4338.205.8

Towelling myself dry on the dusty bank of the lagoon, the sense of tranquility I had felt in the water began to ebb away. As I stood there, the air seemed to shift around me, losing the purity that had enveloped me so completely moments before. Instinctively, I sniffed the air, searching for a clue to this sudden change. Something was different, and it wasn't just the transition from water to land.

I turned my gaze towards what I believed was the direction of our camp, squinting against the light. My heart skipped a beat. *Am I seeing things?* A small trail of grey smoke was snaking its way into the sky, a stark contrast against the clarity of the atmosphere I had become accustomed to. Panic surged within me, icy and sharp.

"The tent!" The words ripped from my throat before I could think. *It has to be the tent on fire. There's nothing else here!* The thought propelled me into action with a sense of urgency I hadn't known I possessed.

Wrapping the towel tightly around my waist, I grabbed my clothes in a hasty bundle and took off towards the camp, my feet barely touching the ground. As I ran, the dampness of my skin mingled with the fine dust of the Clivilius ground, creating a gritty layer on my legs. Each stride sent a cloud of dust swirling into the air, marking my frantic passage.

"Jamie! Fire!" I shouted, my voice strained with fear and exertion, as I neared the final hill that separated me from the camp. The weight of the situation pressed down on me, heavy and suffocating. "Fire!" I called out again, my voice breaking as I crested the peak of the small incline, the imagined sight of our camp in flames already burning behind my eyes.

"For fuck's sake! I know there's a fire!" Jamie's response cut through the air, a mix of irritation and something else I couldn't quite place.

I stopped dead in my tracks, my frantic momentum halted by the unexpected reply. My eyes widened, the adrenaline that had fuelled my sprint suddenly draining away as they settled on the scene before me. The campfire, crackling merrily, was the source of the smoke.

"I got the campfire started," Jamie said, his tone now softer, perhaps sensing my embarrassment.

"Oh," was all I could manage in reply, the heat of my flushed face competing with the warmth of the fire. The embarrassment was a tangible force, washing over me in waves of red. "That's great." My words felt inadequate, a poor cover for the mix of relief and foolishness that tangled inside me.

The small campfire before us crackled and popped, as Jamie tossed another piece of kindling into its heart. "All I could see from over the hill was smoke. I was worried that it may have been the tent. We've got nothing else here," I found myself explaining, my voice tinged with the residual adrenaline from my mistaken panic.

"Obviously," Jamie's reply came with a sneer.

Shrugging off Jamie's remark, I remained standing there, awkwardly holding my clothes under one arm, my mind racing for a solution to dry off without giving Jamie more ammunition for his evidently sharp tongue. Despite the tension, I couldn't help but take a moment to observe him. Luke had chosen well, at least in terms of aesthetics. Jamie, standing a little under six feet, presented a compact yet impressively muscular figure. And on manscaping, my mind added, an involuntary observation as my gaze lingered momentarily on Jamie's well-defined abs, revealed as he casually pulled his t-shirt over his head in a display of nonchalance and confidence.

"Don't let the fire go out," Jamie's voice cut through my thoughts, a clear instruction that brought me back to the present moment and the practicalities of our situation. His directive, simple yet loaded with the unspoken responsibilities that had fallen on our shoulders, anchored me back to the immediate needs of our camp.

Shaking my head in an attempt to dispel the lingering fog of embarrassment and redirect my focus, I voiced the concern that had been gnawing at the edges of my mind. "Are you sure having a fire is the best thing?" The words tumbled out, laced with a hesitance that mirrored my internal conflict. "What if there is something out there and our fire... attracts it?"

Jamie paused, his movements halting midway through the act of unzipping his jeans, a gesture that under any other circumstances might have gone unnoticed. He looked up at me, his expression shifting from one of casual indifference to serious contemplation. "You really think there might be something else out there?"

"Maybe," I shrugged, my response a non-committal veil over the torrent of possibilities that raced through my mind. The truth was, I had no idea what might lurk beyond the flickering reach of our campfire, but the unknown was a fertile ground for the seeds of fear and speculation to take root.

"I'm sure it'll be fine for now. We'll make sure we put it out shortly after nightfall," Jamie offered, a reassurance that seemed as much for his own benefit as for mine. His words, meant to comfort, did little to dispel the cloak of apprehension that had settled around my shoulders. Yet, the practicality of his plan, the promise of caution, was enough to coax a reluctant agreement from me.

Without further ado, Jamie wasted no time in shedding the remainder of his clothes, an act of defiance against the constraints of our situation, and threw them against the tent with a carelessness that spoke of his confidence. Then, with a burst of energy, he sprinted towards the bank of the river, a beacon of youthful vigour and impulsiveness.

"Hey! Wait!" The words escaped me in a rush, a futile attempt to bridge the distance between caution and recklessness. My breath caught in my throat as I watched, the last vestiges of my concern momentarily suspended by the spectacle unfolding before me.

My voice had impeccable timing, catching Jamie moments before he launched himself into the air, poised to embrace the river's cool embrace with the abandon of a child. But as Jamie pulled back, attempting to heed my call, his foot betrayed him, slipping in the soft, treacherous dust that lined the bank.

I couldn't resist—the laughter that had been bubbling just beneath the surface burst forth, a release of tension and absurdity that the situation warranted. As Jamie slid to an ungraceful stop, landing on his rear in a cloud of dust, the laughter overtook me.

"I'm so sorry," I managed to gasp out, my voice hitched between uncontrollable fits of laughter. It was one of those moments where the absurdity of the situation rendered me helpless to the mirth that bubbled up within me.

"What?" Jamie's voice floated back, tinged with confusion and a hint of amusement. He remained grounded, making no immediate effort to rise, as if conceding to the ridiculousness of his predicament.

Just breathe, breathe, I mentally coached myself, attempting to quell the laughter that shook my frame. It was a futile effort; the humour of the moment was too potent, too infectious.

Finally, Jamie pushed himself up, his movements hesitant as he turned on the spot, seemingly disoriented from his unexpected descent. I caught my breath, my laughter momentarily forgotten as I took in his appearance. *What the heck is Jamie wearing?* The question screamed in my head, curiosity piqued by the incongruous choice of attire for our wilderness setting. Yet, deciding discretion was the better part of valour, I opted not to voice my wonder aloud.

Instead, I shifted the topic, pointing in the direction from which I had come. "There's a good little lagoon just over the way, near the end of the river's bend," I offered, hoping to provide Jamie with a chance for a more graceful, and perhaps more private, interaction with the water.

"Thanks," Jamie replied, his voice carrying a note of gratitude, albeit slightly strained as he brushed off the fine layer of dust that had claimed his legs as a casualty of his fall. He then moved past me, a determined stride in his step, leaving a trail of dust in his wake.

I couldn't resist another light chuckle, my gaze inadvertently following his retreat, particularly the dust-covered aftermath of his misadventure. *There's no way that dust didn't get into that skimpy thong*, I mused silently, the amusement a welcome distraction from the tension of our recent days. It was a small, private amusement that lightened the weight on my shoulders, if only for a moment.

"Ahh, shit!" The exclamation tore from me as I suddenly became aware of the heat creeping up the towel wrapped around my body. In my distraction, I had edged too close to the campfire, the flames eagerly latching onto the corner of my towel. Panic replaced amusement as I hastily discarded the towel, now alight, onto the ground, frantically rolling it in the dust to smother the flames.

Standing there, momentarily exposed and slightly singed, the warmth of the fire against my skin was a stark contrast to the cooling of the afternoon air. *At least Jamie should be at the lagoon for a while*, I reassured myself with a wry smile, finding a sliver of solace in the thought. It was a moment of vulnerability, tempered by the small comfort that, for now, Jamie's attention would be elsewhere, allowing me a brief respite to collect myself and perhaps salvage what dignity remained after the day's escapades.

❖

Pushing back the tent flap, I was momentarily blinded by the harshness of the bright afternoon daylight. Instinctively, my hand came up to shield my eyes from the glare.

"Now, where's Jamie?" Luke's voice reached me, grounding and familiar, as he approached the tent.

"He's gone to bathe," I replied, my voice carrying a hint of pride as I recounted my discovery. "I found a nice lagoon just around the riverbend," I said, my smile broadening at the memory. The lagoon had been an unexpected treasure in the midst of this barren, unforgiving wilderness—a small haven of tranquility and a rare luxury that seemed almost out of place in our rugged existence. The pleasure of the water, so intense and personal, had been a profound experience, one that I felt might be best savoured in solitude. The thought of sharing it, even with my brother, brought a complex mix of emotions. I shifted uncomfortably, the mere recollection of the water's embrace stirring a warmth within me that was ill-suited for the company I was in.

"I'll have to check it out tomorrow," Luke's voice pulled me back from my reverie.

I found myself shifting my weight again, an awkward attempt to adjust to the persistent urges my thoughts had provoked. It was a physical manifestation of the sensual memories of the lagoon that stirred within me.

"Mmm, smells delicious!" The words escaped me before I could rein in my senses, my attention abruptly captured by the scent emanating from the pizza boxes Luke was carrying. It was an olfactory feast, a sudden and stark contrast to the blandness of dust. For a moment, all thoughts of the lagoon were swept away by the tantalising promise of a familiar comfort from our world—a taste of delicious normalcy in the midst of our extraordinary circumstances.

I almost lunged towards Luke, drawn by the irresistible aroma of the pizzas, my nose eagerly tracing the air above the boxes as if to capture every nuance of the scent. Taking the boxes from him, we made our way together to the small campfire. The thought of sharing a meal, especially one as unexpectedly luxurious as pizza, felt like a small victory.

By this point, the pervasive dust of Clivilius had made its claim on everything, a relentless invasion that seemed futile to resist. So, with a resigned air, I plonked myself down onto the ground, the fine particles puffing up around me in a small cloud of defeat. It seemed petty, now, to fuss over the omnipresent dust when there were far more pressing concerns at hand—like the gnawing emptiness of my stomach.

"I'll get you some chairs tomorrow," Luke offered, squatting down beside me with a practicality that was both comforting and slightly amusing in the context of our current situation.

"That'd be nice," I responded, though my mind was only half on the conversation. The thought of chairs, while appealing, paled in comparison to the immediate, visceral need to eat. It was a stark reminder of the basic necessities that had taken precedence since our arrival in Clivilius. My stomach underscored this point with another loud gurgle, as if to chastise me for my brief distraction from its urgent demands.

Opening the first box, I eagerly grabbed myself a slice of pepperoni pizza. The sight of it, so familiar and yet so incongruous in our current setting, sparked a hunger I hadn't fully acknowledged until now. "I didn't realise I was so hungry," I admitted, a bit sheepishly, as a droplet of saliva betrayed my anticipation, falling onto the dust below.

Luke's laughter rang out at my eagerness, a sound that, for a moment, cut through the heaviness that had clung to me since our arrival. I mumbled through a mouthful of pizza, the taste exploding in my mouth in a riot of flavour that seemed almost too intense after the blandness of our recent meals. A rogue piece of pepperoni, having made a bid for freedom, ended up on my singlet. Without hesitation, I picked it off and popped it into my mouth, determined not to waste a single bit of this unexpected feast.

"You haven't changed," Luke laughed.

"Nope," I replied, swallowing the last of my mouthful before attacking the next with unabated zeal.

The two of us, seated side by side in the Clivilius dust, formed a picture of brotherly bonding in the midst of desolation. Conversation was sparse as we focused on the simple pleasure of eating pizza and sipping the chilled Chardonnay that Luke had somehow managed to procure. For a moment, as I closed my eyes, allowing the flavours to fully envelop my senses, a profound sense of peace settled over me. The bustle of my previous life seemed a universe away. No nagging wife. No bickering children. Just the stillness of an alien landscape and the comfort of familiar food and drink.

But then, as quickly as it had come, the peace was shattered by a sudden, piercing thought. *My children.* The realisation hit me like a physical blow, a wave of guilt and longing that was almost overwhelming. For the last few hours, I had been so completely absorbed in the novelty and the struggle of our situation here that they had slipped from my immediate concerns. Now, the thought of their faces, their voices, the warmth of their presence, surged through me with an ache that was both sweet and agonising. I missed them. Terribly.

In an attempt to quell this sudden onslaught of emotion, I mechanically shoved another half-slice of pizza into my mouth. The action was automatic, a physical response to the turmoil that churned within. The food, once a source of solace, now tasted of distraction, a feeble attempt to fill the void that the thought of my children had opened.

The stillness of the Clivilius landscape, so alien and yet momentarily comforting, now seemed to mock me with its tranquility, a stark reminder of the distance—physical and emotional—that lay between me and my family.

"Oh my God. Food!" Jamie's exclamation cut through the quiet early evening air, his voice a mixture of surprise and unabashed delight. It was a reaction that, under normal circumstances, might have seemed exaggerated, but here, in the vastness of Clivilius, it felt entirely appropriate.

"And wine," Luke chimed in, his tone proud as he held up the half-drunk bottle of Chardonnay like a trophy.

"Well, you two look like you've given it a fair go already," Jamie joked, his eyes sparkling with a mix of humour and hunger as he settled into the dust beside us.

We? The thought flickered through my mind as I glanced across at Jamie, now an integral part of this impromptu picnic. "Well, Luke has," I laughed, redirecting the jest towards Luke, who seemed to have taken the lead in our consumption of the wine. My laughter was genuine, but it masked an underlying discomfort. As I took another sip of the wine, my face involuntarily scrunched with distaste. Truth be told, I wasn't much of a wine drinker. The sharp tang of the Chardonnay clashed with my palate, a reminder of my usual preference for sweeter, less sophisticated beverages.

I'll make sure I ask Luke to bring something a little more sugary, next time. The thought was both whimsical and serious. *Not that I drink much alcohol anyway, but if I'm going to drink...* The sentiment trailed off in my mind, an unfinished musing that reflected a broader truth about our current existence. We were far from the choices and comforts of home, yet even here, we sought to carve out moments of preference, of life as we knew it.

The wine, the pizza, Jamie's arrival—they all wove together into a tapestry of the familiar within the unfamiliar, a comforting illusion of normalcy against the backdrop of our extraordinary circumstances. Yet, as I sat there, sharing laughter and food with my companions, I couldn't help but feel a pang of longing for the simple things taken for granted, for a time when the choice of drink was the most mundane of decisions.

I looked up at the clear sky, noting how the sun began its slow descent behind the distant mountains, painting the horizon in hues of orange and pink. It would be dark soon, and the chill of the Clivilius night wasn't far behind.

"Well," Luke announced, pushing himself to his feet with a sense of finality that momentarily pierced the tranquil moment. He brushed the dust from his clothing in a gesture that seemed as much about preparation to leave as it was a dismissal of the day's trials. "Better get back. Don't want Gladys to finish all the wine in the house," he added, the grin on his face failing to mask the underlying reluctance in his voice.

Gladys, the name flickered through my mind as I closed my eyes briefly. *Oh yes, Beatrix's sister.* My interactions with her had been limited, yet memorable. She possessed a quirkiness that was both refreshing and endearing.

"So, that's it then?" Jamie's voice, tinged with a mix of resignation and disappointment, cut through my reverie.

Luke's response was tender, a simple act of affection as he kissed Jamie on the forehead—a gesture that spoke volumes of their relationship. "Yeah," he affirmed, his voice steady yet soft. "But I promise I'll be back first thing in the morning."

"Fine," Jamie replied, his shrug not quite masking the disappointment that clouded his features. "I wish we could go with you." The sentiment, simple and raw, echoed my own thoughts.

My eyes began to burn again. *I wish I could go with Luke too.* The thought was a pang of longing, a desire for return to a life that now seemed as distant as the setting sun. But the reality of our situation was inescapable. Clivilius had spoken to me, its voice a constant echo in my mind, a reminder of the rejection by the Portal. The finality of that rejection—*We would never leave*—was a weight that settled coldly in my stomach.

"Good night, Luke," I managed to say, my voice barely above a whisper, heavy with the acknowledgement of our entrapment.

"Night, Paul," Luke replied, his farewell casual yet loaded with the gravity of our shared predicament. He waved, a solitary figure retreating into the encroaching darkness, leaving behind a silence that felt both oppressive and profound.

Jamie and I settled into the dust, a makeshift campsite that had become our dining room for the evening. We shared the remnants of our pizza and the wine under a sky that transitioned from the warm hues of sunset to a deep, impenetrable black. The fire, our beacon and companion, crackled softly, its glow dimming as the night claimed its dominion.

"It's so quiet," I remarked, the silence enveloping us so completely it felt like a tangible presence. I stretched my legs out in front of me, muscles aching from the day's exertions and the unfamiliarity of the ground beneath me.

"I know," Jamie agreed, his voice a soft echo in the stillness. "And dark." He gestured upwards, towards the night sky, a canvas devoid of light. "Have you noticed that there aren't any stars?" His curiosity piqued, adding another layer of mystery to our already baffling situation.

I tipped my head back, letting my gaze wander across the expanse above us. The blackness was absolute, a void where I expected the twinkling of distant suns. "And no moon either," I observed, the absence of its familiar glow adding to the eerie atmosphere.

"What do you think that means?" Jamie's question hung in the air.

"What do you mean?" I countered, genuinely perplexed. My mind, tired from the day's events and the constant barrage of the unknown, struggled to grasp the implications of his question. To me, the absence of stars and moon merely signified an even darker night ahead, a practical concern that paled in comparison to the broader, more existential questions that Clivilius posed.

If courage had not eluded me at that moment, I might have suggested we keep the fire burning throughout the night, a beacon against the darkness that seemed to press in from all sides. Yet, I hesitated, uncertain of Jamie's reaction to what might be perceived as an irrational fear. After all, our situation was already fraught with challenges; admitting to a fear of the dark, even in a place as alien as this, felt like a vulnerability I wasn't ready to expose.

"Well," Jamie began, a thoughtful edge to his words. "Doesn't the moon normally affect the oceans and tides?" His question, simple on the surface, hinted at the deeper, unsettling uncertainties that this starless, moonless night had unearthed within us.

I shrugged, a gesture born of confusion and a deep-seated unease that seemed to grow with every passing moment. "I guess," I replied, the words heavy with my own doubts. "But all we've seen is a river. We don't even know there are any oceans here." The admission felt like conceding to a broader, more profound disorientation regarding our place in this world—or indeed, if it was a world at all.

"There has to be!" Jamie declared with a conviction that I envied. "We have to still be on Earth, somewhere." His assertion felt like a desperate grasp at the familiar in a sea of unknowns. But his certainty only served to deepen my own confusion.

"I'm so confused," I confessed, my hand instinctively going to my head as if to physically grasp the elusive answers. "None of this makes any sense," I mumbled, my voice trailing off into the darkness. The questions circled in my mind like vultures. *Are we still on Earth? Are we somewhere else? Will I wake up in the morning and find that it's all just a strange, terrifying dream?* The possibilities seemed endless, each more disconcerting than the last.

Jamie, perhaps sensing the futility of our speculation, or maybe just weary from the day's emotional toll, rose to his feet. With a decisive movement, he tossed the pizza boxes into the fire. The cardboard caught quickly, erupting into a brief but bright display of flames that seemed to fight back the darkness, if only for a moment, before dying down to mere embers. "Kick some dust on those embers when you turn in, won't you," he said, his tone casual but carrying an implicit trust that I would see to our safety for the night.

"Sure," I replied, the weight of the night suddenly pressing down upon me. "I won't be far away." My words were a promise, not just to attend to the fire, but an unspoken vow that in this unfamiliar, unsettling world, we would not let the unknown divide us. As Jamie retreated, I remained seated, alone with my thoughts and the dying fire.

The night stretched on, a canvas of unending blackness, as I pondered our situation. The absence of the moon, the unfamiliarity of the landscape, and the pressing silence seemed to conspire, creating a sense of isolation that was both profound and deeply personal. In this moment, on the edge of an unknown world, the questions of our existence and our place within the cosmos seemed to loom larger than life itself, a reminder of our insignificance against the backdrop of the universe.

SETTLEMENT

4338.205.9

I lay quietly on the mattress, the fabric slightly rough against my skin, a reminder of our rudimentary living conditions here in Clivilius. Jamie's soft snores provided a comforting, if unexpected, backdrop to my swirling thoughts. The closeness was unfamiliar, yet in this unfamiliar environment, even the small warmth from another human was a comfort not to be underestimated. A single pillow lay between us, a meagre barrier that underscored our shared predicament. It was all we could spare, and though it was a small inconvenience, the necessity of sharing a blanket seemed to amplify the situation's intimacy and its discomfort.

The thought crossed my mind, not for the first time, that Luke could have at least provided us with two blankets. The oversight seemed minor in the grand scheme of our survival, but in the quiet of the night, such small comforts took on greater significance. I made a mental note, firm in my resolve, to ensure that Luke brought additional bedding with the new tents tomorrow. The darkness enveloped us so completely that writing down this reminder was impossible, leaving me to rely on a memory that often proved frustratingly unreliable.

But what would never escape my mind were memories of my kids. Vivid images of Mack and Rose played across the canvas of my mind like scenes from a life that felt both achingly close and impossibly distant. I could see them running around the Zinc Lakes, their laughter echoing against the backdrop of the churning mines, a soundtrack of our daily lives in the outback. The vivid green of the grass underfoot and the playful chase of mallard ducks brought a bittersweet pang of longing to my heart. I could almost feel the mist of the water fountain on my face, a fleeting respite from the relentless heat of the midday sun. The ache for my children was a constant, a deep-seated longing that this alien landscape could do nothing to alleviate.

And then there was Claire. My thoughts shifted to her—sporadic, lively, troubled Claire. The memory that surfaced was not a pleasant one, tinged with the sharpness of our last argument. The image of the window, the roses, and the thorns invaded my thoughts, a vivid reminder of the tumultuous state of our relationship. The argument, centred around my habitual prioritisation of work over family, had been abruptly cut short by Luke's call. At the time, it had seemed like a reprieve, an escape from the immediate conflict.

But now, lying here, the question of whether that interruption had been fortunate gnawed at me. That very call was the reason I found myself in this current predicament, far from home, far from the unresolved tensions with Claire, and immeasurably far from my children's laughter. The irony of the situation was not lost on me; in my attempt to escape the difficulties of one aspect of my life, I had been thrust into an entirely new set of challenges, ones that made the previous seem trivial by comparison.

The realisation that these memories, both sweet and painful, would never leave me was both a comfort and a curse. They were a link to a world I had been forcibly ripped from, a constant reminder of what I was fighting to return to. Yet, they also underscored the profound isolation of my current situation, the physical and emotional distance that lay between me and the life I knew.

Despite the deep yearning within me to hold my children again, to feel their warmth and hear their laughter, a part of me was also becoming increasingly resolved to face our current reality head-on. The idea of making this new, alien settlement work began to take root in my mind, an unexpected sprout of determination amid the desolation of Clivilius. *Settlement...* the word echoed in my thoughts, highlighting its anonymity, its lack of identity. *It needs a name*, I mused, the realisation bringing a sense of purpose, however small, to our plight.

Letting my thoughts drift off, I allowed the mental exhaustion and the emotional turmoil of the day to wash over me. My eyelids fluttered several times, heavy with fatigue, as they fought for the rest they so dearly sought. The darkness behind my closed eyes became a canvas for my thoughts, a space where the practicalities of survival mingled with the more abstract notions of home and belonging.

"Bixbus!" The name erupted from me, unintentionally aloud, breaking the silence of the night. The sound of it seemed to hang in the air, a tangible manifestation of my subconscious efforts to anchor us to this place. *Yes*, I thought this time, more deliberately, embracing the name fully. *Bixbus.* It had a strange ring to it, alien yet oddly fitting for our new home. The act of naming it felt like a small victory, a way of claiming a piece of this world as our own, of imposing order on the chaos that had been thrust upon us.

BLACK FIRE

4338.205.10

My eyes fluttered open, or at least, I believed they did. Darkness, thick and absolute, pressed down upon me, as if the very shadows had conspired to smother my senses. A wave of panic rose within me as I sat up abruptly, the sweat that had gathered among the sparse hairs on my chest now felt like icy fingers tracing my skin. A shiver coursed through me, a bead of sweat tracing a cold path down my back, amplifying the sense of dread that filled the air.

"Rose!" The name tore from my throat, a scream born of agony and desperation. I reached out into the oppressive blackness that enveloped me, but it was as if the darkness swallowed every movement, rendering my hands invisible even to my own eyes. The sensation, or lack thereof, was disorienting.

Suddenly, the walls of the tent began to shudder and shake with violent intensity, as if caught in a maelstrom unseen but fiercely present. The sound that accompanied the turmoil was akin to a million tiny bullets, a relentless hiss that seemed to target the very core of my being. Instinct took over, and I curled into myself, pressing my stomach against my legs in a futile attempt to shield myself from the unseen assault. "Make it stop!" The plea erupted from me, a desperate cry for relief as I clutched at my ears, trying to block out the cacophony that only grew louder, more insistent.

The shaking of the tent escalated, the very fabric of our makeshift shelter threatening to give way under the unseen force. Poles rattled ominously in the far corner, a sound that spoke of imminent collapse. Fear, raw and unyielding, gripped me, a visceral response to the unknown forces that besieged us.

As I sat back up, my breaths came heavy and laboured, each inhale a desperate fight for air. My hands instinctively clutched at my throat, as if I could physically pull the oxygen into my lungs. "It's going... to kill... us," I managed to croak out, the words slicing through the dense atmosphere of fear that had enveloped me. The terror that gripped me was palpable, a raw, unfiltered dread that seemed to seep into the very fabric of the tent.

"Paul? What's wrong?" Jamie's voice pierced the darkness, laced with concern and confusion. The calmness of his tone, so at odds with the chaos of my own feelings, only served to amplify my panic.

"Clivilius is going to kill us," I whispered back, the words barely a breath, yet heavy with the weight of my conviction. The terror of our situation, our first night in this alien hell, seemed to crystallise in that moment, the reality of our peril striking me with merciless clarity.

Then, cutting through the night, a voice—a young girl's voice—called out. *Daddy!* The familiarity of it, so unexpected and out of place, sent a jolt through me. "Rose. Is that you?" I cried out, the hope and disbelief mingling with a surge of emotion so intense it overwhelmed me. Hot tears streamed down my face, a tangible manifestation of the fear, the longing, and the sheer intensity of the moment.

"What the hell, Paul?" Jamie's voice, now tinged with alarm and irritation, called out from the darkness. His confusion attempted to remind me of the absurdity of my reaction, yet the fear had rooted itself too deeply within me to simply shake off.

Suddenly, a rough hand gripped my forearm, a touch so unexpected and firm that it sent me into a frenzy. I screamed, a primal sound born of fear and survival instinct, as I yanked my arm free and scuttled across the floor of the tent. My hands moved in a constant, desperate search for an escape, for any way out of the enclosing darkness that seemed to press in from all sides.

The terror of the moment was all-consuming, a blend of reality and nightmare that left no room for reason. Clivilius, with its unknown threats and unfamiliar landscape, had become a crucible, testing the limits of my endurance, my sanity. In that moment of absolute fear, the lines between the real and the imagined blurred, leaving me caught in a spiral of panic and desperation, the darkness not just a physical barrier, but a manifestation of the deep-seated fear that Clivilius had instilled in me.

"Paul! Come back!" Jamie's voice reached out to me, a lifeline thrown across the chasm of panic that had engulfed me. But his call fell on deaf ears. The name *Rose* echoed in my mind, a beacon of fear and determination. She was out there, alone in this oppressive darkness, and every paternal instinct within me screamed to find her, to protect her.

"I'm coming, Rose," I cried out, desperation lending strength to my voice as I wrestled with the tent's zipper. The flap danced a violent tango in the unseen wind, lashing out like a living thing. As I pushed my way through the small opening, the zip of the flap struck my cheek with a sharp sting.

"Paul! Stop!" Jamie's voice, edged with desperation, called out again. But the urgency of the moment propelled me forward, beyond reason, beyond caution.

Scrambling to my feet, the sting of Clivilius's dust became immediately apparent. It felt as if every inch of my exposed skin was under assault by invisible needles. I closed my eyes tightly, an instinctive attempt to shield them from the onslaught. My hands rose to protect my face, a feeble barrier against the abrasive air. I dared to peek through my fingers, but it was an exercise in futility. The darkness was absolute, a smothering cloak that rendered me blind despite the absence of dust in my eyes.

"Paul, where are you? Talk to me," Jamie's voice cut through the darkness, a note of command in his tone that sought to pierce the veil of my panic.

"Jamie," I managed to reply, my voice a mix of fear and confusion. "Where are you?" The physical distance between us felt insurmountable, the darkness a divide that could not be easily bridged.

Daddy! The soft voice, so familiar and yet so out of place, called to me again, a siren song that drew me further into the unknown.

A small glimmer of light punctured the darkness ahead, a beacon amid the oppressive black. "I see you. I'm coming, Rose," I declared, each word a promise, a vow. Moving toward the light was a herculean task. The confusion swirling within me was disorienting, the simple act of putting one foot in front of the other a challenge that seemed beyond my capacity.

"For fuck's sake, Paul! Stop!" Jamie's voice cut through the wind, a sharp demand that momentarily pierced the fog of my panic. I swivelled on my heels, disoriented, the source of his voice eluding my senses. The darkness seemed to swallow the sound, making it impossible to pinpoint its origin. Squinting between my fingers, the faint glow that I had convinced myself was a sign of Rose's presence was now directly in front of me. *She must be close,* I thought, desperation lending me a foolish courage.

"Ouch!" The exclamation burst from me as pain lanced through my foot. The still-warm embers of our campfire, forgotten in my frantic state, seared my skin, a cruel reminder of the reality I was trying to escape. I clutched my burning foot, the sudden pain throwing off my balance as the gusty wind seemed to conspire against me, pushing me towards an even greater danger.

I screamed, a visceral sound of fear and pain, as I realised I was falling, the pit of warm coals below me promising nothing but intense agony. Time seemed to stretch, the fall feeling like an eternity as I braced for the impact, for the pain that would surely end this nightmare. My head spun with such ferocity that I half-expected the darkness to claim me before I ever hit the ground.

Then, unexpectedly, salvation. A hand reached around my waist in a firm grip, pulling me back from the precipice of pain and injury. We landed together with a heavy thud, the ground unforgiving beneath us. Our legs intertwined uncomfortably, a tangle of limbs that was both awkward and, in that moment, incredibly reassuring.

Lying there, momentarily stunned, the reality of what had almost happened began to sink in. The fear and the adrenaline that had propelled me forward were now replaced by a rush of relief so intense it was almost dizzying. Jamie had saved me from a fall that could have ended in serious injury, pulling me back from the edge in the most literal sense.

"Keep your eyes shut," came Jamie's voice, grounding yet urgent in the tumultuous darkness that enveloped us. My initial reaction was one of shock, my hand instinctively recoiling as Jamie reached for it, the sudden contact jarring.

"Give me your fucking hand!" Jamie's demand cut through my hesitation, the urgency in his voice brooking no argument. Feeling defeated and overwhelmed by the situation, I let him take my hand, surrendering to the necessity of his guidance.

As Jamie dragged me along the ground, the indignity of the situation was overshadowed by the surreal nature of our predicament. Dust infiltrated my underwear, an uncomfortable sensation that soon became the least of my concerns as I realised they were gone, lost somewhere in the frantic scramble for safety.

My foot collided with the front tent pole, an accident that seemed to invite further calamity. The gusty wind, relentless and unforgiving, seized the opportunity to wreak havoc. I felt myself dragged across the entrance, a puppet in the hands of the storm, as the front canopy gave way with a distressing ease.

"Shit," Jamie muttered, his voice a mix of frustration and concern as the situation spiralled further out of control.

Exhausted, aching, and numbed by the ordeal, I curled into myself, seeking refuge in the smallest space I could make. My knees tucked in, arms wrapped around them, I began to rock back and forth. This repetitive motion became my entire world. Tears streamed down my face, unnoticed and unchecked, as despair took hold.

It was in this moment of utter vulnerability that I felt a warm presence behind me. Jamie's arms, strong and reassuring, enveloped my naked form, pulling me close against the safety of his chest. The simple act of being held, of feeling another's warmth against my skin, began to pierce the fog of my despair. My rocking slowed, then stopped, as I allowed myself to be anchored by his presence. There, in the darkness, wrapped in Jamie's embrace, I found a semblance of peace amid the storm.

"I'm sorry, Rose," I whispered into the blackness, a confession borne of the heartache and fear that had overwhelmed me. The name, a symbol of all that I longed for and all that I feared to lose, slipped out into the night, a silent prayer for forgiveness, for understanding, in a world that seemed determined to test our very limits. In that moment, held tight by Jamie, the lines between reality and nightmare blurred, leaving only the raw, aching need for connection, for assurance, that we were not alone in this fight.

4338.206

(25 July 2018)

IMAGINING

4338.206.1

Slowly, I opened my eyes to a world transformed by the morning light filtering through the fabric of the large tent. As awareness crept back to me, I found myself lying near the centre, the cold, plastic base beneath me an uncomfortable reminder of our makeshift living conditions. A lingering sense of dread hovered at the edge of my consciousness, the remnants of the previous night's terror still palpable in the air. The sensation of being held, of strong arms wrapped securely around me, remained vivid, a fleeting comfort amidst the chaos.

"Rose!" The name burst from me as the memories of the night's events began to crystallise with sudden clarity. Sitting upright in a rush, the blanket that had been my only cover slid from my body, its movement across my skin igniting a trail of fire that seemed to consume me. I shivered, not from cold but from the pain that flared with each movement, a harsh reminder of the ordeal I had endured.

"Ouch!" The exclamation was involuntary as I attempted to stand, my right foot protesting the weight with a sharp, piercing pain. Instinctively, my hand flew to the source of the discomfort, and I found myself wobbling, unsteady and disoriented, before landing back on the tent floor with a heavy thud. The impact sent another jolt of pain through me, drawing tears to my eyes not just from the physical hurt but from the emotional turmoil that churned within.

My body ached, each bruise and abrasion a testament to the night's struggles, but it was the memory of Rose's voice, calling out to me in the darkness, that cut the deepest. The physical pain, intense as it was, paled in comparison to the ache in my heart. The thought of my daughter, real or imagined, reaching out to me in a moment of fear, and my inability to protect her, to reassure her, weighed heavily on me. It was a burden that the morning light could not dispel, a shadow that clung to me despite the new day.

Crawling across the ground felt both humbling and necessary, the blanket clutched in my grasp a makeshift shield against the chill of the morning. As I navigated my way through the tent's open flap, the act of standing was a cautious negotiation, my right foot a traitor that threatened to buckle under any semblance of pressure.

With the blanket wrapped securely around my waist, I limped towards the edge of our temporary shelter, the canopy's farthest reach offering a vantage point into the vast unknown of Clivilius. "Rose!" My voice, fuelled by a mixture of hope and desperation, cut through the silence. "Where are you?" The absence of an answer, save for the echo of my own voice, was a weight upon my heart.

A voice, firm and grounding, reached out to me from the left. "You had a nightmare, Paul," it informed me, a statement that carried with it a mix of relief and disbelief. "Rose isn't here." The words were meant to reassure, yet they sowed seeds of confusion in their wake.

I shook my head, struggling to align this reality with the vividness of my nightmare. "I don't understand," I admitted, my gaze finding Jamie sitting at the edge of the river, a solitary figure against the backdrop of tranquility. His invitation to sit beside him felt like an anchor, a point of stability in the shifting sands of my understanding.

Hesitation gripped me as I took in the scene around us. The tent's left wing had succumbed to the night's fury. The ground, once marred by the evidence of our presence, now bore a fresh layer of dust, as if Clivilius itself sought to erase our footprint, to render us ghosts upon its surface. The sight of Jamie, seemingly at peace by the water's edge, offered a stark contrast to the turmoil within me.

Approaching him, the disparity between the calm exterior and the storm of emotions within me was palpable. Jamie's feet, idly kicking at the water, seemed to mock the intensity of the night's events, a reminder of the fine line between reality and the nightmares that haunted us. In this moment, on the cusp between the known and the unknown, the physical and the psychological scars we bore were a testament to the fragility of our existence in Clivilius, a world that offered no easy answers, only the relentless passage of time and the slow, steady erasure of what had come before.

"The water will help soothe your foot," Jamie's suggestion came as a gentle encouragement, his voice carrying the warmth of concern. With a hesitant motion, I swept the blanket aside and looked down at my feet, the sight greeting me was one of discomfort—both feet were an angry red, the sting palpable even without any contact. *Maybe Jamie's right*, I found myself conceding silently. The thought of the cool river water against my skin offered a sliver of relief in my mind.

As I made my way to the river's edge, I couldn't help but notice the similar marks of distress on Jamie's skin. His arms, exposed and vulnerable, bore the telltale signs of our ordeal. Settling myself gingerly beside him, I took extra care with the blanket, a barrier against the elements and a shield for my modesty.

The moment my foot touched the water, a sigh of relief escaped me, unbidden but deeply felt. "That does feel good," I admitted, the sensation of coolness against the heat of my burns bringing an immediate, though temporary, respite. A newfound sense of self-consciousness washed over me, and I found myself adjusting the blanket around my waist, ensuring I remained covered.

Allowing my eyes to close, I surrendered to the sensation of the water enveloping my feet, the occasional sharp pang of pain serving as a reminder of the night's events. Despite the discomfort, the water was a balm, its gentle flow offering a moment of peace amid the turmoil of memories and confusion.

The events of the last night lingered at the edge of my consciousness, fragmented and disorienting. The sound of Rose's voice, so clear and so desperate, haunted me still. It had felt so real, so undeniable in the moment. *Maybe Jamie can help me understand*, I found myself thinking, the need to piece together the events, to make sense of the nightmare, growing more pressing. The possibility that Jamie might shed some light on the situation, might help reconcile the dissonance between what I had experienced and the reality we faced, was a small beacon of hope in the fog of confusion.

"Last night was a fucking disaster," Jamie's words cut through the calm brought on by the river, snapping me back to a harsher reality.

I found myself at a loss for words, the events of the night still a jumbled mess in my mind. "I guess," I murmured, my gaze drifting across the river, seeking something in its flow that might make sense of the confusion. "What happened to my foot?" The question hung between us, a tangible reminder of the physical consequences of the night's madness.

"You don't remember?" Jamie's incredulity was palpable, a mirror to my own confusion.

My face contorted as I strained to piece together the fragments of memory, but they slipped away, elusive and fragmented. I shrugged, an admission of defeat.

"You went running out of the tent in pitch blackness, in the middle of a fucking dust storm and trod on hot coals from last night's campfire," Jamie recounted, the words painting a vivid picture of my panic-driven folly. "And all for a voice that wasn't real."

Burning anger flared up, a visceral response to his dismissal of my experience. "How do you know it wasn't real?" I found myself demanding, the conviction in my own recollection clashing with his skepticism. "I heard Rose as clear as I can see this water right now."

Jamie's heavy sigh served as a prelude to his words, delivered with a slow, deliberate calm. "Pure blackness can make the mind go crazy," he suggested, a theory that offered little comfort but couldn't be easily dismissed.

My initial resistance softened, giving way to contemplation. *Is Jamie right?* The question wormed its way through my defences, planting seeds of doubt. *Is my mind going crazy already?* The thought was unsettling, a possibility that threatened the very foundation of my sense of self.

Daddy, the voice echoed again in my mind, a haunting reminder of what had driven me into the night. Despite Jamie's logical explanations, the emotional pull of that moment was undeniable. And with it came a renewed determination, a resolve that felt both desperate and essential. *If I'm going to be trapped in Clivilius forever*, the thought solidified with a clarity that brooked no argument, *I need my kids here with me.* The realisation was a beacon, guiding my next steps. Making the settlement thrive, ensuring our survival, became more than just a necessity—it was a mission, a way to forge a semblance of home in the vast unknown, driven by the love for my children and the unyielding desire to reunite with them, against all odds.

"I'm going to go fix the tent," Jamie announced, his voice carrying a pragmatic resolve that momentarily lifted the veil of uncertainty that had settled over me. "And this sun is feeling very warm already. You'd better get some clothes on. I hate to say it, but we may be spending a lot of time in the tent until we can get more shelter." The advice, though practical, served as a stark reminder of our precarious situation, exposed to the elements with limited resources at our disposal.

As Jamie walked away, his figure a blend of determination and resignation, I turned back to the river, seeking a moment of solace in its cool embrace. Lifting my burnt foot from the water, I noted with a mixture of relief and concern that the redness persisted, though the pain had ebbed. The thought of treating it properly crossed my mind, accompanied by the realisation of our limited medical supplies. "Shit!" The exclamation burst from me as the reality of our circumstances once again came into sharp focus. *I'll have to get Luke to bring some cream first!* The notion was a reminder of our reliance on Luke for supplies, a dependency that chafed against my desire for autonomy.

With a cautious effort, I got to my feet, the action more deliberate than graceful, and limped over to Jamie. "Have you seen Luke yet this morning?" The question was as much about gauging Luke's whereabouts as it was an attempt to reconnect with Jamie.

"Nope," Jamie replied, his tone laced with a bitterness that seemed to go deeper than the immediate frustrations of our situation. "Luke seems to be working to his own fucking agenda." The harshness of his words, the underlying resentment, struck a chord within me, a dissonance that resonated with my own feelings of isolation and helplessness.

I frowned. "Do you really have to be so negative? And do you have to swear every second sentence?" I asked, the irritation evident in my voice.

"Yes," Jamie answered defiantly, a spark of rebellion in his eyes. "Yes, I fucking do." The response, so sharp and unyielding, was a reminder of the raw edges that our circumstances were exposing in each of us, the ways in which this unsettled environment was stripping away the veneers of civility and exposing the raw nerves beneath.

If the darkness and the unknown threats of Clivilius weren't enough to send my mind into a frenzy, Jamie's demeanour threatened to push me over the edge. With a mix of resignation and resolve, I pushed my way back inside the tent. *I may as well get dressed. That's something I can actually do.*

❖

"Hey, Jamie?" My voice was casual, an attempt to bridge the gap that had formed between us with a question that now seemed trivial, even misguided, in the vast context of our current situation.

Jamie, his back to me, paused in the act of pulling a fresh t-shirt over his head, a soft gasp marking his surprise at the question. There was a moment of adjustment, a physical settling into the new garment before he responded. "Yeah?" His voice carried a hint of curiosity, a willingness to engage despite the suddenness of my inquiry.

"What did you like least about life back on Earth?" As soon as the words left my mouth, I regretted them. The question, intended to spark a meaningful conversation, felt flat and poorly considered in the moment.

"Hmm," Jamie mused, his reply coming after a brief pause. "Not sure. Life is pretty good." His answer took me by surprise, contradicting the impression I had formed based on Luke's descriptions over the years. I had been led to believe Jamie found little joy in life, yet here he was, offering a perspective that challenged my assumptions.

Jamie's gaze met mine, a cautious evaluation that slowly morphed into a slight grin, as if he sensed the dissonance between my expectations and his response. "Were you expecting something different?" he prodded, the amusement in his voice clear.

Embarrassment flushed my face, a tangible sign of my discomfort. "I... uh... that's not what I meant," I stammered, struggling to articulate my thoughts amid the unexpected turn of the conversation.

"Really?" Jamie pressed, his interest piqued. "Then what did you mean?" His question, straightforward yet laden with the potential for deeper exploration, prompted a pause. I realised the importance of my next words, the need to carefully construct my reply if I hoped to subtly guide Jamie towards understanding the significance of creating a space that could welcome my children—a goal that remained unspoken between us.

"I mean—" I started, halting mid-sentence as I sought the right approach. The pause was pregnant with possibilities, a moment of recalibration as I navigated the delicate balance of revealing my true intentions without making them explicit.

"Hmm," Jamie teased, the lightness in his tone offering a reprieve from the tension. He seated himself beside me on the mattress, the physical proximity a reminder of our shared reality, of the need to work together despite the undercurrents of misunderstanding and unspoken plans that lay between us. The moment was a crossroads, an opportunity to bridge the gap with honesty and shared purpose, even as I sought the right words to mask the true depth of my intentions.

My mind raced, teetering on the edge of persuasion and honesty. The excitement in my voice was genuine as I envisioned the possibilities, yet it masked the underlying challenge of conveying the full breadth of my hopes without revealing too much. "We get to leave all of the dramas of earth life behind and start fresh." The words hung between us, a loaded statement that invited scrutiny. I paused, watching Jamie closely for any sign of agreement or skepticism.

Jamie's eyebrow arched, a silent, visual prompt that urged me to elaborate. "Go on," he said, his interest piqued or perhaps merely amused by my tentative optimism.

Encouraged, I plunged ahead. "Think about it. We don't have to go to work. I mean, yeah, we may need to work here so that we don't die, but it's not the same thing as having set hours to be working for someone else." The distinction felt important, a key selling point to this unorthodox freedom we'd been thrust into.

"And?" Jamie prompted.

"And," I continued, my thoughts gathering momentum. "And we get to leave all the annoying, stupid people behind. All the politics. All the dumb rules." The words spilled out, a mixture of frustration with our old lives and a burgeoning hope for what lay ahead. It was an appeal to the part of us that yearned for simplicity, for a life unencumbered by the societal norms we'd unknowingly chafed against.

"And family?" Jamie's question sliced through the optimism, pinpointing the heart of my internal conflict with surgical precision.

His insight into my greatest vulnerability didn't surprise me, but it steeled my resolve. "Not necessarily," I countered, my voice a blend of defiance and wishful thinking. The implication hung in the air, a delicate balance between the desire to escape and the bonds that tethered us to our previous lives.

"How so?" Jamie wasn't letting me off easy. His question demanded an explanation, a justification for the hope I clung to despite the overwhelming evidence to the contrary.

"What if we created a new civilisation here? One where we could bring only the family we wanted? Only the people who would participate and contribute productively to the society?" The words tumbled out of me, a mix of hope and desperation, as I laid bare the vision that had begun to form in my mind. It was a bold proposition, one that sought to reimagine our grim circumstances as an opportunity, however far-fetched it might seem.

I watched Jamie closely, searching for any sign of agreement or at least, intrigue, in his response. His face was a study in contemplation, the gears turning behind his eyes as he weighed the possibilities I'd presented.

"Don't you think that's even just a little exciting?" I pressed, eager to ignite in him the spark of optimism that was slowly kindling within me. "Don't you get it? We can create our own rules. Our own culture. Our own society." The words felt powerful, transformative, even if they were born from a place of sheer necessity.

Jamie's gaze met mine, a moment of unspoken communication that seemed to stretch between us. "After last night, do you really believe any of that is true?" His question was a bucket of cold water, a reminder of the harsh reality we'd endured and the monumental challenges that lay ahead.

"I do," I replied, the words firm, imbued with all the conviction I could muster. I had to believe in the possibility of a better future, not just for my sake, but for the sake of my children, for the sanity that teetered on the edge of despair. The alternative was unthinkable.

But Jamie's skepticism remained apparent. "As soon as Luke returns, I'm going to try and leave Clivilius again," he declared, his decision a clear indication of his doubts about our chances of making a life here. With a resigned gesture, he let himself fall back onto the mattress, closing his eyes and resting his arms behind his head, a physical withdrawal into his own thoughts and uncertainties.

I was left to sit in silence, contemplating the enormity of the task ahead. Persuading Jamie, convincing myself of the feasibility of this nascent dream, seemed like daunting obstacles on a path fraught with uncertainty. A sudden pain shot through my foot as I accidentally shifted my weight onto the burn, a sharp reminder of the immediate physical realities that compounded our existential plight. The river's cool embrace called to me, a temporary relief from the physical and emotional turmoil that defined our existence in Clivilius. It was a small comfort, yet in that moment, it was everything.

DROP ZONE

4338.206.2

The sound of soft footsteps approaching snapped me back to the present, a subtle reminder of Jamie's presence, though I didn't feel the need to turn and acknowledge it directly.

Jamie settled himself beside me, his body folding into the dust with a resignation that seemed to mirror the resignation in his voice. "There's nothing else to do," he stated, a flat declaration that hung between us, laden with an unspoken acceptance of our situation.

I continued to stare across the river, the gentle flow a stark contrast to the turmoil within. Jamie's words echoed a sentiment I was all too familiar with, yet I wasn't ready to concede. The absence of Luke weighed heavily on us both, a silent spectre of uncertainty that loomed over our makeshift encampment. Jamie's resolve to leave once Luke returned was clear, but my own thoughts on the matter were muddled, caught between a desire to escape and the burgeoning sense of responsibility for what we could create here.

"Well," I ventured, grasping for a semblance of optimism. "We could do with a place near the Portal where Luke can deliver things. We can then work out what to do with them." The suggestion was a shot in the dark, an attempt to inject purpose into our waiting.

Jamie's response was a reflection of his skepticism. "Well, that seems a bit random," he observed.

I couldn't help but chuckle at the absurdity of my suggestion. "It does a bit, doesn't it?"

Jamie's smile, rare and fleeting, was a beacon of shared humanity in the vastness of Clivilius.

Both of us then returned to our silent contemplation of the river, its steady flow a metaphor for the passage of time and the uncertainty of our future. The quiet between us was no longer oppressive but filled with a tacit understanding, a mutual acknowledgment of the challenges ahead and the fragile hope that, somehow, we would find a way to navigate them together.

"I guess it would give us something to do," Jamie conceded, his voice carrying a hint of reluctant acceptance that signalled a shift in his stance. The opening was all I needed, a sliver of common ground from which we could build.

I seized the moment, eager to expand on the idea. "And not just finding a good spot. Getting Luke to leave whatever he brings through the Portal in a single spot will give us something to do, to move it." The plan was forming, a tangible task that could lend structure to our days, a purpose amidst the uncertainty.

"And," Jamie interjected, enthusiasm beginning to colour his tone as he warmed to the concept. "Luke is very intelligent, but he can also be a bit of a scatterbrain."

"Totally," I agreed wholeheartedly. "I don't think it's wise for us to trust Luke to establish a settlement properly." The words were out before I could consider their weight, a candid admission of our need to take control of our situation, to assert some level of order.

To my surprise, Jamie's response was not a verbal one but an action. He rose to his feet, a decisive movement that spoke volumes, and extended his hand to help me up.

I accepted his hand and stood, momentarily caught off guard by the physical support. For a brief moment, I watched

Jamie's back as he walked away, a silent figure moving with purpose.

"Well, you coming then?" Jamie called back over his shoulder, his voice carrying a blend of challenge and invitation. "It was your idea after all." The tease was evident, a playful nudge that broke through the residual tension and solidified our newfound resolve.

A wide grin spread across my face, an involuntary reaction to the progress we'd made. In that moment, the path forward seemed a little less daunting, the prospect of working together not just a necessity but a source of hope. *Progress, indeed.*

❖

By the time I had hobbled over to the Portal, Jamie was deeply engrossed in his task, dragging a small rock through the dust with a focus that was both admirable and slightly intimidating. The line he was creating in the ground was a tangible sign of our commitment to this new beginning, a boundary marking the start of something that was still too nebulous to fully comprehend.

Taking my cue from Jamie's determined efforts, I set about gathering larger rocks from the surrounding area. Each stone felt significant as I placed them down, small piles in each corner and at regular intervals along each edge of our designated site. The physical act of defining our space lent a sense of reality to our plans, a solid foundation on which to build our hope.

"There," I announced, a sense of accomplishment threading through my voice as I wiped the sweat from my brow. The task had been more arduous than I anticipated, the sun beating down on us with an intensity that seemed to underscore the seriousness of our endeavour. My actions, though small in the grand scheme of things, felt like a declaration, a statement of intent in the face of overwhelming odds.

"Looks alright," Jamie observed, his gaze sweeping over our newly marked territory with a nod of approval. The simplicity of his acknowledgment felt like a small victory, a sign that perhaps we were on the right track. "You got a name for it?"

"Hmm," I hesitated, the weight of the question prompting me to pause and consider. A name wasn't just a label; it was a declaration of our intentions, a marker of our efforts to carve out a semblance of civilisation in Clivilius. "Yes," I finally declared, a burst of inspiration cutting through the uncertainty. "The Clivilius Delivery Drop Zone," I announced, a surge of pride lifting my words. The name felt like a fitting tribute to our efforts, a nod to the practical purpose of the site and its significance in our bid to establish a foothold.

Jamie's laughter, sudden and unexpected, cut through my moment of triumph.

"What?" I couldn't help but ask, a mix of hurt and curiosity colouring my voice. I had expected skepticism or perhaps even indifference, but not laughter.

"Nothing. It's as good a name as any," Jamie assured me, still chuckling. "But I'll just call it Drop Zone. It's easier." His words, light and devoid of malice, suggested a compromise, a way to bridge the gap between my grandiose vision and practicality.

"Drop Zone," I repeated, rolling the name around in my mind. It was succinct, efficient, and somehow right for the rugged simplicity of our lives in Clivilius. "I like it!"

❖

"Do you hear that?" Jamie's question halted me in mid-motion, his grip on my arm preventing the pebble in my hand from joining its predecessors in their dusty flights across the land.

I paused, tuning my ears to the distant sound that had caught Jamie's attention. "I think so," I answered, the faint noise slowly becoming discernible. "Is that... it sounds like a reversing vehicle?" The suggestion seemed absurd, yet the unmistakable beep of a vehicle moving backwards was hard to dismiss.

"It does, doesn't it?" Jamie's response carried a mix of excitement and disbelief. "And it sounds like it's coming from the direction of the Portal. It must be Luke!" His optimism was infectious, yet a part of me balked at the idea.

Luke? The thought echoed loudly in my mind. *Luke, of all people, reversing a vehicle through the Portal?* The notion was almost laughable. Luke's aversion to driving was well-known, making the scenario Jamie proposed seem all the more implausible. *Why on Earth would he be reversing a truck?* And the logistics of driving it through the study wall, the entry point of our arrival in Clivilius, presented a puzzle that my mind struggled to piece together.

Despite my reservations, Jamie was already moving, his jog towards the Portal a clear indication of his intent to investigate. I followed as best I could, my injured foot a painful reminder of the previous night's drama.

"Shit," I muttered under my breath. The burn, though not serious in appearance, was agonisingly tender, and the absence of proper footwear only compounded my discomfort. Each step kicked up dust that seemed to seek out the raw skin, a harsh and unwelcome addition to the burn's sting.

The journey to the Portal, typically a short trek, felt interminable given my injury. Jamie's figure grew smaller in the distance, his pace unfettered by physical ailments, while I lagged behind, each step a test of endurance. The possibility of Luke's return, under such bizarre circumstances no less, added a layer of urgency to my movements, propelling me forward despite the pain.

As I hobbled after Jamie, the sound of the reversing vehicle grew louder, a tangible promise of answers just ahead. The curiosity, mingled with a dash of skepticism, fuelled my determination. What we would find at the Portal remained to be seen, but the prospect of any change to our current predicament was enough to quicken my pace, pain or not.

Limping over the crest of the small hill, the sight that greeted me was almost comical—a small truck awkwardly making its way backwards through the Portal, with Jamie animatedly waving his hands, attempting to direct it. The sight of him trying to guide the vehicle, as if his gestures could somehow compensate for Luke's notorious lack of driving skills, was enough to draw a chuckle from me. If that really was Luke behind the wheel, Jamie's efforts were predictably futile.

"For fuck's sake, Luke!" Jamie's exasperated cry cut through the air, confirming my suspicions about the driver's identity.

"I told you," I muttered to myself, the scene unfolding before me proving my point. The near miss as the truck almost collided with Jamie was classic Luke—reckless, impulsive, but somehow always managing to pull through by the skin of his teeth.

By the time I reached them, Luke was already out of the truck, jumping down with a mixture of gusto and relief. Jamie's frustration was palpable as he confronted Luke. "What the fuck are you doing, Luke? You know you can't drive! You almost hit me!" His complaint was valid, yet there was an underlying concern that belied his harsh words.

I couldn't help but roll my eyes at the exchange. Jamie's decision to get so close to the truck, knowing full well Luke's driving capabilities—or lack thereof—struck me as more reckless than brave. *Jamie's more stupid than I thought*, I thought, unable to suppress a shake of my head.

"You shouldn't have got so close to me, then," Luke retorted, his defensive stance typical of the banter that seemed to define their relationship.

Watching them, I was reminded of an old married couple, bickering over something trivial yet filled with underlying affection. The urge to laugh bubbled up within me, a momentary distraction from the weight of our situation. Yet, as quickly as the amusement came, it was replaced by a pang of sadness. Memories of my last night with Claire, filled with arguments and unresolved tensions, surged to the forefront of my mind, casting a shadow over the momentary levity.

The reminder of what—and who—I had left behind, the unresolved issues that hung between Claire and me, made my heart heavy. My worries, far bigger and more complex than a poorly executed reverse job, loomed large, and the laughter died in my throat.

"What happened to you?" Luke inquired, prompted by the sight of my bare, injured foot and my uneven walk.

"I burned it," I responded with a straightforwardness that belied the complexity of the situation.

"Burned it? How?" Luke's confusion was evident.

Not entirely sure how to distill the night's events into a narrative that Luke would grasp without further bewildering him, I glanced at Jamie, hoping he could articulate the sequence of events more succinctly than I felt capable of.

"Hmm," Jamie began, his tone dripping with sarcasm—a precursor to the blunt summary I knew he was capable of delivering. He paused, perhaps for dramatic effect, then laid out the events with unerring accuracy, "No light, hot coals, and a fucking dust storm." The simplicity of his summary, though laced with his characteristic bluntness, captured the essence of the ordeal with surprising precision.

Luke's subsequent look of inquiry towards me demanded confirmation. "Yeah. That's a pretty accurate summary," I admitted, finding myself unexpectedly admiring Jamie's ability to encapsulate the chaos of the night in a single sentence.

"Oh," was all Luke managed to say, his response falling flat in the wake of Jamie's vivid recounting, his face a mask of disappointment or perhaps disbelief.

Jamie's frustration was palpable as he threw his hands up in the air. "Is that all you have to say? Oh?"

Luke's shrug was noncommittal, his response—or lack thereof—highlighting his apparent struggle to find the right words. "What do you want me to say?" he asked, genuinely at a loss.

"I don't know," Jamie retorted, his expectations of Luke clearly unmet. "But surely you could do a little better than just, oh?"

I frowned, an observer to the familiar dance of their disagreement. *Here they go again*, I thought to myself, a part of me relieved that their exchange, though heated, was not directed at me. It was a small consolation, but in that moment, it was enough to inject a faint glimmer of humour into the tension that hung between us.

"So, what's in the truck, Luke?" I ventured, eager to steer the conversation away from the brink of another round of bickering. The tension that had been building seemed to dissipate at the question, a welcome reprieve from the discord.

The cessation of their argument allowed a moment of calm, one that I welcomed with a silent sigh of relief. The anticipation hung in the air as we all turned our attention to the truck.

With a dramatic flourish that was characteristic of Luke, the back door of the truck was flung open, crashing against the side with a resounding clang. "It's all the stuff from your list," he announced, his grin wide, showcasing a mix of pride and excitement at the delivery.

My reaction was immediate, my earlier frustrations and concerns momentarily forgotten in the face of this tangible progress. "Oh, that's great," I exclaimed, the reminder of the list and its contents injecting a fresh wave of enthusiasm into my veins. The unfortunate events of the previous night had pushed the list, and the hope it represented, to the back of my mind.

"I need the two of you to unpack the truck. I'll come and collect it in an hour or so, once the other tents have arrived," Luke instructed, laying out the plan with a straightforwardness that left little room for argument.

I gestured towards the area we had marked out earlier, the rectangle of ground now designated for this very purpose. "There's a spot over there where you can leave all the things you bring through the Portal," I explained, my voice steady, outlining our makeshift logistics strategy. "Jamie and I can take care of it from there."

"Oh, cool," Luke responded, his casual acceptance marking a smooth transition from potential conflict to collaborative effort.

"It's the Clivilius Delivery Drop Zone," I announced, unable to keep the pride from my voice, my smile broadening as I shared the name we had settled on for our newly established area.

"I love it!" Luke's enthusiasm was infectious, his approval coming in the form of a hearty thumbs up.

"I just call it the Drop Zone," Jamie interjected, his tone carrying a hint of dismissiveness towards the formality of the name I had chosen. His preference for brevity was a stark contrast to Luke's and my own excitement over the official designation.

"Jamie helped," I quickly added, eager to give credit where it was due and perhaps bridge the gap between Jamie's brusqueness and the moment of collective achievement. I nodded towards Jamie, hoping to acknowledge his contribution in a way that would smooth over any perceived slight.

However, Jamie's reaction was not what I had anticipated. His glare was sharp, a clear indication that my attempt at inclusivity had somehow missed the mark, making me feel suddenly uneasy under his gaze. "You say that like you both expected that I wouldn't," he retorted, the words carrying an undercurrent of hurt, his pout a visible sign of his displeasure, as he huffed his way closer to the back of the truck,

"You better drive the truck over there for me," Luke instructed, tossing the keys in my direction.

With each step towards the truck, a sharp pain reminded me of the burn on my foot.

"I can do it, if you like?" Jamie's offer came at a moment of weakness, his hand outstretched, ready to take on the task himself.

I paused, considering his proposal, but a mix of pride and determination pushed me to decline. "Nah, It's all good. I'll manage. Thanks though." My words were genuine, appreciating his willingness to step in, yet not ready to admit just how much the injury was affecting me.

"Sure," Jamie replied, his voice neutral, stepping back to allow me to proceed.

Gingerly, I positioned myself behind the wheel of the truck, the familiar feel of the driver's seat offering a fleeting sense of control. "I want to try and leave again," Jamie's voice filtered through the open door, a statement directed at Luke.

With a sense of resolve, I slammed the door shut, cutting off their conversation and enveloping myself in the relative silence of the cabin. The brief respite from our harsh reality was welcome, even if I knew it was temporary. I had a feeling that it was going to be a very long day.

As I navigated the truck towards the Drop Zone's designated entrance, a semblance of normalcy played in my mind. There was technically enough space for me to drive through anywhere, but adhering to the boundaries we had set somehow made the situation feel more manageable, less chaotic. The entrance, marked by piles of rocks significantly higher than the rest, served as a makeshift gate to our burgeoning Drop Zone.

Bringing the truck to a stop just inside the Drop Zone, a moment of exhilaration washed over me. Stepping down from the vehicle, the anticipation of discovering what Luke had brought us mingled with the pain from my foot. Despite the discomfort, the prospect of unpacking supplies, of tangible progress, fuelled a sense of purpose and hope.

Tuning out the noisy chatter of Luke and Jamie, who had distanced themselves about twenty meters from me, I focused on the task at hand. The back of the truck greeted me with a resounding clang as I swung it open, the sound momentarily cutting through their conversation. Inside, shadows obscured the cargo, my eyes taking a moment to pierce the dimness that enveloped the truck's contents.

"Cement, cement mixer, sheds, tools," I narrated softly to myself, itemising the essentials Luke had managed to procure. A sense of appreciation for his efforts briefly lightened my spirits—Luke had indeed done well, securing not just the basics but the backbone of what could be our first storage. However, this initial relief quickly gave way to the realisation of the task ahead. A small furrow creased my brow as the logistics of our situation settled in. *I'll need to enlist Jamie's help to unpack the truck,* I acknowledged silently, the magnitude of the job becoming increasingly apparent.

I glanced back towards Luke and Jamie, noting the animated nature of their conversation. The volume of their chatter had escalated, a clear sign that their discussion, whatever its content, was growing more intense. Despite the distance, the energy between them was palpable, a stark contrast to the quiet determination that filled me as I stood at the threshold of the truck.

"Still can't leave, then?" I ventured towards Jamie, who seemed to embody defeat as he sat sulkily in the dust, it was the only logical conclusion I could make. The silence that followed my question hung heavily in the air, an unspoken yet clear acknowledgment of my assumption.

"Oh, also," Luke's voice broke through the tense silence, bringing an unexpected request into the mix. "I need your wallets."

The request caught me off guard, a mix of confusion and curiosity swirling within me. *What on earth does Luke want our wallets for?* The thought barely had time to form before Jamie voiced the skepticism I felt.

"What for?" Jamie's question was laced with a hint of accusation.

"Those tents are expensive," came Luke's simple yet loaded explanation. The implications of his statement began to dawn on me, a mixture of disbelief and concern brewing.

"How much did you spend?" Jamie's question was pointed, demanding transparency.

Luke's hesitation only served to heighten the tension between us. "How much?" Jamie pressed, unwilling to let the matter drop.

"The credit card is almost maxed out," Luke finally admitted, his words dropping like a bombshell.

Jamie's reaction was immediate, his frustration manifesting in a physical gesture as he kicked at the dust. "Shit, Luke."

"It's not like you can use any of it here anyway," Luke countered, a defensive edge to his voice that did little to soothe the growing unease.

I grimaced at Luke's attempt at justification. *Poor form, little brother,* I thought to myself, the situation rapidly deteriorating.

Jamie's anger flared, his words cutting sharply through the tension. "Oh, fuck you. Just rub it in, why don't you!? I get it, we're stuck forever in this fucking hole of a dustbowl and it's all thanks to... guess who!?" His frustration was palpable, a raw expression of the helplessness he felt.

Seeking to somehow diffuse the escalating argument, I reached into my pocket, retrieving my wallet. Its presence, forgotten until now, seemed almost trivial in the grand scheme of our current reality. "Here," I said, extending the wallet towards Luke, a gesture meant to bridge the gap between necessity and resentment.

"You can't be fucking serious!" Jamie's outrage at my compliance was explosive, a clear sign of his vehement disagreement with the situation.

I shrugged, a feeble attempt to convey my resignation to the circumstances. *What else can I do?*

Luke stepped over to take my wallet, his request extending beyond the physical handover. "I'll need you to write down all your bank account details too," he said, adding a layer of gravity to the situation that I hadn't anticipated.

"What sort of details?" My question was laced with caution, the implications of his request slowly dawning on me.

Luke met my gaze squarely, his intent clear and unnervingly direct. "Everything," he asserted. "Online logins, pin codes. Over the next few days, I'm going to convert as many of your assets into cash as possible." The seriousness in his voice was unmistakable, a declaration of a plan that felt both desperate and final.

A wave of fear washed over me, the enormity of Luke's proposal striking me with the force of a physical blow. My eyes widened as the implications took root, a sense of vulnerability engulfing me. The thought of relinquishing such control, of exposing every financial detail of my life, was overwhelming. I felt a sudden nausea at the prospect, a visceral reaction to the perceived invasion of my and my family's privacy and security.

In a moment of panic, I acted instinctively, snatching the wallet back from Luke's grasp. The sudden movement caught him off guard, his surprise mirrored in the way he threw his hands up.

"What's up?" His confusion was evident, a stark contrast to the decisive tone he had employed just moments earlier.

"I can't let you do that, Luke," I found myself saying, the words tumbling out in a rush of emotion and resolve. "I need to think of my children." The thought of Claire and the kids, of their well-being and financial security, crystallised my opposition. "Claire still has access to those accounts. She'll need the money to take care of the kids, especially now that I have no way of providing them any further support." The admission was a painful reminder of my current helplessness and the responsibilities that lay beyond the confines of Clivilius.

The rapidity of my response left me dizzy, a tumult of thoughts and fears swirling within me. I blinked rapidly, an attempt to refocus, to steady the turmoil that threatened to overwhelm me.

Luke's expression shifted from confusion to understanding. "Of course," he conceded, his voice softer, tinged with regret. "I understand." The acknowledgement was a small comfort, a recognition of the complexities and connections that remained tethered to a world we could no longer claim as our own.

"Here. Take mine," Jamie's voice cut through the tension, his offer catching me off guard. "It's just the two of us anyway. You may as well have it," he said, a gesture so unexpected it momentarily silenced the unease that had settled over us. His wallet arced through the air, landing with a soft thud at Luke's feet, a tangible symbol of his willingness to contribute, to sacrifice for the collective need.

Luke bent to retrieve the wallet, his movements gentle. "Thanks," he said, his smile soft and laden with gratitude. It was a rare glimpse into the depth of their relationship, a moment of vulnerability and mutual understanding.

I found myself caught in the observation of this exchange, a witness to a side of Jamie I had perhaps too hastily overlooked. Despite his brusqueness, his earlier willingness to comfort and protect me in a moment of vulnerability flashed through my mind, reminding me of his capacity for compassion. It had been Jamie's arms that had provided solace in the darkness, his presence a beacon in the tumult of fear and confusion. A surge of guilt washed over me for not fully acknowledging the complexity of his character, for underestimating the breadth of his empathy.

Maybe... My train of thought was suddenly derailed by Jamie's exclamation.

"Shit, Luke. This is insane," he blurted out, the gravity of what we were about to undertake hitting him anew. His words echoed my own fears, a vocalisation of the dread that lay heavy on my heart.

"I know," Luke's response was resigned, a verbal shrug in the face of our unprecedented circumstances. "But this is just how it is now."

His words, simple yet profound, hung in the air, a sombre acknowledgment of our new reality. My head bowed, weighed down by the acceptance of our predicament. "I'll go and get some paper," I murmured, the need to contribute, to participate in our collective survival, pushing me to action despite the heaviness that threatened to immobilise me.

And so, I retreated back to the tent, each step a mixture of determination and despair. The act of fetching paper, mundane in any other context, felt like a small but significant assertion of agency in a world where so much had been stripped away.

❖

Jamie had done a commendable job repairing it, yet the string winds last night had turned the left wing of our tent into a disarrayed mess, with sheets of paper scattered like leaves in a storm. The urgency that had propelled me moments ago seemed to dissipate as I surveyed the scene before me. There was a certain solace in the task at hand, a reprieve from the relentless pace of our new reality. Thus, with no particular desire to hasten back to the Portal and face whatever awaited me there, I allowed myself a moment of deliberate slowness. Dropping to my knees, I methodically began to gather the strewn paper, each sheet a tangible connection to a world that felt increasingly distant.

The act of collecting the paper was meditative. The tent, for all its imperfections, offered a semblance of shelter, not just from the elements, but from the weight of our circumstances. As I crawled, retrieving each piece, I found myself grappling with the duality of our situation—caught between the need to press forward and the desire to hold onto the fragments of the life I had known.

With a single sheet of paper and pen in hand, I emerged from the tent, stepping back into the uncertain daylight of Clivilius. The security of the tent, transient as it was, had provided a brief respite, a moment to gather my thoughts and brace for what lay ahead. The open air of Clivilius greeted me with a palpable sense of expectation, a reminder of the vast unknowns that stretched beyond the horizon.

❖

Shuffling over the final small rise, the unexpected sight that greeted me drew an involuntary smile. Luke and Jamie, momentarily lost in a passionate kiss, presented a beautiful contrast to the tension that had permeated their interactions up until now. "So, you've made up then, I see?" I couldn't resist the urge to tease, even as I intruded upon their intimate moment.

Startled, they broke apart, the space between them widening as Jamie reflexively held Luke's shoulders at arm's length. The moment of surprise quickly gave way to an awkward pause, a silent acknowledgment of my presence.

I tried not to look down, but Jamie's arousal was all too obvious through his thin pale beach shorts, stretching its way down his left leg. I forced myself to look at Jamie's chest instead, as I waited patiently.

Jamie scribbled down his bank details, the act itself a reluctant surrender to our grim circumstances. Once done, he handed the paper over to Luke with a simple, "That's it."

Luke's response was tender, a firm squeeze of Jamie's shoulder that seemed to convey a multitude of unspoken promises. "I'll spend it carefully," he assured Jamie. Then, turning towards the Portal, he stepped through its swirling, electric colours, disappearing from sight as the Portal's colours vanished, leaving behind a palpable sense of finality.

My gaze shifted to Jamie, whose expression had morphed into one of profound sadness. The juxtaposition of his forlorn demeanour against the backdrop of their recent embrace was jarring. I found myself wanting to reach out, to ask what had transpired between them to cast such a shadow over the moment, but Jamie preempted any attempt at conversation.

"I want to be alone," he said, his voice devoid of its usual fire, his gaze fixed firmly away from mine. With those words, he turned and walked off, leaving me to contemplate the scene alone.

I watched Jamie's retreating figure, his silhouette growing smaller against the vast, dusty landscape of Clivilius. The distance between us seemed to grow with each step he took, not just physically but emotionally, a gap widened by unasked questions and unshared pains. The sight of him walking away, so clearly burdened by a weight I could neither lift nor share, filled me with a sense of helplessness.

"Hmm," I murmured, the sound more a reflection of my internal state than a response to any external query. With a noncommittal shrug, I moved towards the truck, its presence in the Drop Zone a reminder of the work to be done.

Discovering the truck's automatic tray was an unexpected boon. "Well, that's a bit handy," I remarked, a small smile breaking through as I considered the ease it would lend to my unloading efforts.

Carefully, mindful of the sharp pain that shot through my foot with every step, I began to unload the truck. Each item I pulled from the back—cement, tools, the cement mixer—was handled with an unusual level of care and attention. Organisation was not typically my forte, but in this moment, as I laid out our supplies, there was a sense of ceremony to my actions. It felt... *special,* imbued with a significance that went beyond the mere act of unloading goods.

I thought back to my conversation with Jamie, to the hope and determination that had underpinned my words. *We really do have a chance to create a new, thriving settlement.* The thought was a beacon, a guiding light as I surveyed the goods spread before me. *We could really do it.* A sense of conviction settled in my bones, a belief in the potential of what we were building here.

Yet, as the engine of the truck roared to life under my hands, a shadow of doubt crept in. *But what happens when the money runs out?* The question loomed large, its weight threatening to undermine the fragile optimism I'd nurtured. I pushed the thought aside, unwilling to succumb to the fear of uncertainty. *Luke's creative,* I reassured myself with a firm nod. *He'll figure it out.*

With a sense of resolve, I manoeuvred the truck between the two stacks of entrance rocks, parking it next to the Portal, ready for Luke's collection.

PAINFUL REVELATIONS

4338.206.3

Moseying casually around the Drop Zone, I found myself adrift in a sea of uncertainty, not particularly sure where to begin my search. I chose a spot on the soft, fine dust that blanketed the ground like a thin layer of forgotten snow that refused to melt. Sitting there, I let my gaze fall onto a picture plastered on the side of one of the larger boxes – a large, green garden shed, so vivid and out of place in this barren landscape. It seemed to mock me with its promise of normalcy in a world that was anything but.

"Hey! You actually going to do anything with that besides stare at it all day?" Jamie's voice sliced through the silence, jolting me out of my reverie.

The sound of his voice, so familiar yet unexpected, released me from my pointless trance. I turned my head towards him, the words stumbling out of me. "Umm. I'm not really sure," I replied, the honesty in my voice surprising even myself.

Jamie moved in closer, his presence sending small puffs of dust into the air as his feet dragged across the ground with a deliberate slowness. "It's a lot of stuff," he said calmly.

I turned my full attention to Jamie, my eyes narrowing as I studied his face more closely. There was something undeniably different about him. His usual brooding demeanour had been replaced by something else, something... calmer. Jamie almost brought an air of peacefulness with him, a tranquility that felt both unusual and unsettling. It was as if he carried with him a bubble of serenity, undisturbed by the entropy that defined our surroundings.

"What?" Jamie asked, his eyebrows arching in curiosity as he noticed my fixed gaze on him.

I blinked quickly, breaking the intense eye contact between us. My eyes widened as a thought began to form, unbidden, in the back of my mind. *I wonder...* The thought lingered, unfinished, as I grappled with this new perception of Jamie.

"How was your walk?" I asked, feigning a casual interest that belied the eager anticipation swirling within me. My voice, I hoped, carried a tone of nonchalance, but internally, I was fighting the urge to let a wide grin spread across my face. I knew where Jamie had been, and the thought of it filled me with curiosity.

Jamie shrugged, his response as noncommittal as his gesture. "Fine," he said, his voice flat, giving nothing away. Yet, there was something in his demeanour that suggested otherwise.

"Find anything interesting?" I prompted further, my curiosity barely contained. I was determined to probe gently, to peel back the layers of Jamie's recent experience without revealing too much of my own interest. His suddenly calm demeanour, the casual way he stood there with his shoulders relaxed, was at complete odds with his usual restlessness. It made me almost certain he had encountered the lagoon, that mystical place that had had a profound effect on me.

"Hmm. Not really," Jamie replied, his voice laced with a disinterest that didn't quite reach his eyes. It was as if he was trying to maintain a façade of indifference, but the subtle shifts in his expression betrayed him.

There was a moment of silence between us, thick with unspoken thoughts and questions. The lagoon, that serene and mysterious place, was teetering on the edge of my tongue, begging to be acknowledged. I bit down on my lower lip, holding the word back, fearing that mentioning it outright might shatter the delicate moment we were sharing.

"The lagoon is nice," Jamie finally said, breaking the silence with a casualness that felt rehearsed.

Aha! I told myself, a surge of triumph coursing through me. *I knew it!* The knowledge that Jamie had experienced the lagoon's tranquil beauty, just as I had, filled me with a sense of camaraderie. "It is," I agreed, my voice soft, accompanied by a gentle nod.

Then, we fell silent again, the air around us filled with the weight of our discoveries and the unspoken thoughts that lingered like ghosts.

"So..." I started, my voice laced with a tentative eagerness as I sought to engage Jamie further, buoyed by his uncharacteristically mellow mood. "This is pretty much everything from the first list that I gave Luke." My eyes briefly scanned the collection of materials and tools scattered around us

Jamie's eyebrows arched in genuine surprise. "Really?" he queried, his tone mixing incredulity with a hint of respect. "You've both actually done a really good job."

I couldn't help but chuckle at his astonishment, the sound echoing slightly in the open space between us. "You sound surprised," I remarked, finding a sliver of humour in our dire situation.

"Well," Jamie continued, his gaze drifting from the pile of supplies to me, a playful yet skeptical glint in his eyes. "You've managed to get us all this stuff, but do you actually know what to do with any of it? Guessing from the way you've been staring at that box for so long, I'd guess you've got no clue."

"Umm... well..." I stammered, the words tumbling out in a hesitant admission of my inadequacy. "No, not really," I confessed, feeling a wave of defeat wash over me. My expertise, if it could be called that, was confined to the sterile predictability of office life—hours spent in front of a computer screen, punctuated by the occasional, mind-numbing meeting. Hardly the skill set required for the task at hand. "But really, how hard can it be to put a few sheds together?" I added, trying to infuse a bit of bravado into my voice, despite the sinking feeling in my stomach.

Jamie positioned himself behind me, his gaze joining mine as we both stared at the picture of the shed, as if willing it to offer up its secrets. The silence stretched between us, heavy with the unspoken acknowledgment of our mutual cluelessness.

"I think we're a bit fucked," Jamie finally said, his voice low and devoid of his earlier amusement. The words hung in the air, a stark, unvarnished truth that neither of us could deny.

I groaned loudly, the sound a visceral response to the grim reality of our situation. Deep down, I had harboured a faint hope that Jamie possessed some untapped reservoir of practical skills, a hope that now seemed as flimsy as the paper instructions we lacked. The realisation that Jamie might be as out of his depth as I was struck a chord of panic within me. Up until that moment, I had clung to the notion that together, we could blunder our way through this project. Now, faced with the daunting reality of our incompetence, I couldn't help but feel a profound sense of dismay. *How were we supposed to build a future here, when the simplest of tasks felt insurmountable?*

"But..." Jamie's voice trailed off slowly, a hint of contemplation in his tone that immediately caught my attention. A spark of hope began to flicker within me, faint yet persistent, as I clung to the possibility that Jamie might have a solution, or at least the beginnings of one.

Jamie continued, breaking the brief silence that had fallen between us. "But I do know that before we can start working on the shed, we need to pour the concrete foundations." His words carried the weight of practical knowledge, a reminder of the essential first steps we had overlooked in our eagerness to make progress.

"Of course," I replied, nodding with feigned assurance, as if the idea had been on the tip of my tongue all along. Internally, I kicked myself for not considering the basics of construction. The fact that Jamie had to point it out was a small blow to my pride. It seemed so obvious now, a fundamental prerequisite for any stable structure, and yet it had completely eluded me until he mentioned it.

I rose to my feet, infused with a sudden surge of energy at the prospect of taking tangible action. "Let's get it started then," I declared to Jamie, my excitement momentarily overshadowing the daunting task ahead of us.

"Hang on a sec," Jamie interjected, his hand grasping my arm just as I reached out to grab the first bag of cement mix. His caution tempered my haste, pulling me back from the brink of a potentially rash decision.

"What?" I asked, a trace of irritation threading through my voice. *What does he want now? Can't we just get on with it?* My impatience to move forward was palpable, but Jamie's intervention suggested there was more to consider.

"Have you actually ever laid concrete before?" Jamie inquired, his question hanging in the air like a challenge to my unspoken assumptions.

I shook my head, the admission of my inexperience leaving me somewhat deflated. "No," I confessed, the word tasting like defeat on my tongue.

Jamie gently pushed me aside and took the initiative, grabbing the first bag of cement mix and turning it over to reveal the instructions on the back. I watched him intently, a mix of anticipation and frustration building within me.

"What's it say?" I asked, unable to mask my impatience. Each second that ticked by felt like a missed opportunity, a delay in our progress.

"Not much," Jamie replied after a moment, his voice tinged with a hint of disappointment. "It only explains how to mix the concrete. But I am pretty sure we need to prep the ground first." His conclusion seemed to stem from a place of logical deduction rather than concrete knowledge, pun unintended.

"Oh," I said, my gaze drifting over the array of tools and materials scattered around us. An idea sparked in my mind, born out of desperation rather than expertise. "We can use the pickaxe to dig the foundation hole."

Jamie laughed at my suggestion, the sound light and teasing in the heavy air. "Now you just sound like you're throwing words together." His amusement, though gentle, underscored the absurdity of my attempt to grasp at solutions, highlighting my ignorance in the face of a task that required far more skill and preparation than I had anticipated.

"Yeah, I kinda am," I conceded with a broad smile, the absurdity of the situation not lost on me. Despite the daunting task ahead and Jamie's gentle ribbing, I couldn't help but feel a flicker of determination. I walked over to collect the pickaxe, the weight of it reassuring in my hands. "We may as well give it a try," I suggested, turning back to Jamie with the pickaxe in hand. I hoped the gesture would encourage him, show him my readiness to tackle the challenge, no matter how ill-equipped we seemed.

Jamie took the pickaxe from me with a nod, a silent agreement to my unspoken plea. "You'd better let me do the digging," he said, a playful smirk on his face as he glanced down at my foot. "You're already crippled," he joked, pointing at my red foot, which was a vivid reminder of my less-than-stellar physical condition.

I offered no objection to his teasing. Truth be told, I wasn't afraid of hard work, but if Jamie was willing to take the lead on this, I had no qualms in stepping back. After all, teamwork was about playing to each other's strengths and compensating for weaknesses.

Jamie walked to the edge of the Drop Zone, the pickaxe slung over his shoulder with a casual ease. "Where do you want it?" he called out, his voice carrying back to me over the short distance.

I joined Jamie at the edge, peering out over the vast, open expanse that stretched before us. The empty landscape was a blank canvas, waiting for us to impose some semblance of order and purpose upon it. "We could put the sheds anywhere really," I mused aloud, my voice tinged with the weight of decision. The vastness of Clivilius offered endless possibilities, yet that very expanse made the task of choosing a spot seem all the more daunting.

"Think, Paul. It has to be practical," Jamie interjected, his tone firm yet not unkind. His words snapped me back to the reality of our situation. It wasn't just about placing a shed; it was about planning, about foreseeing the needs of a future we were still trying to piece together.

"Well..." I began, my voice trailing off as I mulled over our options with a newfound seriousness. The decision's weight felt heavy on my shoulders, a tangible reminder of the responsibility Jamie and I carried. "If they were near the Drop Zone, we wouldn't need to carry items too far," I reasoned out loud, trying to visualise the logistics in my head. The idea seemed practical at first glance, minimising the immediate effort required to move our supplies.

However, as I delved deeper into the thought, a critical flaw in my initial plan became apparent. "Oh... Yes... But then we'd still need to carry stuff to the campsite, which is where it'd most likely be required." The realisation dawned on me like a slow, breaking wave; convenience now could lead to hardship later. "If we built the sheds near the campsite, someone would need to move things there initially, but it would be closer and easier access for everyone else." My voice grew more confident as I spoke, the plan solidifying in my mind with each word. It was about more than just Jamie and me; it was about building a foundation for a community, however uncertain that future might be.

"Everyone else?" Jamie interjected, his question cutting through my thoughts like a knife.

I bit my tongue, a momentary frustration flaring within me. *Surely Jamie doesn't think it's going to just be the two of us forever?* The thought was a silent rebuke to his implied doubt, a reminder of the hope and vision that had propelled us this far. "We're building the sheds near the campsite," I declared, more boldly than I felt. It was a decision made not just for our immediate convenience but for the future we were trying to build.

"Okay then," Jamie conceded with a simplicity that belied the complexity of our endeavour. He collected the shovel and pickaxe, a silent symbol of his acceptance, and began walking towards the camp, the tools dragging a line in the dust behind him, marking our path forward.

I sighed, the reality of our decision settling in. "I'll grab the cement," I called out, my voice carrying a mix of determination and resignation. I heaved the bag of cement into the wheelbarrow, its weight a physical manifestation of our burdens. Along with a few other smaller items that would fit, I prepared to follow Jamie, my pace slow and measured.

The journey was punctuated by the wheel snagging in the dust, each stop to adjust the pile of unstable contents a reminder of the challenges we faced. Each time the wheelbarrow lurched, my grimace reflected not just the physical strain but the mental and emotional toll of our task. We were laying the groundwork for something far greater than just a few sheds; we were building the foundation of our future, brick by brick, with every snag in the dust a small obstacle in the grand scheme of our shared endeavour.

❖

As Jamie swung the pickaxe with determined force into the ground, the sharp edge sliced through the layer of dust with ease before striking the hard surface beneath with a resounding crack. The sound echoed in the open space. He poised himself for another swing, muscles tensed and ready.

"Wait!" I couldn't help but cry out, an instinctive reaction to what I perceived as a potentially misguided effort.

Jamie paused mid-motion, the pickaxe frozen in air, and turned his gaze towards me, a mixture of confusion and expectancy in his eyes. "What?" he asked, his voice laced with both curiosity and a hint of frustration.

"That crust is really firm," I observed aloud, my tone cautious. The realisation that the hardened ground beneath the thin veil of dust might actually be an asset rather than a hindrance was a new and unexpected development. "Maybe we should just leave it and only move the few inches of dust?" I suggested, the idea forming more clearly as I spoke. "I reckon the concrete will set better on that solid ground." It was a gamble, relying on my limited knowledge of construction, but it felt like a sound hypothesis.

Jamie considered my suggestion for a moment, his expression contemplative. Then, with a nod, he conceded,

"That's actually not a bad idea." The approval in his voice was unexpected but welcome, a sign that we were finally starting to operate on the same wavelength.

I breathed a sigh of relief, a weight lifting off my shoulders. *Finally*, I thought, *a small but significant victory*. We were starting to get along, to truly collaborate on this daunting task. The early tension that had hovered between us like a thick fog was beginning to dissipate, replaced by a burgeoning sense of teamwork and mutual respect.

"I'll go get us some water for the concrete mix," I announced, eager to contribute further and maintain the momentum of our newfound cooperation.

"Sure," Jamie replied, a simple acknowledgment that carried with it a sense of agreement and partnership. He set aside the pickaxe and picked up the shovel, adapting to the new plan without hesitation.

Collecting the large plastic bucket, I set off toward the river, the anticipation of the task ahead mixing with a slight apprehension about my ability to carry it out. The journey, though familiar, felt different this time, imbued with the weight of responsibility resting squarely on my shoulders.

As I knelt down on the bank, the coolness of the earth seeped through the fabric of my pants, grounding me in the moment. I lowered the bucket into the clear, inviting water, watching with a childlike fascination as the water resisted entry, swirling around the rim in a playful dance before conceding, allowing the bucket to fill. The simple act of collecting water, so mundane yet so vital, reminded me of the precarious balance of our existence here.

Heading back to camp, I was acutely aware of every step on the uneven ground, my sore foot a constant reminder of my vulnerability. Then, without warning, a sharp pain shot up my leg, as if lightning had struck from the earth itself, causing my knee to buckle. "Shit," I cried out, the expletive torn from me as I landed heavily in the dust, a cloud of fine particles rising around me like a mocking spectre.

Lying there for a moment, frustration knotted my brow as I watched the precious water spill from the bucket, greedily absorbed by the parched ground beneath. It was a disappointing reminder of the challenges we faced, not just in building a physical structure but in surviving here, in this unforgiving landscape.

With a half-full bucket as my reluctant companion, I trudged back to the river, each step full of the determination that had taken root within me. The quick refill was a silent act of defiance against the setbacks that seemed all too eager to test us.

On the walk back to the shed site, I paced myself, mindful of the lessons learned from my previous fall. The realisation that this was just the first of several trips to the river cast a shadow of pragmatism over my initial enthusiasm. I couldn't afford to be careless; the success of our endeavour depended on the accumulation of small victories, each bucket of water a building block in the foundation we were striving to lay.

Arriving back at the site with the full bucket of water, I set it down with a deliberate care, mindful of not repeating my earlier mishap. I turned my attention to the concrete mix bag, studying the instructions printed on its back with a concentration borne out of necessity. *It doesn't look too difficult,* I thought, a flicker of optimism breaking through the daunting prospect of what we were about to undertake. With a measure of confidence, I tipped half the contents of the first bag into the wheelbarrow, the dry powder forming a small mountain in the centre.

"I'll pour, you stir," Jamie instructed, his voice pulling me back from my contemplation. He walked over to join me, a determined stride in his step that I hadn't noticed before.

"You finished clearing the dust already?" I asked, genuinely surprised. Jamie's efficiency was a welcome contrast to the slow, painstaking process I had envisioned in my mind.

"Yeah, I think it's as good as it's gonna get," he replied, a hint of resignation in his tone that suggested he had come to terms with the imperfections of our workspace.

I casually glanced over at Jamie's handiwork, my eyes quickly finding the small, visible lumps that smattered the site. *Oh no,* I thought to myself, a sinking feeling in my stomach as I contemplated the potential impact of those blemishes on the stability of our foundations. I opened my mouth to point out the concerns, the words teetering on the edge of my tongue, but then thought better of it. *At least Jamie tried.* Honestly, assessing my own skills, or lack thereof, I admitted silently that I probably couldn't do a better job. "Great," I said instead, picking up the stirring stick with a feigned enthusiasm that masked my internal reservations.

After making quick work of the first ten kilograms of concrete mix, I walked back to the Drop Zone for the second bag. The return journey offered me a moment of reflection, a chance to weigh the pros and cons of our methods. The wheelbarrow, which I had initially thought would ease our burden, became a source of frustration as it repeatedly got stuck in the uneven ground. The cement mix, heavy and unyielding, seemed to mock my efforts with each step. *The cement mix is heavy, but the number of times that wheelbarrow got stuck...* I mused, the wheels digging obstinate trenches in the soft earth. *Carrying is definitely less of a hassle!* I finally decided, a conclusion reached through the trial and error that seemed to characterise much of our endeavour.

"Stop!" Jamie's voice cut through the air sharply, halting my movements just as I was about to tear into the new bag of concrete mix. His tone was urgent, a clear indication that something was amiss. "This isn't looking right," he added, a note of concern threading through his words.

"Really?" I queried, my brows furrowing in confusion. From my perspective, everything seemed to be proceeding according to plan, or at least, as close to 'plan' as we could manage given our circumstances. "It looks fine to me."

Jamie shook his head, his expression one of unmistakable dissatisfaction. "Nah. It shouldn't be clumping like that. And see how it is seeping into the surrounding dirt," he said, his finger pointing towards the far corner of our makeshift worksite. His observation drew my attention to the inconsistencies in the mixture, something I had naively overlooked.

"Hmm," I mused, taking a closer look at the areas Jamie highlighted. The evidence was hard to ignore, and a small part of me knew he was right even before my pride allowed me to admit it. "You might be right."

Jamie gave a small shrug, a gesture that seemed to carry a mix of resignation and frustration. It was clear he was as invested in the success of this project as I was, yet equally aware of our limitations.

"We could probably fix it," I said, my voice laced with a forced optimism. Despite the growing evidence to the contrary, I clung to the hope that there was still a way to salvage our efforts.

"I dunno," Jamie replied, his skepticism mirroring my internal doubts. "Maybe we should ask Luke to bring us a short how-to guide for laying concrete for a small shed?" His suggestion was practical, a concession to the fact that we were out of our depth.

I took a moment to survey the mess that lay before us. The uneven, partially mixed concrete that now marred the landscape was a testament to our inexperience. "You're probably right," I conceded with a soft sigh, my smile strained as I attempted to mask the depth of my disappointment. This task, which I had so naively assumed would be straightforward, had quickly devolved into a glaring symbol of our inadequacy. *And we couldn't even get that right! What hope did we really have?* The question loomed large in my mind, a shadow cast over our ambitious endeavour.

We need someone with better handyman skills, I concluded silently, the thought a bitter pill to swallow. The realisation that our survival and success depended not just on our willingness to work hard but on acquiring the necessary skills and knowledge was a sobering one.

"Well..." Jamie stood there, hands planted firmly on his hips, his eyes scanning our surroundings with a mixture of frustration and resignation. It was clear he was at a loss, grappling with the reality of our situation and the dwindling options before us.

My stomach chose that moment to betray my own growing concerns, emitting a loud, unmistakable gurgle that echoed awkwardly between us. I rubbed it tenderly, a futile gesture aimed at quelling both the hunger and the rising anxiety within. "I'd suggest we eat. But even that is a little challenging at the moment," I managed to say, the irony of our predicament not lost on me.

Jamie's reaction was immediate and visceral. "Fuck it!" he exclaimed, his voice tinged with a blend of anger and desperation. With that, he turned on his heel and started walking briskly towards the Drop Zone, leaving me to digest the sudden shift in his demeanour.

And there we go, I sighed silently, a sense of resignation settling over me. *Jamie's calm has come to an end.* "Where are you going?" I called out, curious despite the obvious tension in his stride.

"To the Drop Zone," he shouted back without breaking his pace, the distance between us growing with each step.

"What for?" I asked, my curiosity piqued as I hurried to catch up, my sore foot protesting with every rushed step.

"To look for food," Jamie replied, his voice firm. It was a plan born out of necessity, a testament to our dire situation.

"But I just came from there and—" I began, my voice trailing off as something extraordinary caught my attention and halted my words mid-sentence.

The Portal, a marvel of swirling colours and energetic sparks, sprang to life in the distance. Its mesmerising display was a rare beacon of hope and wonder in our otherwise bleak surroundings. The larger streams of light collided with one another, sending sparks flying into the air in a breathtaking spectacle.

"Luke?" Jamie turned to me, his question hanging in the air, laden with hope and anticipation.

I knew the question was rhetorical, a shared acknowledgment of the one variable in our predicament that remained constant. Yet, I couldn't stop myself from responding. "I guess so," I answered.

We stood there, transfixed, as the small truck made its way through the Portal, its emergence into our world as surreal as ever. True to our suspicions, Luke was perched high in the driver's seat, a sight that somehow managed to blend the mundane with the extraordinary.

"Were you expecting anything else?" I found myself asking Jamie, my voice tinged with a mix of surprise and skepticism. In my mind, Luke's role had been to retrieve the truck I had emptied, not to arrive with another load. Besides, my understanding was that everything we had initially requested had already been delivered.

"Oh," Jamie responded, the gears turning in his head. "It could be the tents Luke said he had ordered." His speculation made sense, yet the method of delivery seemed excessive for something as simple as tents.

"In a truck?" My question hung between us, a reflection of the puzzlement that mirrored my own thoughts.

"Who knows," Jamie retorted dryly, a hint of resignation in his voice. "This is Luke we're talking about, remember." His reminder was unnecessary; Luke's unconventional methods were well-documented in our shared experiences.

"True," I conceded, acknowledging the unpredictability that seemed to be a hallmark of our plight.

The truck halted abruptly, a mere ten metres from the Portal, its sudden stop sending a cloud of dust swirling into the air.

"You're not even going to drive it into the Drop Zone?" Jamie's voice carried a mix of annoyance and disbelief. His expectation that the truck would be brought closer seemed reasonable under the circumstances.

As I reached out, my fingers brushing against the keys that dangled from Luke's grasp, his reaction was swift and unexpectedly sharp. "No!" he barked, pulling away before hurrying to the back of the truck.

Without hesitation, Jamie and I followed, our curiosity piqued by Luke's abrupt manner.

"But..." I began, the question dying on my lips as Luke cut me off.

"There's no time to move it. The delivery guy is in the toilet. We only have a matter of minutes to get all these boxes out!" The urgency in Luke's voice was palpable, a clear indication that the window of opportunity was narrow and closing fast.

"Shit!" Jamie's expletive was a succinct summary of our collective sentiment. The simplicity of our task had suddenly escalated into a race against time, a frantic effort to unload the truck's contents before the delivery driver's return.

"Tents?" I asked.

"Yeah," Luke confirmed. With a swift motion, he swung the truck's back doors open. The clang of metal on metal was so loud in the quiet of our surroundings that it felt like a physical blow, reverberating through the air and setting my ears ringing with a sound akin to an endless roll of thunder.

"Shit, Luke!" Jamie exclaimed, his hands flying up to cover his ears in a vain attempt to shield himself from the sudden onslaught of noise.

I found myself doing likewise, pressing my palms against my ears until the ringing subsided to a tolerable level. "Oops," came Luke's sheepish reply, a single word that did little to capture the discomfort his actions had caused.

Unperturbed, Luke reached up to grab the metal pole just inside the door, using it to hoist himself into the truck with ease. I watched him for a moment, marvelling at how the most mundane actions had taken on a new significance in our altered reality.

"How many are there again?" I asked, my voice louder than necessary in the aftermath of the noise. I reached up to take the first box from Luke, the weight of it surprising in its heft.

"Three," Luke answered, his voice steady and matter-of-fact as he passed another box down.

"At least that will give us something to do," I commented, tossing the words in Jamie's direction with a hint of irony. Our days were filled with tasks, yet the arrival of the tents presented a tangible project, something with a clear beginning and end.

Jamie reached out to take another box from Luke, his movements deliberate but lacking enthusiasm. "True," he agreed, the word heavy with resignation rather than excitement.

The three of us worked quickly, efficiently unloading all the tent boxes from the truck. We didn't bother moving them to the Drop Zone straight away, a decision born out of practicality rather than laziness. Watching Luke select each box with a haphazard carelessness, it was clear they would require some sorting before we could even think about setting them up.

"Thanks," Luke huffed, his breath coming out in short, laboured puffs as he jumped down from the back of the truck. With a quick gesture, he indicated for us to take care of the back doors while he made his way to the front of the vehicle, disappearing from sight with a purposeful stride.

"You coming back soon?" Jamie's voice carried a mix of hope and resignation as he called after Luke, the mention of hunger adding a layer of urgency to his question. But there was no reply, Luke's silence speaking volumes.

Jamie and I exchanged a glance, a silent communication that conveyed our shared expectations—or lack thereof—regarding Luke's unpredictability. *Typical chaotic Luke*, I mused internally, as we managed to close the truck doors far more gently than they had been opened.

"Odd," Jamie voiced his observation, the word hanging in the air between us as Luke and the truck vanished as quickly as they had arrived, leaving us alone with the boxes.

I picked up the corner of one of the larger boxes, my curiosity piqued. "What is?" I inquired, genuinely unsure of what Jamie found strange this time.

"The Portal is still open," he replied, his gaze fixed on the mesmerising display of colours that danced within the frame of the Portal.

"Luke must be coming back then," I reasoned, trying to inject a note of optimism into the situation. It was a small hope, but hope nonetheless in the face of our many uncertainties.

Jamie, drawn like a moth to a flame, stopped just an inch away from the vibrant display. *Oh no, here we go again*, I thought, a sense of dread settling in as I anticipated what was coming next.

True to form, Jamie extended his hand towards the swirling colours, a gesture born of an irresistible combination of curiosity and the faint hope of understanding—or perhaps influencing—the Portal's mysteries.

I shook my head in resignation. *Why does Jamie insist on trying when it just makes him more and more frustrated?* It was a question I had asked myself countless times, each instance ending in the same predictable frustration for Jamie.

Dragging the box along the ground, I set my sights on the Drop Zone, determined to at least accomplish the task of moving the supplies, even if everything else around us was shrouded in uncertainty.

"Fuck!" Jamie's exclamation sliced through the air, an obvious indicator of his failed attempt to interact with the Portal.

"No luck then?" I couldn't help but call out, my words laced with a sarcasm born of familiarity with the routine.

In response, Jamie's middle finger was all the answer I needed, a silent but eloquent reply that spoke volumes of his irritation.

"Figures," I scoffed under my breath, my attention turning to the second box. The physical exertion of the task at hand was beginning to take its toll, a bead of sweat forming at my forehead a testament to the relentless sun above.

"Where are you taking that?" Jamie's voice sliced through the air, a mix of curiosity and demand that instantly put me on edge.

"Why do you care?" My response came out sharper than I intended, a snarky retort flung over my shoulder without pausing to gauge its impact.

"What the hell is that supposed to mean?" Jamie's tone escalated, his footsteps quickening to catch up to me, injecting a note of confrontation into the already tense atmosphere.

I stopped in my tracks, the weight of my earlier words and the exhaustion bearing down on me making my shoulders slump. "Look, I'm sorry," I said, my voice softer now, tinged with genuine remorse. I shook my head, a mix of frustration at the situation and at myself for snapping. "I'm just tired and my whole body is aching."

Jamie's response was a short huff, a sound that seemed to carry all the weight of the world in it. I braced myself, expecting a retort or a continuation of our spat.

"It's okay," Jamie huffed again, his voice unexpectedly softer. "I get it." His simple acknowledgment acted as a balm, easing the tension that had quickly built between us.

I looked up, meeting Jamie's gaze, searching his face for any sign of lingering annoyance or sarcasm. Instead, I found an expression of understanding, perhaps even empathy.

"That dust storm last night was pretty brutal," Jamie offered, shifting the topic away from our earlier friction. In a gesture that seemed to underscore his point, he lifted his sweaty t-shirt to reveal his chest, marked by a vivid redness and a large welt sitting ominously between his pectoral muscles.

"What the fuck!" The exclamation burst from me before I could temper my reaction, my concern overriding any previous irritation. "What the hell is that?" I asked, stepping closer, my eyes widening at the sight of the injury.

Jamie's action of letting his top fall back into place was almost dismissive, but the seriousness of what he'd just revealed lingered in the air. "I think one of the hot coals struck me," he said, his voice carrying a note of nonchalance that didn't quite mask the underlying discomfort.

"Shit, Jamie! I'm so sorry!" The words tumbled out, a rush of concern flooding through me. The thought that Jamie had been hurt, and the possibility that I could have been responsible, even indirectly, sent a pang of guilt through me.

"I don't think it was you," Jamie replied, his tone reassuring despite the circumstances. "I think it just got caught in a gust of wind."

My head began to spin with a mixture of confusion and guilt. *Why hadn't Jamie told me about his injury earlier?* Here I was, hobbling around all morning, wallowing in self-pity over my foot, and expecting Jamie to shoulder the burden of our workload. As the realisation dawned on me, my eyes started to water, the guilt burrowing deep into my heart. The sight of Jamie's chest, marked by that vivid, angry welt, was a stark visual evidence of the pain he must be in. "But you wouldn't have been out there if not for me," I managed to say, my voice barely above a whisper.

Jamie picked up the corner of the box I had let fall to the ground. "If we're going to set these up down by the river with the other tent, we may as well take these boxes straight there rather than bother with the Drop Zone," he suggested with a level of calm that seemed almost inhuman under the circumstances. Then, without waiting for my response, he turned to walk away.

I stared after him, my disbelief mixed with a rising admiration. *How is he staying so calm?* The question echoed in my mind, especially when his burn seemed far more serious than the minor injury I had been nursing on my foot.

"Jamie!" I called out, my voice laced with concern and urgency.

He waved for me to follow him, continuing his stride with a determination that belied the pain he must have been feeling.

"Jamie!" I called out again, my voice louder, more desperate as I hobbled to catch up. "You need a doctor!"

Jamie whipped around so suddenly, it was as if he had reached his breaking point. "We don't have a fucking doctor!" he exclaimed, the harshness of his words cutting through the air between us.

I stopped mid-step, the raw emotion visible in Jamie's eyes, tears swelling up and breaking the façade of calm he had been maintaining. The sight of his vulnerability, so rare and stark, brought a lump to my throat.

Jamie sniffed deeply, trying to regain control over his emotions, a silent struggle that spoke volumes of his resilience and pain.

Moved by a wave of spontaneous emotion, I closed the distance between us, hobbling over with as much speed as my injured foot would allow. I wrapped my arms around him, drawing him into a close embrace, an attempt to offer comfort in the only way I knew how. "I'm so sorry, Jamie," I whispered into his shoulder, my voice thick with emotion. But before I could continue, before I could find the words that might offer some solace, we were interrupted, leaving my apology hanging incomplete.

The abrupt sound of a dog barking snapped us out of our emotional moment, drawing our attention away with such immediacy it felt like being jerked into a different reality. In my surprise, Jamie's reaction was swift, pushing me away as he spun towards the source of the sound.

The barking continued, a sound so out of place in our current surroundings that it momentarily disoriented me. "Henri!" Jamie's voice, infused with a mix of disbelief and joy, cut through the air as he dashed toward the small, enthusiastic source of the noise.

Rubbing at my eyes, I questioned the reality before me. *Are we both having the same hallucination? Or is Henri really in Clivilius?* The sight before me seemed too surreal, too starkly opposed to the harshness of our current life.

Jamie reached the dog in moments, bending down to scoop the chubby Shih Tzu into his arms. The dog's tail wagged furiously, its small tongue lavishing Jamie's face with affectionate licks. Watching them, a smile broke through my own confusion and worry, a brief respite in the form of this joyful reunion.

However, the lightness of the moment evaporated as quickly as it had appeared when Luke stepped through the Portal, another dog, Duke, cradled in his arms. The atmosphere shifted palpably as Jamie's voice rose in anger and disbelief. "Luke! What the fuck are you doing! Why the fuck did you bring them here?" His scream sliced through the air.

Luke, taken aback by Jamie's reaction, gently set Duke down in the dust. Duke immediately began to explore his new environment, his nose to the ground, sniffing around with curiosity. The tension in the air was palpable, the sudden arrival of the pets casting a long shadow over the joy of their unexpected presence.

"What the fuck, Luke?" Jamie's voice was a mixture of anger and disbelief, echoing loudly in the tense air between them. His frustration boiled over into physical action as he shoved Luke hard in the chest, a move that caused Luke to stagger backwards, unprepared for the force of Jamie's emotions.

Luke's response was immediate, his face contorting into an expression of stern defiance. "Fuck off, Jamie!" he retorted with equal volume, the anger palpable in his voice as he pushed back, his hands finding Jamie's chest with significant force.

The impact elicited a sharp cry of agony from Jamie, who stumbled backwards, his hands instinctively reaching for the site of pain. The sudden escalation from verbal to physical confrontation seemed to freeze the air around us, my attention torn between the innocent exploration of Henri and his older brother through the dust and the rapidly intensifying conflict before me.

"Is that blood?" The question from Luke broke the heavy silence, his voice dropping to a mix of concern and disbelief as he took a cautious step towards Jamie.

Jamie's denial was quick, a shake of his head accompanied by a feeble, "It's nothing," an attempt to downplay the severity of the situation.

"Nothing?" Luke's skepticism was evident, his voice sharp as he moved closer, dismissing Jamie's protests with a swift motion. He forcibly moved Jamie's arm away and lifted his shirt, revealing the extent of the injury beneath.

The sight that greeted us was shocking. The welt on Jamie's chest had ruptured, oozing blood and pus in a vivid display of the injury's severity. My gasp was lost among the collective intake of breath from those around me.

Luke's reaction was one of blatant fear, his eyes widening as he took in the full extent of Jamie's injuries, his earlier anger replaced by a dawning realisation of the seriousness of the situation.

Jamie, however, maintained a steady gaze on Luke, his voice low and haunting. "You've sentenced us to death, Luke," he said, his words soft yet carrying a weight that seemed to echo around us. "Welcome to the fucking nightmare."

The words hung heavy in the air, a sombre pronouncement that seemed to encapsulate the direness of our predicament. The presence of Duke and Henri, which should have been a source of joy, now underscored the harsh reality of our situation in Clivilius—a reality marred by danger, uncertainty, and now, the immediate threat to Jamie's health. The conflict between Luke and Jamie, sparked by fear and frustration, had laid bare the fragility of our existence in this alien place, a reminder that our survival hung by a thread, every decision, every action fraught with potential disastrous consequences.

ALLEGIANCE

4338.206.4

Sitting beside Luke on the mattress, the air was thick with the residue of tension from his and Jamie's recent altercation. The silence between us felt heavy, charged with unspoken thoughts and regrets. Luke had been rendered speechless, a rare occurrence, visibly shaken by the confrontation and Jamie's subsequent rejection of his attempted help. Watching Jamie walk off to the river to tend to his wound, left a palpable void in the camp.

Now, Duke was making his rounds around the tent for what seemed like the fourth time, his nose diligently mapping out his new environment. Henri, in stark contrast, had claimed a spot on the mattress with an air of finality, curling up comfortably in a corner as if he'd been doing so for years. The thought fleetingly crossed my mind that Duke would probably get along well with Charlie. They seemed like they would be fast friends, if only circumstances were different. But I quickly squashed the thought, echoing Jamie's earlier sentiments. As much as seeing Charlie would brighten my spirit, introducing more pets to Clivilius under these conditions was far from prudent.

I turned my gaze to Luke, taking in his slumped posture and the distant look in his eyes. We've weathered many storms together, yet the sight of him so deeply affected was unsettling. My forehead creased with worry lines, a physical manifestation of my concern. Luke had always been the tough one, the backbone in many ways of our duo. To see him this despondent, so utterly devoid of his usual resilience, was disconcerting.

Yet, there was a part of me that knew Luke's usual nonchalance wouldn't serve us here. If he maintained a too-laid-back attitude towards our dire circumstances, the harsh reality was that our chances of survival would dramatically decrease. His reaction, though painful to witness, was a necessary adjustment to the extreme circumstances of our situation. It was a reminder that our current existence in Clivilius balanced precariously on the edge of survival, where every decision, every action, could mean the difference between life and death.

"He needs a doctor, Luke," I found myself saying with a firmness that betrayed my growing concern for Jamie's well-being. The injury was far more serious than any of us had initially realised, and it was pressing down on me with an undeniable weight.

Luke paused, the silence stretching between us as he processed my words. "I know," he finally admitted, his voice carrying a hint of resignation. "I'll take care of it."

"How?" The question escaped me before I could temper it with tact. "Are you sure bringing another person here is the best idea?" The risks of introducing another individual into our precarious situation were not lost on me, yet the alternative was watching Jamie suffer, an option I found intolerable.

Luke's stare then became challenging, as if he was ready to confront not just the question but the implications behind it. "So, you agree with Jamie, do you? You think being here is a death sentence?" His words, sharp and probing, sought to dissect my loyalties and beliefs about our situation in Clivilius.

"Luke, that's not what I said," I countered defensively, the tension evident in my voice as I struggled to navigate the conversation without exacerbating an already delicate situation. My mind raced, weighing every word before it left my lips.

"But?" Luke pressed, his single word a prompt for me to elaborate, to reveal the depth of my concerns and perhaps, in doing so, betray a rift in our unity.

I hesitated, the weight of the decision pressing heavily on me. *Is this really a path I want to go down?* The thought of adding to Luke's burdens with my doubts was unpalatable, yet the reality of our incompetence in handling even basic tasks was undeniable. I sighed gently, a quiet resignation to the complex web of loyalties and responsibilities that bound us.

I closed my eyes, seeking a moment of clarity amidst the turmoil. "Luke," I began again, my tone softer, more reflective. "Yeah," Luke's response came, an invitation for me to continue.

"We need someone with decent handyman skills. Jamie and I suck. We can't even lay a concrete slab for the shed." My admission was both a concession to our limitations and a reluctant acknowledgment of the necessity for additional help.

"I shouldn't be surprised," Luke's words carried a mix of humour and understanding, a brief moment of levity in an otherwise tense exchange.

My gaze met Luke's, my expression earnest. "But don't tell Jamie I told you that," I implored, the last thing I wanted was for Jamie to feel undermined or for my words to be construed as siding against him. "We're struggling enough as it is. The last thing I need is for him to think that I agree with you, that we should start bringing more people here."

"Of course," Luke agreed, his tone indicating a deep understanding of the delicate balance I was trying to maintain. "I understand."

"Thanks." My gratitude was genuine, a small beacon of hope in the uncertainty that enveloped us.

"Shit," Luke's exclamation, sharp and sudden, cut through the stillness of the moment, propelling him to his feet with an urgency that seemed out of place in our brief respite from Jamie's painful revelations.

"What?" My question was instinctive, a reflex to his sudden change in demeanour. The eerie vibe of urgency emanating from Luke sent a tingle down my spine, a premonition that something was amiss, even as he tried to downplay it.

"Oh. It's nothing," Luke's response came too quickly, his attempt at nonchalance not quite masking the undercurrent of concern in his voice.

Luke and Jamie and their bloody nothings, I mused silently, a wry smile touching my lips despite the tension. *Honestly, they really are as bad as each other.* Their propensity for underplaying serious matters was both infuriating and endearing, a trait that seemed to bind them even in the most trying of times.

"I'd better get going then," Luke said, his voice softer now, a hint of reluctance threading through his words as he gave Duke a quick scratch on the head. His gaze then shifted to Henri, who lay lightly snoring, blissfully unaware of the complexities surrounding him. "Now, be good. Both of you," he instructed, the affection in his tone belying the hesitancy of his departure.

I chuckled. Henri didn't seem the least bit concerned by his new environment. *If only it really were that simple. Just find a spot to get comfortable in and the rest will be taken care of.*

"Take good care of them for me, won't you?" Luke's request pulled me back from my reverie, a solemn reminder of the responsibilities now resting on my shoulders.

I nodded, my agreement silent but firm. I understood the implicit trust Luke was placing in me, an acknowledgment of the challenges he faced that left little room for the care of our four-legged companions. The task of starting a civilisation in this alien world was daunting, consuming all of Luke's time and energy, leaving him torn between his duties and the welfare of Duke and Henri.

Luke's brow furrowed. "I never meant for them to enter like this," he admitted, his voice laden with regret.

"I know," I responded, my words aimed at offering solace. It was important that Luke understood that, despite the upheaval and the heartache of being torn from familiar surroundings, I didn't view him as a villain in our narrative. The complexity of our situation, fraught with danger and uncertainty, didn't allow for simple judgments or blame.

Leaving Henri comfortably asleep on the mattress, a picture of blissful ignorance in this chaotic new world, Duke and I trailed after Luke towards the Portal.

"Luke, wait!" My voice echoed slightly, cutting through the silence as Luke prepared to step through the Portal. He paused, a sign of his willingness to listen despite the clear intention to leave.

"Can you print us instructions for laying a concrete slab for a shed?" I asked, the request born out of our earlier conversation and the realisation of our limitations in handling even the most basic tasks of survival here.

"Sure thing," Luke responded, his grin a brief flash of camaraderie in the midst of our ongoing struggle. With a final wave, he disappeared through the Portal, leaving Duke and me to face the realities of Clivilius once again.

❖

Duke jumped up at my leg, his simple act of affection grounding me in the moment. "Well, Duke," I said, bending down to scoop him up into my arms, "What are we going to do with you?" His response was to lavishly cover my cheek with rough, eager licks, a reminder of the uncomplicated love and loyalty our four-legged friends offered us.

"We'll bring you Charlie," I found myself promising him, my decision solidifying with the words. "You'll like her." The thought of adding another member to our small, burgeoning family here in Clivilius brought a flicker of warmth to my heart, a small moment of hope that our isolation might be temporary.

Turning back towards the Drop Zone, a sigh escaped me. "Shit," I muttered under my breath as the realisation hit—Luke had forgotten to take the empty truck back with him. A minor oversight in the grand scheme of things, yet indicative of the myriad of challenges and distractions that constantly vied for our attention.

Duke's subsequent lick across my cheek pulled me from my thoughts, his simple, joyful demeanour a welcome contrast to the complexities of our human concerns. "You're right, Duke. Oh well, indeed." His presence was a gentle reminder not to dwell too much on the things I couldn't control.

As we headed back to the camp, I couldn't help but notice that the thick layers of dust covering the ground of Clivilius seemed particularly tough on Duke, his short legs struggling against the soft, treacherous terrain that threatened to swallow him with every step. Picking Duke up, I carried him the remainder of the distance.

"We'd better check on your other dad," I told Duke, a sense of responsibility washing over me. It was time to see how Jamie was faring after his encounter with the river, to offer whatever support I could.

Duke's bark, full of energy and agreement, echoed my sentiments.

Lifting my head, I scanned the surroundings with a growing sense of panic. Jamie was nowhere in sight. "Shit,

shit, shit," I muttered under my breath, my gaze darting upstream and then swiftly downstream towards the lagoon. The possibility of Jamie venturing as far as the lagoon sent a wave of nervousness crashing through me. The lagoon... its serene beauty and the strange, unsettling effect it seemed to have on me lingered at the back of my mind, fuelling my apprehension. *I know I have to check on Jamie, but maybe we shouldn't be at the lagoon at the same time...* The thought echoed, a reminder of the unexplained turmoil that place stirred within me. *I had never doubted my sexuality before, but that lagoon... What was it doing to me?* The question hung heavily in my mind, a mystery I was determined to unravel.

"Jamie!" My voice broke the silence as I jogged downstream towards the lagoon, calling out for him periodically. Duke, loyal as ever, tried to keep pace, but the thick, clinging dust proved too much for him, and with a reluctant glance back at me, he turned and headed towards the safety of the tent.

Reaching the lagoon, I continued to call out. "Jamie!" My voice echoed off the water, the only reply the gentle lapping of the waves against the shore. "Where the hell are you?" Frustration laced my words as they dissipated into the air, unanswered. My forehead creased with worry, the tight knot in my stomach growing with each passing moment of silence.

The pain in my foot, a constant reminder of our harsh environment, flared with intensity, urging me to sit and tend to it in the cooling embrace of the lagoon's water. But the urgency to find Jamie overshadowed my physical discomfort. The thought of anything happening to him under my watch was unbearable. *Luke would never get over it if something tragic happened to him. And I'd be all alone here,* the realisation hit me with a cold dread. The thought of solitude in this vast, unfamiliar world, without Jamie's presence, was a scenario I couldn't—and didn't want to—contemplate.

"Jamie!" The scream tore from my throat, raw and filled with a desperation I hadn't known I possessed. "Where the hell are you?" My voice echoed off the silent expanse of the lagoon, unanswered. Spinning on my good heel, my movements were too quick, too frantic, leaving me dizzy and nauseated. It was then, through the disorienting swirl of my surroundings, that I caught sight of it—a large hill, looming ominously on the other side of the lagoon.

With a sense of urgency propelling me forward, I forced my aching body up the steep incline of the hill. Each step was a battle against both the terrain and my own physical limitations. By the time I reached the top, I was gasping for breath, my body bent double as I tried to recover. My hands clamped down on my knees, a futile attempt to steady myself. It was in this moment of forced pause that I noticed the redness on my arms—another reminder of the harshness of this environment.

After a few minutes, with my head thrown back in an attempt to catch my breath, the reality of my situation hit me. "Shit," I cried out into the unforgiving sky. "I'm going to burn to a crisp out here." The thought spurred a new wave of panic. *I have to find Jamie, and fast.*

Lifting my head slowly, the landscape unfolded before me as I looked up from between my arms. "Holy crap!" The words slipped from me in a whisper of awe mixed with fear. Just a few meters from where I stood, the ground took a sharp, rocky drop, revealing cliffs that stretched for several kilometres on both sides of the river. From the safety of the lagoon, it had been impossible to tell the cliffs were there.

The river, a serpentine ribbon of blue, cut through the barren landscape, stretching into the horizon where it disappeared from sight. On the far side of the river, beyond the intimidating presence of the cliffs, the terrain flattened out, extending towards the distant mountains. These majestic peaks rose sharply from the ground, their silhouettes a testament to the raw, untamed beauty of this world.

With my hand raised to shield my eyes from the relentless glare of the sun, I squinted towards the horizon, trying to discern any sign of Jamie in the vast expanse. To my right, the landscape on my side of the river was a tapestry of gentle, dusty hills that cascaded down to the cliff's edge—a boundary between the rolling terrain and the sheer drop beyond.

Despite the overwhelming sense of emptiness, I couldn't help but find a harsh beauty in the scene before me. The sun painted the landscape in vibrant strokes of browns, oranges, and yellows, each shade blending into the next, contrasted against the clear blue of the river below. It was a beauty that was both striking and unforgiving, a reminder of the vastness of the world we now inhabited.

Yet, the breathtaking view offered no comfort in the absence of Jamie. Closing my eyes, I took a deep breath, trying to expel the growing sense of dread and helplessness with each exhale. *If Jamie is out here, there's no way I'm going to find him now.* The thought was a bitter pill to swallow, a concession to the reality of our situation that I was reluctant to accept.

With a heavy heart, I began the trek back to the tent site, each step a physical manifestation of my defeat. My body ached, and my spirit was weighed down by sorrow. My head, once filled with determination, now sagged under the burden of a hundred terrible thoughts. The world around me felt both vast and oppressively small as I reentered the tent

"You look worse than I do," the familiar, croaky voice broke through the silence, pulling me out of my reverie.

My head snapped up in surprise, relief flooding through me at the sight of Jamie. "Where the hell did you go? I've been searching for you," I blurted out, the frustration and worry of the past hour condensed into a single question.

"I know," Jamie replied, his voice weak but filled with an apologetic tone. "I could hear you calling out, but every time I try to move, it starts to bleed again."

I stared at Jamie's bare chest, where he lay on the mattress, the welt that marred his skin looking more menacing with each passing moment. "The water didn't help then?" I asked, hoping against hope that he had found some relief.

Jamie shook his head, a gesture laden with defeat. "I didn't make it to the river." He took a laboured breath before continuing, "I went too far upstream and then I collapsed before I had the chance to get in the water."

"Probably just as well," I found myself saying, trying to find a silver lining in the situation. "Or you could have collapsed in the water." The thought sent a shiver down my spine, the potential consequences too dire to fully contemplate.

"I know. Thankfully, Duke found me." The mention of Duke brought a small smile to my face, the loyal dog proving once again to be more than just a pet.

"And how did you make it back here?" I asked, my curiosity piqued as I gave Duke a quick scratch behind his ear, a silent thank you for his role in Jamie's return.

"Luke," Jamie said simply. "Duke fetched Luke and he carried me."

"Luke was here?" The question was rhetorical, my mind already piecing together the events that had transpired.

"Yeah. He brought in Duke and Henri's beds and box of toys," Jamie added, managing a faint smile as he gestured around the tent.

I couldn't help but smile back. "At least he gets some things right."

Jamie's smile, though faint, was a clear indication of the deep bond between him and Luke. Observing their interactions over the years, I've always sensed a profound connection, one that went beyond mere companionship. Yet, their reluctance to openly acknowledge the depth of their relationship puzzled me. *Why do they feel the need to hide their feelings for each other?* I wondered. *After all, they've been together for a decade.* The complexity of their dynamics, the unspoken emotions and the silent strength of their bond, was something I had yet to fully understand.

"I'm going to start putting up another one of these tents," I announced to Jamie, wanting to ensure he was comfortable before I began. "Do you need anything first?"

"No," he replied, his voice weak but resolute. He shook his head slightly. "I think I might try and get some sleep."

"Good idea," I responded, supportive of his decision to rest. Turning away, I made my way to the corner of the opposite wing of the tent where my suitcase lay. I quickly changed into a pair of jeans and a long-sleeved shirt, topping off my ensemble with my favourite cap. Despite knowing the outfit would result in discomfort due to the heat, the necessity to protect my already drying skin from further damage outweighed my concern for personal comfort. The harshness of the Clivilius sun was unforgiving, and my skin had reached its limit of exposure.

❖

Approaching the Drop Zone to collect the tent boxes, I noticed the absence of the small truck that had been there before. It clicked in my mind that Luke must have taken it back when he brought over Duke and Henri's beds and toys. It was a moment of realisation that perhaps I had been too quick to judge Luke's contributions; he was doing what he could, in his own way, to help us manage.

I found a large box with a blue, plastic strip on top and started the laborious task of dragging it through the thick dust back towards our campsite. The work was monotonous and physically draining. The heat bore down on me mercilessly, mixing with the dust to create a gritty film on my skin. Sweat plastered my clothes to my body, and fatigue tugged at my muscles. Despite the exhaustion, the relentless churn of thoughts and worries in my mind spurred me on, not allowing me the luxury of rest.

As I neared the end of my task, moving the last of the boxes, the Portal caught my attention once again. The familiar burst of colours across its screen heralded Luke's return, this time driving another small truck into the Drop Zone. I paused in my work to watch him navigate the vehicle with a level of ease and confidence that spoke of his growing familiarity with the process. He steered the truck with surprising skill through the narrow passage between two rock stacks and into the Drop Zone, an expression of his commitment to aiding our survival efforts.

I had no idea what to expect. My latest requests to Luke had been focused on personnel, not supplies. So, when the truck ground to a halt in the Drop Zone, my curiosity piqued. Opening the back, I peered into the dim interior, the low light casting shadows on the contents.

"An assortment of shelving," Luke declared, materialising beside me as if summoned by the very act of my investigation.

"Shelving?" I echoed, the word feeling foreign in the context of our current situation. "What for?"

"For the sheds," Luke replied, his tone suggesting that the purpose should have been self-evident.

I couldn't help but let out a slight, incredulous laugh. "I think we're a bit far from needing shelves," I admitted, my initial enthusiasm for Luke's arrival ebbing away like water in sand. The reality was quite different to the one Luke seemed to be imagining—we were still grappling with the basics of construction. "We still haven't finished the first concrete slab."

Luke's response was nonchalant, almost as if he had anticipated the course of our conversation. "Oh, that reminds me," he said, reaching into the back pocket of his jeans to retrieve several folded pieces of paper. "The concrete instructions," he announced, extending the paper towards me.

"Thanks, Luke," I responded, accepting the papers with a mix of gratitude and resignation. The physical weight of the instructions in my hand felt like a tangible representation of the responsibility resting on my shoulders. Without even glancing at the contents, I tucked the papers into my back pocket, their existence a reminder of the tasks that lay ahead.

Helping Luke unload the boxes of shelving from the truck felt somewhat surreal, given our current priorities. Nonetheless, we worked together to stack them neatly in their designated corner of the Drop Zone, a witness to Luke's planning, even if it seemed misaligned with our immediate needs.

"I'll be back soon," Luke announced with a sense of urgency, his figure quickly disappearing into the cab of the truck. The engine roared to life, a sound that momentarily filled the expanse of the Drop Zone before fading away as Luke and the truck vanished through the Portal. The colours of the Portal, vibrant and mesmerising, followed suit, leaving behind a silence that seemed to amplify my solitude.

I turned to face the large stacks of shelving boxes, their presence almost mocking in the vast emptiness of the Drop Zone's borders. I shook my head slowly, a mix of disbelief and resignation washing over me. *Luke's priorities seem a little off,* I couldn't help but think. Despite the logic that might have driven his decision, the timing felt completely ill-conceived.

Pulling the folded paper from my back pocket, I carefully unfolded it, my eyes quickly scanning the concrete laying instructions Luke had provided. The precision of the instructions was apparent, an appealing contrast to the ambiguity that often shrouded our daily existence here. Yet, even with such clarity, the task ahead seemed daunting, reinforcing the reality of our situation—so much to do, with so few hands to do it.

"Oh, Luke," I murmured to myself, a sigh escaping as I refolded the paper and tucked it away. "Please bring us a handyman soon." The sentiment felt like a prayer, a plea for relief in the face of overwhelming odds.

With the instructions secured in my pocket once again, I turned my attention to the last tent box, its blue plastic strip a beacon of my immediate focus. *The tent is your priority now,* I reminded myself, the resolve hardening within me.

INTERVENTION

4338.206.5

Taking a moment to step back and admire my progress was a rare indulgence in the midst of our ongoing struggle to adapt and survive. Surprisingly, the second tent, though not yet halfway completed, was really starting to take shape. It was a visual testament to the effort and determination I had poured into the task, a small beacon of progress in the vast, uncertain landscape of Clivilius.

However, my moment of quiet satisfaction was abruptly shattered by the sound of Luke calling out my name. The voice, unmistakably his, cut through the silence, originating from the direction of the Portal. *What does he want now?* I couldn't help but wonder, a mix of irritation and curiosity pulling me away from the task at hand. The half-made shelter stood as a silent witness to my efforts, its incomplete form a reminder of the work that still lay ahead.

As I began to drag myself away from the tent, Luke's voice reached me once more, this time with a message that immediately captured my full attention. "Food!" he announced, the single word carrying across the dust hills, igniting a spark of anticipation within me.

At the mention of food, my earlier reservations and fatigue momentarily faded into the background. Food was a commodity that had taken on a new level of importance, a scarce yet vital source of energy and comfort. Without needing any further encouragement, my legs responded with a newfound vigour, propelling me towards the Drop Zone at a pace driven by the promise of sustenance.

"I don't have time to help you move them," Luke's voice was matter-of-fact, his hands busily placing another three shopping bags beside the cluster already gathered in the dust next to the Portal. The urgency in his voice hinted at the tight schedule he was operating under. "I have another delivery arriving within the hour."

"Another food delivery?" My curiosity piqued as I reached for the first of the bags, the weight of it reassuring in my grasp.

Luke nodded, confirming my guess. "Yeah, I made two online grocery orders from two different supermarkets last night." The simplicity of his statement belied the complexity of our situation—relying on deliveries from another world for nourishment.

"Oh, I didn't realise." My response was tinged with both surprise and a newfound appreciation for Luke's efforts to ensure our well-being.

Without another word, Luke stepped back into the swirling colours of the Portal, disappearing from sight. The seamless manner in which he navigated between worlds was both fascinating and unsettling. In less than a minute, he re-emerged, this time with another four shopping bags in hand. "There should be enough non-perishables to last you at least a few days," he mentioned, his tone casual, as if delivering groceries across dimensions was an everyday task. Then, just as quickly as he had reappeared, he vanished once more, the Portal closing behind him, its colours fading into the background.

"Bye, Luke," I called out to the now silent Portal, a small smile playing on my lips despite the oddness of the situation. *Luke really is odd sometimes*, I mused internally, the thought accompanied by a gentle shrug of my shoulders.

Carrying the bags of grocery supplies back to the tent, I decided it was best to place them under the shade of the first tent's canopy for the time being. The plan was to store the food in the second tent once it was fully set up—a task that still required my attention and effort to complete.

No sooner had I set down the bags than Duke and Henri emerged from the tent, their curiosity piqued by the new arrivals. They eagerly poked their noses into each bag, their faces comically intrusive as they searched for any hidden treats. "I don't know if there's anything for you," I told them, trying to manage their expectations while secretly hoping Luke had thought to include something for them too. They deserved a bit of comfort just as much as Jamie and I did.

To my amusement, Duke's head dove deep into one of the bags, his body wiggling in a mix of excitement and determination. Moments later, he triumphantly emerged, a packet of dog treats clenched gently in his mouth. "Well," I couldn't help but chuckle at the sight, "I guess there is something for you after all." Duke's reaction, his tail wagging in a blur of motion, was a heartwarming sight.

"Bring them here then," I instructed, extending my hand to retrieve the treats. But Duke, ever the playful soul, deftly evaded my attempt and darted into the tent with his prize.

Following Duke into the tent, the light-hearted atmosphere was momentarily interrupted as Jamie, with a quick movement, snatched the packet of dog treats from Duke's mouth. "Luke's brought us a heap of groceries," I announced preemptively, forestalling any questions Jamie might have had.

"Thank fuck. I'm starving," Jamie responded with a hint of relief in his voice, his movements careful as he propped himself up to a sitting position. He then proceeded to open the bag of treats, distributing one to each of the eagerly waiting dogs.

"So, you're feeling better then?" I inquired, observing him closely. Jamie's condition had been a constant source of worry, and any sign of improvement was welcome news.

"I think so. I think I actually fell asleep," he admitted, a note of surprise in his voice as if the very act of resting had been an elusive luxury.

I chuckled at his realisation. "Yeah, you did." It was good to see him getting some much-needed rest, a brief respite from the discomfort and stress.

Jamie offered a faint smile, a subtle acknowledgment of the moment's tranquility.

"Well now that you're awake, I may as well bring these bags inside. It'll be better than leaving them outside in the heat," I suggested, thinking ahead to the practicalities of preserving our newly acquired supplies.

"I'll help you," Jamie offered, showing a willingness to contribute despite his recent revelation. He attempted to push himself up from the mattress, a gesture of determination that was both admirable and concerning.

"No," I insisted firmly, the protective instinct kicking in. "I think you had better take it easy for the next few days." The last thing I wanted was for Jamie to overexert himself and exacerbate his condition.

Jamie slowly settled back down, the realisation dawning that perhaps rest was the most prudent course of action. "Maybe just for the rest of today," he conceded, a compromise that reflected his reluctance to remain inactive but also an understanding of the necessity to heal.

❖

As I sifted through the Drop Zone, my focus solely on the elusive box of tent pegs, the familiar burst of colours from the Portal caught my attention. The sight was always a prelude to something new, something unexpected. Now, it heralded the arrival of a tall, slender woman whose entrance seemed almost serene against the backdrop of swirling energies. Her long, blonde hair, cascading around her shoulders, caught the light in a way that made it seem almost ethereal, especially against the vibrant hues of the Portal. Dressed in professional attire—long navy slacks and a crisply fitted white button-down shirt—she presented a stark contrast to our dust-covered, makeshift camp. Her steps, confident and unfazed, turned her black shoes a shade of brown as they met the soft, omnipresent dust of Clivilius.

"This is Glenda," Luke announced with a volume that filled the space between us, his presence quickly materialising beside the newcomer. "Glenda is a doctor in Hobart," he added, a visible sense of accomplishment lighting up his features.

I was utterly gobsmacked. Luke had actually done it; he'd brought a doctor into Clivilius. The reality of it left me momentarily speechless, my mind racing. *How the hell did he manage to pull that off?* The question echoed through my thoughts, mingling with a surge of relief and disbelief. Luke's ability to navigate our needs with tangible solutions was a cornerstone of our survival, but this... this was beyond anything I had anticipated.

The arrival of Glenda, a doctor, no less, into our fold was a game-changer. It was a beacon of hope, not just for Jamie's immediate needs but for our overall chances of maintaining health and safety in an environment that was anything but forgiving. The implications of having medical expertise readily available were vast.

Glenda extended her hand toward me, her gesture one of professional warmth. "It is a pleasure to meet you..." she began, her voice trailing off invitingly for my name.

"Paul," I filled in quickly, taking her hand in a firm shake, trying to convey a sense of gratitude and respect in the gesture. "I'm Luke's brother."

"Of course," Glenda replied, her accent thick, adding an intriguing layer to her presence. *German? Or maybe Swiss?* It was hard to pinpoint, but it lent her an air of worldly experience. "I see the resemblance now," she observed, a slight smile touching her lips as she made the connection.

"Paul burnt his foot last night," Luke interjected, drawing Glenda's professional focus toward me. "He seems to be doing okay with it, but I reckon a bit of medical attention wouldn't hurt."

"Sure," Glenda responded without hesitation. Turning to me, she commanded gently, "Show me your foot," her tone leaving no room for protest.

Her efficiency caught me off guard. Glenda hadn't even been in Clivilius for five minutes, and already she was ready to dive into her role as a doctor. Her eagerness to help, despite the unfamiliar surroundings and the abruptness of her arrival, piqued my curiosity about what had motivated her to join us in this uncertain world. Yet, any reservations I had about revealing my injury were swiftly overshadowed by the realisation of how much we needed her expertise.

I obliged, lifting my leg toward her with a mix of reluctance and relief. The action felt oddly personal in the context of our brief acquaintance, yet necessary under the circumstances.

"Oh, no, no. Not yet," Luke's voice cut through the air, halting the process before it had even begun. His concern was palpable, adding a layer of urgency to the situation. "There is another man, in far more need than Paul," he explained, his tone heavy with worry.

"Take me to him," Glenda responded immediately, her professionalism shining through her prompt readiness to assist. "And I shall take a look."

Luke's gaze shifted to me, seeking information. "Where's Jamie?" he inquired, his voice laced with concern.

I swallowed hard, the weight of the situation pressing down on me. "He's resting in the tent. I think he has a fever," I admitted, the words feeling inadequate to convey the seriousness of Jamie's condition.

"Shit," Luke exclaimed, his frustration evident. "What happened? I thought he was feeling better?"

"He seemed much better when we ate. But soon after... He looks pretty bad," I explained, struggling to keep my voice steady as I recounted Jamie's rapid decline.

Glenda wasted no time. "Take me to him. Now," she commanded, her tone leaving no room for delay.

Surprised by Luke's deference, I found myself taking the lead as he gestured for me to guide Glenda to Jamie. Despite the gravity of the situation, I couldn't help but feel a sense of appreciation for Luke's respect in allowing me to direct Glenda to where Jamie rested. With a sense of purpose, I navigated through the dust, leading the way to the tent site, each step fuelled by a mixture of hope and apprehension. The presence of a doctor offered a glimmer of hope in what had quickly become a dire situation.

❖

As we approached the site, Glenda's sudden exclamation, "Oh my God!" pierced the air, her concern palpable and immediate. Her eyes quickly assessed the scene, landing on the half-built tent with evident alarm. "He's not trapped under there, is he?" she asked, already moving toward it with a sense of urgency that spoke volumes of her dedication to her profession.

The misunderstanding, though tense for a moment, was almost comical under the circumstances. I couldn't suppress a chuckle, appreciating the absurdity of the situation amidst our concern for Jamie. "Oh, no," I quickly reassured her, gesturing towards the actual shelter where Jamie was resting. "He's in the fully built tent," I clarified, hoping to alleviate her immediate worry.

"Thank God," Glenda breathed out, her relief audible as she redirected her steps towards the intended destination. Her reaction, a mix of professional readiness and human concern, was a comforting reminder of her presence and purpose here.

"That one is just my attempt to put a tent up by myself," I added, feeling a slight flush of embarrassment as I admitted to the incomplete structure. It stood as an expression of my efforts, however inadequate they might seem in the shadow of Glenda's swift professionalism.

"Oh, I see," she responded, a hint of understanding in her tone.

As Luke held back the tent flap, allowing Glenda and me to step inside, the atmosphere was heavy with anticipation and concern. "Jamie?" Luke's voice, soft and filled with worry, cut through the silence, but Jamie remained unresponsive, a silent testament to the severity of his condition.

Glenda wasted no time, moving quickly to Jamie's side with a sense of purpose that was both reassuring and alarming. "He's not good. Not good at all," she announced, her professional assessment of Jamie's condition coming after a brief examination of the burst welt on his chest. Her words, stark and unfiltered, sent a chill down my spine.

"What happened here?" Glenda's question was directed at Luke, but it was I who responded, feeling a need to provide some explanation for the bizarre and unfortunate accident. "A hot coal struck him in the middle of the night," I explained, hoping to convey the seriousness of the situation without delving into the chaotic details of that night.

Glenda's reaction—a look of wide-eyed bewilderment—was understandable. The circumstances under which Jamie had been injured were as extraordinary as our current living situation. "It's a long story," I added quickly, hoping to steer Glenda's focus back to Jamie's immediate needs rather than the peculiarities of our predicament.

"Later, then," Glenda agreed, her attention returning to Jamie. Her professional demeanour, a blend of concern and determination, was a small comfort in the face of my growing apprehension.

As I stood there, watching Glenda work, I realised I had been biting the inside of my left cheek, the taste of blood an unpleasant reminder of my own anxiety. The tension was palpable, each of us wrapped up in our worries yet united in our hope for Jamie's well-being.

"I need a cloth," Glenda voice broke through my thoughts, her focus unwavering as she prepared to address Jamie's condition with the seriousness it demanded. Luke's panicked gaze met mine, a silent plea for reassurance in a moment teetering on the brink of crisis.

I moved quickly, my hand finding Luke's shoulder in a gesture meant to steady us both. "I've got this," I whispered, injecting a confidence into my voice that I hoped was more convincing than I felt. Rifling through my suitcase, I found a clean t-shirt, the best substitute we had under the circumstances. "It's clean. It's all we have," I offered, somewhat apologetically, as I handed it to Glenda.

"Seriously?" Glenda's question, directed at Luke, was laden with disbelief. Her gaze sought confirmation, a silent inquiry into our level of preparedness.

Luke's response was a resigned nod, coupled with an apologetic shrug. "I'm sorry, Glenda," he admitted, the simplicity of our supplies laid bare in this moment of need.

Turning her attention back to Jamie, Glenda muttered a terse "shit" under her breath—a faint utterance that nonetheless resonated heavily in the tense air of the tent. My body shivered in response, every instinct on high alert.

"He has severe swelling in the upper left of the small gap between his pectoral muscles," Glenda observed, her professional assessment tinged with concern. As she gently probed the area, she announced, "I need to relieve some of the pressure."

"Okay," Luke and I responded in unison, our voices a blend of apprehension and resolve.

"Someone will need to hold him," Glenda instructed. "And take those dogs outside."

As Luke stepped forward, I intercepted him, the urgency of the situation lending firmness to my voice. "I think you better take the dogs," I stated, recognising the need for him to manage the pets and leave the medical intervention to Glenda and me.

After a brief moment of hesitation, Luke acquiesced, gathering Duke and Henri with a gentle urgency. He led them outside, sealing the tent behind him to ensure a controlled environment for Glenda to work. The zip's closure marked a delineation between the severity of our predicament and the focused effort to aid Jamie.

Kneeling beside Glenda, I felt the gravity of the situation weigh heavily upon me. Her instructions were clear, yet the task at hand seemed daunting. "Hold his shoulders down," she directed, her voice steady and authoritative.

As I reached across her to comply, our arms brushed awkwardly—a reminder of the cramped space and the urgency of our actions. "It'd be best if you sit on his waist,"

Glenda suggested next, her advice practical yet something about the positioning felt inherently uncomfortable to me. "Lightly," she quickly added, sensing perhaps my hesitation. I did as instructed, positioning myself cautiously atop Jamie's waist, keenly aware of his vulnerability and my responsibility to keep him still. "He's likely to try and move suddenly," she warned, her tone implying that what was to come might not be pleasant.

My mind was a whirlwind of concern and confusion. I understood the necessity of Glenda's presence and her medical expertise, yet the specifics of her intended procedure were a mystery to me. Jamie, for his part, remained oblivious to the preparations, his slumber undisturbed by our quiet but tense conversation.

Observing Glenda's actions, I noticed her attention was fixed on a small lump near Jamie's left pectoral muscle—a detail that had escaped my notice until now. She prepared the area with a makeshift sterility that the clean t-shirt offered, her fingers delicately probing the flesh surrounding the lump. It was evident she was assessing the situation, determining the best course of action to alleviate Jamie's discomfort. Yet, without any visible tools for incision and no prior sterilisation of the area, doubts clouded my mind. *How is she planning to proceed without making an incision? And without sterilised equipment?* The questions lingered, unanswered.

Despite my apprehensions, I reminded myself to trust in her expertise. *She's the doctor. Leave it to her,* I silently reassured myself, trying to quell the rising tide of worry.

"You ready?" Glenda's voice cut through the tense silence, her focus unwavering from the spot on Jamie's chest she had identified as needing attention.

"Ready," I managed to reply, my voice betraying the anxiety I felt. The seriousness of the moment, the anticipation of what was to come, left a tightness in my chest.

Glenda's posture shifted slightly, a silent signal of her preparation. *Don't hesitate now, Glenda,* I thought, my mind racing with a mix of fear and hope.

Then, with a precision that spoke of her expertise, Glenda pressed her fingertips firmly into Jamie's chest. The reaction was immediate; Jamie's body tensed sharply beneath me, his sudden movement restricted by my hold on his shoulders.

His eyes snapped open, and a scream of pain escaped him —a sound so raw it pierced straight to my core. Instinctively, my grip on his shoulders tightened, an effort to both comfort him and hold him steady against the reflex to move away from the source of his pain.

Outside, Duke's barking added to the chaos, his protective instincts riled up by Jamie's scream.

"Jamie!" Luke's voice joined the tumult, filled with concern and confusion.

"Stay out!" Glenda commanded firmly as Luke attempted to enter.

Duke, driven by loyalty and distress, growled menacingly, his protective nature putting him on edge as he ran up behind Glenda.

"Get them the fuck out!" Glenda's focus remained unshaken, her directive clear amid the unfolding drama. Her priority was Jamie's well-being, and despite the pandemonium, her determination to alleviate his suffering was evident.

The tension in the tent was palpable, a thick, heavy air that seemed to press down on all of us. My grip on Jamie's waist had loosened momentarily as my instincts kicked in to protect Glenda from Duke's protective aggression. "Don't you move," she commanded sharply, her focus unwavering from the task at hand. Her stern gaze was enough to snap me back into position, a reminder of the critical role I played in this precarious procedure.

Jamie's pain-filled screams cut through me, each cry sending a wave of helplessness and sympathy coursing through my veins. My heart ached for him, my eyes watering in response to his agony. Luke's timely intervention, pulling Duke away from Glenda, was a small relief, but my attention was quickly drawn back to the grim task at hand.

"Hold him. It's nearly there," Glenda's voice, firm and authoritative, anchored me despite the emotional turmoil I felt. Her instruction was a lifeline in the tempest of Jamie's cries and the unsettling atmosphere that filled the tent.

Curiosity and dread mingled as I glanced down at Glenda's work. The sight of grey and yellow pus being expelled from Jamie's chest was horrifying, but it was the appearance of a small, black mark that truly caught my attention. *What the hell is that?* The question echoed in my mind, a mix of fear and fascination at the foreign object that had caused so much pain.

"Last time," Glenda announced, her tone indicating the culmination of her efforts. The final push was met with another of Jamie's screams, a sound so raw and pained that it seemed to resonate with the very walls of the tent.

Then, suddenly, there was a pop—a sound so unexpected and grotesque in its implications that for a moment, time seemed to stand still. A long, black splinter, accompanied by a gooey, gunky mess, oozed its way out of Jamie's chest, marking the end of Glenda's procedure. The relief I felt at the removal of the object was quickly overshadowed by the foul odour that followed, an assault on the senses that made my stomach churn.

As Glenda methodically cleaned the area with the t-shirt, she brought the long, charcoal splinter close to my face, prompting an involuntary cringe. "I'm guessing nobody knew that was in there?" she queried, her tone implying both curiosity and a hint of incredulity at the discovery.

I shook my head, too appalled to offer a verbal response. "I certainly didn't," I managed to say after a moment, my voice muffled as I pressed the back of my hand against my mouth, a feeble barrier against the revulsion threatening to overcome me.

Thankfully, Jamie's body ceased its squirming, his breathing slowing to a more regular pace, signalling that the worst was likely over. "I need some clean water," Glenda announced, her voice cutting through the heavy silence that had enveloped the tent.

"I'll get it," I volunteered quickly, eager for any excuse to step away from the stifling atmosphere and the lingering odour of infection. Climbing off Jamie's waist, I welcomed the fresh air that greeted me as I exited the tent.

"Who the fuck are you?" Jamie's voice followed me out, his question directed at Glenda in a confused, albeit characteristic, manner. My eyes rolled at his query. *Yep,* I thought, a mix of relief and sarcasm threading through my mind, *The Jamie we know and love is back.* Despite the situation, his gruff inquiry was a sign of his resilience, a trait that, under different circumstances, might have elicited a gentle rebuke rather than a sarcastic thought.

Stepping outside, I relayed Jamie's condition to Luke. "I think he is alright," I said, trying to infuse my words with reassurance, despite the tumultuous events I'd just witnessed.

Luke's response was a silent nod, his actions—wiping away another tear—speaking volumes of the worry and relief that battled within him.

"I need to get them some water," I reiterated, feeling the weight of responsibility settle back onto my shoulders. As I squeezed Luke's shoulder, a gesture meant to convey both comfort and solidarity, I moved past him, determined to fulfil Glenda's request.

❖

Gathering the water had proven to be a more time-consuming task than I had initially thought. By the time I made my way back to the tent, Luke was already on his way out, his movements quick, driven by a purpose that immediately set off alarms in my mind.

"Everything okay?" I asked, the concern evident in my voice. Luke's rush could only mean that Jamie's condition was fluctuating, and not necessarily for the better.

"For now," Luke responded, his words offering a temporary relief but also hinting at underlying issues. "But I need to go back to Hobart for some medical supplies." His statement was a sobering reminder of our precarious situation, reliant on resources from a world away.

I let out a soft sigh, a mix of frustration and helplessness swirling within me. "I wish I could come and help you," I said, the sentiment genuine. The limitations of our existence in Clivilius were never more apparent than in moments like these, where even the simplest forms of assistance were constrained by the boundaries of this world.

"If you could come with me, I wouldn't be needing any help to start with," Luke shot back, a hint of bitterness perhaps, or maybe just a raw acknowledgment of our reality. His words stung, not because they were meant to wound, but because they laid bare the truth of our situation.

I remained silent, at a loss for words. *What am I supposed to say to that?* Luke was right. If Jamie and I could simply leave Clivilius, none of us would be facing these dangers, these constant threats to our well-being.

"Got to go," Luke said, urgency propelling him forward as he took off in a sprint towards the Portal. I watched him go, a mix of admiration and envy for his ability to move between worlds, a freedom that Jamie and I sorely lacked.

Standing there, with the water in my hands and Luke disappearing over the crest of the hill, I was reminded of the stark realities of our new life. The physical distance between Clivilius and Hobart might as well have been a chasm, one that Luke could cross, but Jamie and I could not.

Ducking to enter the tent, I was acutely aware of the water I carried, cautious not to spill a drop. The scene inside was not what I had expected. "Are you okay, Glenda?" I blurted out, noticing her position on the tent floor, extending a dog treat towards Duke with a wariness that seemed out of place. My gaze then fell to her arm, wrapped in one of my fresh t-shirts. "What happened?" I hurriedly asked, my concern for her immediate well-being momentarily overriding my curiosity about the broader situation.

"I'm fine," she assured me, her voice steady despite the circumstances. "It's just a surface wound. This shirt is just a precaution until Luke gets back with some antiseptic." Her calmness in the face of injury was reassuring, yet it did little to quell the storm of questions brewing in my mind.

"But, what..." I faltered, struggling to articulate the confusion and concern swirling within me.

"Duke doesn't like her," Jamie interjected from his position in the tent, his voice carrying a chill that matched the coldness of his gaze. "And neither do I," he concluded, his words sharp and unforgiving.

"Jamie!" I couldn't help but scold him, taken aback by his harshness towards Glenda, whose only intention had been to help.

"She shouldn't be here," he insisted stubbornly, his refusal to see reason frustrating me further.

Glenda's glance in my direction held a clear warning—a plea for me to leave the matter alone. But the injustice of Jamie's words propelled me forward. "If she wasn't here, you'd be bloody dead within a few days!" I retorted, my frustration boiling over. The truth of my words hung heavy in the air, a blunt reminder of our constant battle for survival and Glenda's crucial role in it.

Jamie averted his gaze, a quiet moan escaping him as he attempted to shift positions, only to be met with a gentle admonition from Glenda. "You'd best stay on your back for now," she advised, her attention returning to her patient with a professionalism that underscored her commitment to his care.

Closing the distance between us, I approached Glenda, my movements deliberate. "I've brought you some clean water," I announced, nudging Duke aside with my foot to place the small bucket before her. The gesture was simple, yet it felt like a silent acknowledgment of the tension that permeated the tent. Without waiting for a response, I turned and exited the tent, the weight of the confrontation lingering heavily on my shoulders as I stepped back into the uncertainty of Clivilius.

UNBRIDGED

4338.206.6

Walking the short distance to the river felt like a brief escape from the turmoil that had engulfed the tent. As I arrived at the river's edge, I stood there, arms folded tightly across my chest, my stance more a reflection of my internal unease than the chill in the air. The water, gently gurgling past, offered a soothing soundtrack to my tumultuous thoughts. It had to be no more than twenty meters wide at this point, I guessed, my eyes tracing its serpentine path as it meandered through the landscape.

"It's a good spot for a nice bridge," Glenda's voice, soft and unexpected, broke through my reverie.

I gave a little jump, the surprise of her presence snapping me out of my deep thoughts. Turning my head to look at her, I found a small smile tugging at the corners of my mouth, despite the sombre mood that had taken hold of me. "It is," I replied, my voice steadier than I felt.

Glenda moved in beside me, her presence a comforting warmth. "It's oddly beautiful, isn't it?" she observed, her gaze not on the river, but on the larger scene that unfolded before us. The way the late afternoon light danced on the water's surface, the gentle swirls of the dust in the breeze, it all painted a picture of serenity that stood in opposition to the chaos that had unfolded in the tent.

"It is," I replied again, my agreement automatic as I took in the scene anew through her eyes. The beauty of it all, in such an unexpected moment and place, struck me, lending a fleeting sense of normalcy to the otherwise extraordinary circumstances we found ourselves in.

"How are you so relaxed with all of this?" I asked her, my curiosity piqued.

Glenda folded her arms across her chest, mirroring my earlier posture, and shrugged lightly. "I'm a doctor. It's my job to be calm," she said, her tone matter-of-fact yet tinged with a softness that suggested an underlying strength. It was a simple explanation, but one that spoke volumes about her character and the resilience she possessed.

I smiled, a genuine expression of admiration and gratitude for the perspective she brought to our predicament. "Fair call," I acknowledged, the weight of my own worries momentarily lifted by the interaction.

"We will build a bridge," declared Glenda confidently, her voice cutting through the ambient sounds of the river with an assurance that felt both inspiring and jarring against the backdrop of our situation.

"We can't," I found myself saying, almost instinctively, shaking my head in disbelief. The idea seemed as distant as the world we'd left behind—beautiful to imagine but impossible to reach.

"Can't?" Glenda echoed, turning to face me, her eyebrows raised in challenge. "Of course, we can."

"We don't have any materials," I replied, my voice laced with a mixture of frustration and resignation. The lack of materials wasn't my only concern, though it was the most tangible. Beneath the surface, a sea of doubts swirled. Even if we did have the materials, the task of building a bridge loomed like a mountain before us—daunting, insurmountable. I had no idea where we would even begin. The engineering, the construction, the planning... it was all foreign territory.

"Luke will get them for us," she said, nudging my crossed arms with her elbow, a light touch that carried the weight of her conviction. Her confidence was unyielding, a fortress against my doubts.

"And I thought you were the optimistic one." Her words, delivered with a playful smirk, were a gentle rebuke, a reminder of the roles we had seemingly swapped in the face of adversity.

My eyes narrowed in thought, not in skepticism but in contemplation. Her unwavering belief, her ability to see beyond the immediate obstacles, was a beacon in the fog of my uncertainty. "I am," I finally said, the words emerging slowly, deliberately.

"Glenda! Paul!" Luke's voice, edged with urgency, sliced through the quiet murmur of the afternoon air.

"Come," Glenda beckoned, her voice a mixture of command and invitation. I couldn't help but smile at her words, finding solace in her confidence and determination. It was comfortably different to the atmosphere that Jamie often cultivated with his never-ending supply of criticism and discouragement. Glenda's presence was like a lighthouse guiding ships through a stormy sea—her resolve, a welcome breath of fresh air.

We followed Luke inside the tent, the fabric flaps parting to reveal a scene that tugged at the heartstrings. I caught sight of Jamie hastily wiping away tears from his face—a rare glimpse into his vulnerability.

"You okay?" Luke's concern was palpable as he dropped the bags he was carrying, his actions punctuating the urgency of his query. He rushed to Jamie's side.

"Yeah," Jamie sniffed, his voice breaking through the mask of toughness he so often wore. "Just in a lot of pain."

"You'll be right now," Luke assured, his tone gentle yet filled with an unspoken promise. "I've got you some strong pain medication."

"Grab that spare blanket and spread it across the floor over there for me," Glenda instructed, her gaze locking onto a blank space along the backside of the tent. I moved to comply, my actions automatic, driven by a desire to be useful in a moment filled with so much uncertainty.

As I laid the blanket out, creating a makeshift workspace, I watched Glenda with a sense of awe. She began to sort through the bags of medical supplies with a methodical precision, each movement deliberate and purposeful. The items were placed down on the blanket before her, transformed from mere objects into tools of healing under her skilled hands.

"I'm pretty sure I've got all the items on the list without an asterisk," Luke said, his voice a mixture of hope and hesitation. "But I'll have to go back now and check the supply room for the rest."

"Yes. I will need the antiseptic and antibiotics. I can't dress Jamie's wounds properly without them. Go," Glenda insisted, her tone brooking no argument. Her focus was laser-sharp, the urgency of her request underlined by the critical nature of the supplies.

Jamie moaned again, a sound that cut through me, a visceral reminder of his pain and our collective vulnerability. He shifted his weight, seeking a fraction of relief in a new position.

"Just try and relax," Glenda's voice was soft yet firm. "Not much longer now and I'll have something to take the pain away and help you sleep." Her words were a promise, a beacon of hope in the shadow of discomfort.

Jamie exhaled loudly, his breath a release of more than just air—a release of tension, of fear, perhaps even a surrender to the care he was under.

Well, if you don't need me, Glenda, I'll go and see if I can finish getting this other tent up," I said, keen to move along, to find a task that would not just occupy my hands but also offer a distraction from the helplessness that gnawed at the edges of my mind.

"That's fine," Glenda replied, her attention already turning back to Jamie, to the critical task at hand. "I'll come and help you when I've sorted Jamie."

Her response, though brief, carried with it an undercurrent of solidarity. In that moment, I understood the unspoken balance of our makeshift family: each of us playing our part, supporting one another through actions both big and small. As I stepped out of the tent, the fabric flap closing behind me, I felt the weight of the afternoon air. It was a reminder of the world outside, of the tasks awaiting us, and of the resilience required to face them. Setting up the other tent wasn't just about providing shelter; it was about creating a semblance of structure. And so, with a deep breath, I moved forward, determined to add my contribution to our collective survival.

❖

As the dwindling sun's rays stretched across the sky, casting long shadows and painting the horizon in hues of orange and pink, Glenda and I found ourselves in the quiet companionship that comes with shared tasks and mutual understanding. We had finished erecting the tent together, our movements synchronised in a dance of necessity rather than conversation. Silence had been our soundtrack, punctuated only by the rustling of fabric and the occasional clink of metal tent pegs. Afterward, I had busied myself with getting the campfire going, a task that offered both warmth and usefulness, while Glenda had taken on the responsibility of organising our food and medical supplies in the newly pitched shelter.

The campfire crackled and popped, a comforting sound in the growing evening chill. Wiping the last of the sauce from my paper plate with my finger, I tossed the plate into the flames, watching as it curled and blackened, consumed by the fire's insatiable appetite. Moments later, Glenda, who had been rhythmically tapping her empty plate against her knee, mirrored my action. The repetitive tapping, a seemingly absent-minded action, had caught my attention, and I found myself watching her more closely.

The moment her plate left her hand, I noticed her fingers immediately took its place, dancing nervously on her thigh. It was a small gesture, but in the quiet of the evening, it spoke volumes. "Everything okay?" I ventured, breaking the silence that had settled between us.

"Ahh, yeah," she replied, her voice carrying a hint of hesitation as she rubbed the hand that had been tapping along her thigh. The quick, almost reflexive movement did little to mask the underlying tension I sensed in her.

I wasn't convinced. The unease that seemed to radiate from her was palpable, and concern tightened its grip around my heart. "You sure?" I pressed gently, hoping to offer an opening should she need it. "I'm here if you need to talk."

Her response was almost immediate, a swift "I need to check on Jamie," as she got to her feet with a speed that suggested a desire to escape rather than address whatever was weighing on her mind.

As she walked away, the flickering light of the campfire casting her shadow long and wavering against the ground, I couldn't shake the feeling that there was indeed more on Glenda's mind than she was willing to share. Her quick departure, the nervous tapping, the brief and unconvincing reassurances—it all painted a picture of someone grappling with concerns they felt unable to voice.

Sitting there, watching the flames dance and consume everything thrown into them, I felt a sense of isolation creep in. It wasn't just the physical distance Glenda had put between us by walking away; it was the emotional distance, the barriers we all sometimes erect when we're struggling to cope. In that moment, I realised that despite our proximity, despite the shared experiences and the camaraderie that had momentarily begun to blossom among us, there were still chasms that remained unbridged, secrets and fears that lay hidden in the shadows, just beyond the reach of the campfire's light.

※

The return of Glenda from attending to Jamie marked a subtle shift in the atmosphere beside the campfire. Her presence seemed to carry a heavier weight this time. As she settled herself back into the dust beside me, the fine particles billowing softly around her, I couldn't help but notice the weariness etched into her features, a silent testament to the burdens she bore.

"How is he?" The question slipped from my lips, filled with genuine concern, not just for Jamie's well-being but for Glenda's too.

"Still in a lot of pain," she admitted, her voice tinged with a hint of frustration and helplessness that anyone in her position would feel. "I've changed the dressing on his wound and given him some more painkillers and a few sedatives. He should be out for the rest of the night." Her words were clinical, yet beneath them lay a layer of deep care and concern for Jamie's suffering.

"Thank you, Glenda," I found myself saying, the gratitude in my voice deep and profound. "I'm not sure we would have survived here long without you." It was the truth, unvarnished and simple. Glenda had become our beacon of hope in a situation that often seemed bleak and unforgiving.

At my words, Glenda shifted awkwardly in the dust, the movement betraying a discomfort with the praise or perhaps with the weight of responsibility that had been thrust upon her. "Is this all of you?" she asked, a question that seemed to come from a place of deep contemplation.

"Yes," I replied, puzzled by the direction of her inquiry.

"There's been nobody else?"

"No," I answered, my curiosity piqued. "Were you expecting more?" I couldn't help but probe further, sensing an undercurrent of something unspoken, a hidden layer of concern or doubt within her.

"Oh... um... no," Glenda stammered, her response coming out more as a hurried evasion than a clarification. The moment stretched between us, filled with a palpable awkwardness that neither of us seemed able to dispel.

We continued to sit in that awkward silence, the minutes stretching into what felt like an eternity. All the while, I listened to the fire crackle, its sounds a soothing yet sombre background to my racing thoughts. The flames, with their relentless consumption of the wood, seemed almost like a metaphor for our situation—constantly burning through resources, through hope, leaving behind nothing but ashes and the lingering warmth of our shared humanity.

"You know you can't go back," I found myself saying to Glenda, the statement carrying more weight than a question ever could. It was an acknowledgment of our situation, a mutual understanding of the point of no return that we had crossed.

"I know," she replied, her voice steady yet laden with an unspoken mix of acceptance and resignation. Her simple acknowledgment sent us spiralling back into a silence that was both reflective and charged with the weight of our reality.

The silence stretched on, a tangible entity that seemed to envelop us, until Glenda broke it with a question that had been lingering in the air, unasked yet palpable. "So, what did actually happen last night?" Her inquiry, gentle yet probing, sought to pierce the veil of uncertainty that had shrouded the events of the previous night.

I weighed my response carefully, aware that the full truth might be more than either of us was prepared to handle in this moment. I recounted the tale of the dust storm and the overwhelming darkness that had enveloped us, a narrative that, while true, omitted the chilling encounter with the night terror. It was a deliberate choice, a bid to spare her from the added burden of knowing every harrowing detail. *I've given her enough to think about already*, I rationalised, hoping the partial truth would suffice for now.

Glenda's gaze drifted upwards, seeking out the sky that had turned the same eerie black as the night before. "It's very dark. There is no moon, or stars here?" she pondered aloud, her question voicing a sense of disorientation and loss—a yearning for the familiar comfort of celestial bodies that seemed absent in this place.

"I don't think so," I replied, my own voice tinged with a hint of regret. "At least we didn't see anything last night."

"Oh, I see," Glenda murmured, her attention returning to the fire. The light from the flames reflected in her eyes, casting a warm glow on her face, yet unable to dispel the growing shadows of concern.

As I observed her, lines of worry etched themselves deeper into her expression, a map of the stress and challenges she had faced. *She must be nearing her early forties,* I mused, noting the graceful way she carried the weight of her experiences. Despite the hardships, Glenda seemed to be ageing with a resilience and strength that was as admirable as it was enviable.

In that moment, seated by the fire under a starless sky, the contrast between the darkness above and the flickering light before us served as a metaphor for our current existence—caught between the unknown and the faint hope that sustained us. Glenda's concerns, mirrored in her furrowed brow, were a reminder of the complexities and uncertainties we faced, not just in our surroundings, but within ourselves.

"Glenda," I whispered, breaking the silence that had once again settled around us like a thick blanket.

"Yes, Paul," she responded, her voice carrying a note of readiness, as if braced for whatever concern or confession I was about to voice.

"The dark can be a scary place here," I admitted, the words feeling both vulnerable and true. "I'm going to keep the fire going all night tonight." It was a declaration as much as it was a reassurance to myself—a way to ward off the shadows that seemed to press in closer with each passing hour.

"Do you feel safe here?" Glenda's question cut to the heart of our situation, simple yet profound in its implication.

I paused, considering the reality of our circumstances. "Nothing about this place seems particularly safe," I confessed. The admission felt heavy, laden with the weight of our collective unease. "But I think having the light is the best thing for us, if we are going to avoid a repeat of last night's fiasco." It was a tactical decision, born of necessity rather than comfort, a small beacon of hope in the form of a flickering flame.

Glenda shifted uncomfortably in the dust again, her movements reflecting the internal turmoil that seemed to grip her. "I think we should build some security for our settlement. And soon," she urged, her voice laced with a sense of urgency that belied a deeper concern.

I eyed Glenda cautiously, her suggestion sparking a mix of curiosity and apprehension within me. *What isn't she telling me?* The question echoed in my mind, a silent alarm that hinted at unseen dangers lurking just beyond the firelight's reach. "I'll have a chat to Luke about it tomorrow," I told her, attempting to offer some measure of reassurance.

Although, to be honest, I wasn't sure what good that would do right now. In the brief time since our arrival, our accomplishments had been modest at best and disastrous at worst. In two days, all we had managed to do was put up two tents, botch a slab of concrete, and nearly kill Jamie. The idea of building any form of security felt daunting, almost laughable in the context of our current capabilities. It was a task that seemed leagues away from the immediate, tangible goals of simple survival—shelter, food, and safety from the elements. And yet, Glenda's insistence suggested it was not only necessary but urgent.

As I sat there, watching the flames dance with a hypnotic, mesmerising glow, I couldn't help but feel the weight of the challenge ahead. Building security, both physical and psychological, in this Clivilian environment was going to be a monumental task.

"You'll take the first watch then," Glenda's proposition, practical as it was, underscored the needs of our situation. Her rising from our shared spot by the fire, the simple act of brushing dust from her slacks, seemed to punctuate the end of our fleeting respite.

"First watch?" My question echoed faintly, a verbal grappling for understanding, even though I already knew the answer. It was an acknowledgment of our new reality—a night segmented into shifts of vigilance, a necessity born from the unknowns that might lurk in the darkness beyond our campfire's light.

"Well, you can't very well sit there awake all night," Glenda pointed out, her voice carrying a blend of logic and concern. "I'll switch with you when I check on Jamie during the night."

"Sure," I agreed, my assent automatic, yet imbued with a deep-seated appreciation for her thoughtfulness. As I turned back to the fire, its flames a mesmerising dance of light and shadow, I felt a solitary weight settle upon my shoulders. It was a responsibility not just to the flames before me, but to the safety and well-being of our makeshift family.

Glenda's departure was marked by a pause, a moment of hesitation that drew my attention away from the hypnotic flames. "Oh, Paul?" Her voice, calling out before she reached the sanctuary of the food and medical tent, held an unexpected note of curiosity.

"Yeah?" My response, slightly apprehensive, sought to bridge the distance between us.

"Does our little settlement have a name yet?" The question, seemingly innocuous, carried an undercurrent of significance. It was about more than just a name; it was about identity, about laying claim to a piece of this world as our own.

I smiled, despite the seriousness of our conversation and the weight of the night ahead. "Bixbus."

"Hmm, odd name," Glenda mused, her voice carrying a mix of amusement and contemplation. And without another word, she turned and disappeared into the tent, leaving me with the fire, the night, and my thoughts.

❖

The passage of time felt interminable, each minute stretching into an eternity as I kept my solitary vigil by the fire. Eventually, the discomfort in my leg grew too insistent to ignore, compelling me to stand and stretch, dispelling the numbness that had crept into my muscles. The act of standing felt like a small rebellion against the lethargy that threatened to envelop me.

Compelled by a mixture of concern and a need for movement, I made my way over to Jamie's tent. The action was almost stealthy, a quiet intrusion into the sanctuary we had created for him. As I pulled back the flap, the ambient light from the fire cast flickering shadows across the interior, painting a scene of fragile tranquility. Jamie was lost in sleep, his light snores a comforting sign of life in the silence that filled the space.

Duke lifted his head to acknowledge my presence, his eyes meeting mine in a silent exchange of understanding before he settled back down. Henri, unfazed by my intrusion, gave a tired snort and rolled over, his soft snores a constant, somewhat reassuring background noise. I was impressed with their unwavering presence by Jamie's side since Glenda's treatment.

Returning to the fire, I tried to find solace in its warmth and light. The dust, omnipresent and seemingly invasive, offered a soft cushion against the hard ground, yet comfort remained elusive. I shifted positions frequently, a restless attempt to find even a modicum of ease in the discomfort.

The restlessness within me grew, an unquiet spirit that refused to be stilled. In response, I fed the fire, throwing several large chunks of wood onto the flames. It was a determined effort to keep the darkness at bay, to ensure that our beacon of light and warmth did not falter. The fire responded, crackling and brightening, a defiant blaze against the encroaching night.

Eventually, I lay down on my back, my gaze drawn upward to the dark, lifeless sky. It was an expanse that offered no comfort, no familiar points of light to anchor to. Blinking rapidly, I fought against the weight of exhaustion that pressed down on my eyelids, the heaviness a tangible force in the battle to remain vigilant.

I have to stay awake, I chided myself, the mantra an attempt at a lifeline in the struggle against sleep. *I... must... stay...*

4338.207

(26 July 2018)

THE BODY

1338.207.1

Waking up to the gentle, albeit unexpected, affection from Henri was disorienting yet oddly comforting. The small, furry face peering into mine, followed by a quick lick on the cheek, was a jolt back to reality from the depths of an unintended slumber. I gently pushed Henri away, my movements sluggish as I fought the fog of sleep that clung stubbornly to my senses. Sitting up, I felt the stiffness in my neck protest, a physical reminder of the makeshift bed of dust I had chosen over vigilance.

"You must have been tired," Glenda's voice reached me, laced with a mix of amusement and concern.

Looking up, I found her standing just outside the supply tent, her silhouette framed against the backdrop of our nascent settlement. "Yeah, I was," I admitted, the acknowledgment coming with a tinge of embarrassment. I had not intended to fall asleep; the realisation that I had done so without noticing the transition from night to day unsettled me.

As Glenda approached, her presence seemed to anchor me back into the moment, her steps stirring up small clouds of dust that danced in the morning air. "You fell asleep pretty quick," she observed, her words doing little to fill the gaps in my memory of the previous night. The mention of breakfast, offered in the form of a muesli bar, was a welcome distraction, yet my thoughts were already drifting towards the idea of cleansing the night's weariness from my body and spirit.

"Thanks, but I think I might go have a quick wash first," I said, my decision made as I shook the dust from my hair, feeling it cascade down in fine particles that glittered momentarily in the morning light.

"In the river?" Glenda's question, though expected, carried a note of caution.

"Yeah," I replied. "It's all we've got."

"Fair enough," Glenda conceded, her voice softening. "But make sure you eat when you get back. You need to keep your strength up." Her words, practical and motherly, were a reminder of the challenges that lay ahead. The mention of setting up a third tent and pouring concrete, tasks that seemed daunting in the context of our limited resources and manpower, brought a sense of urgency back into focus.

"Oh," was all I could manage.

"Yes. I found your concrete instructions," Glenda said, her smile conveying a mix of reassurance and determination.

As I stood, the ritual of brushing dust from my clothes had become almost second nature. My face contorted involuntarily as I took in the sight of my attire, each layer of dust a testament to the day's, or rather, the night's slumber. The realisation of my own need for cleanliness was immediate and undeniable as I raised my arm for a quick, confirming sniff. *Yep*, the verdict was clear in my mind, a wash was not just needed; it was essential.

With a sense of purpose, I entered the tent, my anticipation of a quick grab-and-go for my washing essentials halted by the sight that greeted me. The mattress lay empty, an unspoken question hanging in the air, its usual occupant nowhere to be seen. "Where are Jamie and Duke?" The query was out before I could temper my surprise, directed towards Glenda as I poked my head back outside, seeking reassurance or at least an explanation.

"They've gone for a walk. He seems much better this morning," came Glenda's response, her words floating back to me with a casualness that belied the underlying relief. The news that Jamie was feeling well enough to venture out was a bright spot in the otherwise mundane start to the day.

"That's good," I replied, the sentiment genuine as I retreated back into the tent. The relief I felt at Jamie's improvement was a small buoy of hope in the ongoing saga of our survival. My attention then turned to the task at hand—locating fresh clothes and a towel amidst the organised chaos of our supplies. My fingers eventually found what they were searching for, but not without a brief battle with the various items that had become our makeshift home's decor.

Lifting the towel I had managed to unearth, I brought it to my nose, the action instinctive. The smell that greeted me was an unpleasant reminder of our current living conditions—stale and slightly damp, the scent of use without the luxury of proper drying. *We need to find a way to hang up wet belongings soon*, I mused, the thought more a mental note to address later. The realisation was a practical one, born from the necessity of maintaining not just personal hygiene but a semblance of broader cleanliness in our day-to-day lives.

Stepping outside, the contrast between the dim interior of the tent and the bright world beyond was striking. For the first time since I had awoken, I fully registered the warmth of the sun's rays, a comforting presence in the vastness of the blue sky above. It was a moment of unexpected beauty, a gentle reminder of nature's indifference to our struggles and fears. "Do you know which way they went?" I asked, my voice carrying a hint of apprehension. The last thing I wanted was an awkward encounter with Jamie on his return.

"They've headed downstream," Glenda responded, her finger pointing towards the gentle flow of the river, her casual mention of a lagoon sparking my interest. Jamie's decision to venture towards that particular spot was a testament to his improving condition, a fact that brought an unspoken relief.

At first, I was hesitant to share the treasured location, but part of me was curious whether the lagoon had the same surreal effect on everyone. "Yeah," I replied, my voice carrying across to Glenda with a note of encouragement. "It's a nice spot. There's nothing there except water and dust, but you should check it out sometime."

Glenda's reaction, a nod filled with contemplation, signalled her interest, yet her practicality shone through in her response. "I might wait until I have some clothes to change into," she said, her words reflecting a pragmatic approach to the adventure.

As I walked past Glenda and the campfire, embarking on my journey towards the river, I could feel the weight of her gaze on me. It was an unsettling sensation, a silent scrutiny that seemed to pierce through the back of my head, making my steps feel heavier than usual. The unease that settled over me was palpable, a testament to the vulnerability that accompanies being observed when one is about to undertake a task as private as washing away the grime of survival.

My discomfort peaked when the realisation hit me—I had chosen the direction leading towards the lagoon, where Jamie and Duke had ventured. The thought of potentially encountering them, especially in a state of undress, sent a wave of embarrassment crashing over me. "Oh," I scoffed under my breath, the absurdity of my oversight dawning on me. In an attempt to correct my course, I spun around, my cheeks aflame with a flush that felt hot enough to rival the warmth of the morning sun. "I'll go upstream," I announced to Glenda, my voice a mix of determination and chagrin. The gesture of pointing, as if to solidify my new decision, was more for my benefit than hers.

Glenda's response was a smile, a simple, understanding curve of her lips that offered a semblance of comfort amidst my self-conscious fluster. Then, turning away, she headed towards the Portal, her movements marking a return to the tasks at hand and leaving me to my revised plan.

I gave myself a mental shrug, trying to shake off the residual embarrassment. I'd circle back to Glenda later, perhaps after regaining a bit of dignity along the riverbank. Not wanting to venture too far, my eyes began to scan the landscape ahead with increased scrutiny, searching for a spot that offered both privacy and proximity to the water. The task of finding a suitable place to undress and cleanse myself, while seemingly simple, carried with it a heightened sense of awareness of my surroundings. Every shift in the breeze became a signal to be interpreted, a potential indicator of privacy or exposure.

❖

The decision to stop was born out of frustration more than satisfaction with the location. The landscape around me offered little in the way of privacy, just the modest shield of small hills dotting the otherwise open and unforgiving terrain. With resignation setting in, I began the awkward process of disrobing in what felt like an expanse of vulnerability, the barren land stretching out in all directions with not nearly enough coverage for comfort.

As the zipper of my jeans hissed open, a sudden bark shattered the quiet, slicing through the stillness and immediately seizing my attention. It was a sound unmistakably familiar, yet alarmingly out of place in the serenity of my intended solitude. "Henri?" The name slipped out as a whisper, a query into the silence as I paused, my senses heightened, straining against the distance for any further sign.

Then, as realisation dawned with the clarity of the danger it suggested, a single, emphatic "Shit," escaped me. The bark wasn't just a call; it was a warning, a harbinger of something amiss. My actions became frantic, the previously leisurely task of undressing now a rushed attempt to make myself presentable in the face of urgency. The zip was yanked carelessly, a hasty movement born of the sudden fear that coursed through me, igniting a cascade of alarm bells in my mind.

Shoving my feet back into my shoes with an urgency that bordered on panic, the thought of something seriously wrong back at camp propelled me forward. Each second seemed to stretch, elongating with the growing dread that something had happened in my brief absence.

With my heart hammering against my ribcage, I turned back towards camp, the need to understand and possibly confront whatever had prompted Henri's alarm consuming all other thoughts. The tranquility of the morning, once a backdrop to a simple task of cleansing, had morphed into a pressing need to return, to ensure the safety of those who had become more than just fellow survivors—they were my responsibility, my community.

Racing back to camp, the urgency in my voice carried across the distance as I called out for Henri, my concern for the little dog now intertwined with a deeper sense of alarm. "Henri! Henri!" My shouts echoed, a desperate attempt to locate him, to assure myself he was safe.

As the camp came into view, Henri's form materialised at the river's edge, his small frame tense, barking incessantly in a display of distress that was impossible to ignore. My heart skipped a beat at the sight, the cause of his agitation quickly becoming horrifyingly clear. There, in the shallow embrace of the river, lay a young man, his body partially submerged, face down in the water. The gentle bobbing of the current, in stark contrast to the scene's gravity, seemed to mock the perilous situation with its calmness. His boots, caught on a rock, prevented him from being carried further downstream, an accidental anchor to this grim tableau.

"Shit!" The expletive burst from me as I rushed forward, adrenaline propelling me to action. Dropping to my knees at the riverbank, I was overcome with a mixture of fear and determination. The need to act was immediate, every second crucial.

"Paul, what's going on?" Luke's voice, tinged with concern and confusion, reached me from a distance.

"Help me!" My scream was a plea for immediate assistance, my voice straining with the effort. "Hurry, he needs help!" The words were a clarion call, a summons for aid in a moment that allowed for no hesitation.

Luke joined me without a moment's delay, sinking to his knees beside me. "Shit," he whispered, the curse a shared sentiment of shock and realisation.

Reaching across the water, my initial attempt to roll the man was clumsy, resulting in little more than nudging the body closer to Luke. Without hesitation, I found myself entering the river, the coolness of the water enveloping me as it quickly rose to my waist, its depth catching me off guard.

"Help me roll him," I urged, my voice carrying a mix of determination and anxiety. Luke joined me in the water. "Go," he said, ready to assist. "I've got him."

Glenda's count down, "Three. Two. One. Roll," might have seemed superfluous in the urgency of the moment, but it provided a necessary cadence to our actions. As we turned the body, Glenda worked to free the man's feet from the entrapment of the rocks.

The sudden exclamation, "Who the fuck is that?" jolted us, an unexpected voice piercing the tense air. The young man's face, now visible and bobbing in the water, was unfamiliar, his identity a mystery that only deepened the urgency and confusion of the moment. "No idea," I found myself whispering, a response more to myself than to the question posed by the unknown voice.

"Is he breathing?" Glenda's question, filled with concern, cut through the chaos.

"I don't think so," Luke's grim assessment came as he checked for signs of life.

"Quick, bring him to shore," Glenda urged, her voice a beacon of action in the panic.

"No," I countered abruptly, my discovery halting any further attempts at rescue. My eyes, wide with shock, were fixed on the young man. "I don't think it will help," I said, my voice barely above a whisper, the revelation of the cause of death—a slit throat—rendering any attempt at resuscitation futile.

"Fuck!" the voice exclaimed again, the terror and disbelief palpable in the air.

The tension hung in the air as Glenda's gasp sliced through the grim silence. "We should bring the body in anyway."

"What good will that do?" Luke questioned, his voice laced with apprehension. "If he's been murdered and someone comes looking for him, perhaps we shouldn't be the ones caught with his body." His words painted a grim picture of the potential dangers we faced, not just from the elements, but from other, more malevolent human forces.

My hands, betraying my inner turmoil, began to tremble uncontrollably. The reality of murder, of other people out there capable of such violence, was a shock to my system. *What the hell is going on?* The questions whirled through my mind, a maelstrom of fear, confusion, and disbelief.

The nameless voice, aligning with Luke's cautious stance, only added to the weight of the decision before us. Yet, despite the fear and the logical arguments for caution, I found myself agreeing with Glenda. "Yes," I said, my voice firmer than I felt. "Regardless, he deserves a proper burial." The assertion was a reflection of a fundamental belief in human dignity, a conviction that even in death, especially under such tragic circumstances, respect was owed.

Luke's scoff, "Proper burial! You don't even know the guy," highlighted the divide in our perspectives. His pragmatism, though understandable, clashed with the more humanistic approach Glenda and I seemed to be leaning towards.

"If we bring him in, I can do a rough autopsy," Glenda suggested, her voice steady.

"Is that really necessary?" Luke's challenge was predictable, his focus on the pragmatic, the immediate. "I think it's pretty obvious what happened to him."

The conversation, the debate over what to do next, was almost too much to bear. A wave of acidic bile rose in my throat, a physical manifestation of the horror and revulsion that the situation evoked within me.

"A rough autopsy might be able to tell us more of a story of how he met his fate," Glenda explained, her rationale clear.

The sensation was overwhelming, a visceral reaction that I couldn't control. The taste of bile, acidic and relentless, clawed its way up my throat as the surrounding arguments became a distant cacophony. My focus narrowed to the internal battle raging within me, the imminent expulsion of my stomach's contents becoming my sole reality. The tears that blurred my vision, a mixture of physical reaction and emotional overload, were a testament to the severity of the moment.

Just as the nausea reached its peak, I managed to turn away, a small mercy to spare my companions from the brunt of my sickness. However, the riverbed beneath me proved to be an unreliable ally, shifting unexpectedly and sending me beneath the water. The shock of the cold water compounded my distress, leaving me gasping and disoriented.

As I floundered, my arms and legs moved of their own accord, desperate to right myself and regain some semblance of control. The river water, an unwelcome intruder, forced its way into my mouth, adding insult to injury. When I finally managed to surface, coughing and spluttering, my immediate concern was for the young man we had been trying to save.

"Where's the body?" The question burst from me, a mix of panic and confusion. My eyes, still stinging from the tears and now the river water, sought out Luke. The sight of him, as drenched and dishevelled as I felt, somehow brought a momentary flicker of solidarity.

"Shit... shit!" The words echoed in the thick, humid air, a chaotic mantra that seemed to amplify the panic setting into our bones. Luke's voice cut through the clamour, desperate and tinged with an urgency that sent a shiver down my spine. "Where's Jamie?" he asked, his voice laced with panic.

I stared at him, feeling a mix of confusion and suspicion. My eyes narrowed instinctively, as I tried to decipher the sudden shift in his demeanour. *Why the sudden concern for Jamie? What had changed in the mere moments since we had last spoken about him?* "He went for a walk to the lagoon," Glenda's voice broke through my thoughts, calm yet carrying an undercurrent of worry that I hadn't detected before.

"Lagoon?" Luke's voice quivered slightly, betraying his confusion.

"Downstream," I found myself saying, the word leaving my lips with a mixture of reluctance and resolve.

"Shit," Luke muttered under his breath, his eyes darting back to meet mine, wide with realisation and fear. "We need to retrieve that body. Now!"

I felt a jolt of surprise at his words, a sharp contrast to his earlier stance. "But... but you just said," I stammered, my voice faltering as I grappled to keep up with Luke's thinking.

"Forget what I said. You were right. We are better off keeping the body," Luke interjected, his voice firm, leaving no room for argument as he clambered onto the riverbank with a sense of purpose that was almost palpable. And then, without another word, he took off in a sprint, his figure quickly distancing himself, following the body as it bobbed and floated downstream.

I stood there for a moment, stunned, wiping a smidge of vomit from the corner of my mouth with the back of my hand. The acrid taste lingered, a distasteful reminder of the horror we were now facing.

"Go!" Glenda's voice snapped me out of my daze, her hand pushing against the back of a young man who stood frozen, caught in the headlights of the unfolding chaos. "Fuck off," he muttered, dodging Glenda's second attempt with a deftness that spoke of his desire to remain uninvolved.

I felt a surge of determination as I pulled myself from the river, the water clinging to my clothes, adding weight to my already heavy heart. "I'll go," I announced, stepping forward, my voice carrying a resolve I wasn't sure I felt.

"Introductions can wait," Glenda said, her eyes urging me to follow Luke without delay.

Brushing past the young man, who looked at me with a mix of confusion and relief, I took off in a sprint. Luke wasn't too far ahead, despite his head-start. Ignoring the sharp twang of pain that shot through my foot with every step, I kept my focus steady. Luke had always been the faster one, but this wasn't a race I was willing to lose. Not now.

"Luke! Stop!" I cried out. My heart pounded in my chest, a relentless drumbeat that echoed my racing thoughts. *What were we doing?* The situation was spiralling, and with every step, I felt the weight of our decisions pressing down on me, a burden I wasn't sure we were prepared to carry.

Luke didn't stop, but his pace slowed considerably, a tacit acknowledgment of my presence as I caught up within seconds. Our footsteps synchronised, a rhythmic thud against the soft dust.

"Why is that body suddenly so important to you?" I asked, my voice strained from both the run and the weight of confusion pressing down on me.

"He's Jamie's son," Luke replied, his voice barely above a whisper, yet it cut through the air with the sharpness of a knife.

I slowed my pace, my feet dragging as if the ground beneath them had turned to quicksand. I shook my head, trying to dispel the fog of disbelief clouding my mind. "Are you serious? Since when did Jamie have a son?" The words felt foreign, as if I was talking about a stranger rather than someone I had known for the good part of a decade.

"Long story," Luke said, his eyes fixed on the path ahead, as if the answers lay just beyond our sight. "And Jamie doesn't know he's dead."

The weight of his words anchored me to the spot. Grabbing Luke's arm, I yanked us both to a sudden stop, our momentum halting as abruptly as my racing heart. I glared at my brother, the brother I thought I knew inside and out. "But you already knew," I accused, the words heavy with betrayal and hurt.

Luke swallowed hard. "Yes," he slowly replied, his admission hanging between us like a dense fog.

"Shit," I said, the word a mere whisper, as the shock of the news began to settle in the pit of my stomach. I gradually released my grip on Luke's arm, my fingers uncurling as the initial surge of anger gave way to a deep, gnawing sense of betrayal. I thought we told each other everything. But now, standing here in the shadow of this revelation, I wasn't so certain anymore.

Luke pulled himself free, a gesture that felt symbolic of the growing distance between us. "I had nothing to do with it. I swear." His voice was earnest, desperate even, but it did little to bridge the chasm that had opened up between us.

"I highly doubt that," I replied, my words laced with a bitterness that surprised even me.

Luke huffed with frustration, the sound harsh in the quiet that surrounded us. "We don't have time for this, Paul," he said, his voice urgent, as he tried to coax me back into motion.

But I resisted, firmly planted in my spot, my heart racing not from the run but from the tumult of emotions raging within me. *How could he do this?* I asked myself, incredulously, the question echoing in my mind.

"I'll tell you about it later," Luke urged, his gaze imploring me to understand, to trust him despite the secrets he'd kept. "There's a lot you don't know."

Another twang of betrayal, sharper and more painful than before, coursed through my heart, leaving a sting that was hard to ignore. "Obviously," I sneered, the bitterness of the situation coating my words like a thick, unpalatable syrup. The revelation Luke had dropped on me cast a long, dark shadow not just on our immediate mission, but on the very foundation of trust and brotherhood I had always believed was indestructible between us.

As the reality of the situation sank in, my eyes widened in a mix of shock and begrudging acceptance. *Now that,* I had to concede silently, *Luke was most certainly correct about.* The weight of the secret he had been carrying, the revelation of Jamie's unknown son, it all added layers of complexity to what I had initially thought was a straightforward albeit grim circumstance.

The landscape around us began to change as we neared our destination. The river widened, its banks spreading out as if to welcome us into the open jaws of the lagoon. "There it is!" I cried out, my voice laced with a mix of desperation and determination, as I spotted the body floating downstream, its presence a reminder of the grim reality we were trying to outrun.

"We're never going to catch it before it reaches the lagoon," Luke huffed beside me, his breath heavy with exertion and a hint of defeat. His words felt like a cold splash of water, damping the flicker of hope that had ignited within me at the sight of our morbid target.

"What do we do?" I asked, my heart pounding against my ribcage, the fear of the consequences if Jamie were to spiral further out of control, becoming a tangible presence that threatened to choke the very air around me.

"I'll run ahead. If Jamie is there, I can distract him," Luke suggested, his plan sounding more like a desperate gamble than a well-thought-out strategy.

"Distract him?" I echoed, the confusion evident in my tone. The pieces of the puzzle were starting to come together, but the picture they were forming was one I wasn't sure I wanted to see.

"Yes," Luke answered, his voice carrying a determination that seemed to cut through the uncertainty of the moment. "You need to make sure the body doesn't stop. It has to keep going downstream."

The very thought made my stomach churn. The dead body, now a silent player in our twisted scenario, floating downstream to an unknown destination was a morbid image that would likely haunt me for years to come. *Where would he end up?* The question echoed ominously in my mind. *We have no idea what's out there.*

"Are you sure, Luke?" I found myself asking, the doubt in my voice a clear reflection of the turmoil swirling within me. "You know nothing stays hidden forever."

"Yes," Luke said firmly, the resolve in his voice brooking no argument. "I'm sure."

His assurance did little to quell the storm of emotions raging within me. As I watched Luke prepare to sprint ahead, a sense of foreboding settled over me, a dark cloud that seemed to whisper that we were stepping further into a web of lies and secrets from which there would be no easy escape.

Duke's bark, a familiar sound that usually brought a sense of comfort, now carried an ominous note as it drifted towards us on the gentle breeze. The situation we were in, the mission we had embarked upon, lent a sinister undertone to even the most mundane of sounds.

Luke and I jogged to the top of the final hill, our bodies tense with anticipation and dread for what awaited us. The crest of the hill offered us a panoramic view of the lagoon, a natural beauty that under different circumstances would have been a sight to behold. Instead, it was the backdrop to a grim tableau that I was reluctantly a part of.

"Look, there's Duke and Jamie," I pointed out, my voice strained as I spotted them on the far side of the lagoon. The relief of seeing them, however, was short-lived.

"Shit," Luke cursed under his breath, his gaze locked onto something beyond them. "And there's the body."

My eyes quickly followed the direction of Luke's pointing finger, and a knot formed in my stomach. He was right. The relentless current had carried the body to the mouth of the lagoon, where it had unceremoniously washed up, getting caught on a shallow dune that lurked just below the surface of the water. The glimmering surface of the lagoon, usually a peaceful sight, now seemed to mock us with its tranquility, hiding the grim reality that lay just beneath.

"Go!" Luke insisted, his urgency palpable as he shoved me in the direction of Jamie's lifeless son. The physical push felt like a jolt, not just to my body but to my psyche as well. I was being propelled towards a reality I wasn't sure I was ready to face.

The weight of the situation bore down on me as I made my way towards the lagoon. Each step felt heavier than the last, as if the very earth beneath me was trying to hold me back, or perhaps, give me a moment to gather the courage I would need to face what was coming.

INFECTED - PART 1

1338.207.2

I stood on the bank of the lagoon, my expression clouded with unease. The young man's body lay on the other side, an inert reminder of the unpleasant task at hand. The mouth of the lagoon stretched before me, no more than five metres across, yet the thought of crossing it filled me with an overwhelming sense of dread. It wasn't just the physical distance; it was the emotional chasm that seemed to widen with every second.

I glanced across to the right, seeking a sliver of distraction. It seemed Luke had managed to catch Jamie just in time. Duke was weaving playfully around their feet, oblivious to the sombre undercurrents of our gathering. For a fleeting moment, I envied Duke's ignorance.

The sun's relentless pursuit had almost succeeded in drying my clothes, a minor victory in the grand scheme of things. With a heavy heart, I began to remove my shoes, socks, and jeans, the fabric feeling cumbersome and heavy, much like the burden we were shouldering. Each piece of clothing I set aside felt like stripping away another layer of denial about the reality we were facing.

My heart pounded against my ribcage, a frenetic drumbeat echoing the turmoil within. I stared at the water's surface, which glimmered deceptively calm under the sun's gaze. The terror of what lay beneath, of what crossing that water symbolised, gnawed at me. *It's only a few metres away,* I tried to convince myself, a mantra that felt as hollow as it was intended to be comforting.

With a deep breath, I attempted to steel my resolve. Carefully, I extended my foot towards the cool embrace of the water. The moment my skin made contact, a shiver ran up my spine, and the familiar zing of sexual pleasure raced up my leg. I gasped. My groin pulsated with an intensity I'd never experienced before. My eyes closed tightly as I fought the sexual urges roaring through my entire body.

The lagoon, with its serene appearance, was a stark contrast to the tumult of emotions raging within me. Each step I took into the water felt like a descent into a realm where the lines between right and wrong, between duty and despair, blurred. The coolness of the water enveloped my feet, a chilling reminder of the task that lay ahead.

As I waded through the lagoon, the weight of the situation settled heavily upon me. This wasn't just a physical crossing; it was a passage through the murky waters of moral ambiguity, of decisions made in the shadow of desperation. With each step, I felt the water's resistance, as if it were questioning my resolve, testing my willingness to proceed despite the uncertainty that lay on the other side.

The distance might have been mere metres, but with every step, the journey felt longer, weighted down by the gravity of my actions and the potential consequences they harboured. As I moved closer to the young man's body, the reality of what I was about to do became ever more tangible. This was more than just freeing a body; it was about confronting the fragile thread that ties us to life and the unpredictable nature of the choices we make.

Planting my feet firmly into the submerged dune, I found myself standing over the body, a surreal and haunting tableau that seemed more like a scene from a grim narrative than reality. The head, its slackness a silent testament to the violence inflicted upon it, was resting against the bank of the lagoon, almost as if seeking solace in its final resting place. A deep gash marred the throat, a wound so severe it seemed to speak volumes of the story leading to this moment.

I reached down, my hands hovering momentarily before grasping the shoulders with an uncertainty that belied my resolve. Giving them a timid yank, I hoped for movement, but the body remained stubbornly in place, as immovable as the heavy guilt that weighed on my heart. I sighed, a sound that seemed to dissipate into the still air, carrying with it the burden of the task at hand.

I'm going to have to get closer and throw more strength at my efforts if I'm going to get this body back into the river so it can disappear downstream, I thought, a burdened determination setting in. The very notion of making a body "disappear" was something I had never imagined I would contemplate, let alone act upon. Yet, here I was, caught in the throes of a situation that demanded actions far removed from the realm of what I considered moral and just.

Staring down at the blank face, a visage now devoid of the life and stories it once held, I took a deep breath. The face, unseeing yet accusing in its silent repose, seemed to pierce through the veil of my intentions, questioning the very essence of what I was about to do. *Alright, let's try that again*, I resolved, trying to muster a courage I wasn't sure I possessed.

A clammy hand, unexpectedly animate, shot up from the water and clasped my forearm with an eerie tightness. The chipped fingernails, like the remnants of a life once lived, dug into my flesh with an urgency that belied their owner's deathly state. In that moment, as the young man's eyes snapped open, staring into mine with an impossible vitality, the boundary between life and death seemed to blur.

My face contorted in sheer terror, an instinctive reaction to the surreal horror unfolding before me. "Luke!" I screamed, my voice piercing the stillness of the lagoon, a desperate plea for help in a situation that defied all logic. Frantically, I brushed at the hand gripping my arm, but it clung to me with a supernatural strength. I winced in pain as the sharp, broken fingernails carved into my skin, sending a trail of deep red blood trickling down my forearm, staining the lagoon's clear waters with an ominous tint.

The fingers felt unnaturally cold and rigid against my skin, like the touch of death itself. In a frantic bid for freedom, I tore at them, each movement fuelled by a primal urge to escape. Grasping the middle finger, I yanked it backwards with all the force I could muster. The sound of bone snapping echoed eerily, a grotesque testament to the desperation of my actions. A ghostly gasp, seemingly exhaled from the dead lips, filled the air, a sound so chilling it seemed to freeze the very atmosphere around us. The stench of rotting flesh assaulted my senses, a nauseating reminder of the macabre reality I was grappling with. Mercifully, the hand released its grip, and the arm fell back into the water with a splash, retreating to the depths from whence it came.

In my panic to distance myself from the nightmare, my movements were hasty and uncoordinated. My feet, seeking purchase on the slippery pebbled bottom of the lagoon, betrayed me. I lost my footing, the stability of the ground beneath me as elusive as the peace I had hoped to find in this grim task. Floundering backwards, I plunged into the water with a great splash.

The cold embrace of the lagoon enveloped me, a stark contrast to the fevered chaos of my thoughts. Every rational part of my being screamed that what had just transpired was impossible, yet the marks on my arm, the lingering pain, and the blood mingling with the water were evidence of a terrifying reality. As I struggled to regain my footing, to surface from the literal and metaphorical depths into which I had been plunged, the isolation of my position struck me with full force. Out here, in the midst of this desolate beauty, we were confronted not just with the consequences of our actions, but with the fragile line between life and death, and the haunting possibility of what lies beyond.

❖

"Shit, Luke! Who the fuck is that?" Jamie's voice, thick with panic and disbelief, reached my ears as I gasped for air, breaking the surface of the lagoon. The chilling episode with the dead body's hand still echoed in my mind, leaving a trail of fear that seemed to grip my very soul. I scrambled towards the water's edge, the urgency of Jamie's shout propelling me forward despite the numbing terror that threatened to paralyse me. On hands and knees, I clawed my way across the soft dust on the bank of the mouth of the lagoon, every muscle in my body tensed, my heart pounding against my ribcage like a caged animal desperate for escape. The proximity to the dead body, now identified with a name, sent another jolt of fear through me, freezing me in place.

"Holy fuck!" Jamie's scream pierced the heavy air again. "What the fuck is Joel doing here?"

His words, a confirmation of the identity of the deceased, sent a shockwave through my already reeling senses. Joel. A name that transformed the previously anonymous tragedy into a personal nightmare. The ground beneath me seemed to shift, our situation taking on a new, horrifying dimension. My mind recoiled at the implication, refusing to accept the truth that was unfolding before us. The thought that it wasn't just a random dead guy, but Joel, someone intimately connected to Jamie washed up at our camp, was a reality too gruesome to comprehend.

My body shuddered uncontrollably, a physical manifestation of the inner turmoil that raged within me. The sheer brutality of the situation, the recognition of Joel's body, it all became overwhelmingly real in that moment. If my stomach hadn't been wracked by the events of the day, leaving it pitifully empty, I was sure a volcano of vomit would have erupted from me. Instead, only a vile dribble of acidic bile managed to escape, running down my chin to drip into the dust below, a bitter testament to the horror and disbelief that choked me.

The taste of bile in my mouth, the stench of death that lingered in the air, and Jamie's anguished cries created a sensory maelstrom that I struggled to navigate. My hands, now planted firmly in the soft dust, trembled under the weight of our grim discovery. The realisation that our quiet campsite had become the scene of a chilling mystery was a pill too bitter to swallow. The implications were terrifying, the questions numerous, and the fear of what this meant for all of us hung heavily in the air.

"He's still breathing!" Jamie's call, laden with a mixture of disbelief and urgency, cut through the dense air, shattering the morbid silence. Terror surged within me, my eyes widening in shock as I fought to suppress another onslaught of acid threatening to escape my throat. I rolled onto my bum, my movements awkward and heavy, as I stared across the lagoon at the body I had presumed dead, now a source of bewildering horror.

Jamie, oblivious to the chilling encounter I had just experienced with the body, stood behind the man's head, embodying a mixture of determination and concern. He bent down, his hands reaching for the man's shoulders in a gesture of aid. Panic gripped me; I wanted to scream, to warn Jamie of the macabre twist this situation had taken. But my voice betrayed me, offering nothing but another dribble of burning acid that seared my throat and spilled onto the dust.

Luke, with a decisiveness that seemed to cut through the chaos, grabbed hold of Jamie's shoulders and yanked him back with a firmness that spoke volumes. Jamie's reaction was immediate and visceral, a swipe at Luke born of confusion and adrenaline. "What the fuck did you do that for?" he yelled, his voice tinged with anger and disbelief, spitting saliva into the air as if to punctuate his frustration.

"Take a look at his throat," Luke yelled back, his command slicing through the tension like a knife.

Jamie, his emotions a tumultuous storm, turned back to the body, crouching over it with a mixture of curiosity and dread. "What the fuck?" The disbelief in his voice mirrored the shock that rippled through me, a shared horror at the unfolding scene.

"Jamie, stop!" Luke's insistence was a desperate plea, a command laced with an understanding of the danger that lay in ignorance. Yet, Jamie, driven by a need to help, reached underneath the body's shoulders, beginning to drag him from the lagoon with a resolve that bordered on reckless.

A loud gasp diverted my attention from the grim tableau before me. Glenda and the new stranger, now part of this nightmare, had arrived at the scene. Glenda, without hesitation, broke into a jog around the perimeter of the lagoon, her actions guided by a sense of urgency as she made her way to Luke and Jamie.

"Jamie!" the stranger called out, his voice carrying across the water. So, the stranger knows Jamie, a realisation that dawned on me amidst the turmoil. Questions began to swirl through my mind, each one a thread in the tangled web of confusion and fear that this day had woven. Yet, the intensity of the moment, the sheer incredulity of the situation, rendered me mute, unable to articulate the whirlwind of thoughts racing through my mind.

"What the fuck have you done, Luke?" Jamie's voice, raw and teeming with accusation, tore through the tense air as he lost his balance and tumbled to the ground alongside the body. It was a sight that would remain etched in my memory, the embodiment of chaos and despair. Tears, a rare sight, broke through Jamie's normally impenetrable facade, revealing a vulnerability that was as shocking as it was heart-wrenching. "Help me take him back to camp," he pleaded, his voice quivering with emotion

"Wait," Glenda interjected, her voice a beacon of calm in the storm. Her insistence on assessing the situation before acting was like a lifeline in the tumultuous sea of panic and fear that had engulfed us.

With the bleeding of my arm nearly halted, I dragged myself to the edge of the lagoon, my heart pounding against my ribcage, loud and insistent, as if trying to drown out the noise around me. *What would Glenda find?* The question cascaded through my mind, each imagined answer a hammer blow to my already fragile state of being. The possibility of danger, of infection, of death itself, loomed over me like dark clouds on the horizon.

Glenda, with a focus and precision that bespoke her strength, crouched beside the body that had been the source of so much dread. "He's breathing," she announced, her voice cutting through the thick tension.

Gasps, mine included, punctuated the moment. *How is that even possible?* The thought echoed in my head, a refrain of disbelief in the face of the inexplicable. *This is fucking insane!*

"But barely," Glenda continued, her clinical assessment painting a picture that was both hopeful and horrifying. "I think he may actually be alive. But I don't understand how that is possible. His colour suggests he has lost so much blood that his circulatory system has collapsed." Her analysis, so precise and unflinching, was a cold splash of reality. Her gaze then met Jamie's, a silent exchange of resolve and determination. "You're right," she said calmly. "I agree we should bring him back to camp."

"What? Seriously?" Luke's disbelief mirrored my own, a reflection of the surreal turn the unfolding drama had taken.

I took a deep breath, trying to ground myself amidst the whirlwind of emotions and physical discomfort. My palms sank into the dust as I pushed myself up, a futile attempt to regain some semblance of control. But within seconds, my head began to spin, a dizzying carousel that refused to slow. Sinking back to my knees, my breathing became laboured, a struggle for air that felt as if I were trying to breathe through a cloth. My wounded arm, a reminder of the nightmare we had stumbled into, shook uncontrollably. I clasped both hands tightly, a vain effort to quell the trembling that seemed to have taken root deep within me.

The realisation that we were about to embark on a journey back to camp, carrying with us a man who had brushed so closely with death, was overwhelming. The implications of our actions, the potential dangers, and the sheer absurdity of the situation were a maelanage of thoughts and fears that threatened to consume me.

"You coming, Paul?" Glenda's voice, clear and steady, reached out to me across the distance, a lifeline thrown in the midst of turmoil. Her call was a reminder of the collective burden we were shouldering together.

I looked up, my gaze lifting from the dust and disorder at my feet to the scene unfolding before me. Luke, Jamie, and the young man, whose name still remained a mystery to me, were already making their way up the first hill, the body cradled between them in a sombre procession. The sight was jarring, an eerie contrast to the serene landscape that surrounded us. Each step they took seemed to mark the rhythm of a silent, mournful march

I swallowed hard, fighting back another surge of bile that threatened to rise. The acidic taste lingered in my throat, a bitter reminder of the day's harrowing events. "I'll meet you there soon," I called out in reply, my voice barely masking the unease that lay beneath. It was a promise, a declaration of my intent to follow through despite the turmoil churning inside me.

Without another word, the group continued on their way, their figures gradually diminishing in the distance. I watched them for a moment, a mix of admiration and apprehension filling me. The solidarity and determination they displayed were both comforting and daunting. Here we were, bound together by a series of events that none of us could have anticipated, each step forward a venture into the unknown.

Turning back to my throbbing arm, the sight that greeted me was one of subtle horror. The skin immediately surrounding the three distinct fingernail cuts had transformed into a dark grey, an unnatural shade that seemed to pulse with a life of its own under my gaze. The urge to touch, to somehow understand the change through tactile sensation, surged within me. Yet, as my hand hovered over the discoloured skin, a primal instinct of self-preservation kicked in, and my hand recoiled as if repelled by an invisible force.

The potentially contaminated waters of the lagoon loomed in my mind as a warning, urging me to seek a cleaner source for what I hoped could be a form of relief, or even healing. Thus, I crawled over to the edge of the river, each movement deliberate, fuelled by a mix of hope and desperation. The cool water appeared almost inviting. Taking a deep breath, I braced myself for what was to come and thrust my arm into the flowing liquid. The sting that followed was both immediate and intense, a sharp sensation that seemed to penetrate deep into the very fibres of my being. Small trails of blood, escaping from the fingernail cuts, mingled with the water, creating ephemeral tendrils that danced away with the current, as if carrying a piece of my fear with them.

My heart raced, pounding against my chest with a ferocity that mirrored the turmoil of my thoughts. I watched, mesmerised, as the dark grey skin around each cut gradually lightened, returning to its normal flesh colour. The transformation, though slow, was a spectacle of nature's resilience, a small victory in the face of the unknown. Soaking my arm in the refreshing embrace of the river for almost ten minutes, I clung to the hope that this natural remedy could somehow reverse the damage, heal the wounds completely.

Yet, as the minutes passed, it became evident that the water's healing touch had its limits. The wounds remained, a visual reminder of the ordeal, unchanged despite the passage of time. *Is this as much as the water can heal me?* The question echoed in my mind, a whisper of doubt amidst the crashing waves of fear and uncertainty. *Could I still get infected? Or... am I already infected?*

In the silence that followed, a resignation settled over me, soft as the fall of dusk. "It doesn't matter now," I whispered softly to myself, a surrender to the inevitable. Lifting my arm from the river, I watched as the small droplets of clear water fell from my skin, each one returning to its source with a purity that seemed to mock my current state. The sight was a poignant reminder of the cycle of nature, of the ebb and flow of life and the inevitability of our actions and their consequences. *What is done is done.* The acceptance of this was both a weight and a release, a realisation that, regardless of what the future held, the present moment was all that I could truly grasp.

GUARDIAN

1338.207.3

As I neared camp, the sight of Luke emerging from the tent with a sense of urgency painted a stark contrast against the backdrop of our makeshift refuge. "Luke, wait!" I called out, my voice tinged with a mix of concern and confusion. "Where are you going?"

"I have to find Cody," he replied without breaking his stride, his determination evident as he continued towards the Portal.

Curiosity, mixed with a hint of alarm, propelled me into a gentle jog to keep pace with my brother. "Who's Cody?" I asked, the name unfamiliar, adding yet another layer of complexity to the already bewildering situation.

Luke stopped abruptly, turning to face me. For a moment, he seemed lost in thought, his eyes scanning the horizon as if searching for answers in the desert that surrounded us. Then, leaning in close, he shared in a hushed tone, "He's a Guardian."

The word 'Guardian' hung in the air between us, heavy with implications I could scarcely grasp. "What the hell is a Guardian?" I gasped, my mind racing to make sense of this new revelation.

"Like me," Luke stated bluntly, the simplicity of his answer doing nothing to quell the storm of questions brewing within me.

"What... how...?" I stammered, struggling to piece together the fragmented puzzle.

Luke shook his head, a gesture of frustration or perhaps confusion. "I don't completely understand it myself yet," he admitted, an acknowledgment of the profound uncertainty that seemed to shadow us at every turn.

For a fleeting moment, a spark of optimism ignited within me. "But there are more of... you?" I asked, clinging to the hope that perhaps we were not as alone in this fight as we had feared. *Anything*, I thought, *to bolster our chances of survival*.

"Yes," Luke confirmed. "But don't tell the others yet. Not until we know it's safe."

"Safe?" The word echoed hollowly in my mind, dousing the flicker of hope with cold apprehension. My heart sank, the brief surge of optimism quashed by the weight of Luke's caution.

Luke's next words were heavy with implication. "I still don't know who killed..." He hesitated. "Who, ah, slit Joel's throat. Cody thinks whoever did it mistook Joel for me."

The revelation struck me like a physical blow. "Shit, Luke," I gasped, the danger we faced suddenly taking on a more personal and immediate threat.

"I need answers," Luke declared, his voice laced with a determination that was both admirable and terrifying. With that, he resumed his brisk pace, leaving me to process the whirlwind of information he had just imparted.

"So, does that mean Joel is really dead?" I found myself asking, the weight of the situation making my steps heavier as I struggled to keep pace with Luke. The absurdity of what had transpired, coupled with the uncertainty of our next steps, made each word feel like a burden.

As we neared the Portal, it erupted into life, its colours swirling in a dazzling display of energy that captivated and unnerved me in equal measure. I halted, momentarily caught in the spectacle, my mind racing with questions about its operation. The absence of any visible mechanism, save for Luke's proximity, lent an air of mystique to the device. *It's a fascinating phenomenon, if not somewhat disturbing,* I mused, the memory of the eerie Clivilius voice echoing in my mind, its cryptic messages a source of ongoing intrigue and unease.

"Luke," I called out, an urgency in my voice that halted him in his tracks, just seconds from stepping through the Portal. He turned, an expectant look on his face.

"Don't get yourself killed, okay? We still need you." The words tumbled out, a mix of concern, plea, and a stark reminder of the danger he was in.

Luke offered a small, reassuring smile, a rare glimpse of warmth amidst recent events. "I'll do my best," he replied, his voice carrying a weight of promise and determination. Then, with a step that seemed both bold and inevitable, he vanished into the mesmerising colours of the Portal, leaving me alone with my thoughts and fears.

Guardians... The word lingered in my mind, a concept both comforting and daunting. I took a moment to gather my scattered thoughts, the throbbing in my arm a constant reminder of the immediate dangers we faced. Glancing down, I noticed with a grimace that the skin around the wounds was turning grey once again. *Is this a normal reaction from a wound like this?* Doubt and concern swirled within me, a tumultuous mix that offered no clear answers. *I really have no idea.*

The last thing the camp needed was more panic, more questions without answers. Yet, as I stood there, contemplating the uncertain path ahead, I knew that silence was not an option. It was time to seek out Glenda. Her expertise, her calm demeanour in the face of the unknown, offered a sliver of hope that perhaps there might be a way to understand, to counteract the unsettling changes my body was undergoing.

KAIN

1338.207.1

As I approached the camp, the unfamiliarity of the situation seemed to crystallise with the sight of the young man stepping outside the tent. "What's going on in there?" I inquired, my curiosity piqued by the activities that were unfolding without my presence.

The man stopped in his tracks, clearly startled by my sudden question. It was then, for the first time, that I really took the opportunity to assess him from head to toe. He wasn't particularly tall, I estimated around five foot five, but what he lacked in height, he made up for in physical presence. His well-defined biceps hinted at a lifestyle more active than sedentary, suggesting agility and strength rather than sheer bulk. *Luke has chosen well, it seems,* I thought with an inward scoff, recognising the potential value this young man could bring to our precarious situation.

"Glenda is going to do some surgery," he finally responded, his voice carrying a weight of seriousness that immediately drew my attention back to the matter at hand.

"Surgery?" I echoed, the word slicing through the fog of my thoughts like a scalpel.

He swallowed hard, his Adam's apple bobbing in a visible sign of nervousness. "Yeah. She is going to stitch his throat back together." The simplicity of his statement belied the complexity of the procedure about to be undertaken.

My chest constricted with a mix of anxiety and apprehension. "So, Glenda really thinks he might be alive?"

The idea seemed to hover on the edge of possibility, teetering between hope and disbelief.

"Yeah, I guess so," he shrugged, his nonchalance a stark contrast to the turmoil churning inside me.

"Shit," I muttered, the situation's absurdity becoming more apparent with each passing moment. "This isn't making any sense."

"That's a bit of an understatement," he scoffed.

Closing my eyes, I took a moment to breathe deeply, seeking a fleeting sense of calm. It was then I realised I still hadn't caught the name of this new ally, this unknown variable in our increasingly complicated equation. Extending my right hand toward him, I broke the ice. "Paul," I announced, introducing myself. "I'm Luke's brother."

There was a moment of hesitation, a brief interlude where uncertainty and alliance weighed equally in the balance. Then, his grip met mine, firm and resolute. "Kain," he introduced himself.

In that handshake, there was a silent exchange of mutual respect and recognition of the shared trials we were about to face. Kain—his name now a fixture in the tapestry of our struggle—represented both an unknown factor and a potential asset.

"You know Jamie then?" I found myself asking, curiosity piqued as I released Kain's hand, the connection between him and the turmoil that had engulfed us suddenly taking on a new dimension.

"Yeah, he's my uncle," Kain replied, a fact that added layers to the complexity of our situation. It wasn't just strangers brought together by fate; there were familial bonds intertwined with the unfolding events.

"I see," I said, absorbing this new information. It was clear now that Luke's influence extended beyond the immediate crisis. The pieces of the puzzle were slowly coming together, but each new piece seemed to add more questions than answers. "So, how did you end up here?" I probed further, eager to understand the sequence of events that had led Kain to us.

Kain huffed, a prelude to the story he was about to share. "My mother sent me to check on Uncle Jamie. She hadn't been able to contact him for a few days. So, I went over and Uncle Jamie wasn't there. Luke told me that he was out and would be back soon. And that's when it got weird."

"Weird?" I echoed, my interest piqued. The situation was already beyond normal, but any additional information could be crucial.

Kain tilted his head, as if sifting through his memories for the details that would best explain his experience. "Well..." he began, hesitation lacing his voice before he paused again, collecting his thoughts. "Well, I was about to leave but then Luke suggested I hang around and wait for Uncle Jamie to get home. He insisted that he wouldn't be much longer."

I couldn't help but interject, "Well, that doesn't seem too weird," before the full weight of our reality crashed back down upon me. Jamie would never be going home—a fact that cast a shadow over Kain's seemingly mundane encounter.

The realisation hit me with a pang of guilt. In our world, now skewed by mysterious portals, Guardians, and the looming threat of an unknown assailant, what constituted as 'weird' had taken on a whole new meaning. Kain's story, under any other circumstances, might have seemed like a simple case of miscommunication or perhaps a mild inconvenience. Yet, here and now, it was a thread in a larger tapestry of confusion, danger, and the unknown.

Kain's frown deepened. "I guess not," he conceded, his story painting Luke in a light that was both concerning and mystifying. "But then I had to go to the bathroom, and when I came out, Luke asked if I minded helping him with something downstairs. I can't even remember what he wanted now. It all happened so quickly. As we approached the top of the stairs, there was a bright flash of colour when Luke slid the door open and then I felt something shove me in the back. I'm pretty certain it was Luke."

My face contorted in concentration, trying to piece together Luke's actions with the brother I knew. "So, Luke had no idea that you were coming?" The question lingered in the air, a futile attempt to find logic in what seemed to be a hastily executed plan.

"I don't think so," Kain replied, his uncertainty mirroring my own. The idea that Luke had orchestrated this without prior knowledge of Kain's visit added an element of spontaneity to his actions that was both intriguing and disconcerting.

A grimace took over my expression as I processed Kain's account. The realisation that Luke might have acted impulsively, or perhaps with a calculated risk, left me torn between concern and a begrudging admiration. *Perhaps my brother is far more devious than I anticipated.* The thought was unsettling, yet in our current predicament, Luke's audacity could indeed prove to be an asset. The notion that we had an extra set of hands, especially under such bizarre circumstances, was undeniably a point in our favour.

But then again, Luke had essentially kidnapped the poor guy, and he couldn't be older than twenty-five. The ethical implications of Luke's actions weighed heavily on me, casting a shadow over the relief of having Kain with us. *Is Luke spiralling out of control?* The question echoed in my mind, a haunting possibility that I couldn't entirely dismiss.

The complexity of our situation seemed to grow with each passing moment, each new revelation adding to the tangled maze of motives, actions, and consequences we found ourselves in. As I stood there, contemplating the moral quandary that Luke's actions presented, I couldn't help but feel a surge of protectiveness towards Kain. Despite the unexpected manner of his arrival, he was now part of our group, thrust into the unknown just as we were.

"I'm sorry for what my brother has done," I found myself saying, the weight of Luke's actions pressing heavily upon me. "I really am." My apology, sincere as it was, felt inadequate under the circumstances, a meagre offering in the face of Kain's unforeseen ordeal.

Kain's response was a shrug, a non-verbal expression that spoke volumes of his current state of resignation or perhaps confusion. It was hard to tell which.

"So, if your mother sent you, does that mean you still live with her?" I ventured cautiously, aware that each question unwrapped another layer of Kain's life, revealing the stakes involved for him personally.

At the mention of his living situation, Kain's eyes began to swell with emotion. "Both me and my fiancée live with my parents," he revealed, his voice carrying a tremor of vulnerability that struck a chord within me.

"What's her name?" I probed gently, feeling a bond of empathy towards Kain's predicament deepen.

"Brianne," he replied, the simplicity of his answer belying the complexity of emotions behind it. "She's six months pregnant."

"Shit," escaped my lips before I could censor the reaction. The news hit me with the force of a physical blow, my eyes widening in shock. *Did Luke know that when he pushed Kain?* The question haunted me, echoing the fear that Luke's actions might have repercussions far beyond what I initially realised. *I hoped not. Luke could do some serious familial damage.* Yet, the uneasy feeling twisting in my gut suggested otherwise. My brother may be erratic at times, but ignorance was not a trait he possessed.

"Is there really no way to go back home?" Kain's voice, tinged with a mix of hope and despair, broke through my ruminations.

I shook my head, the gesture laden with regret. "Not that we know of." The finality of my words hung between us, a brutal reminder of the uncertain future we faced.

Kain's heavy sigh was a palpable release of pent-up tension, his gaze dropping as he grappled with his situation.

The furrow deepened across my forehead as I contemplated our next steps. "I know this is an unfortunate situation," I started, choosing my words with care. "But the truth is, Jamie and I could really use your help right now." I paused, watching Kain intently, gauging his reaction, preparing myself for any possible refusal or resentment.

To my relief, and slight surprise, Kain slowly raised his head, a glimmer of resolve in his eyes. "What can I do to help?"

A faint smile began to form on my lips, a rare moment of relief. *Well, that was easier than I expected.* "Follow me," I said, leading the way. Kain's willingness to help, in spite of his own dire circumstances, was a beacon of hope in the overwhelming darkness. As we set off together, I couldn't help but feel a renewed sense of purpose, a reminder that even in the darkest times, the human spirit's resilience and capacity for cooperation can shine through.

❖

Taking our time, Kain and I meandered towards the Drop Zone, our designated area that had quickly become a vital lifeline for our survival in this new world. As we walked, I found myself explaining the significance of this spot to Kain, whose understanding of our situation was still in its infancy. "This is where Luke delivers most of the things he brings to the new world," I told him, my voice tinged with a mix of awe and resignation. It was up to us, I emphasised, to regularly monitor the site for drop-offs. Luke, in his mysterious ways, had already on more than one occasion dropped items there without any prior announcement or explanation.

As we arrived, I gestured towards the boxes that lay scattered around the area. Among them were the unassembled pieces of what would become our additional tents, alongside materials meant for the construction of sheds that would offer us some semblance of storage. The sight of these supplies, still untouched and packed as they were delivered, served as an uncomfortable reminder of the sheer magnitude of work ahead of us.

Kain's gaze followed mine, taking in the assortment of boxes and materials. I could see him mentally cataloging each item, the wheels in his head turning as he began to grasp the scope of our day-to-day reality. The responsibility of keeping an eye on the Drop Zone, of ensuring we didn't miss any crucial supplies, suddenly felt less burdensome with Kain by my side. His presence, initially an unintended consequence of Luke's actions, was quickly becoming an asset I hadn't realised we so desperately needed.

The quiet solidarity between us as we surveyed the area spoke volumes. Here we were, two individuals thrown together by fate, now bound by a shared purpose. The task ahead—to build, to maintain, to survive—seemed daunting, yet somehow more achievable with Kain's silent promise of assistance.

"And you haven't started constructing any of the sheds yet?" Kain's question, simple as it was, felt like a spotlight on our inadequacies, our struggles to adapt to this new world and its demands.

I grimaced, the memory of our attempt souring my expression. "Well... I'm pretty sure we screwed up the first slab of concrete we tried to lay." The words came out reluctantly, an admission of our lack of experience and perhaps, our desperation to get things started in a situation where every little bit of progress counted.

Kain chuckled at my confession, a sound that surprisingly didn't grate on my nerves but instead offered a moment of comfort. "You better show me then," he said, his response not mocking but genuinely offering assistance.

Trudging through the brown and red Clivilius dust, the landscape around us a constant reminder of how far from home we truly were, we stopped at the site of our failed attempt. The mess that was supposed to be the base for the first shed lay before us, a debacle of our inexperience.

"Yeah. That's pretty much fucked," Kain observed matter-of-factly upon seeing the disaster we'd made. His bluntness, rather than offending, somehow put me at ease. It was refreshing, in a way, to deal with our situation with a bit of humour, even if it was dark. And then he added, "I helped my father put our garage together, so these should be pretty straightforward."

"Straightforward," I laughed, the absurdity of everything momentarily lifting as I entertained the thought of something in this place being simple. "And just how big was this garage?"

"Oh, it was ten metres by ten metres." The casualness with which he shared this detail only added to my growing respect for him.

Impressive, indeed. My eyebrows shot up in acknowledgment of his experience. Perhaps, with Kain's know-how, we stood a chance at not just surviving but establishing something resembling a functional camp.

Kain then moved on to the second slab, crouching down with a focus that was both intense and reassuring. His brow furrowed in concentration as he examined our work, the silent assessment hanging in the air between us.

"We followed instructions for that one," I called out, a defensive note in my voice I hadn't intended.

"It shows," Kain responded after a moment, rising to his feet. His words, "It's a little rough, but I think this one will actually be okay for what we need," washed over me like a wave of relief.

"Really? That's the best news I've heard today." The gratitude in my voice was palpable. In this world, where every small victory felt monumental, Kain's assurance felt like a beacon of hope.

"It looks like we already have so much work to do. The less rework the better," Kain noted, his gaze sweeping over our makeshift camp with a pragmatism that was both necessary and welcome.

I smiled to myself, feeling a surge of appreciation for Kain. I liked him—a lot. He was both smart and pragmatic, qualities that were invaluable in our current situation. The thought crossed my mind that if Luke could bring us someone with just a little more experience, I could really see our settlement not just surviving but thriving.

"Well, let's get to it," Kain announced, his voice pulling me from my thoughts as he started another trek back to the Drop Zone.

I quickened my pace to catch up. "So, what do we do first?" I asked, curiosity piqued as we approached the two piles of stones marking the site's entry. "Dig up that first slab of concrete?"

Kain turned to me, his expression a mix of bewilderment and amusement. "Shit, no. There's no point touching that for now. We'll get the slabs done for a few more sheds first. We have to let them cure for seven days."

"Cure for seven days," I echoed, the concept foreign and intriguing. "What the hell does that mean?"

He smiled softly, a gesture that carried both patience and a hint of camaraderie. "It means that once we've poured the concrete, we have to leave the slabs for seven days before we can build the sheds on them."

"Shit," I muttered, a mix of surprise and embarrassment colouring my tone. "I've never heard of that before."

"I'm not surprised," Kain replied with a slight chuckle, his tone light and devoid of any malice.

I swallowed any offence I might have felt. It was clear Kain didn't mean to belittle my ignorance. And besides, he was right—I really had no idea when it came to construction. Standing there, on the brink of a learning curve as steep as the one before us, I realised that even the simplest of tasks in this new world was going to be far from simple.

❖

Working under the close direction of Kain, we made surprisingly quick work of setting the next slab of concrete. His guidance felt like a beacon in the murky waters of my inexperience. Each step he outlined was clear, methodical, and imbued with a sense of purpose that was infectious. As we mixed, poured, and levelled the concrete, I found myself marvelling at the process—a blend of science and art that had previously been foreign to me.

Kain's confidence was a constructive contrast to the apprehension that had initially clouded my thoughts. With each instruction he gave, I felt my own confidence grow. It was as if his knowledge was a torch, illuminating the path forward, dispelling the shadows of doubt that lingered in my mind. The rhythm of our work became a dance of sorts, a physical manifestation of hope and determination that pushed back against the uncertainty of our situation.

As the concrete spread across the mould, smoothing out under our tools, I couldn't help but reflect on the significance of what we were doing. It wasn't just a slab of concrete; it was the foundation of something greater—a sign of our resilience, our refusal to succumb to despair. The act of building, of creating something tangible in this new and unpredictable world, felt like a declaration of our intent to survive, to thrive even, against all odds.

Feeling somewhat more comfortable with the process of laying concrete, and perhaps because of that growing ease, the two of us began to drift into a little non-work-related conversation. It was a welcome diversion, a brief respite from the constant focus on survival and the tasks at hand.

"So, you've been separated from your family too?" Kain's question cut through the air, simple yet loaded with the weight of our shared circumstances.

"Yeah," I responded, the mention of my family stirring a tumult of emotions within me. "I have two kids. Mack is ten and Rose is six." Just saying their names out loud felt like a bittersweet reminder of what I was fighting for.

"Oh," Kain replied softly, his reaction a mixture of empathy and sorrow. It was clear he understood the pain of separation all too well.

"I miss them terribly," I found myself admitting, more to myself than to Kain. It was a truth that needed no elaboration, a sentiment that anyone in our position could understand without further explanation.

Kain's attention seemed to fixate on the concrete, a deliberate focus that suggested he was grappling with his own thoughts, his own losses. I watched him closely, sensing that there was more he wanted to say, a turmoil beneath the surface waiting to be acknowledged. *Should I ask? Or should I just leave Kain to his own thoughts?* The dilemma hovered in my mind, a decision between pushing for more or respecting his silence.

Before I could resolve my internal debate, Kain voiced his own question, preempting mine. "Have you considered bringing them here?" The inquiry, loaded with implications, momentarily caught me off guard.

"I have," I replied, hesitating as I considered how much to share. It was evident that Kain's own situation, Brianne and their unborn child, loomed large in his thoughts, perhaps mirroring my own concerns for my family.

"And?" Kain prompted, his interest clear, urging me to continue.

The risk of revealing my plans weighed heavily on me, the potential for backlash a tangible concern. *But surely the risk is worth it*, I reasoned, the need to connect, to share our hopes and fears, momentarily outweighing the caution. "I've already made up my mind that I want to bring them here. That's why I'm so determined to get this small settlement functioning as soon as possible," I said, pausing to gather my thoughts before adding, "I don't want them to forget me," the words leaving my lips with a heaviness that felt like a physical burden.

Kain's reaction was immediate, his face tightening as his bottom lip quivered, a visible manifestation of the emotions my words had stirred within him. "How long have you been trapped here for?" he asked, his voice barely above a whisper.

"This is our third day," I replied, the brevity of our ordeal somehow magnifying the absurdity of our situation.

"Really? Is that all?" Kain's surprise was palpable, a reaction that spoke volumes of his own disorientation, his own grappling with the passage of time.

His reaction prompted a thought; maybe Kain wasn't as close to his uncle as I had supposed, if he hadn't realised he had only been missing for a few days. The realisation that our perception of time, of connection, of loss, was as varied as our backgrounds, served as a reminder of the individual burdens we each carried. Yet, in sharing these burdens, in opening up about our fears and hopes, perhaps we could find a way to lighten the load, to forge ahead with a shared purpose that made the unbearable, if not bearable, then at least more manageable.

"Paul! Kain!" Glenda's voice pierced the relative calm of our small construction site, pulling me out of the reverie of thoughts and plans swirling in my mind.

My head snapped toward the sound, eyes focusing on the tent where Glenda and Jamie were struggling with a task that seemed both urgent and precarious. They were attempting to carry Joel, a sight that immediately set off alarms in my mind. Watching Jamie stumble, my heart lurched as Joel's body crashed to the ground in an unsettling echo of helplessness. Glenda, caught off guard by the sudden shift in weight, wobbled precariously before her knees gave way, sending her crashing into the dust alongside Joel.

The urgency in Glenda's call had now transformed into a visible crisis, propelling Kain and me into immediate action. We rushed over, our movements fuelled by a mix of concern and adrenaline. As we reached them, Glenda was already brushing off her knees, attempting to regain her composure.

"I'll take him," I found myself saying, stepping forward to lift Joel's shoulder before Glenda could object. It was a reflexive offer, born out of a desire to alleviate her burden, to somehow make right the unsettling scene before us.

Glenda's nod, heavy with silent appreciation, was a brief exchange of mutual understanding.

"Where are we taking him?" Kain's voice, steady yet tinged with confusion, broke through the momentary silence as he lifted Joel's other shoulder, ready to assist without hesitation.

"To the lagoon," Glenda instructed, her voice carrying a weight of authority.

The lagoon? The question echoed loudly in my mind, a silent scream of confusion and concern. *Why are we taking him back to where we found him?* The rationale behind Glenda's instructions was lost on me, shrouded in a mist of uncertainty that no one seemed inclined to dispel.

I never verbalised my questions, the urgency of the situation leaving little room for debate. Similarly, neither Glenda nor Jamie offered any further explanation, their focus solely on Joel. As we moved beyond our campsite, the weight of Joel's limp form a sombre reminder of the grave circumstances, I couldn't help but feel a deepening sense of foreboding.

INFECTED - PART 2

1338.207.5

We took turns supporting Joel's lifeless body as we journeyed across the barren land, a landscape that seemed to reflect the hopelessness of our situation. The weight of his unconscious form was a constant, unnerving reminder of the fragility of life in this new and unforgiving world.

Jamie, driven by a sense of urgency that seemed to consume him, rushed into the lagoon ahead of us. His actions, frantic yet focused, set the pace for our grim procession. When we finally arrived at the water's edge, Kain and I carefully helped to lower Joel into the cool embrace of the lagoon. "Make sure he is on his back," Glenda shouted, her voice cutting through the flurry of movement and the gentle lapping of the water against the shore.

Kain splashed into the lagoon, steadying Joel from opposite Jamie, his actions a clear demonstration of his readiness to dive into whatever tasks were necessary, literal or otherwise. I watched for a moment, caught up in the urgency of their movements, before deciding to take a pragmatic approach. Not wanting to get completely wet for the second time today, I bent down to untie my shoes, thinking to join in without soaking myself further.

"No," Jamie interrupted sharply, his voice cutting through my intentions. "Kain and I have got him covered," he insisted, his tone brooking no argument but also hinting at a depth of determination that I hadn't fully appreciated before.

I paused, my hands frozen on my shoelaces. "You sure?" I asked, skepticism laced with a hint of relief. The prospect of wading back into the water wasn't particularly appealing, but leaving the heavy lifting to Jamie and Kain felt equally troublesome.

"Certain," Jamie called back, his assurance ringing clear across the water as they began to slowly wade deeper from the shore, their movements deliberate and focused.

"Can you see?" Glenda's voice, tinged with concern, broke through my hesitation. She shifted her weight back and forth, straining for a better view.

"No," I admitted, giving up on my half-hearted attempt to join them. I retied my shoelace, resigning myself to the role of a spectator, steadying myself on my feet. "It would be nice if they didn't keep their backs to us. I can't see much at all." The frustration of being unable to witness what was happening, of being sidelined in this critical moment, gnawed at me, even as I understood the necessity of their positions.

Then, breaking the tense silence, there was a loud gasp for air—a sound so fraught with life and desperation that it momentarily stunned us all.

"What's happening?" Glenda shouted, her voice a mix of fear and hope.

Jamie turned to face us, his movements swift, a large smile spreading across his face that was as bright as it was unexpected. "He's breathing again," he yelled out, the joy in his voice echoing across the lagoon, bouncing off the water and reaching us with a clarity that was almost palpable.

Glenda exhaled loudly, her relief audible in the quiet that followed Jamie's announcement. The tension that had wound its way around my heart began to loosen, replaced by a burgeoning sense of wonder and disbelief. *Joel's breathing again?* The thought reverberated in my mind, a mixture of relief and a thousand questions. "How was this possible? What does this mean for Joel, for us?"

Glenda shrugged, her response tinged with uncertainty and awe. "I'm not sure, but it seems there is something about the lagoon that is keeping Joel alive," she replied, her voice reflecting the mystery that enveloped us.

I smiled, partly in relief, partly in wonder. I hadn't realised that I had spoken loud enough for her to hear. But then, my expression transformed as curiosity took hold. "You mean he wasn't actually dead when we first found him in the river?" The question hung between us, loaded with implications that neither of us were fully prepared to unpack.

Glenda paused, her face contorting in thought as she mulled over the possibilities. "I really don't know," she finally said, her admission highlighting the limits of our understanding.

Rubbing at my forehead, I felt the weight of our ignorance and the magnitude of the unknown pressing in.

"What's going on out there?" Glenda's voice pierced the heavy air once more, her concern palpable as she began to remove her shoes and socks, prepared to dive into the lagoon herself.

"It's okay," Jamie called back, his voice a mix of determination and reassurance. "We've got it under control."

"But I really should examine..." Glenda's insistence was cut short as I reached out, grabbing her arm with a gentle firmness. "Maybe we should just leave them be," I suggested, my words a plea for patience in the face of her scientific curiosity and professional concern.

Bewilderment washed over Glenda's features, her mind grappling with the conflicting desires to intervene and to observe.

I concealed a slight chuckle, the situation's irony not lost on me. *This must be torture for her*, I realised. On the verge of what must be the biggest health miracle of her lifetime, and she was being denied access to examine the fascinating specimen. "Just for a little while," I insisted softly, offering a compromise. "You can examine him when Jamie has calmed down," I added, hoping to soothe her frustration with the promise of future investigation.

"Fine," she acquiesced, her tone a mixture of resignation and impatience as she sank into the dust beside me. "But I'm not giving them too long."

"Fair enough," I agreed, recognising the futility in pushing her further. I should be grateful I had persuaded her this far.

We sat in silence, the lagoon's gentle waves lapping at the shore providing a serene backdrop to our tumultuous thoughts. My attention, however, was split. While part of me remained concerned for Joel and curious about the mysterious properties of the lagoon, another part was captivated by Glenda's struggle. Watching her wrestle with her professional instincts versus the situation's demands was unexpectedly compelling. The dynamics at play—between science and the supernatural, between action and observation—underscored the complexity of our predicament. In this moment, it wasn't just about Joel's recovery but about how each of us was navigating this uncharted territory, balancing our roles, our knowledge, and our emotions against the backdrop of the unknown.

❖

"Why don't we head back to camp for a bit," I suggested, pushing myself to my feet with a sense of purpose. I tried to mask the underlying concern for my arm with a casual tone. "Jamie's got a loud voice; he'll yell out if he needs us." I gave Glenda's elbow a gentle tug, signalling it was time to leave the water's edge. At first, she resisted, her body tensed with a mix of professional duty and personal interest in the unfolding situation by the lagoon. Despite her initial reluctance, we eventually started our quiet walk back to camp, each step taking us away from the immediate tension but not from the undercurrent of unease that seemed to permeate the air.

We hadn't gone far when Glenda stopped abruptly, her gaze fixed on my arm. "What's wrong with your arm?" she inquired, her tone shifting from curiosity to concern, her head nodding toward the limb in question.

Reacting instinctively, I whisked my arm away from her view, a feeble attempt to deflect her attention. "Oh, it's nothing," I replied, hoping my voice sounded more convincing than I felt.

Glenda, however, was not to be deterred. She reached across my body with determination, her fingers wrapping around my arm with a firmness that demanded compliance. "This doesn't look like nothing," she stated, her voice carrying a weight of seriousness that made my heart sink. "Tell me what happened."

Feeling the tremble begin in my lower lip, I bit down hard, trying to steady myself against the surge of emotions her question unleashed. The flesh around the three small holes had darkened further since the incident, a visual testament to the bizarre and frightening encounter with Joel. "Joel dug his fingernails into my arm when he first… woke up," I managed to say, the words feeling inadequate to describe the surreal nature of the event. I hesitated at "woke up," unsure if that term truly captured the essence of what had transpired.

"That was when you screamed?" Glenda pieced together, her memory connecting my reaction to the moment of Joel's unexpected resurgence.

My face flushed with embarrassment, the heat rising as I nodded in confirmation. "Yeah."

The shift in Glenda's expression was immediate, her professional curiosity now marred by a deeper, more contemplative concern. Her face turned serious with thought, reflecting the unusualness of the situation and the potential implications of my injury.

"Is it bad?" I asked, my voice laced with a caution that betrayed my fear of the answer. I didn't really want her to respond, hoping perhaps that my question could remain rhetorical, unanswered.

"Well, it's not bloody good," Glenda replied, her bluntness slicing through my thin veil of hope like a sharp knife.

I chuckled nervously, a sound more of discomfort than amusement. *Glenda certainly knows how to put things bluntly*, I thought, her straightforwardness a grounding force in the midst of our surreal circumstances.

"Come," she instructed, a tone of authority mixed with a hint of an idea sparking in her voice. I found myself following her, driven by a mix of curiosity and trust.

We quickly made our way back to camp, the urgency of her stride compelling me to match her pace. "Wait here," she instructed before disappearing into the supply tent. Left to my own devices, I shifted my weight from foot to foot, the nervous anticipation building. *What did Glenda have in mind? But then again, she did save Jamie's life, so I don't have any reason not to trust her*, I reminded myself, trying to quell the rising tide of anxiety.

When Glenda emerged, bandages in hand, her determination was palpable. "We need to go back to the lagoon," she announced, already moving away.

"Glenda, wait!" The words tumbled out of me before I could stop them. "It's only a minor wound. I'm not sure we need the lagoon." My protest was half-hearted, a part of me still clinging to the hope that maybe, just maybe, we could handle this without returning to that place of mystery and fear.

Glenda stopped and eyed me cautiously, her gaze probing. "Go on," she encouraged, sensing there was more I hadn't shared.

"Well," I began, dragging out the word as I tried to marshal my thoughts. "I've already washed it in the river by the lagoon and the flesh seemed to return to normal within a few minutes. So..."

"And then without the water it turned grey again," Glenda finished my sentence, her mind working quickly to piece together the implications. "Interesting. Let's try this river water then," she said, nodding toward the river running behind the tents, her decision made with a characteristic blend of curiosity and decisiveness.

"It can't hurt. Can it?" The question was more to myself than to Glenda, a verbal manifestation of my lingering doubts.

Glenda shrugged, a gesture that encapsulated her uncertainty. "We shall see." Her response, while noncommittal, carried an undercurrent of hope, a willingness to explore all possibilities in the face of the unknown.

As we made our way to the river, the juxtaposition of hope against the backdrop of uncertainty, of seeking answers in the same waters that both threatened and offered salvation, was not lost on me. In this new world, where the line between life and death seemed as mutable as the waters of the lagoon, every decision carried weight, every action a potential ripple in the pond of our survival. And as we prepared to test the healing properties of the river water, I couldn't help but wonder what other secrets this land held, and whether we would be prepared to face them.

❖

"Go," Glenda prompted, her voice firm as she pointed at the clear, flowing water just a few inches below where we knelt along the riverbank. The seriousness in her tone, combined with the urgency of our situation, left no room for hesitation.

I submerged my arm into the water, bracing myself for the familiar, comforting tingling sensation I had come to associate with the healing properties of these mysterious waters. Instead, a strong, unexpected burning sensation surged through my arm, catching me completely off guard. Instinctively, I began to retract my arm, the pain overwhelming, but Glenda's hand shot out, grasping my arm with surprising strength. "That wasn't long enough," she said, her determination evident as she thrust my arm back under the water's surface.

"It's burning!" I shouted, panic edging into my voice as I struggled against her firm grip. The sensation was unlike anything I had anticipated, a fierce, consuming fire that seemed to gnaw at my flesh.

"Wash your arm," Glenda instructed, her tone brooking no argument, even as she acknowledged my discomfort with a brief, sympathetic glance. "I don't think I should touch it." Her words, though confusing at first, began to make sense as I considered the potential risks of contamination—both to me and to her.

My heart raced, shock and a burgeoning sense of betrayal mingling as I wrestled with Glenda's unexpected assertiveness. Yet, as I forced myself to focus on the wound submerged just below the surface of the water, a grudging realisation dawned on me. She was right. With a resigned sigh, I ceased my struggles and began to gently swirl the water around my arm, watching with a mixture of awe and disbelief as the skin gradually began to return to its normal colour. The intense burning that had initially seized me slowly ebbed away, replaced by a dull ache that seemed almost welcome in comparison.

The transformation was mesmerising, a tangible sign of hope in a situation fraught with uncertainty and fear. As the minutes passed, the pain and the initial panic gave way to a profound sense of relief. Glenda's unyielding stance, though jarring, had guided me through the pain to a semblance of healing, a reminder that sometimes, the path to recovery requires us to endure discomfort, to trust in the process, even when every instinct cries out against it.

Sitting back on my heels, I lifted my arm from the water, noting with a mixture of relief and astonishment that the evidence of the trauma had faded significantly from my skin.

"Give me your arm," Glenda ordered, her voice carrying a sense of urgency that snapped me back to the present.

As I extended my dripping arm toward her, Glenda began to wrap the wound tightly with the bandages she had prepared. Suddenly, she stopped, her hands pausing mid-motion, which immediately sent a wave of panic through me. "What's wrong?" I asked, my voice tinged with the anxiety that Glenda's hesitation had sparked.

"I'm not sure if it will make any difference, but it's worth a try," she murmured, more to herself than to me. Her words, cryptic and laden with uncertainty, did little to ease the growing sense of unease within me.

"What is?" I pressed, desperate for any sliver of understanding.

Without answering, Glenda carefully unwrapped the bandage from around my arm and submerged it in the river. Watching her, a realisation dawned on me—a glimmer of understanding amidst the fog of uncertainty. *Ahh*, I thought. *Now I understand. Even if it makes no difference, it's a genius idea to try.*

Glenda looked up, catching my gaze with a hint of satisfaction in her eyes. "It might help to keep the properties of the water on the wound for longer. If we can change the dressing whenever it completely dries out, with a bit of luck, your wound should heal fully," she explained, her smile reflecting a blend of hope and determination.

I shrugged, the gesture a silent concession to her plan. "Go for it."

With a renewed sense of purpose, Glenda wrapped the soaked bandage around my wound once more. Yet, as she worked, her brow furrowed in concentration, a clear sign that her mind was already racing ahead to the next challenge.

The return of her concentration face reignited the nerves I had briefly managed to quell. I was quickly learning that Glenda's focused expression was a harbinger of concern, a visual cue that more obstacles lay ahead.

"The sun is too hot," she observed, breaking the silence that had settled between us. "I'll have to find something to protect it, try to keep it moist for longer." She rubbed her temples, a gesture of deep thought, as she murmured, "But what?" The question, though whispered, echoed loudly in the silence that followed.

Closing my eyes, I allowed myself a moment of raw honesty. *This place is a fucking disaster*, I thought, the words a silent acknowledgment of the overwhelming challenges we faced.

WOMAN OF MYSTERY

1338.207.6

Standing on the riverbank behind the tent, I watched the last few drops of water from the freshly soaked bandage disappear into the lifeless dust below, each drop a fleeting testament to the transient nature of our current existence. The action, so mundane yet so laden with significance, served as a reminder of the delicate balance we now found ourselves trying to maintain.

Yesterday's conversation with Glenda echoed in my mind, her words casting long shadows over my thoughts. She was right: *This is the perfect spot to build a bridge.* As I gazed across the river, the vision of it began to take shape in my mind's eye, a simple yet sturdy wooden structure that arched gracefully from shore to shore. I could almost see the small wooden slats criss-crossing their way along the span, bound by the upper railing that would reach chest height, providing not just passage but a semblance of safety.

Turrets guarding the entrance on either side painted a picture of medieval fortifications, a simple layer of security that seemed both whimsical and desperately necessary. In this new world, where the unknown lurked at the edge of every decision, the thought of having a means to protect ourselves from an enemy seeking to cross, or offering us a route of escape across the river, felt both comforting and chilling.

As the vision of the bridge solidified in my mind, I realised that it represented more than just a physical crossing; it was a bridge between our past and our future, a tangible link between the world we had lost and the one we were striving to build.

"Yes!" I cried out, the idea crystallising in my mind with such clarity it felt like a revelation. "That's what we need."

"What is?" The sound of Glenda's voice, close behind me, jolted me from my thoughts.

I turned quickly to face her, the excitement still bubbling inside me. "I was just thinking about what you said yesterday, about building a bridge." The words tumbled out in a rush, my enthusiasm barely contained.

"Oh... and?" Glenda prompted, her interest piqued, her gaze steady and encouraging.

I gestured towards the river, my arm sweeping across the landscape as I shared the vision that had taken root in my mind. As I spoke, Glenda nodded, her expression thoughtful, absorbing every detail of the plan I laid out before her. *Did she approve?* The question lingered in my mind, a silent plea for her support.

"And if we make them tall enough, I can imagine those turrets would provide a spectacular view over the land," Glenda added, her voice tinged with a smile. Her words, an endorsement of the idea's potential, filled me with a sense of validation.

I grinned, buoyed by her response. "So, my simple idea has your approval then?" I joked, the tension of anticipation easing into a playful banter.

Glenda's laughter, light and genuine, was a sound of agreement and camaraderie. "I think it's the perfect combination of daring further exploration and security. A balance of beauty and practicality."

"Exactly!" I exclaimed, a swell of pride and a newfound sense of ownership coursing through me as I envisioned the future we could build here. I smiled to myself, lost in the thought of my children enjoying the fruits of our labour. Little

Rose would love playing in the reeds, her laughter mingling with the quacks of ducks and the serene sounds of swans gliding across the lagoon. And Mack, I could just see him, claiming one of the turrets as his own fortress, a king surveying his domain with the imaginative seriousness only a ten-year-old could muster.

"We have to make this work, Glenda," I found myself saying, the weight of my decision pressing down on me, tempering the brief flight of fancy. "We just have to." The determination in my voice was mirrored by the resolve in my heart. This wasn't just about survival anymore; it was about creating a space where hope could flourish, where my children could find joy and laughter.

Glenda's expression mirrored the truth of my words, her face growing serious. "I know," she replied, her voice firm, resolute. Yet, as I studied her face, I saw something more beneath the surface—a pain and sadness that ran deep, hints of stories untold, of burdens carried silently. It was a reminder that each of us brought our own ghosts to this place, our own wounds that needed healing.

With time, I hoped that Glenda would open up to me. The foundation of our small community had to be built on trust as much as on hope. If I was going to protect this community, there could be no secrets, no surprises lurking in the shadows of our collective future.

As if sensing the shift in my thoughts, Glenda's soft smile returned, a gentle push against the heaviness of our conversation. "Shall we get this next tent up then?" she suggested, gesturing to the vacant space beside the medical tent.

"May as well," I agreed, the pragmatic part of me taking over once again.

❖

"God, I can't believe we're almost done!" The words burst from me in a mix of relief and disbelief as I surveyed our progress. The tent, a symbol of both shelter and practicality, stood nearly complete before us. "Glenda, you are an expert with tents!" I called out, my voice carrying across the tent to where she worked meticulously.

"I've had plenty of practice," came her modest reply, a hint of a smile in her voice that spoke volumes of her experiences.

"Really?" My curiosity was piqued. The ease with which she handled the tent, her calm amidst my struggle, hinted at a backstory I was eager to hear.

"These are a lot simpler than the large medical tents we used in Borneo." Her casual mention of Borneo, as if it were a routine part of her life, only added layers to the mystery that surrounded her.

"Borneo? What were you doing there?" I couldn't help but ask, my interest now fully captured by the snippets of her past she had let slip.

"Oh," Glenda chuckled, the sound rich with memories. "That's a very long story. Perhaps we save it for the campfire sometime," she suggested, her voice carrying a promise of stories to come.

"Fair enough," I replied, intrigued but willing to wait for the tale. My attention turned back to the task at hand, the tent that was our immediate challenge. In my distraction, the tent wobbled ominously the moment I released the unstable pole.

"Aargh!" Glenda's cry of frustration cut through the air, pulling me back from my thoughts.

"Glenda! You alright?" Concern laced my words as I rushed to her side of the tent, ready to assist.

"Yeah," she said, her voice muffled as she extricated herself from under the fabric. "I just can't get this darn pole to stay right."

"Here, let me try," I offered, reaching under the fabric to find where Glenda's hand gripped the pole. Together, we navigated the awkward angles and the stubbornness of inanimate objects.

"It should just..." I murmured, trying to solve the puzzle of the pole and fabric.

"Am I losing my mind?" Kain's voice, tinged with confusion and disbelief, suddenly entered the camp.

Both Glenda and I attempted to turn our heads, seeking out Kain.

"I don't understand any of this," he said, his voice a blend of bewilderment and frustration as he shook his head slowly.

Glenda pushed her head further away from the edge of the tent, a manoeuvre that gave her just enough space to articulate her thoughts without the fabric muzzling her words. "Just give yourself a few days to adjust," she huffed, the effort of wrangling the tent not diminishing the firmness in her voice. "It'll all start to make sense in a few weeks."

"It will?" My skepticism was barely veiled, my head poking out from underneath the sagging fabric in search of some assurance, some hint that the bewildering reality we found ourselves in would indeed become more manageable with time.

"Sure," Glenda affirmed, though her quick retreat back into the task at hand did little to bolster my confidence.

My gaze shifted to Kain, who stood by the remnants of the cold campfire, his posture betraying a similar skepticism. "So, how is Joel doing anyway?" I asked, hoping for some sliver of good news regarding his situation.

Kain paused, the question seeming to weigh heavily on him. "He's... umm... he's alive, I guess." His hesitation, the uncertainty in his voice, spoke volumes.

"That's great..." My attempt at optimism felt hollow, even to my own ears.

Glenda, ever alert, seized an opportunity to redirect the conversation. "Hey, Kain," she called out with a purpose that seemed too convenient to be coincidental, "It looks as though we've left the tent pegs for the next tent back at the Drop Zone. Would you go have a look, please?"

"Sure," Kain replied, his nonchalant shrug masking any thoughts he might have had about the timing of Glenda's request.

"Thanks. It's probably a small, rectangular box." Glenda's instructions floated after Kain as he walked away, leaving us in a bubble of temporary privacy.

Waiting until Kain was safely out of earshot, I couldn't help but express my incredulity. "Really?" I shot at Glenda, my tone laden with disbelief. "You want to tell me what that was really about?"

"What?" Glenda's response was the picture of innocence, her face betraying nothing that might suggest an ulterior motive. "I remembered I left them on top of one of the larger boxes. I meant to go back for it."

I eyed her suspiciously, my mind racing through the possibilities. *What more can I do? If Kain returns with a box of tent pegs, I'll know Glenda was genuine. Either that or she's very good at spontaneity.* The thought lingered, an unsolved puzzle. "You're a woman of great mystery, Glenda, I'll give you that," I conceded, the honesty in my words reflecting both my frustration and my growing respect for her. Glenda's ability to navigate the unfamiliar with such poise and foresight was as baffling as it was admirable.

❖

In Kain's absence, Glenda and I had managed to complete the third tent and made significant progress on the fourth, despite the complication of missing pegs. It was a testament to our growing proficiency and perhaps, to a certain degree of determination that seemed to fuel our actions in this new, challenging world.

I paused in my efforts, glancing up at the sky where the sun hung low, casting long shadows and bathing the landscape in a warm, golden hue. The mountains in the far distance seemed to cradle the light, holding onto the day for as long as possible. "There can't be more than an hour or so left of daylight," I called out to Glenda, my voice carrying a note of urgency. "I'm going to check on Jamie and Joel," I announced, feeling a need to ensure their well-being

"Alright," Glenda replied, her voice steady and focused. "I'll get the fire started."

Taking the gentle hills with steady strides, I approached the top of the highest peak before the lagoon. My anticipation grew with each step, a mix of concern and curiosity driving me forward. As I neared the crest, my breath caught in my throat, a sudden constriction that forced me to cough lightly several times as I struggled to regain my composure. My eyes scanned the scene below, searching for signs of Jamie and Joel.

Are my eyes deceiving me? The sight that greeted me was both unexpected and heartening. Two figures were making their way up the hill with slow and steady steps.

"Jamie!" I called out, my voice tinged with surprise and relief. "Is that Joel?" The question, rhetorical as it might have been, was driven by a need for confirmation, for reassurance that what I was seeing was indeed real.

"Come and help us," Jamie called back, his free arm beckoning me. His tone, a mix of exhaustion and determination, spurred me into action.

Carefully, I jogged down the dusty incline, my steps cautious as I approached. The sight of Joel, up and moving, was a welcome one, yet I couldn't help but feel a sense of apprehension. As I slid underneath his free arm to support his weight, I tried not to stare. The rough stitching that held his neck together was hard to ignore.

"Thought I'd better get him back to camp before dark," Jamie's voice broke through my contemplation, urging us into motion with a sense of urgency that was palpable in the dimming light.

"Good idea," I echoed, agreeing without hesitation. The practicality of his suggestion was undeniable; navigating the uneven terrain with Joel in his current state would only grow more challenging as night fell.

The journey back was arduous, each step a testament to our collective will to persevere. The grunts and strained breaths that accompanied our efforts blurred, making it hard to distinguish who was struggling more with the burden. Curiosity, however, got the better of me. "Hurt your foot?" I couldn't help but inquire, noting the particular heaviness in Jamie's steps.

"Yeah," Jamie grunted in confirmation, his voice strained with the effort of moving forward. "The hill where you found us was a bit rough," he added, his explanation terse but laden with the unspoken hardships they must have endured.

"Has he spoken yet?" The question lingered in the air, my curiosity for Joel's condition growing with every laboured step we took.

"Not really," came Jamie's reply, his words painting a picture of the uncertainty that still clouded Joel's recovery.

Turning my attention to Joel, I sought to offer a gesture of comfort, a connection in the midst of the turmoil that surrounded us. His wide, beautiful eyes met mine, a silent communication that transcended words. "You've got your father's eyes," I told him tenderly, hoping to ground him in the familiarity of family, of belonging. "Let's get you home."

Jamie's quiet scoff at my words was almost lost in the shuffle of our movement, but its significance wasn't lost on me. I knew all too well the skepticism, the underlying tension that it represented. Yet, I was in no mood to argue, not now. The priority was getting Joel safely back to camp, to the semblance of security and care that awaited him there.

After what felt like an eternity of torturous silence, punctuated only by the sound of our steady breathing and the uneven thud of our footsteps, the camp finally came into view. A wave of relief washed over me, so intense it was almost tangible. Supporting most of Joel's weight had drained me more than I had realised.

"Glenda!" I called out, my voice cracking slightly with the effort.

Jamie let out a heavy sigh beside me, a sound that seemed to carry the weight of the world. It was a mirror of my own relief but tinged with an underlying exhaustion.

Glenda and Luke hurried over as we approached, their faces etched with concern. The sight of us, bedraggled and weary, must have been a shock.

"He's bleeding!" Glenda's cry cut through the air, her medical instincts kicking in immediately. "Luke, get me some tissue from the medical tent," she directed, her tone brooking no argument.

Luke, however, stood frozen, as if momentarily overwhelmed by the situation.

"I got it!" Kain's voice, strong and sure, broke through the hesitation. He emerged from the medical tent with a sense of purpose, rushing over to hand the tissues to Glenda.

"Ta," she replied, a simple acknowledgment as she took the tissues and immediately pressed a wad of them up to Joel's dripping nose. "Let's get him sitting," she instructed, her focus entirely on Joel's well-being.

Together, Jamie and I guided Joel to sit on a large log by the campfire, the warmth of the flames a stark contrast to the chill of the evening air. Kain followed, silently ready to assist further if needed.

"Not too close," Glenda insisted, her attention divided between treating Joel and ensuring his safety from the campfire's heat. "Is it just his nose?"

"I think so," Jamie responded, his voice low and filled with an unspoken concern that mirrored my own.

"I didn't even notice it was bleeding," I admitted, guilt mingling with surprise at my oversight. In the midst of everything, it was easy to miss the small details, even when they were as glaring as a bleeding nose.

Glenda knelt in front of the drooping Joel, who was still being supported on either side by me and Jamie. Her voice carried a mix of concern and bafflement. "I don't understand how," she murmured, her gaze fixed on Joel, searching for an explanation that seemed to elude her.

Jamie shook his head, a gesture of disbelief or perhaps resignation. "I didn't give him any, but he seems to have plenty of it now." His words were cryptic, sparking a flicker of confusion within me.

Plenty of what? I found myself wondering, my head tilting slightly as I tried to piece together the puzzle. The conversation felt like a riddle, each word adding layers to the mystery rather than clarity.

"Yes," Glenda agreed, her attention never wavering from Joel. I watched, fascinated and a little apprehensive, as she poked Joel's arms and legs in several places. "There is definitely blood in his veins now," she announced, her tone suggesting that this was both unexpected and significant.

I released my breath, the pieces of the conversation finally clicking into place in my mind. *Of course! What else would they have meant?* The realisation that Joel's recovery, or at least part of it, involved his blood, something so fundamentally essential yet so bafflingly restored, was a moment of clarity amidst the confusion.

"It's a medical anomaly!" Glenda declared, her voice carrying a mix of excitement and wonder as she rose to her feet, accepting the whiskey bottle Luke offered to her. "You had better lie him down again once the bleeding stops," she advised, her professional opinion mingled with the practical steps that followed such a discovery. Then, without hesitation, she took a swig from the bottle, perhaps seeking solace in its contents from the day's surreal developments.

Luke's laughter, loud and clear, broke through the tension, a reminder of the camaraderie that bound us together in these strange times.

I glanced up at the dimming sky, noting the encroaching darkness that signalled the end of another day. "Nightfall can't be too far away now," I observed aloud, already turning my thoughts towards the practical needs of our group. "I'll prepare us some food," I announced, ensuring that Joel was sufficiently supported by Jamie before I moved away, ready to contribute in the way I knew best.

"I'll help you," Kain quickly chimed in, his offer a reminder of the solidarity that had become our greatest strength.

TRADITION

1338.207.7

As the darkness enveloped our campsite, the atmosphere shifted from one of survival to something resembling normalcy, if only for a moment. Our bellies full and the bottle of whiskey making its rounds added a warmth that wasn't just from the campfire. A loud cackle, surprising even to myself, erupted from my mouth, cutting through the stillness of the night and filling the empty darkness with a moment of cheer.

"Shh," Glenda hushed, her finger pressed to her lips in a playful yet earnest gesture. "The zombie is sleeping," she whispered, her attempt at solemnity crumbling into a fit of giggles. Her laughter was infectious, a reminder of the lighter moments we could still share amidst the uncertainty.

Kain's chuckle resonated loudly, his amusement clear. "Well, I didn't know how else to describe him." His comment, a reference to Joel's miraculous recovery and current condition, was both apt and humorously grim.

"Are we sure it's safe in there? We don't really know what's going on," I found myself saying, leaning forward with a not-so-quiet voice that betrayed my lingering concern. Despite the laughter and light-hearted banter, the reality of our situation, the unknowns surrounding Joel's condition, hovered at the back of my mind.

"Oh," Luke sighed heavily, his patience with the topic seemingly thinning. "Don't be so stupid, Paul." His retort, though sharp, was not unexpected.

"Ah," I gasped, feigning hurt feelings in an attempt to lighten the mood further.

Luke staggered to his feet, using Glenda's shoulder as a makeshift support. "Of course, it's safe," he muttered, his voice a mixture of assurance and slight irritation as he made his way past me, heading toward the silent tent where Joel and Jamie rested. His movements, slightly unsteady, betrayed the effect of the whiskey more than any concern about Joel's condition.

"Is he alright?" Kain leaned in, his voice hushed, a note of genuine concern laced with the alcohol-induced bravery to ask.

"Oh, he's fine," I answered, dismissing the concern with a slight wave of my hand.

The three of us fell into a calm silence, a respite that felt almost surreal given the chaos that had become our new normal. I stared at the empty plate at my feet, its barren paper surface a reminder of the meagre dinner we had managed. *I should've made more sandwiches*, I realised, as my stomach responded with a betraying gurgle. Hunger was a constant companion, yet in the face of this world's unending uncertainties, even basic needs became secondary. I was pretty certain we were all guilty of neglecting our health to some extent, all except Glenda, of course. Her reminders about nutritional needs were as frequent as they were well-intentioned, a beacon of care in our fragmented existence.

"Well, dinner was tasty," Glenda offered, her voice cutting through the stillness with a warmth that felt both comforting and misplaced. "I wonder whether now might…"

"Shh," I hushed her, cutting off her words with a sharpness that surprised even me. A sudden, instinctual alertness took hold as my ears picked up on something—a discordant harmony of voices, their pitch and tension rising in a way that set every nerve on edge. It was emanating from the tent, a cacophony that promised nothing good.

Quietly, I pushed myself up from the log that had been my seat, my actions deliberate. As a dark figure burst from the tent, my heart skipped a beat. I recognised Luke immediately—his silhouette unmistakable even in the fleeting shadows.

"Luke!" I called out, desperation tinting my voice, a futile attempt to bridge the distance he was determined to put between us.

But Luke didn't stop. Instead, he broke into a run, his form swallowed by the darkness that stretched like a chasm between us. I stared after him, my mind a whirlwind of confusion and fear. *What the hell just happened? Is he hurt?* My body tensed, ready to sprint after him, to cross the void his departure had created.

However, Glenda's hand shot up, warning me off with an abrupt gesture. Her eyes, wide with a mix of caution and fear, locked onto mine, silently urging me to reconsider. In that moment, our world seemed to shrink to the space between us, filled with unspoken worries and the heavy weight of decision.

In the distance, the night was momentarily chased away by the surreal glow of Portal colours, painting our rugged surroundings with fleeting, ethereal light. The display was both beautiful and heart-wrenching, a reminder of the vast, unpredictable universe that now cradled our fates. As quickly as it appeared, the light show vanished, leaving behind a darkness that felt even more profound.

My face tightened into a deep frown, the muscles around my mouth and eyes contracting with a mixture of frustration and concern. *Luke's gone.* The words echoed in my mind like a haunting refrain. *He's left us again.*

"Yep, looks like it's definitely you and me tonight, Paul," Kain's voice broke through my thoughts, his tone attempting levity but failing to mask the underlying tension.

"I guess so," I sighed, the weight of the situation settling heavily upon my shoulders. "I might get used to this dust yet," I said with a half-hearted attempt at humour, sitting back on the log and absently patting the ground with my foot, sending small clouds of dust swirling into the air.

"Oh no," Glenda interjected. "There's a sleeping bag for you in the other tent."

"Really?" I asked, my surprise genuine. The thought of a sleeping bag, an artefact of comfort in this desolate world, felt almost luxurious. "That should make a nice change." I looked over at Kain, offering a semblance of a smile. "But the tent's all yours," I said casually, though a part of me craved that minor comfort. "I'll sleep out here again tonight. I don't want to let the fire completely burn out." My gaze lingered on the flames, their flickering light a fragile barrier against the encroaching darkness.

Kain looked at me, his surprise evident. "Don't like the dark?" he probed, an undercurrent of curiosity in his voice.

"Hmph," I managed, a non-committal grunt, as I glanced across at Glenda, seeking an ally in my ambiguous response. "Something like that."

"Is there something out there?" Kain pressed, his voice lowering to a cautious whisper. "Other people maybe?"

"Not that we know of," I replied quickly, too quickly perhaps. *But is that really true?* I couldn't help but question myself. Luke had shared whispers of a Guardian named Cody, a figure shrouded in mystery who was supposedly out there, somewhere in the vast unknown. He hadn't shown up at camp, at least not within the sphere of my awareness. *He must be somewhere out there,* I mused, my gaze drifting beyond the firelight to the expanse of darkened emptiness that stretched before us.

The night seemed to hold its breath, the silence a canvas on which my fears and speculations painted vivid pictures. The idea of Cody, a Guardian lurking unseen, added layers to the night's shadows, each movement of air or crackle of firewood a potential signal of his presence. And yet, the part of me that clung to the remnants of hope wondered if perhaps his existence out there could be a beacon, a sign that we were not alone in this struggle to survive and make sense of a world turned upside down.

"But," Kain's voice cut through the tension that hung like a thick fog around us, his words louder, more forceful than before, "If Luke is telling the truth about not bringing—" He paused, the weight of his thoughts momentarily halting his speech before he pressed on, "About not bringing Joel here, then who did? And how did they get him here without any of us seeing something? There isn't exactly any cover here. And he looked like he'd spent a fair amount of time in the water already."

Yes, of course! My mind screamed in silent revelation. *If we follow the river upstream far enough, we'll likely find the source of Joel's...* My thoughts trailed off, a mixture of dread and determination settling in. The mystery of Joel's appearance wasn't just a puzzle; it was a gaping hole in our understanding of this place, a place that seemed to defy the very laws of nature and humanity we thought we knew.

Glenda shifted uncomfortably on her log, her movements drawing my attention away from the spiralling thoughts. Her constant shuffles, the physical manifestations of her anxiety, were beginning to grate on me, adding to the already overwhelming tension.

"Do you know something that you're not telling us?" I asked, my voice carrying an edge of suspicion and frustration.

It wasn't just the situation with Joel that bothered me; it was the ever-present feeling that we were all holding back pieces of a puzzle only solvable through collective honesty.

Glenda hesitated, her eyes darting between Kain and me, as if measuring the weight of her words against the potential consequences of sharing them. "I'm just as confused as the two of you are," she said finally, her voice a mix of resignation and defensiveness.

Kain's breathing quickened noticeably, a physical testament to the rising fear and uncertainty that seemed to suffocate us. "I don't think we're safe here," he whispered, the words barely escaping his lips, as if saying them louder might make them more real.

I let out a soft sigh, the sound more a release of pent-up frustration than anything else. Here I sat, caught in a web of mysteries and half-truths, with a woman who played her cards close to her chest and a young man whose fear seemed to amplify with every breath. And then there was Luke, with his erratic behaviour and enigmatic warnings, and Jamie, whose newfound obsession with his son painted a picture of desperation and denial. According to Luke, Joel should be nothing more than a memory, yet here we were, grappling with a reality that seemed to mock the very essence of logic and loss.

"Right now, we don't have any other option," I said, trying to inject a note of certainty into my voice. The flickering shadows cast by the campfire seemed to dance with my words, creating an eerie ballet of light and darkness. "I'm sure Luke would have warned us if it wasn't safe." My statement hung in the air, a fragile banner of hope in the uneasy silence that enveloped us.

Kain scoffed loudly, a sound that cut sharply through the night. "Luke doesn't know everything." His skepticism was palpable, a tangible force that seemed to add weight to the growing unease within me.

My eyebrow raised in suspicion at his quick dismissal. I knew that was indeed an understatement—Luke's knowledge, or lack thereof, had been a recurring theme in our struggles. *But does Kain know something else too?* The question wormed its way through my thoughts, unsettling me further. *Is he hiding something that could put us all in danger?* My stomach growled uneasily, a reminder of the physical demands that mirrored our psychological turmoil. *We can't afford to be divided,* I realised. *We need a leader, someone with the skills and charisma to unite our growing settlement, to navigate the treacherous waters of uncertainty that lay ahead.*

"We'll just have to watch out for each other," I told them emphatically, trying to bridge the gaps of mistrust and fear with words of solidarity. "We're all we've got right now," I said pointedly, glancing across at Glenda, hoping to find some semblance of agreement or reassurance in her eyes.

Glenda shifted uncomfortably again, her movements betraying an inner turmoil or perhaps a reluctance to confront the reality we faced. "I think it's time for bed," she said abruptly, slapping both her thighs in a motion that seemed to signal a retreat more from the conversation than the night. Without another word, she got up and left the warmth of the campfire.

Probably a good idea, although that was a bit sudden, I mused, watching her retreating back. The night air felt cooler now, the absence of her presence making the darkness seem more oppressive. "I'll go grab a sleeping bag," I said to Kain, pushing myself up from the ground, my limbs stiff from sitting. The action felt like a physical attempt to shake off the tension that had settled around us. "Does it matter which one?"

Kain shook his head, his gaze lingering on the dying fire. "Nah."

I casually made my way to the tent, the night around me thick with shadows that seemed to stretch and reach out with every step I took. As I let myself inside, the darkness enveloped me, a stark contrast to the weak flicker of light from the distant campfire. This tent, the furthest from our makeshift hearth, lay in near complete darkness, the glow barely brushing its entrance with a teasing touch of light. Suddenly, a familiar cry echoed in my mind, *Daddy!* Rose's voice, filled with fear and longing, sent a shuddering wave of terror crashing over me. My heart clenched, a physical reaction to the pain of her absence.

Not tonight, I told the darkness, my voice a silent declaration of defiance. My fingers found the sleeping bag's carry strap, their grip firm and resolute. *Not tonight.* I refused to let the haunting memories and what-ifs consume me, not when survival demanded every ounce of focus and strength.

Moving carefully across the tent's floor, I navigated by memory and the faint glow that filtered in. Pushing my way outside, the cool air hit me like a splash of reality, a reminder of the world beyond my fears. The decision to sleep next to the campfire suddenly felt not just wise but necessary. It was a tether to the present, a guard against the ghosts of the past.

As I crept towards the fire, the figures of two bodies moved quietly by the glow. "Glenda," I whispered into the night, my voice barely louder than the crackling of the flames.

She jumped, and Kain pulled on her hand, helping her to maintain balance on her log.

I couldn't help but chuckle softly at her reaction, an involuntary response that felt strangely out of place in the solemnity of our situation. "Sorry," I whispered, the word floating away into the night as I dropped the sleeping bag into the dust in front of my designated log.

"No, you're not," Glenda replied, but the edge in her voice was softened by a smile that seemed to flicker in the firelight.

I perched on the log, my bum cheeks rubbing against the rough wood as I searched for a sense of comfort. The simple act of settling down for the night had taken on a new meaning here; it was a nightly ritual of finding safety and solace. Each shift, each adjustment, was a small declaration of resilience, of our continued struggle against the darkness, both literal and metaphorical.

"You don't like the tent?" Kain's question broke the quiet of the evening, his eyes darting towards the medical tent as if seeking an answer in its silent form.

"Actually," Glenda began, her voice trailing into a pause that seemed to stretch between us, laden with anticipation. "There's something I think we should do as a group first." The seriousness in her tone, mixed with a hint of vulnerability, piqued my interest. After her abrupt departure earlier, this sudden proposal felt unexpected, almost out of character. *What could Glenda possibly consider so important that she needed to address it now?*

Kain's brow arched, mirroring my own curiosity. "What is it?" he inquired, his voice a mix of skepticism and interest.

"Gratitude," she simply stated.

My head tilted, a gesture of surprise and intrigue. *Well, that was unexpected.* In a world that seemed perpetually on the brink, where survival often took precedence over everything else, gratitude was not a concept that had frequently crossed my mind.

"Gratitude?" Kain's voice carried a note of disbelief, almost a scoff.

"Hear me out," Glenda quickly interjected, cutting off any potential objections with a gesture of her hand. Her insistence demanded our attention, silencing the immediate skepticism that had bubbled to the surface.

Kain fell into a reluctant silence, and I found myself doing the same, a part of me curious about where this was going.

"It's something my father taught me. I've done it every day since..." Glenda's voice faltered, a rare crack in her composed exterior, and she swallowed hard, as if pushing down memories too painful to fully surface. "It's become a nightly tradition for me," she concluded, her voice steadying once more.

"Oh," was all I could manage, softly spoken, as a new layer of Glenda's character was revealed to us. *A woman of mystery, indeed*. This revelation offered a glimpse into her inner world, a personal ritual rooted in resilience and memory.

Glenda knelt in the dust near the soft glowing embers of our fire, her silhouette outlined by the faint light. "Come join me," she encouraged, her tone gentle yet persuasive.

Kain shot a glance my way, uncertainty written across his face. The idea seemed foreign, yet disarmingly simple. *It couldn't do us any harm*, I reasoned, shrugging my shoulders in silent acquiescence before kneeling beside Glenda. The act felt strangely grounding, a physical manifestation of openness to whatever this shared moment might bring.

Kain, however, remained motionless for a moment longer, his skepticism a tangible barrier. "It's okay," Glenda reassured, turning to look up at him with a smile that seemed to bridge the gap between doubt and acceptance. "We're not praying or anything."

Finally, Kain relented, his knees finding the dust opposite Glenda. As we formed a small, unlikely circle around the dying embers, the night around us seemed to hold its breath.

When Kain and I had finally settled into an uneasy quiet, each of us wrestling with our own discomfort amidst the dust at our feet, Glenda broke the silence. "I'll go first," she announced, her voice cutting through the tension like a gentle breeze. I found myself drawn to the warm glow of the fire, its light flickering across her features, painting her with a softness that seemed almost out of place in our harsh surroundings.

"I'm grateful for life," she stated, her words simple yet profound, floating into the night air with a calmness that belied the turmoil of the day.

A whole minute passed, filled with a silence so thick it felt almost tangible. I shifted uncomfortably, the bulk of my weight pressing into my right knee. *Is that it? Is it over?* The questions raced through my mind, an internal monologue of doubt and confusion. But then, a gentle nudge from Glenda's elbow against my ribs pulled me back to the moment. It was a silent prompt, her way of saying it was my turn to find something, anything, to be grateful for.

I took a deep breath, letting the cool night air fill my lungs as I searched for an answer amidst the scatter of my thoughts. *What am I grateful for?* The question seemed almost laughable in the context of our current predicament. *Jamie's moodiness, Luke's absence, the severance from my children, the looming threat of death in this alien darkness...* Yet, despite the despair, I knew there had to be a glimmer of positivity, a single thread to cling to in the overwhelming tapestry of our survival.

Glenda's elbow nudged me again.

"I'm grateful for the river," I finally said, the words escaping my lips before I could fully gauge their weight. A pang of self-consciousness washed over me as I realised how my words might be interpreted. *They wouldn't think I meant more than just its healing properties, would they?* The river, after all, had been a source of refreshment, a beacon in the vastness of our desolation, but to voice such a specific gratitude felt oddly revealing, as if I were exposing a part of myself I hadn't intended to share.

And then, the awkward silence descended upon us once more, a thick blanket that seemed to wrap around us, binding us in a moment of shared vulnerability.

As the silence stretched into an almost tangible entity, a part of me couldn't help but fight the smile that began to tug at the corner of my mouth. That was three times now that Glenda had nudged Kain, her persistence a testament to her determination in this strange ritual of gratitude. It was a small, almost humorous rebellion against the bleakness that surrounded us.

Then, breaking the silence like a sudden crack of thunder, Kain blurted out, "I'm grateful for Uncle Jamie." The words came out in a rush.

My hand shot to my mouth in an instinctive attempt to stifle a scoff, but it escaped nonetheless, a brief, involuntary sound that I instantly regretted. The look of annoyance that flashed across Kain's face was like a physical blow, and I found myself calling out in apology, "Kain. I'm sorry," as he huffed, his body tense with hurt as he stormed off into the darkness beyond the campfire.

As I unfolded myself from the ground, my knees protesting with audible groans of discomfort, I made to follow him, driven by a sense of responsibility and concern. But Glenda's hand on my arm stopped me, her silent plea of "Don't" hanging between us. Her gaze held mine, a depth of understanding in her eyes. "He'll be back. There's nowhere else to go," she whispered, her voice barely audible over the crackling of the fire. Yet, despite her assurance, doubt gnawed at me. The darkness that lay beyond our small circle of light was a vast, unknown expanse, one that I knew all too well could be as unforgiving as it was unyielding.

"Besides, we're not done," Glenda added, her words pulling me back to the present moment. My eyebrow arched in surprise at her declaration. "We're not?" I echoed, my voice laced with a mix of curiosity and resignation.

Glenda turned her attention back to the fire, her profile illuminated by the flickering flames, casting long shadows across her face. The silence that followed was heavy, filled with the weight of unspoken thoughts and emotions. After several minutes, feeling the pull of the ritual's unfinished business, I gave in and dropped to my knees once more, resigning myself to the moment.

Glenda swallowed deeply, a visible effort to compose herself. I caught a glimpse of a tear tracing its path down her cheek, a silent testament to the depth of feeling behind her next words. "I'm grateful for Clivilius," she said, her voice a whisper against the backdrop of the night.

As Glenda disappeared into the medical tent with a haste that spoke volumes of her inner turmoil, I found myself shuffling back to my log, the dust kicking up behind me in a silent testament to the heavy thoughts weighing me down. There, I settled once more, my gaze fixed on the fire before me. Its crackles and pops were a dying chorus, singing the final notes of what felt like our dwindling hope for survival. In the orange glow of the embers, I found myself lost in a reflection, waiting for what would come next, yet unsure of what I was truly expecting.

When Kain re-entered the camp at a brisk pace, his return pulled me from my reverie. He immediately lay down, finding solace by the last warmth of the coals, seeking comfort in the fire's fading embrace. Glenda had been right. Despite the darkness that lay beyond our circle of light, Kain had found his way back to us. His chest heaved with silent breaths, a wordless expression of whatever fears or shadows he had encountered in the night. The sight stirred a deep empathy within me. The unknown terrors of the darkness were a shared dread among us, yet each experience was painfully personal.

My face softened as I observed him. Kain was still so young, barely on the cusp of adulthood, yet soon to face the responsibilities of fatherhood. The thought sent a sharp pang through me, an aching reminder of my own children, whose faces I feared I might never see again. The pain was a raw, jagged edge in my heart, a constant reminder of what was at stake, of what had already been lost.

Compelled by a sudden urge to offer some small measure of comfort, I rose from my seat. The sleeping bag at my feet, momentarily forgotten, now seemed like a small but significant offering. I picked it up and gently placed it beside Kain's resting form, a silent gesture of solidarity. In this world that demanded so much from us, it was these small acts of kindness that kept the ember of humanity alive within us.

Then, quietly, with a care not to disturb the fragile peace that had settled over the camp, I crept towards the tent.

Returning from the tent with the second sleeping bag clutched in my arms, I couldn't help but smile warmly at the sight that greeted me. Kain's belongings, a pair of jeans and a t-shirt, were strewn haphazardly across his log. He looked to be wrapped snugly within the confines of the sleeping bag, his eyes fixed on the vast, empty expanse of the night sky above us.

I undressed down to my underwear, taking care to fold my clothes neatly, a small gesture of order amidst the disorder. Placing them atop my log, I allowed myself a deep breath of relief, the cool night air caressing my skin. Slipping my legs into my own sleeping bag, I welcomed the thought of rest, a precious commodity in these times.

However, the ground beneath me was unforgiving, a small lump of dust making its presence known against my back. I rolled onto my side, attempting to smooth it out with fumbling hands, but my efforts only succeeded in creating another lump. After several frustrated pounds, I resigned myself to the discomfort, rolling back onto my back. *Probably as good as it's going to get*, I thought, a sigh escaping me.

The silence of the night was heavy, filled with the unsaid and the unresolved. "I'm sorry, Kain," I found myself saying, breaking the quiet. My mind, restless and refusing to settle, needed to voice the apology, to acknowledge the moment of discord from earlier.

Kain's response was a soft sigh, filled with a weariness that I felt mirrored in my own bones. "I'm grateful for the light," he said simply, his words carrying a depth of meaning that went beyond the physical. In this world of shadows and uncertainty, the light was more than just a beacon in the darkness; it was a symbol of hope, of the fragile yet persistent will to survive.

A deep line of worry etched itself across my forehead, his words resonating with me. Pulling myself from the sleeping bag, I moved quickly, driven by a newfound determination. After a quick dash to gather what was needed, I returned to place several more logs on the fire. The flames, rejuvenated by the fresh fuel, danced with renewed vigour, casting a warm glow that pushed back the encroaching darkness.

The light will remain tonight, I promised myself silently. *I will make sure of that.*

4338.208

(27 July 2018)

AWAKENING

1338.208.1

Sitting up slowly, the ache in my bones greeted me like an old, unwelcome friend. Despite the discomfort, there was a small consolation—the dust beneath me. It shifted easily under my weight, almost like a natural mattress, moulding itself to the contours of my body. In a world stripped of most comforts, this small adaptation of the earth to my form made the harsh reality of sleeping without a mattress just a tad more bearable.

I glanced over at Kain, who lay in a tangled half-in, half-out sprawl across his sleeping bag and the dust. The sight brought a smile to my face, a rare moment of lightness in the midst of our unusual situation. It was hard to tell whether Kain had been battling restlessness or had found an odd sense of comfort in his unconventional sleeping position.

As the gentle morning breeze brushed against my skin, the hairs on my arms stood on end, a chill running down my spine despite the warmth of the rising sun. The breeze carried with it a small puff of dust, swirling in a miniature whirlwind before dissipating into the air. The sight, rather than being mundane, filled me with a sense of unease. It was a haunting reminder of the dust storm we had endured, the strongest breeze I had felt since that torturous night. The thought of facing another storm so soon sent a shiver of apprehension through me, even as I gazed up at the clear, cloudless sky, questioning the likelihood of a repeat disaster.

Shaking off the dust and the lingering worry, I quickly dressed in yesterday's clothes, the fabric stiff and gritty against my skin. Rolling my sleeping bag with practiced motions, I entered the third tent, the one we had rushed to set up the day before. The large, vacant spaces within it seemed almost mocking in their emptiness. "Well, that was worth the rush to get it up yesterday," I muttered to myself, the words heavy with a mix of sarcasm and resignation. Yet, as I surveyed the space, a different thought occurred to me—having the tent up spared us the task today, a small victory in itself.

"This is my home now," I declared, a statement that was more an affirmation to myself than anything else. Dropping the sleeping bag onto the floor at the back of the central shared living space, I felt a complex mix of emotions. There was a sense of finality in accepting this place as my home. Yet, there was also a subtle undercurrent of defiance and resilience in claiming this space, in making it ours despite everything. The tent, like Clivilius with its vast, empty expanses, was a blank canvas—a place of potential and possibility, a testament to our continued survival and adaptation in a world that had changed beyond recognition.

The realisation hit me with a mix of discomfort and necessity—I really needed a wash, and a change into fresh clothes seemed long overdue. I made a mental note to collect my bags once Jamie woke up.

Stepping out from the tent, the absence of Glenda was noticeable, but my immediate concern led me towards the river located behind our camp. The cool morning air brushed against my skin, a reminder of the day's start and the tasks that lay ahead. Approaching the river, the sound of its flowing water was a welcome respite.

Crouching down by the river's edge, I cautiously began to unwind the bandage wrapped around my arm. The bandage was very dry, a good sign perhaps, but it did little to ease the knot of worry forming in my stomach. My brow furrowed as I contemplated the state of the wound beneath. The fear of finding my skin in a deteriorated condition, possibly turned grey again as it had before, weighed heavily on my mind. Holding my breath, I braced for what I might uncover.

To my profound relief, as the bandage came off and I examined the wound, the greyness had not returned. I exhaled a long, steadying sigh, my shoulders dropping slightly with the release of tension. Closer inspection of the three puncture marks revealed a healing process underway. Gently poking the surrounding flesh, I observed how the skin turned pale under pressure, a sign of blood flow interruption, only to see it promptly return to its normal fleshy pink colour upon releasing my finger. Small scabs had started to form over the puncture sites, a clear indication of the body's natural healing at work.

The sudden sound of Glenda's voice close behind me was enough to almost send me toppling into the river. "That's looking really healthy," she observed, her tone carrying a note of genuine approval.

Caught off guard by her silent approach, I struggled to regain my balance, my concentration shattered. "We'll have to stop meeting like this," I joked, an attempt to lighten the moment. But the joke seemed to fly right past her, leaving a momentary awkwardness hanging in the air between us.

Glenda gave me a sideways glance, her expression unreadable for a moment. "I mean you sneaking up behind me at the river," I clarified, hoping to bridge the gap my attempted humour had seemingly widened.

Her brow narrowed slightly, a sign of misunderstanding or perhaps concern. "Sorry," she said, her voice softening as she crouched down beside me to take a closer look at my arm. I turned my gaze out across the river, shifting my now reddening face away from her direct scrutiny. *Did Glenda not get the humour?* I found myself wondering, a ripple of unease threading through the brief exchange.

After inspecting my arm, Glenda released it and pushed herself to her feet, her movements efficient and focused. "Keep a close eye on it. Notify me immediately if anything changes. And soak the bandages back in the river," she instructed with a professional detachment that belied the earlier awkwardness.

"Of course. I'll watch it closely," I assured her, pulling myself up to stand. As she turned to leave, a thought occurred to me, prompting a spontaneous call. "Hey, Glenda?"

"Yes, Paul?" She paused, turning back with an openness that invited further conversation.

I ventured into the logistical arrangements that had been on my mind. "Are you happy to keep sleeping in the medical tent for now? If so, Kain and I will share that third tent and we can leave Jamie and Joel where they are," I proposed, the practicalities of our living arrangements suddenly pressing. "Oh, and Luke if he ever decides to stay the night," I added, almost as an afterthought, acknowledging the fluidity of our group's dynamics.

"Sure," Glenda responded with a gentle shrug, her demeanour easygoing and accommodating. "I don't have any issues with that."

Relief washed over me, accompanied by a smile. "Great. I'll move my suitcase across as soon as Jamie is awake," I confirmed, buoyed by the ease of the arrangement. Despite the occasional misunderstandings, I found a deep sense of gratitude for Glenda's agreeableness.

"They are both awake now. I was just in with them," Glenda's words caught me off guard as we made our way back to camp.

"Oh," was all I could manage, my surprise evident. "Joel too?" The question slipped out as we walked.

"Yes. He has a broken finger but apart from that, he looks to be making a speedy recovery. It is quite remarkable, really," Glenda explained, her voice carrying a note of professional admiration.

A dryness clutched at my throat, the memory of the sound of bone snapping vividly replaying in my mind, sending an involuntary shudder through my body. "It is very odd," I found myself agreeing, though I strained to keep my voice even and casual. The words felt hollow, a feeble attempt to mask the unease that twisted in my gut. "I may as well move my stuff now then."

"I don't think they'd mind," Glenda remarked.

My voice dropped to a softer register, a reflection of the concern that lingered beneath my composed exterior. "Do you know if Kain slept alright?" The question was directed at Glenda, but my gaze drifted toward Kain, who was showing signs of waking.

"I assume so. I didn't notice anything unusual," she answered, her response straightforward. "Why do you ask?" Her inquiry, simple on the surface, felt laden with a deeper probing for my motives.

"Just making sure we're all safe, I guess." The words were a shield, a vague explanation for the genuine concern that drove me to ask. Safety had become a precious commodity, its assurance found not in grand gestures but in the small checks we made on each other.

"You could ask him yourself, he is awake now," Glenda suggested flatly, her statement a gentle nudge towards direct communication.

"Sure, okay," I agreed, nodding, though the prospect of broaching the subject directly filled me with an inexplicable hesitance. "I'll do that then. I'll just grab my bag first." The smile I offered Glenda was uncomfortable, a poor mask for the mix of concern and responsibility that tugged at me.

Pushing my way inside Jamie's tent, I was acutely aware of the delicate balance we all maintained, each of us orbiting the others in a silent dance of mutual support and individual resilience.

❖

"You two look well," I ventured as I stood up, striving to infuse a note of cheer into my voice despite the complexity of emotions swirling within me.

"Well enough," came Jamie's succinct reply, his voice carrying an undercurrent of resilience mixed with resignation.

"I'm just collecting my suitcase to take to the other tent," I explained, deliberately keeping my gaze away from Joel. The last thing I wanted was to make the situation more uncomfortable than it already was. I hastily gathered the few items of clothing scattered on the floor beside my bag, stuffing them in before zipping it up with a decisive motion.

"Why?" Jamie's voice cut through the air, a note of curiosity or perhaps challenge in his tone.

I paused, the question hanging between us, heavy with implications. "Oh," I began, my voice slightly hesitant as I avoided turning back to face them. "Kain and I thought it would be a good idea if we took the third tent and left you and Joel to have this one," I replied, trying to sound matter-of-fact. "And Luke if he ever stays with us," I added, almost as an afterthought, though the mention of Luke carried with it a weight of unspoken concerns and questions.

"Hmph," Jamie scoffed, a sound rich with skepticism and perhaps a hint of disdain. "I'm not sure Luke will be spending many nights with us."

His words left me momentarily puzzled, my brow furrowing in confusion. Jamie's comment hinted at something deeper, a story untold or expectations unmet regarding Luke. Sure, Luke had been distracted, a shadow figure flitting in and out of our collective existence, but his need for rest, for a place among us, remained undeniable—at least, in my eyes.

With the bag now in tow, I felt the weight of the unspoken hanging heavy in the air. I chose not to press further, to delve into the meaning behind Jamie's words or to challenge the skepticism that laced them. Instead, I let myself out of the tent without another word, the act of leaving marking a silent acknowledgment of the complexities and tensions that wove through our group, binding us together even as they pulled us apart.

❖

"Do you have a preference as to side?" I called out to Kain, my voice echoing slightly as I emerged from the dimness of Jamie's tent into the more open space where our new dwelling stood. The transition from the sheltered interior to the outside world felt symbolic, a step into a new chapter of our shared survival.

"They're both the same, really," Kain replied, his voice stretching as leisurely as his arms above his head. There was a simplicity to his response, a readiness to adapt that I admired.

"Fair enough," I responded with a casual shrug, my mind already turning over the possibilities of our new living arrangement. Carrying my bag into the tent, I chose a corner in the left wing almost instinctively, setting down my belongings with a sense of finality. The act of unravelling my sleeping bag and smoothing it out on the floor, meticulously working out the lumps of dust beneath it, was meditative.

Each thump against the ground served as a reminder of the new reality we were carving out in this unfamiliar world.

"So, this is home," I reminded myself with a murmur, the words barely audible. The thought of personalising this space, of adding the comforts of a large pillow or two, drawers, hangers, and especially some form of light, flickered through my mind like a distant dream. The idea of sleeping here, under the shelter of the tent rather than by the campfire, seemed almost luxurious in its novelty.

A slight grimace marred my expression as I considered the distance between this makeshift home and the possibility of bringing my children here. The ache of missing them was a constant companion, softened only by the hope that they were too engrossed in the joys of spending school holidays with their grandparents to feel the weight of my absence.

"I'm going for a walk to the Drop Zone," I announced, stepping back out into the relentless brightness of the day. The cloudless sky overhead seemed to mock the complexity of our lives on the ground. "Take stock of what Luke's left us."

"I doubt you'll find anything new. I haven't seen him yet this morning," Glenda's words were a gentle reality check. "But I'm sure there might be useful things we didn't notice before," she quickly added, her voice tinged with optimism as she caught the fleeting shadow of disappointment on my face.

❖

Taking my time, I trudged through the thick dust, my footsteps a slow, deliberate dance with the earth beneath me. Each step kicked up clouds of dust that seemed to defy gravity, lingering in the air with a persistence that caught my attention. It fascinated me, this dance of particles, suspended as if time itself had slowed to marvel at their grace. *The dust must be exceptionally fine and light*, I mused, its behaviour unlike anything I'd encountered before, a small wonder in our new world.

As I approached the large, vacant screen of the Portal, I detoured to the right, passing through the small rock-pile gate that served as the Drop Zone's informal entrance. The piles of rocks, haphazard yet deliberate, felt like silent guardians to the trove of discarded hopes and potential resources that lay beyond.

Despite Glenda's earlier prediction, a part of me had held onto a sliver of hope that perhaps Luke had left something new, something overlooked in our previous forays. However, it didn't take long for me to conclude that the Drop Zone remained unchanged since my last visit. Luke had not been here, or if he had, he'd left no trace of his passage. The realisation was a quiet disappointment, a reminder of the unpredictability and often fruitlessness of our scavenging efforts.

NEW TOY

1338.208.2

"Glenda's cooking breakfast," Kain's voice pierced the silence, pulling me back from my reverie amidst the dust and collected items at the Drop Zone.

I looked up, a flicker of surprise crossing my face. "You came all that way to tell me that?" My voice carried a mix of amusement and disbelief. The thought of breakfast seemed almost too good to be true.

Kain laughed, the sound carrying easily in the open air. "She's insisting that we all eat a hearty meal. We need to keep our strength up for the busy day ahead of us," he explained, his grin infectious.

"Sounds like she has plans," I replied, my laughter mingling with his. The prospect of Glenda taking charge, ensuring we were well-fed and prepared for whatever tasks lay ahead, was both comforting and slightly amusing.

"I believe so," Kain affirmed, now standing beside me. "So, what's your assessment?" he inquired, his gaze sweeping over the Drop Zone, curiosity evident in his tone.

Caught off guard by the question, I paused, "Oh," letting the word hang in the air as I gathered my thoughts. I considered the practical needs of our settlement, the balance between immediate necessities and long-term sustainability. "I'd really like us to get some more concrete poured for the sheds. Nearly everything here has been here for less than twenty-four hours and it's already covered in a layer of fine dust," I explained, demonstrating my point by swiping my finger along the top of a large tent box, revealing a layer of dust on my fingertip to Kain.

"I don't think it matters what we do," Kain replied, his tone resigned yet pragmatic. "We're never going to stop that, but the sheds should help."

"Hmm," I murmured, my mind returning to the myriad tasks that awaited us, the constant battle against the encroaching dust a minor yet persistent reminder of the challenges we faced.

"Any more tents?" Kain's question brought me back to the present.

"Yeah," I answered, scanning the area. "Looks like there's only one. We can take the boxes back to camp when we go for breakfast."

"Yeah," Kain agreed with a chuckle, his earlier sombreness momentarily forgotten. "I'm sure Glenda will get it up quick."

I nodded, a sense of admiration in my agreement. "She definitely knows what she's doing with them. Far more than I do," I admitted, the acknowledgment of Glenda's competence and our collective reliance on each other's strengths a grounding thought.

"And me," Kain added sombrely, his voice carrying a hint of self-reflection.

As I glanced over at Kain, I realised that he was grappling with more challenges than I had initially perceived. Despite his youthful age and the noticeable difference in our heights, Kain's dedication and skill had already made a significant impact. His work with the concrete had not only impressed me but also highlighted his valuable contributions to our collective efforts. "Don't doubt yourself, Kain. You've got amazing skills," I assured him, my tone imbued with genuine respect and encouragement.

"Thanks," he responded, his reply brief yet carrying a weight of appreciation. Then, abruptly, his attention shifted, his head snapping up. "Is that a pillow?"

"Where?" I found myself asking, my interest piqued, eyes straining to follow the direction of his pointing finger. The prospect, no matter how slim, stirred a flicker of hope within me. The discomfort of last night's sleep was still fresh, a sore reminder of our austere living conditions.

"Wedged between the two boxes," Kain clarified, his movements quick as he navigated through the makeshift aisles created by our organised chaos. "It is," he exclaimed, his voice lifted in triumph as he retrieved the pillow from its hiding spot.

"Just the one?" The words left my mouth even as a part of me already knew the answer.

"Looks like it," he confirmed, making his way back to me, the pillow in hand.

I couldn't help but frown at the realisation. "Like one pillow will do us much good," I remarked, the bitterness in my voice betraying my frustration. The thought lingered, heavy with irony—how such a small comfort could have significantly improved the quality of my rest last night. Yet, despite the sting of missed opportunity, the discovery of even a single pillow felt like a small victory.

"What are you two creeping about for?" Luke's voice, unmistakable and imbued with his characteristic briskness, sliced through the stillness of the morning as he approached the Drop Zone.

Both Kain and I spun around, the suddenness of his voice jolting us from our focus on the newly discovered pillow. "Hey Luke!" My response was sharp, a mix of surprise and accusation. "When did you drop off the sleeping bags?"

Luke paused, his expression turning contemplative as if trying to recall a detail amidst the blur of his tasks. "Umm," he began, "Would have been sometime late yesterday afternoon or early evening. Why?" His question, simple and direct, seemed oblivious to the undercurrent of frustration his absence had stirred.

My irritation found a voice, tinged with sarcasm, as I snatched the single pillow from Kain and thrust it towards Luke. "Didn't you think it might be a good idea to let someone know?" The words were more a jab than a question, a release valve for the pent-up annoyance at his lack of communication.

Luke's attempt to respond was stammered, cut short by my continued argument. "If Glenda hadn't sent Kain over to collect the box of tent pegs, we wouldn't have had them for sleeping last night," I pointed out, the frustration in my voice rising with each word. I glanced at Kain, seeking an ally in this moment of tension.

Kain, caught in the crossfire, opted for a non-committal retreat, his hands raised in surrender and his head shaking in disbelief as he backed away slowly, unwilling to be drawn into the fray.

Luke's retort came swiftly, his patience evaporating. "I have a lot planned to bring through the Portal for you, and I don't have the time to take it further than the Drop Zone," he countered, his tone edging towards defensive. "Besides, wasn't the Drop Zone your idea? You're the one who told me to leave stuff there."

His words struck a chord, a reminder of the agreed-upon system that now seemed to backfire in the face of practical reality. "Yeah, but you need to at least tell someone," I insisted, my argument losing steam even as I made it.

"I don't have time for that crap, Paul!" Luke's voice snapped, sharper now, his frustration mirroring my own. "You, or someone else, will just have to check frequently."

The confrontation, fuelled by mutual stress and the pressure of our circumstances, left me momentarily deflated. As much as I relished the verbal sparring with Luke, a part of me recognised the validity in his argument. Despite the annoyance it caused, the Drop Zone was indeed my idea, and his contributions, however unannounced, were invaluable. Reluctantly, I backed off.

"Hey, Kain!" Luke's call cut through the tension that had lingered from our previous conversation, shifting the focus entirely. "Do you still have the keys to your ute?"

Kain's immediate response was to pat down his jeans in a near-reflex action, his movements quick and purposeful. When his hand emerged from the back pocket with the keys, a small wave of relief seemed to wash over him. "Actually, I do," he announced, a note of surprise in his voice as if he hadn't expected to find them. The keys dangled in the air between us.

"If you give them to me, I'll bring your ute through," Luke offered calmly, his demeanour unflappable as always.

My eyes widened in response, the implications of Luke's words slowly sinking in. *A ute? Luke's bringing us a ute?* The possibility seemed almost too good to be true.

"Really?" Kain asked, his excitement palpable as he moved closer to hand over the keys.

Luke's nod was all the confirmation we needed. "That's mad!" Kain exclaimed, the keys now securely in Luke's possession. The promise of having a vehicle at our disposal was thrilling.

This is so exciting, I thought to myself, a flicker of personal longing crossing my mind. *I want my car!* Yet, almost as quickly as the excitement had risen, it was tempered by a more pragmatic concern. "But what happens when it runs out of fuel?" I asked, unable to keep the skepticism from my voice.

"I'm working on a solution for that," Luke assured us, though his answer was far from satisfying.

"Like what?" I pressed, seeking a more concrete plan.

Luke's shrug was noncommittal, his response, "I'm not a hundred percent sure yet, but I'm getting there, so I'll let you know when I do," did little to alleviate my doubts.

"That's very vague of you," I remarked, my skepticism deepening.

"Have you spoken to my mother?" Kain asked, interrupting our minor squabble.

"Umm, nope," Luke's response was casual, almost dismissively so, as if the sensitivity of Kain's query barely registered on his radar.

"So, she has no idea where I am?" Kain pressed, his voice laced with an undercurrent of anxiety. It was clear this was more than just a passing concern for him.

Luke shook his head, a gesture that seemed to carry more finality than words. "Not that I know of." His tone was nonchalant, but the implications of his words were anything but.

"Don't you think you should tell her?" The words tumbled out of my mouth before I could stop them, driven by a sense of righteousness. "You know that his fiancée is pregnant, right?" It was a low blow, but I felt the situation warranted it.

"Umm," Luke's annoyance was palpable, a sharp contrast to his previous indifference. "Have you asked me to tell Claire and the kids where you are?" His counter-question was like a slap, forcing me to confront my own hypocrisy.

I fell silent, the weight of his question anchoring me to the spot. I hadn't. And the truth was, I had no intention of letting Luke do that. Not until I was ready for Mack and Rose to join me, preferably without Claire. The silence that followed was heavy, filled with the unsaid and the undone.

"That's what I thought," Luke sneered, his voice breaking the tension. He took a deep breath, as if bracing himself for what came next. "The less anyone outside of Clivilius knows of its existence, the better," he said, his tone firm, leaving no room for argument. "It's safer for all of us that way." His words were like a decree, setting the boundaries of our secrecy.

I nodded, the action more reflexive than anything. My mind was racing, thoughts swirling with questions and concerns. As I studied Luke, I couldn't help but wonder what he was holding back. *Had he found Cody? Did he have more information on the Guardians?* Questions I wanted to ask but didn't dare in front of Kain. *The less anyone inside of Clivilius knows what is really going on, the better. At least until Luke and I could work out what really was going on.* It was a delicate balance, one that we needed to tread carefully.

Kain's hesitation was palpable, a contradiction to Luke's decisiveness. "But I guess I could try and bring your mother through the Portal, if you'd like?" Luke's offer was unexpected, a glimmer of compromise in the rigid stance he'd taken.

"No, I think we could do without her," Kain replied, his voice steady but his body language betraying a hint of reluctance. "For now at least," he added quickly, as if to soften the blow of his words.

My head tilted sideways, an involuntary response to the undercurrents of intrigue that seemed to be unravelling. *A bit of tension there maybe?* It was a rhetorical question, even to myself.

"Well, I'd better go get your ute," Luke announced, his voice cutting through the stillness that had settled around us. His statement seemed to mark the end of our current discussion, a signal that it was time to shift gears—literally and figuratively. He turned to walk away, his movements brisk, a man on a mission.

"Oh. Hey, Luke," I called out, a sudden thought striking me. It seemed only fair to bring this up now. "Can you bring Jamie's car through too?" If Kain was getting his ute, then it was only right. Equality, even in vehicle retrieval, seemed like a small but significant form of fairness.

"Umm, nope," Luke teased, his tone playful yet final. It was a response that irked me, the simplicity of his refusal without room for negotiation.

"Why not?" I couldn't hide the annoyance that crept into my voice. It was frustrating, dealing with Luke's sometimes arbitrary decisions.

Luke's expression shifted, the playfulness draining away to be replaced by a seriousness that was rarely seen. "I need it to drive to Collinsvale," he explained, his tone suggesting that this was a matter of practicality rather than choice.

"Where the hell is Collinsvale?" I asked, turning to Kain for some context.

"Not far from his house," Kain supplied, his voice carrying a note of nonchalance. It was an answer, yet it provided little in the way of real information.

I turned back to Luke, a plan formulating in my mind. "Oh. So, you could walk there then," I said, my words more an assertion than a question. It was a challenge, lightly veiled in the guise of a suggestion.

Kain laughed, a sound that broke the tension that had begun to coil between Luke and me. "It's not that close," he interjected, his amusement clear.

"Gotta go now," Luke said, his voice carrying a finality that ended the exchange. He smiled and waved, a gesture of farewell that was both friendly and dismissive. *It was Luke's way*, I realised; he navigated our demands and the necessities of our situation with a pragmatism that was both infuriating and admirable.

Glenda's familiar yet muffled voice drifted towards us on the listless air. "Breakfast must be ready," I surmised, my voice carrying a mix of hope and hunger.

"We may as well wait for Luke to bring my ute," Kain mused, his gaze fixed on the horizon. His voice held a note of anticipation. "Imagine the others' surprise when we drive it back to camp." The thought brought a smirk to my face, picturing the bewildered expressions that would greet our grand entrance.

"Yeah, it will be a surprise," I concurred, the idea amusing me. Curiosity then nudged my thoughts in another direction. "By the way, have you seen Jamie or Joel yet this morning?"

"Yeah," Kain replied, his attention briefly meeting mine. "I went and saw them just after you left. I'm surprised Luke didn't ask about them."

I turned towards Kain, a thoughtful expression crossing my face. "I think Luke's a bit distracted right now," I offered, trying to excuse his oversight.

Both our jaws dropped in astonishment as the ute came bunny-hopping through the wall of swirling colours, a spectacle that defied the mundane expectations of vehicle arrival. It stuttered and stalled, coming to an abrupt halt. The sight was so unexpected, so out of the ordinary, that we couldn't control our laughter. We doubled over, half bent in stitches.

A sulking Luke stepped from the ute, his expression a mix of frustration and resignation. It was a look that only added fuel to our amusement.

"Luke! Wait!" I called out between bursts of laughter, trying to catch my breath and regain some semblance of composure. Luke stopped in his tracks, yet he didn't turn to face us. His posture stiff, a clear sign of his annoyance.

"I said no," he stated bluntly, his voice cutting through the humour of the moment like a cold blade. It was a reminder of the tension that had preceded his departure.

I stepped beside my brother, placing a hand on his shoulder in a gesture of solidarity. "I know," I said, my voice softening. "It's not about Jamie's car," I continued, lowering my voice further. It was important to make Luke understand that our concerns went beyond the trivialities of the moment.

"Then what is it?" Luke snapped, his patience thin. "I'm already late for breakfast with Karen." His words carried a hint of desperation.

My mouth dropped open, a gape of disbelief that far surpassed my reaction to Luke's erratic driving earlier. "You're going out for breakfast!" The words tumbled out, laced with incredulity. "We're stuck in this dustbowl, and you're going out for breakfast? Unbelievable!" I spun away, a whirl of frustration, my gaze landing on the barren landscape that stretched out beyond us—a brutal reminder of our isolation.

"It's not like that," Luke's voice came from behind me, a hint of urgency as he reached out, his hand clasping my arm, pulling me back from the edge of my annoyance.

I wheeled around to face him, my frustration boiling over. "Then explain yourself," I demanded, my stance rigid, expecting a justification that would somehow make sense of his seemingly frivolous plans.

Luke chuckled softly, a sound that in any other context might have been comforting. But now, it only served to fan the flames of my irritation.

"What?" I barked, unable to mask the annoyance that seeped into my tone.

"You're so funny when you're mad," he said, his grin wide, as if he found genuine amusement in my frustration.

"Oh, shut up!" My protest was half-hearted, a smile threatening to break through despite my best efforts to stay annoyed.

"Ahh," Luke teased, his finger pointing accusatorially at the twitching corner of my mouth—a traitorous sign of my crumbling facade.

I brushed his hand away, a mix of irritation and amusement swirling within me. "Stop being an idiot," I chided, even as the tension between us began to dissolve into the familiarity of our sibling bond. "What do you want?"

"You wanted me, remember?" Luke laughed, his eyes twinkling with mischief.

My face warmed, a blush of sheepish realisation. "Oh yeah," I admitted.

"But first, why are you having breakfast with Karen?" I pressed, curious about the underlying reason for his departure.

Luke's gaze darted about, a signal of his discomfort. Kain, oblivious to our exchange, sat in the front seat of his ute, poised for departure.

"Well?" My impatience was palpable, a prompt for him to divulge his plans.

"I'm hoping to bring her and her husband here," Luke revealed, his voice a soft murmur.

I gasped, the sound sharp in the quiet that enveloped us. My face turned serious, the weight of his intention sinking in. "Are you sure that's a good idea? We're not exactly a thriving community." My words were laced with skepticism, a reflection of the doubts that continued to plague me.

"Not yet you're not," Luke conceded, his agreement a gentle reminder of our shared aspirations. "But you will be."

I eyed him suspiciously, my mind racing with the implications of his plans. "And how can they help?" I asked, my curiosity piqued despite my reservations.

"Their skills will be pretty evident. Give them a warm welcome," Luke replied, his confidence in his decision unwavering.

"Of course," I responded, nodding slowly. In the end, I knew the decision wasn't mine to make. This place was challenging enough without adding unnecessary conflicts. Luke's intentions, though bold, reminded me of the broader vision we shared—a vision of transformation and growth. It was a hard life here, but perhaps I didn't need to make it harder by resisting change.

"Now, what is it you wanted?" Luke's voice pulled me back from my thoughts, his gaze steady and expectant.

"Oh," I started, my mind scrambling to collect the scattered pieces of my brain. "We need some more wood for the campfire." The words felt mundane, yet the need was as vital as any other.

"Sure," Luke replied with a nod, his assurance quick and unwavering. "I'll make sure you have some before nightfall."

"And Kain and Glenda need fresh clothes," I continued, the list of necessities growing as I spoke.

"Okay," Luke nodded once more, the simplicity of his response belying the importance of the task. And with that, he turned toward the Portal, the gateway that connected us to a world we were both part of and apart from.

"And Joel too," I added quickly, the name springing to mind as an afterthought but no less important.

Luke's eyes widened slightly at the addition, a visible sign of the mounting pressures. "I'll get Kain and Glenda's clothes first," he conceded. "But I'll need you to get me Joel's address."

"Why do you need his address?" I questioned, the suggestion seeming to complicate what I had imagined would be a simple task. "Can't you just buy them some new ones? It'd be much easier."

"We're running low on cash," Luke stated flatly, his voice devoid of emotion yet heavy with implication.

"Already?" My exclamation was more of a reflex than a question, a verbal manifestation of the disbelief and concern that knotted in my stomach.

"Yes, already," Luke confirmed, his eyes meeting mine in a brief exchange that conveyed the extent of his admission. "And get me Kain's wallet at some point for me, would you," he added, the request trailing off as he stepped through the Portal, leaving me to ponder the implications of his departure.

I watched as the vibrant colours of the Portal faded, a visual echo of Luke's presence disappearing into another reality. I sighed softly, the sound a whisper in the vastness that surrounded me. "Stay safe, little brother," I murmured into the silence, a silent prayer to the universe.

A loud honk from the horn jerked me out of my introspection, slicing through the still morning air with an urgency that was hard to ignore. I glanced over at Kain, his impatience palpable even from a distance. With a few long strides, eating up the space between us, I found myself sliding into the passenger seat beside him.

"Let's go!" Kain announced, his enthusiasm manifesting in a thumbs-up that seemed to embody his readiness to tackle whatever lay ahead. His energy was infectious, yet something nagged at the back of my mind.

"No, wait!" The words burst from me as the engine roared to life, a beast awakened, eager to be unleashed.

Kain turned to me, his expression a mix of confusion and mild irritation. "What now?" he asked, his patience thinning.

"We may as well pack those tent boxes in the back," I suggested, the practicality of the idea emerging from the remnants of our earlier conversation. It was a logical step, one that would streamline our efforts and minimise unnecessary back-and-forth trips.

Kain frowned.

"It'll save us coming back for them," I pressed, hoping to appeal to his sense of efficiency. The rationale was sound, but it required a brief delay in our departure, a sacrifice Kain seemed loath to make.

"Fine," Kain huffed, his agreement coming as a begrudging exhale. "But make it quick!" His tone left no room for dawdling, a clear directive that haste was of the essence.

"Oh," I laughed, the humour in the situation not lost on me. I clambered out of my seat, a movement more enthusiastic than graceful. "You're helping too." It was a declaration rather than a request, an invitation to share in the labour.

Kain's eyes rolled, a silent but eloquent commentary on his feelings about the plan. Yet, despite his apparent reluctance, his door opened all the same.

❖

Kain manoeuvred the ute with the precision of a seasoned navigator, threading it carefully through the Drop Zone, a no-man's land that lay between us and the rest of Clivilius. The two small rock piles that flanked the path stood like ancient guardians, silent witnesses to our passage. As we cleared them, I noticed the wheels deliberately veering away from the direction of camp, charting a course that was as unexpected as it was unannounced.

Kain revved the engine, a declaration of intent as much as a necessity. The ute responded with enthusiasm, its wheels biting into the dust, sending plumes of red and orange spiralling into the air, painting the sky with the colours of adventure. The dust swirled around us, a tangible reminder of the untamed world we inhabited.

"What are you doing?" I couldn't keep the mixture of apprehension and excitement from my voice, my grip tightening on the side of the seat as if to brace myself against the unknown.

"Just a short detour," Kain replied, his grin infectious, wide enough to dispel any lingering doubts. His confidence was a beacon, guiding us through the uncertainty of the detour. The ute took a sharp turn, skirting the roughly marked perimeter of the Drop Zone, a clear departure from the beaten path.

Laughter bubbled up between us, a shared moment of joyous rebellion against the caution that had begun to define our existence in Clivilius. It was a laughter born of complicity, of shared secrets and the thrill of the unexpected.

The journey was rough, a testament to the untamed nature of the land. The ute churned through the dust, its passage marked by a trail of disruption in the otherwise untouched landscape. We navigated over small hills, each one a minor victory in our impromptu expedition, heading towards the imposing silhouette of the mountains in the distance. Their presence loomed large, a reminder of the vastness of the world beyond our immediate concerns.

My heart raced with the exhilaration of the moment. This detour, this brief escape from the confines of our daily struggles, was a vivid reminder of the beauty and excitement that still existed in the world around us. It was a stark contrast to the often grim reality of our situation in Clivilius, a place where joy was a rare and precious commodity.

As we bounced and jostled along the makeshift path, I found myself reflecting on the moments of happiness that had punctuated my time in this strange, new world. This detour, this moment of unfettered freedom and camaraderie, was undoubtedly one of those moments. *Well, maybe just one exception*, I mused to myself, a smile playing on my lips as I thought of another time, another joy that had briefly illuminated the darkness of Clivilius. In that moment, with the wind in our faces and the untamed world stretching out before us, I was reminded of the unpredictable beauty of life, even in the most unlikely of places.

"How much petrol?" My voice pierced the roar of the engine and the rush of wind, a pressing concern as we neared the crest of another hill. The anticipation of our fuel status hung between us, a tangible reminder of our precarious adventure's limitations.

"Still three-quarters," Kain shouted back, his voice steady and reassuring over the din. The response was a beacon of hope, a promise of continued freedom, however fleeting it might be.

As we reached the summit, my breath caught in my throat. The world unfolded before us in a tapestry of stark beauty, a vast expanse of reds, browns, and oranges that painted the earth in hues of fire and earth. It stretched endlessly, a wild and untamed landscape that spoke of ancient times and secrets buried deep beneath the soil. The dark grey mountains stood as silent sentinels in the distance, their peaks slicing into the clear blue sky, marking the boundary between our little corner of the world and the unknown.

"Floor it!" The excitement was irresistible, a command born of the moment's exhilaration. I wanted to chase the horizon, to defy the constraints of our reality, if only for an instant.

Kain's response was immediate, his foot slamming down on the pedal with a determination that matched my own. The ute leaped forward, a beast unleashed, its engine roaring with newfound vigour. We surged ahead, leaving a billowing cloud of dust in our wake, a testament to our passage through this desolate yet beautiful land.

The thrill was short-lived. Barely a hundred metres into our mad dash, the engine sputtered and died, the sudden silence a disappointing contrast to the moments before. The ute coasted to a stop, its momentum spent, leaving us adrift in the vastness of the landscape.

I turned to Kain, confusion and disbelief etching my features. "What the hell?" My question hung in the air, an echo of our shared dismay.

Kain's hands worked the ignition, the engine chugging in protest as he turned the key several times. But the only answer was silence, a stubborn refusal that left us stranded, the adventure abruptly grounded.

As we disembarked from the ute, the silence of our surroundings enveloped us, the mechanical heartbeat we had become accustomed to during our journey, fading into a distant memory. The act of stepping out felt like a concession to our predicament, an acknowledgment of the unexpected pause in our adventure. We made our way to the front of the vehicle, the ground beneath our feet shifting softly, a reminder of the arid landscape that had claimed our progress.

Kain, with a sense of purpose, lifted the bonnet, and his exclamation, "Shit!" sliced through the quiet. It was a simple word, but it carried the weight of our collective frustration and disbelief.

I peered over his shoulder, the sight that greeted us was one of desolation. The engine, the heart of our ute, was cloaked in dust—a testament to the harshness of the terrain we had attempted to conquer. The fine, pervasive dust clung to every surface, insidious in its infiltration.

"How are we going to clean that?" Kain's question hung between us, a challenge to our resourcefulness in the face of adversity.

Without a clear answer, I acted on impulse, leaning in and blowing hard into the cramped space. The result was immediate—a large cloud of fine dust billowed into the air, a visual echo of my efforts. "Help me blow," I called over my shoulder, a request that was both absurd and essential under the circumstances.

Kain's initial reaction was one of surprise, his eyes wide as he processed the unconventional nature of our solution. Yet, without protest, he shrugged his shoulders—a gesture of resigned acceptance—and joined me. Together, we exhaled forcefully, our breaths merging in a shared endeavour to revive the ute.

"It's working," I observed, a note of surprise in my voice as I stepped back, gasping for fresh air. The process was arduous, a testament to our determination. Over half an hour of almost continuous blowing, interspersed with attempts to coax the engine back to life, became a battle of wills against the elements.

"I'll go give it another shot," Kain announced, determination lacing his words as he climbed back into the driver's seat. I took a few steps back, watching with a mix of hope and exhaustion.

Finally, our persistence was rewarded. A large cloud of loosened dust heralded the engine's triumphant return to life. Relief and triumph flooded through me, manifesting in a wide, albeit tired, grin. I gave Kain a thumbs up—a silent celebration of our victory over the odds.

Then, with a sense of finality, I closed the bonnet, the sound echoing in the quiet that surrounded us. Climbing back into my seat, I settled in, the familiar contours offering a small comfort. The engine's steady hum was a welcome backdrop, a sign of our resilience, and a reminder of the journey that still lay ahead.

The journey back to camp was an ordeal, each metre fought for against the relentless grip of the thick dust beneath us. The ute struggled, its tires grasping for traction in spots where the dust seemed to conspire against us, almost swallowing us whole on several occasions.

"We need some roads," Kain's voice cut through the tension, his words carrying a mixture of frustration and resolve. He glanced at me, as if seeking confirmation or perhaps a shared recognition of the problem. "We need to contain this dust!"

I scrunched my face, deep in thought. The idea of combating the omnipresent dust seemed like a battle against the very nature of this place. *This dust is just not containable,* I lamented internally, the realisation settling in with a weighty sense of resignation.

"Even if we just clear a few trails down to the hard crust beneath, should be good enough to drive on," Kain proposed, his voice carrying a hint of optimism amidst the bleakness of my thoughts.

My eyes widened at the suggestion. *Why didn't I think of that?* The idea sparked a brief flare of hope, a potential solution that seemed so simple yet so effective. But almost as quickly as it appeared, a wave of overwhelming reality crashed over me. "There's so much to do," I murmured, the scope of our task daunting. "Where do we even start?"

"We need a bulldozer," Kain chuckled, the laugh more a release of tension than amusement.

His laughter barely registered before I found myself considering his joke with grave seriousness. "That's actually not a bad idea," I said, turning to him with a look of sudden inspiration. The notion of a bulldozer, absurd as it might have sounded moments before, now seemed like a rational step towards reclaiming some semblance of control over our environment.

"More people?" Kain mused, his gaze fixed on the path ahead, squinting as if the answer might be etched somewhere on the horizon.

"Huh?" The shift in conversation caught me off guard, my mind still wrestling with the logistics of our newfound plan. I turned back to face the front, trying to align my thoughts with the reality that awaited us.

As Kain eased the ute into camp, the sight that greeted us was unexpected. Two unfamiliar figures stood near Glenda, their presence a reminder of the world beyond our dust-enshrouded struggles. "Shit!" The word escaped my lips before I could contain it. "I forgot about Karen!"

THE BUG LADY AND THE DUST REMOVER

1338.208.3

"That was bloody awesome!" Kain's enthusiasm was infectious, his high-five a physical punctuation to our shared thrill. We stood at the front of the ute, its once clean surface now a testament to our adventure, covered in layers of the very dust that had threatened to halt our journey.

"Apart from clogging up the engine!" My laughter mingled with his, the relief of having overcome our mechanical challenge lending a lightness to the moment. It was one of those rare times when the journey itself overshadowed the destination, each obstacle a shared victory.

"Come on," Kain prodded, his eyes sparkling with the residue of our recent escapade. "You have to admit, even that was fun." And in truth, amidst the laughter and the transient worry, it had been.

"Guys!" Glenda's voice cut through our mirth, grounding us with the reminder of our present reality. "We have two new guests." Her announcement was a pivot, a momentary bridge from our shared joy back to the responsibilities that awaited us.

"I wouldn't call them guests," Jamie's interjection was swift, his tone laced with his typical candour. "They're not going anywhere."

And Jamie's back to his usual self, I mused silently as the group lapsed into an awkward silence. His ability to cut through the pretence with his straightforward observations was as reassuring as it was jarring. I may have been a bit late to the introduction, but recalling my promise to Luke, I stepped forward, intent on bridging the gap between our established group and our newest arrivals.

"I'm Paul," I introduced myself, extending my hand in a gesture of welcome. It was a small act, but in the context of our secluded existence, it held the weight of an unspoken pledge of solidarity.

"Chris Owen," the man replied, his grip firm and assured. His appearance, short and with thinning hair, belied a strength that was immediately apparent in his handshake. "And this is my wife, Karen." His introduction was straightforward, a simple declaration that nonetheless hinted at the complexities of their story.

"Nice to meet you, Karen," I continued, turning my attention to her.

As Kain stepped forward to make his introductions, the dynamics of our group subtly shifted, the initial awkwardness giving way to the beginnings of understanding. "Kain," he said

"Ahh," Karen responded, her eyes lighting up with recognition at Kain's mention of being Jamie's nephew.

"I see you've met Jamie," I remarked, gesturing towards where Jamie stood, a stoic figure with Henri, sitting uncomfortably at his feet. *Henri must be feeling adventurous today,* I mused internally, finding a moment of amusement in the rarity of Henri's ventures outside.

"We've only just met," Karen responded, her tone carrying a hint of warmth, perhaps gratitude for the recognition. "But Luke has told us a lot about him over the years." Her words painted a picture of long-standing connections, of stories shared and bonds formed over time.

"Us?" Chris interjected, his confusion manifesting in a furrowed brow. "I've never heard his name before," he admitted, the perplexity evident in his voice and the slight downturn of his expression.

Karen's response to her husband was patient, tinged with an explanatory tone. "Not you, darling. Jane," she clarified, addressing the misunderstanding with a familiarity that spoke of shared histories and private jokes.

"Who's Jane?" Kain queried, his curiosity piqued, a reflection of our collective interest in the unfolding narrative.

"Oh," I exclaimed, a lightbulb moment of realisation. "You must be one of Luke's bus friends." The pieces fell into place, recalling Luke's stories of Karen and Jane, two names that had peppered our conversations over the last few years. Yet, the Karen before us defied the image I had unwittingly constructed—a contrast that served as a reminder of the gap between perception and reality.

"Yes," Karen affirmed, her response simple yet laden with the weight of shared experiences and memories with Luke that we were only now beginning to uncover.

"But where is Luke?" Kain's question redirected our focus, his gaze sweeping towards Chris as if he might hold the answer.

"He's not here," Karen answered for her husband, her voice carrying a hint of resignation or perhaps acceptance of the situation's fluidity.

I exchanged a glance with Glenda, seeking some understanding or insight. Luke's decision to bring the couple here and his implicit trust in me to lead the welcoming committee was clear, but his absence left a void filled with unanswered questions and unspoken expectations.

"Appears this was another accident," Glenda observed, her shoulders slumping in a mix of disappointment and resignation. It was a sentiment that seemed to echo our collective realisation that despite our best efforts, the unpredictable nature of our existence here often left us at the mercy of circumstances beyond our control.

"Figures," Kain muttered, his words barely audible, a verbal shrug that encapsulated the blend of resignation and resilience that had come to define us.

"Not to be rude, but what do you actually do?" My curiosity was genuine, tinged with a hint of skepticism as I struggled to see how Karen's expertise fit into our rugged, survival-driven existence.

"I'm an entomologist," Karen replied, her face alight with a pride that was both infectious and bewildering. Her enthusiasm for her profession was clear, but its relevance to our immediate needs was not.

"A what?" I found myself echoing, the unfamiliar term hanging awkwardly in the air.

"She studies bugs," Kain interjected, his simplification both helpful and seemingly dismissive.

"Oh," was all I managed, my mind racing. *How the heck is this bug lady supposed to help us?* The thought was uncharitable but honest, reflecting my inability to connect the dots between her expertise and our day-to-day challenges.

"Insects," Karen corrected sharply, her glare at Kain a silent rebuke for his oversimplification. "Insects, not bugs." Her distinction made a point, though the significance was lost on me.

"Well," Karen began, launching into an explanation with a passion that was almost tangible. "I work with the University of Tasmania to understand how insects contribute to ecosystems and work with local communities and environmental groups to petition for greater protections," she explained, her words painting a picture of a world far removed from the immediate practicalities of our survival.

"That's great!" I exclaimed, more out of politeness than comprehension. My mind was still trying to bridge the gap between her world of insects and our immediate needs. I turned towards Chris, hoping for something more tangibly useful to our situation.

"I do yard work," Chris stated simply.

Ooh, my internal response was immediate. *A dust remover! Perfect!* His profession, mundane as it might sound, was exactly the kind of practical skill we were in desperate need of.

"Yard work?" Kain echoed.

Chris crouched down, his action drawing our collective attention as he scooped up a handful of the omnipresent dust. "It's everywhere!" I couldn't help but exclaim, feeling an instant kinship with Chris. His observation was so simple, yet it spoke volumes. *I like him already*, I decided, appreciating the practical implications of his skills.

Chris let the dust cascade through his fingers, a silent demonstration of the challenge we faced. "Yeah, I've noticed that," he responded with a calmness that was reassuring. His glance towards Karen was tender, a silent pact between them. "But if this is our home now, we'll find a way."

The statement, so quietly made, was like a lighthouse in the storm of our uncertainty. *Luke is a genius*, I realised with a surge of optimism. In bringing Karen and Chris here, Luke had somehow managed to balance our need for immediate, practical solutions with the longer-term vision of sustainability and ecological balance. Karen's expertise, though initially seeming out of place, offered a broader perspective on our relationship with the environment we were part of. Chris's skills, on the other hand, addressed our immediate challenge of making this place liveable. Together, they represented a blending of the practical and the profound, a reminder that survival was not just about enduring but thriving within the ecosystem we now called home.

"Call me crazy," Karen said, her smile directed at Chris. "But I trust Luke."

Jamie's reaction was immediate, a scoff that cut sharply through the air, his skepticism unmasked and unapologetic. "You're definitely crazy, then," he retorted, his words edged with a sneer that seemed to underscore the divide between hope and reality.

Yet, Karen remained unfazed, a testament to her belief. Her face illuminated with a conviction that seemed to stem from a place of deep certainty. "A beautiful masterpiece starts with a single brushstroke. This is our blank canvas. Let's create a masterpiece. Together." Her words flowed, not just as a retort to Jamie's cynicism but as a vision, a rallying cry for what could be amidst the desolation that surrounded us.

In that moment, my perception of Karen shifted. Here was a woman I had initially doubted, unsure of her place within the harsh reality of our existence. Yet, her optimism, her unwavering belief in the potential of what we could achieve together, struck a chord. Despite my earlier reservations about her expertise in a world that seemed to demand more immediate, practical skills, I found myself unexpectedly inspired. Her optimism, in contrast to the often grim pragmatism that defined our days, offered a different kind of value—a reminder of the importance of hope and vision in the face of adversity.

The couple will make a good addition to the small settlement, I concluded, my earlier skepticism giving way to a cautious optimism. Karen's words, imbued with a sense of possibility, and Chris's practical skills, suddenly seemed not just useful but essential.

"I better check-in with Joel," Jamie's words sliced through the tension that had settled among us. His departure was swift, marked by a light wave and a fleeting expression of courtesy towards our new arrivals. "Nice to meet you both," he offered, before vanishing into the fabric confines of the tent that held so much of our collective concern.

"Joel?" Karen's inquiry, her brow arching in curiosity.

"Jamie's son," Glenda provided, her voice steady but her eyes betraying the complexity of emotions that Joel's situation evoked within us all.

"He's not... been well," I found myself contributing, my gaze flicking to Glenda in a silent plea for guidance. I was treading carefully, wary of dousing the flicker of hope and enthusiasm that Karen and Chris brought with them. "I'm sure he'll be fine after a few days' rest," I hastened to add, an attempt to paint a brighter picture, to preserve the fragile optimism that had just begun to take root among us.

"Yes," Glenda concurred, her sideways glance a silent conversation, an acknowledgment of the delicate balance we were attempting to maintain. "Perhaps you and Kain would be best moving back in there for a short time," she suggested, her nod towards the tent housing Jamie and Joel a directive that sent a ripple of apprehension through me.

My heart sank at the prospect. *Glenda can't be serious*, a thought that was as much a reflex as it was a silent protest.

And then, as if sparked by necessity, inspiration struck. "We have another tent," I declared, the enthusiasm in my voice belying the rapid shift in my emotions. My suggestion, pointing towards the ute, was a lifeline, a tangible solution that suddenly seemed so obvious.

"Brilliant!" Glenda's cry was a mix of relief and approval, a shared recognition of the simple yet effective resolution to our immediate dilemma.

Kain was the first to act, lifting the first of the boxes from the back of the ute. "Looks like they got a little dusty," he observed, the action of blowing the top sending a swirl of red dust into the air.

"Here, let me take that," Chris offered, stepping forward to take the box from Kain. His gesture, simple yet significant, was an act of integration, a physical manifestation of their willingness to become part of our community.

"Thanks," Kain responded.

"May as well put it next to ours, I guess," I suggested, pointing towards the third tent.

Chris nodded and then headed in that direction.

"Tent pegs," I offered, extending the small box towards Karen with a gesture that felt both trivial and essential in the grandeur of our shared endeavours. She thanked me with a nod, her actions brisk as she quickly followed Chris, each step they took together a further integration into our makeshift community.

Turning back to the ute, I hefted the final box, its weight a tangible reminder of the responsibilities we all bore. It was in this moment of transition, as I balanced the load in my arms, that Kain announced his intention to return to the Drop Zone for the concrete.

"Hold up," I found myself saying, my voice a mix of urgency and surprise. The box wobbled precariously as I reached out in a futile attempt to halt Kain's departure.

"What?" Kain's impatience was palpable as he shrugged off my attempt to delay him. "If you want these sheds up, we have to get this concrete poured asap."

I frowned, the logistics of construction and curing times tumbling through my mind. "Five to seven days?" The question hung between us, a verification of our shared understanding.

"Five to seven days," Kain confirmed, his assurance momentarily reassuring. "Although if we're going to keep getting these cloudless skies, we might get away with four."

Glenda's interjection, her confusion mirroring my own earlier uncertainties, was a reminder of the specialised knowledge that our survival had necessitated. "What's five to seven days?" Her query, innocent in its asking, underscored the vast array of skills and information we were all rapidly having to assimilate.

"We have to let the concrete..." I paused, grappling for the correct terminology that Kain had effortlessly used earlier. "Rest," I finally said, the word a poor substitute for the precise process Kain had described but the best I could muster under the weight of her questioning gaze.

"Ah, that makes sense," Glenda's response, a simple acknowledgment, somehow managed to convey understanding. Yet, her acceptance only served to amplify my internal frustration. *Why does everyone act like this should be common knowledge?* The thought echoed in my mind.

"How many sheds?" Glenda's inquiry was practical, a reflection of our shared need to maximise the resources at our disposal.

"Not sure," Kain's response was equally laconic, his gaze fixed on the horizon as if he could summon the answer from the barren landscape itself. "I'll check how many Luke's left us."

"We may as well do as many slabs as possible for the concrete we have," I found myself saying, eager to contribute to the conversation meaningfully. As I looked around at the dusty landscape, a sense of urgency settled within me. The world around us was a canvas of desolation, each grain of sand a silent witness to our struggle. "I don't think we can have too much storage and protection here." My words hung in the air, a reminder of our precarious existence on this frontier of humanity's reach.

"And Luke can always bring us more sheds," Glenda added, her tone imbued with a hint of optimism.

"I'll bring all the concrete supplies we have then," Kain declared, his figure swiftly moving to climb into the front seat.

"I'll come with you," I said, moving toward the passenger side, driven by a desire to be useful.

"No offence," Kain's words were a gentle rebuff, "But maybe you'd be better helping Glenda with the new tent." His decision, while practical, left a sting of exclusion.

"Chris and I can help," Karen's voice, bright and cheerful, broke through my reverie, as she and Chris approached the small group. "We're used to camping when we go on our short trips. Shouldn't take too long."

"That'd be great," Glenda replied.

"Okay," I said, shrugging my shoulders in a gesture of resignation. *Kain doesn't want my help with the concrete, and now Glenda has the new people to help her.* A sense of isolation crept upon me, as if I were adrift. "So, what am I doing now?" My question was a lifeline thrown into the void, a search for connection.

The group fell into silence, a palpable tension that enveloped us like the dust swirling around our feet. I could feel all eyes on me, their gazes weighing heavily. *The lagoon sounds good right now*, I mused silently, yearning for a moment of solitude, a brief escape from the weight of helplessness.

"You're helping us put the tent up," Glenda's voice was decisive, a beacon guiding me back from the brink of isolation.

"Great. Let's get to it," I said, my voice infused with a newfound eagerness.

❖

"I'm going to go check on Kain," I murmured to Glenda, my voice barely rising above the hum of activity surrounding us. She brushed past me, her arms laden with the skeletal framework of another future shelter, another long tent pole balanced precariously against her shoulder.

She paused, her hand finding its way to my shoulder, grounding me amidst my momentary despair. "You okay?" Her gaze pierced through the veil of dust and sweat, seeking out the truth hidden behind my forced bravado.

"Yeah," I managed, contorting my lips into a semblance of a smile. "Tents aren't really my thing," I confessed with a nonchalant shrug, trying to mask the unease that seemed to cling to me like the fine sand underfoot.

"You've done a good job," Glenda reassured me, her voice a soothing balm against the prickling of my insecurities. "I'm sure Kain would appreciate the help too."

"Thanks, Glenda." The gratitude I felt was genuine, a small oasis of warmth in the vast desert of my apprehensions.

"Hey, Glenda, have you seen pole L?" Karen's voice, sharp and clear, cut across the tent site, slicing through our momentary connection.

Glenda's hand tightened on my shoulder, a final, affirming squeeze before she released me back into the whirlwind of our makeshift community. "Let me check," she called out to Karen, her voice carrying over the din of their collective endeavour.

And then she was gone, moving with a purpose that I admired yet was presently struggling to emulate. I watched her for a moment, her figure a constant amidst the flux of our expanding settlement, before turning my attention back to my new task.

Is he going to stay in there all day? The question lingered in my mind like an uninvited guest as I ambled past the tent where Jamie had disappeared earlier to check in on Joel. A flicker of curiosity ignited within me, overpowering my initial reluctance. With cautious steps, drawn by an invisible thread of concern and nosiness, I found myself gravitating towards the tent's entrance.

Gently pushing the flap aside, I peered into the dimly lit interior, my eyebrows arching in mild surprise. Jamie and Joel were ensconced on the mattress, their attention divided between the meagre remnants of food on a plate between them and my sudden appearance. Their faces, etched with the quiet intimacy of shared hardship, turned towards me, marking the end of their secluded moment.

"Sorry, need to get some paper," I muttered, breaking the silence as I navigated towards a small bag of supplies nestled in a corner of the tent. The fabric underfoot whispered secrets with every step I took. "Oh, and I need Joel's address too," I added, the thought springing to mind like a forgotten chore.

"What for?" Jamie's response was sharp, a bark that seemed to slice through the tent's sombre atmosphere.

I met his challenge with a steady gaze, my eyes narrowing slightly. "So Luke can bring him some fresh clothes," I replied, my voice carrying a flat, unyielding tone. There was a brief, charged silence, a standoff not just of words but of wills.

Jamie's demeanour shifted subtly, a silent concession as he gestured for me to pass him the pen and paper. Turning to Joel, his voice softened, "Do you want to try writing?" The question was gentle, an offer of support that seemed at odds with the man I was still getting to know.

"Yeah," Joel's voice was a raspy whisper, a sound of vulnerability and determination intertwined. I watched, a silent observer, as Jamie guided Joel's hand, their actions a delicate dance of patience and care. It was a side of Jamie I hadn't expected, a revelation that unfolded before me in the quiet of the tent.

"Thanks," I said as I collected the paper, the scribbled address a testament to Joel's resilience and Jamie's unexpected tenderness. "Should have it by the end of the day."

"Thanks," Joel's gratitude was palpable, his gaze lifting to meet mine.

"No worries," I responded, the words leaving me with a sense of completion, of having contributed something meaningful, however small. I stepped back into the embrace of the warm sun, leaving the tent and its occupants behind. The exchange with Jamie remained unspoken, yet it hung in the air between us, a silent acknowledgment of something shifted, however slightly, in the intricate web of our survival.

CRANKY DUST

1338.208.1

I wiped the sweat from my forehead, the gritty sensation of dust mingling with perspiration serving as a harsh reminder of the environment's unforgiving nature. My feet dragged through the thick, omnipresent dust, each step a laborious effort that echoed the desolation of our surroundings. Pausing, I shook out the fine, pervasive dust from my shoes for what felt like the umpteenth time, my mind bitterly comparing this to the more forgiving sands of a beach—or even the rugged terrain of Broken Hill. This was a different beast altogether, a relentless, suffocating blanket that seemed to seep into every crevice, both physical and emotional.

The sudden, familiar rumble of the ute's engine cutting through the still, heavy air propelled me into action, my jogging pace a futile attempt to escape the omnipresent dust cloud that trailed my every move. As I approached, Kain greeted me with the window wound down, the interior of the vehicle a brief, tantalising glimpse into a world less choked by dust.

"No Luke?" I inquired, the question hanging between us, laden with unspoken concerns and the weight of our collective dependence on each other's roles in this precarious balance of survival and construction.

"Nope," Kain's response was succinct, a verbal shrug that did little to assuage the knot of worry forming in the pit of my stomach. I couldn't help but wonder about Luke's whereabouts and the silent pressures we all navigated beneath the surface of our makeshift community.

"Need a lift back?" Kain's offer broke through my reverie.

"Nah. All good," I replied, brandishing the pen and folded paper I had been safeguarding in my back pocket as if they were talismans against the uncertainty of our situation. "I'll do an inventory and then I'm going to make Luke some lists." My voice carried a determined undertone, a commitment to getting things done.

Kain's laughter, light and unburdened, floated through the air. "Your inventory will be easy," he joked, a moment of levity in the face of our daunting reality. "I think it's mostly just large shed materials left."

His words, though meant in jest, anchored me back to the purpose of my endeavour. The task of inventory, simple as it might appear, was a linchpin in the delicate machinery of our operations. I was acutely aware of the weight of responsibility that came with construction, far removed from the hobbyist projects of my past. This wasn't about assembling a child's playhouse or piecing together a computer desk; the stakes were infinitely higher, with real consequences for failure.

"They're making quick work with the tent. I'm sure Glenda will enjoy helping you with the slabs," I offered, an attempt to bridge my concerns with the ongoing efforts back at camp.

"Okay," Kain's response was terse, the finality of the conversation underscored by the revving engine and the subsequent kick-up of dust as he drove the ute back towards camp.

I stood there, a solitary figure amidst the swirling dust, watching the vehicle's rear tires bite into the soft earth. The worry lines deepening on my forehead were a mirror to the tracks left by the ute, a physical manifestation of my internal fears. *He'll be lucky if he doesn't get bogged*, I thought.

❖

    The Drop Zone, a sprawling expanse of dust and ambition, had quickly sapped what little energy I had mustered that morning. After a solitary, contemplative lap around the perimeter, I found myself gravitating towards an unassuming box, its surface dust-coated yet inviting. Settling down, the heat enveloped me like a suffocating blanket, and a sense of exhaustion washed over me, leaving me feeling utterly deflated. With a heavy sigh, I smoothed out a piece of paper along my thigh, the texture of the material a startling reminder of the roughness of my hands, dry and gritty from the relentless dust.

    Despite the overwhelming odds, a flicker of hope persisted within me—hope that Luke might procure the right materials for my ambitious project. It was a long shot, given our isolated circumstances and the specific needs of the Drop Zone, yet the possibility of contributing to something tangible spurred a rare surge of optimism. So, with deliberate care, I began to jot down the requirements in very general terms at the top of the page: long posts and shade cloth – the Drop Zone needs some shelter. The words, simple yet laden with the weight of our collective need for respite from the relentless sun, seemed to echo the urgency of our situation.

    Time became a blurred notion, lost amidst the concentration and the relentless heat that made the sweat trickle down my face incessantly. It was during this haze of focus and discomfort that the bright colours of the Portal abruptly shattered my concentration, its vibrant swirls igniting a spark of excitement within me. The arrival of the charcoal BMW, gliding to a stop just a few meters from the Drop Zone's modestly pillared entrance, was a spectacle that momentarily lifted the oppressive atmosphere. Admiration washed over me, a brief respite from the day's drudgery.

Yet, as the vehicle came to a halt, a flicker of curiosity morphed into intrigue. I squinted against the glare, the silhouette of an additional passenger momentarily catching my attention. The question of who it could be lingered in the air, an unresolved puzzle that was quickly overshadowed by the sudden appearance of a large golden retriever leaping from the car. The dog's majestic form, a burst of energy and fur, trotted past with an air of purpose, oblivious to my presence. Its bark, both joyful and commanding, seemed to herald its arrival as it made a beeline towards the camp.

"Lois!" Luke's voice cut through the stillness as he emerged from the car.

What the hell is Luke thinking bringing yet another dog here! My frustration bubbled up, manifesting in a silent, theatrical gesture of disbelief towards the sky. In this landscape, every new mouth to feed was another day's worth of resources stretched thinner.

"Glenda's," Luke explained briefly, as if the mere mention of her name should clarify any and all concerns.

I could only offer a noncommittal shrug in response, the dog already forgotten as my interest pivoted towards the vehicle. "Nice car," I commented, my fingers tapping against its hood with an appreciative rhythm. The sleek lines of the BMW contrasted sharply with the rugged backdrop of the desert. "Do we get to keep it?" I asked, half-joking yet secretly hopeful.

"Of course," Luke responded, his casual affirmation catching me off guard. "The keys are in the ignition."

"Sweet," I murmured, allowing myself a moment of unabashed pleasure as I sank into the front seat. The interior's cool luxury was a refreshing departure from the harsh, unforgiving environment outside.

"Have you got Joel's address yet?" Luke inquired, snapping my attention back to him.

"Yeah," I replied, fishing the torn piece of paper from my back pocket and handing it over. A grin tugged at my lips as I watched his reaction, knowing full well the assumptions that would dance through his mind. "Joel wrote it," I hastened to add, eager to absolve myself of any blame for the illegible scrawl that barely passed for an address.

"Oh," Luke murmured, his reaction subdued, betraying a hint of surprise. "Nice."

"Hey!" I called out, extracting myself from the cocoon of the car as Luke began to distance himself. "Are you going to help?" My gesture encompassed the vehicle, heavily laden with supplies that whispered promises of progress and backbreaking labour in equal measure.

"Can't," Luke replied with a straightforwardness that bordered on dismissive. He brandished the torn piece of paper like a shield, a flimsy excuse that nonetheless granted him passage away from the physical toil awaiting us. "Joel's waiting," he called over his shoulder, his form retreating towards the swirling colours of the Portal.

Then, just like that, he was gone, swallowed by the kaleidoscopic gateway that connected our worlds. The Portal's vibrant hues faded, leaving me alone with the car, its cargo, and a sense of abandonment that was becoming all too familiar in this landscape of survival and sacrifice.

Closing the car door behind me, I felt a surge of excitement mixed with a touch of reverence for the task at hand. Turning the key in the ignition, the car purred to life, a symphony of mechanical perfection that momentarily eclipsed everything else. A wide grin spread across my face, unbidden yet genuine, as I whispered to no one in particular, "Such a beautiful car." My eyes danced over the interior, taking in the luxury of the leather that peeked out from under an assortment of pillows, blankets, and an array of bags and cases—a juxtaposition of opulence and practicality that somehow seemed fitting for our odd existence.

With a final, affirming rev of the engine, I guided the shiny vehicle over the crest of the first hill, the thrill of the drive igniting a flicker of joy within me. Plumes of dust billowed into the air behind me, marking my passage through this desolate landscape. "Woo!" The exultation slipped from me as the car fishtailed down the hill, a moment of exhilaration that was abruptly snuffed out as the vehicle came to an unexpected and jarring halt.

I attempted to restart the car, turning the key with a mixture of hope and urgency. The engine obeyed, humming back to life, but my relief was short-lived. Pressing the accelerator only resulted in the back wheels spinning helplessly, digging themselves deeper into the unforgiving dust until they, and my spirits, ground to a halt. Climbing out to assess the situation, the depth of it hit me hard. The wheels had buried themselves so deeply that the bottom of the bumper was barely an inch above the ground. "Shit!" The word was a cry of frustration, echoing starkly against the silence of the barren landscape.

With a huff of disappointment that felt heavy in my chest, I resignedly removed the key from the ignition, my actions mechanical as I began to unload several bags from the car. To my chagrin, they turned out to be dog food—a small consolation, but one I clung to nonetheless. I couldn't bear the thought of returning to camp completely empty-handed, not after the brief taste of freedom the car ride had offered.

And so, with my enthusiasm deflated and the weight of failure pressing down on me, I began the short but now seemingly insurmountable trek back to camp. The bags felt heavier with each step, a physical manifestation of my disappointment. I was almost there, on the cusp of a small victory. Yet, as I marched back to face the others, the dust clinging to my boots and the dog food cradled in my arms, I couldn't help but feel the sting of what could have been.

❖

As I made my way into the heart of our burgeoning camp, the declaration fell from my lips with a mix of resignation and determination, "We need a road." The moment my presence was noted, Lois, a bundle of unrestrained joy, abandoned Joel's side to greet me. Her tail was a frantic pendulum of excitement as she bounded towards me, her enthusiasm a stark contrast to the weight of the situation I was bearing.

Tossing the car keys to Glenda with a casual flick of my wrist, I set down the bags of dog food with a thud, the dust rising around us like a slow exhale. Crouching to meet Lois, her affectionate lick across my cheek sparked an immediate smile. "Ooh, you're a gorgeous girl," I murmured, my fingers lost in the thick fur of her head, each scratch a momentary escape from the harsh reality awaiting us just over the hill.

"My car's here?" Glenda's voice, tinged with a mix of surprise and concern, cut through the moment. The keys dangled from her hand, a symbol of both hope and the complications that came with it.

"Yeah," my response was distracted, my attention wholly claimed by Lois, whose demands for affection provided a brief, cherished respite. "It got bogged just over the hill." The admission was made with a heavy heart.

"We definitely need a road," Kain's laughter, light and mocking, attempted to slice through the tension.

"I wouldn't be laughing if I were you," I retorted, the jest tinged with an edge of reality. The question that followed was a mock challenge, a reflection of the daunting task that lay ahead. "You want to be the one to collect the stuff in it or dig it out of the dust?"

"Honestly," Glenda exhaled in a huff. "This camp is like living with a bunch of children sometimes." Her stride towards the car, with Lois and Duke trailing loyally behind, was a mix of determination and resignation, bracing herself for yet another obstacle.

Kain and I exchanged a glance, an unspoken acknowledgment of the absurdity and complexity of our situation. Jamie's joke, "I don't think she's got any children," was a light-hearted attempt to ease the tension, a brief interlude of humour in our otherwise unfortunate circumstances.

"I heard that!" Glenda's call, sharp and clear, reverberated back to us, a reminder of her ever-vigilant presence.

"Come on," Kain urged, nodding towards Glenda's retreating figure. His suggestion, simple yet laden with the unspoken understanding of shared burden, propelled us into action.

As we made our way across the uneven terrain, the absence of our newest additions to the camp sparked a question that had been lingering at the back of my mind. "Hey, where are the new people?" I voiced out, curious about their whereabouts.

"Karen and Chris?" Kain echoed, as if to confirm whom I was inquiring about amidst our ever-growing assembly of Bixbus settlers.

"Yeah," I affirmed.

Jamie's shoulders lifted in an indifferent shrug, his silence speaking volumes of our collective awareness—or lack thereof—of each other's movements.

"They've gone for a walk," Kain finally disclosed, filling in the gaps of our fragmented community tapestry.

"Oh, the lagoon?" The question left my lips tinged with a knowing smile, the mention of the lagoon bringing forth images of tranquility and sensual energy.

"Pretty sure they went upstream," Kain corrected, his answer redirecting my mental map of their possible retreat.

Our focus shifted abruptly as Jamie, crouching beside the car's hopelessly buried back wheel, let out a mix of astonishment and amusement. "Fuck! You've done a good job, Paul," his voice was laced with a sarcastic commendation, drawing a tight line of frustration across my forehead.

"It all happened so quickly," I defended, the words barely covering the embarrassment and haste that had led to the car's unfortunate demise.

"I bet it did," Jamie retorted, the undercurrent of humour in his voice matched by Kain's soft chuckle. The camaraderie, though strained by the situation, was a thin veneer over the underlying tension. Rolling my eyes, I turned away, eager to escape the spotlight of their amusement.

"You're not staying, Paul?" Glenda's voice called out, a mix of surprise and reproach halting my retreat.

"I don't think Luke's done yet," I replied, the words, while true, were a thin veil for my desire to distance myself from the immediate failure and perhaps find solace in whatever new arrival lay ahead. My steps, determined yet heavy, carried me away from the group.

The sound of soft steps trailing behind me prompted a pause in my stride. Turning slightly, I saw Lois, her attention momentarily caught by the mundane allure of the desolate landscape. "Come on, Lois," I encouraged, a faint smile breaking through as she dutifully followed, after stopping to sniff at nothing-in-particular and squatting to pee.

❖

"Luke!" The call left my throat more as a plea than a summons, echoing off the dusty landscape as Lois and I stood sentinel atop the final hill. The sight of him, hastily abandoning an armful of belongings by the Portal only to vanish without a trace, sparked a flare of frustration within me. The fact that he hadn't even bothered to take it to the Drop Zone, where every resource was precious and accounted for, struck me as both reckless and disheartening.

By the time Lois and I made our way down to the Portal, the heat and the exertion were evident in her laboured panting. The air was thick, almost tangible with the heat that shimmered off the barren earth. "We'll just see what Luke is doing and then we'll get you back to camp for some water," I assured her.

Lois's attempts to find a comfortable position to rest, her awkward shuffling and resettling, painted a picture of discomfort that resonated deeply with me. When she finally stood still, her gaze lifted to mine, eyes brimming with a sadness that mirrored my own sentiments. The dust, invasive and relentless, seemed to sap the vitality from us both. "I know," I found myself empathising openly as I crouched to offer her a comforting pat. "This dust is horrible, isn't it?" The words were a whispered acknowledgment of our shared plight, a moment of connection in the midst of our struggles.

Faced with the task of dealing with the abandoned suitcase, my gaze drifted back towards camp, the distance looming like a chasm filled with heat and exhaustion. My eyes closed against the daunting prospect, a silent plea for respite from the relentless sun. *It's too far*, the thought echoed in my mind, a sentiment that bore the weight of the day's challenges and the cumulative toll of our circumstances. The very idea of undertaking another trek back to camp, under the scorching sun and with the dust swirling around me, felt like too much to bear in that moment. With a resigned determination, I lifted the suitcase, I carried the suitcase to the Drop Zone.

Bending to collect the second suitcase, the world around me felt like it was closing in, the boundaries between frustration and resignation blurring. Then, as if on cue, Luke materialised through the swirling colours of the Portal.

"Who's all this for?" The question burst from me, a mix of curiosity and a growing frustration that I found increasingly difficult to keep at bay.

"Oh," Luke began, his casual demeanour in stark contrast to the tension I felt. "The suitcases are for Karen and Chris, the large backpack over there is for Kain, and these," he gestured with a nod towards the small bags still clutched in his grasp, "are Joel's."

I was about to respond, to articulate the mixture of disbelief and concern that was brewing within me, when Luke cut me off with a continuation that felt almost dismissive in its casualness. "And I may as well bring a few things through with me whenever I come and go from different locations, so expect the random."

Random! The word echoed in my head like a siren, its implications unsettling. This randomness, this unpredictability, it was the straw that broke the camel's back, shattering the fragile veneer of my composure. "You can't just bring random crap through," I found myself saying, the volume of my voice a testament to the mounting pressure within.

"It's not crap! These are people's belongings!" Luke's retort was swift, his frustration mirroring my own as he dropped the bags in a gesture of defiance.

"What the hell are they supposed to do with it all?" My voice rose in anger, a part of me detachedly recognising the irrationality of my outburst, yet powerless to rein it in. "It's not like we have anywhere to put anything! Hell, we don't have houses. We may as well be living in dog kennels!"

"Far out, Paul!" Luke's exclamation, his hands thrown up in a gesture of exasperation, felt like a physical blow. "Give me a break. I'm only trying to make things more comfortable and homely for you all."

"Homely!" The word tasted bitter as I spat it back at him. "You can hardly call this homely!" In a fit of frustration, I scooped up a handful of the omnipresent dust, throwing it into the air as if to punctuate my point. "This fucking dust is everywhere and it is driving me fucking nuts!"

Luke's response was laughter, a sound that felt jarringly out of place in the heat of our argument. The sound grated on my already frayed nerves.

"Just fuck off, Luke," I muttered, a mixture of anger and resignation fuelling my words. Hefting the backpack over my shoulders and grabbing another smaller bag, I turned to Lois. "Come on, Lois," I urged, the desire to escape the immediate tension overwhelming. "Let's get you some fucking water."

As we began our retreat, a heavy sigh escaped me, a sound laden with weariness and a dawning realisation. *I'm starting to sound like Jamie already.* The thought was sobering, a reflection of the strain that this new existence imposed on me, warping my interactions and testing my limits in ways I could never have anticipated.

STRATEGIC MANAGER

1338.208.5

The campfire's crackles erupted into a cacophony as Kain, with a casual toss, added another log to the burgeoning flames. Tiny sparks, like fleeting stars, danced through the evening air, embarking on short-lived journeys propelled by the whims of the gentle breeze. This same breeze, a traitor of sorts, guided a fresh plume of smoke directly across my line of sight. Instinctively, I averted my gaze, my eyes squinting, battling against the ashen assault that threatened to invade them. The sharp sting was imminent, a sensation all too familiar in these gatherings around the fire.

"Sorry," Kain's voice pierced through the crackling backdrop, laced with a hint of amusement and concern. "Didn't mean to do that."

"All good," I managed, my voice carrying a lightness, a practiced ease that didn't quite mask the fleeting irritation. My hand waved dismissively, an unspoken pact of camaraderie amidst our shared, rugged conditions.

"Butter chicken for you?" Luke's question redirected my attention from the fire's unpredictable temperament to a more immediate, and certainly more appealing, matter at hand. He extended towards me a plastic container, its contents hidden yet betrayed by the tantalising aroma that immediately commandeered my senses. It was full, promising a hearty meal, the spicy curry's scent weaving its way into my very being, stirring an almost forgotten sensation of homely comfort.

"Yeah, thanks," I responded, my gratitude genuine, my anticipation palpable.

"Chicken tikka?" Luke's inquiry was now directed at Karen, moving the moment along, yet my focus remained fixed on the container now in my grasp.

I found myself momentarily distracted by the sauce, its rich, creamy texture teasing the edges of the lid. With a careful lift, the container revealed its treasures—a perfect harmony of butter chicken paired with rice, a thoughtful, perhaps necessary, combination given our current scarcity of dining ware. Luke's wisdom, or maybe his experience, shone through in this small, considerate act. It was a luxury, this combination, especially when the camp's resources were stretched thin by the ever-growing number of settlers. Each new face around the fire, each new mouth to feed, added layers to our communal narrative, a story of survival, of makeshift families formed not by blood but by circumstance.

As I licked the sauce from the corner of the container, I couldn't help but reflect on our situation. The camp, with its flickering flames and shared meals, was a microcosm of the world outside—chaotic, uncertain, yet filled with moments of unexpected warmth and generosity. The number of settlers, the scarcity of plates, these were but surface concerns masking the deeper, unspoken challenges we faced. Yet, in this moment, with the spice of the curry igniting my taste buds and the camaraderie around the fire warming my soul, the hardships seemed a little less daunting.

"Lois, sit!" Glenda's voice, firm yet affectionate, cut through the evening's calm as she addressed the overzealous retriever. I couldn't help but smile, watching the scene unfold. Lois, whose energy seemed inexhaustible, had taken a particular liking to Duke, shadowing him with a persistence that was both amusing and admirable. Duke, for his part, found sanctuary nestled between Jamie and Joel's feet, a living bridge between two people he adored.

I glanced down at my own arm, where my wound marred my skin. Comparing it to Joel's recovery — his resilience a beacon of hope in these often trying times — I allowed myself a moment of optimism. *Surely, if Joel could bounce back with such vigour, my own healing was just a matter of time.* This thought, a small flicker of positivity, was a rare and cherished visitor.

From a distance, Henri's satisfied snort reached my ears, pulling me from my reverie. I chuckled, the sound a spontaneous reaction to the dog's antics. Henri, ever the elusive character, had spent the better part of the day in a self-imposed exile, seeking refuge from the lively bustle that Lois and the increasing human presence brought to our enclave. However, the moment Jamie relocated the dogs' beds closer to the fire — an attempt, perhaps, to foster a sense of community among our non-human companions — Henri emerged. With a precision that rivalled even the most adept of navigators, he found his way to the beds, claiming a spot as if guided by an internal compass.

Despite the openness of his new resting place, Henri seemed content, a king in his court, so long as his peace remained unbroken. Observing him, I realised that Henri's demeanour mirrored our own delicate balance of adaptation and resistance. In this makeshift family of settlers, animals, and shared hardships, each of us sought our own patch of comfort, our own piece of stability. Henri's choice to join us, yet on his own terms, was a reminder of the resilience and adaptability that defined our collective existence. As the fire crackled and the night deepened, these moments of connection, of shared spaces and silent understandings, wove the fabric of our unconventional community tighter, binding us with threads of mutual respect and unspoken camaraderie.

It was in the midst of these reflective musings, as the din of conversation naturally ebbed to the rhythm of communal dining, that I found an opening to voice my concerns. The remnants of my earlier irritations had dissolved into a calm determination, spurred on by a series of interactions with Luke that left me contemplating the logistics of our daily lives here. This moment felt ripe for discussion, an opportunity to address what I perceived as a growing oversight in our camp's operations.

"Ahem," I ventured, an attempt to herald my forthcoming points despite the flutter of nerves that seemed to dance uneasily in my stomach. I didn't pause for dramatic effect or to ensure I had everyone's undivided attention; the matter felt too pressing, too integral to our collective well-being to delay. "I need everyone to check in at the Drop Zone regularly to see whether Luke has brought any of your belongings. Or perhaps there might be something there that you find you need."

Chris, the voice of reason, nodded in agreement. "That sounds reasonable enough," he chimed in.

"Reasonable?" Karen's voice sliced through the burgeoning consensus, her incredulity directed not just at my suggestion but at her husband's quick endorsement. "It's a long way to walk just to check. I'm too busy to wander over to simply... check."

Jamie was quick to align with Karen's stance, their mutual dissent a testament to the diverse priorities within our group. "I'm with Karen on this one," he affirmed. "Too busy."

Their objections, sharp and swift, struck a chord of frustration within me, a reaction I struggled to keep sheathed. "Busy!? All you've done is sit in the tent for the past two days!" The words escaped me, a reflexive retort that I immediately wished I could reel back in. My attempt at fostering a sense of responsibility and communal effort had inadvertently veered towards confrontation.

"Fuck off, Paul!" Jamie's outburst, punctuated by the unfortunate demise of his saucy chicken morsel, marked a sudden escalation in the tension that had been simmering beneath the surface of our conversation. The piece of chicken, now a casualty of our heated exchange, seemed almost symbolic of the delicate balance I was trying to maintain.

"Didn't you want to be responsible for managing the Drop Zone anyway?" Luke's question came with a sideways glance, a hint of challenge mingled with genuine curiosity in his tone. It was a reminder of our earlier conversations, of the roles we had all tentatively embraced.

"I'm happy to wander over. It'll be a nice break, and good to see what's there," Chris interjected, his voice carrying a note of unwavering support that momentarily lifted the tension. He punctuated his willingness with a forkful of food, as if to underline the simplicity of the task at hand.

"You make a good Drop Zone Manager, Paul," Glenda added, her encouragement offering a soft counterbalance to the brewing discord.

"Well, he is shit at building things," Kain muttered, almost under his breath. The comment, though meant as a jest, landed with the weight of truth. It wasn't my craftsmanship, or lack thereof, that hurt, but the reminder of my limitations.

"I think our settlement has more chance of thriving if we each focus on our own strengths," Glenda continued, her gaze shifting momentarily to Kain, whose attention swiftly returned to his meal, an unspoken acknowledgment of her point. Her words were a testament to the delicate balance of our collective survival—each of us contributing what we could, in the ways we knew how.

Glenda's eyes found mine again, her look conveying a mix of empathy and resolution. "With Luke bringing supplies through so quickly now, perhaps it would be best if the Drop Zone had a dedicated manager." Her suggestion, framed as a gentle proposition, felt like the closing argument in a case I was destined to lose.

I shrugged, a gesture of surrender rather than agreement. My earlier aspirations to instil a sense of shared responsibility within the camp seemed naïve now, crumbling under the reality of our disparate capabilities and priorities. "Fine. I'll be responsible for notifying people when things arrive for them and for keeping the Drop Zone in some sort of order."

"Marvellous," Karen's single word, laced with a hint of sarcasm, yet not entirely devoid of gratitude, echoed the complex tapestry of our interactions.

"But... if I am going to be going back and forth so often, we need to do something about this bloody dust! We need to build a road." The words tumbled out before I could second-guess them, my frustration with the camp's current infrastructure—or lack thereof—spilling over. The dust, omnipresent and relentless, was more than just a nuisance; it was a tangible barrier to efficiency, a constant reminder of the harshness of our environment.

"That sounds fair enough," Glenda's response was swift, her tone imbued with a practicality that I had come to rely on. Her agreement felt like a small victory, a sign that my concerns were not only heard but validated.

"I can help with that," Chris chimed in, his hand shooting up with an enthusiasm that was both heartening and slightly amusing. He reminded me of a diligent student, eager to contribute to a collective project, his spirit undampened by the magnitude of the task at hand.

"Yeah, I guess we could all pitch in," Kain added, his commitment more measured, his gaze wandering around the group as if seeking a consensus.

"I'll help, too," Joel's voice cut through the conversation, stronger and more determined than I had yet to hear. His recovery, both physical and mental, was evident in his willingness to be a part of this communal effort, a testament to his resilience.

As assent rippled through the group, I felt a shift within me, a buoyancy returning to my spirit. The daunting prospect of managing the Drop Zone, compounded by the physical toll of navigating the dust-ridden paths, seemed less overwhelming now. With the prospect of a road, a literal and metaphorical pathway to easing our daily burdens, the task felt more manageable. Besides, it would spare me the challenge of construction work, a field where my skills were notably lacking.

No sooner had we settled on a plan than the group seamlessly returned to their previous engagements, their conversations and meals resuming as if uninterrupted. The ease with which we navigated from debate to decision, from individual concerns to collective solutions, was a reminder of the unique dynamics at play within our settlement.

As the chatter swelled around me, my thoughts lingered on the road ahead—both the literal task of building it and the metaphorical journey we were all on. This road would be more than just a solution to a logistical problem; it would be a symbol of our ability to come together, to transform challenges into opportunities. In the dust we sought to tame, I saw the embodiment of the adversities that had brought us together, and in the road we planned to build, a testament to what we could achieve as a unified community.

As the sun dipped below the horizon, painting the sky in shades of twilight, the camp's energy shifted. The day's work and discussions faded into memory, giving way to the casual camaraderie of the evening. Amidst the growing din of laughter and spirited conversations, a distinct sound caught my attention—a raspy humming, gentle yet persistent, carried to me on the cool evening breeze.

Joel?

The recognition sparked a mixture of surprise and curiosity within me. Joel's voice, unmistakable in its gravelly tone, seemed to weave through the air, drawing closer until the humming evolved into words. The transformation from a simple melody to lyrics felt almost magical in the growing night.

"*Let us celebrate our story,*
The words we've yet to write..."

The simplicity and depth of the words struck a chord within me. There was something profoundly moving about hearing Joel sing, his voice carrying a weight of emotion and resilience that resonated deeply. As I listened, a sense of familiarity tugged at the edges of my consciousness. *Where had I heard this tune before?* It felt like a distant memory, a song from another life, yet it was undeniably present, sung by a man whose strength I was learning to admire.

The melody, with its haunting beauty, seemed to encapsulate our collective experience—our struggles, our hopes, and the unwritten future that lay ahead of us. Joel's performance, unassuming yet powerful, served as a reminder of the human spirit's capacity to find beauty and meaning amidst adversity.

As the simple lyrics and melody enveloped me, I found myself reflecting on our journey, on the stories we were living and those yet to be told. The song, in its gentle insistence, seemed to invite us all to embrace the uncertainties of tomorrow with the same courage and solidarity that had brought us this far.

Glenda's sudden movement shattered the spellbinding atmosphere Joel's singing had woven around us. She stood up abruptly. The abrupt change in the air seemed to startle Joel, his voice trailing off as his cheeks flushed a deep shade of embarrassment. The intimate circle of our gathering, momentarily disrupted, turned their collective attention towards Glenda, curious and slightly apprehensive.

"Please, don't stop. You have a beautiful voice," Glenda's words were a gentle encouragement, an olive branch extended to Joel to bridge the brief chasm her movements had created. Her sincerity, evident in her tone, coaxed a small smile from Joel. With a hesitant nod, he found his voice again, the melody resurfacing, soft and more hauntingly beautiful than before, as if Glenda's interruption had lent it a new depth.

Joel's hum filled the air once more, the tune weaving its magic anew, as Glenda disappeared momentarily into her tent. The anticipation of her return hung palpably in the air, a silent question mark that danced around the firelit faces of our assembly. When she reemerged, violin in hand, a collective breath seemed to be drawn. The instrument, an unexpected addition to our simple gathering, promised a convergence of talents that none of us had foreseen.

I watched, utterly captivated, as Glenda raised the violin to her shoulder, her bow poised with the confidence of a seasoned maestro. Then, with a grace that mirrored the elegance of the melodies Joel produced, she began to play. The violin's voice, rich and emotive, harmonised with Joel's tune in a way that felt almost predestined, as if the song had been waiting for this very moment to be fully realised.

"You know this song?" Karen's inquiry, whispered in a tone of awe, reflected the wonder that had gripped us all.

"Not until now," Glenda responded without missing a beat, her focus unwavering, her fingers moving with a precision and passion that breathed life into the notes. Her words suggested an impromptu performance, yet the synergy between her violin and Joel's voice spoke of a deeper, intuitive connection between the musicians and the music.

Brilliant! If only I had a piano, I mused silently, my fingers instinctively tapping against my thighs as if to find their own place within the burgeoning orchestra. The rhythm of my impromptu drumming mirrored the beat of the song, a subconscious contribution to the ensemble that filled the night air.

As Joel's voice continued to weave its spell around us, effortlessly pouring out the lyrics that had already carved a niche in my memory, Luke took it upon himself to play the role of our benevolent host. With a careful, almost reverent tread, he moved around the circle formed by our gathering, his hands diligently offering drinks to ensure that no one was left wanting.

I found myself drawn deeper into the mystique of Joel's song, the lyrics resonating with a poignant clarity that seemed to echo the very essence of our collective journey. Joel's voice, rich and full of an indefinable emotion, repeated the same four lines, each repetition imbuing them with greater depth and meaning:

"Let us celebrate our story,
The words we've yet to write.
How we all wound up with glory,
In the worlds we fought to right."

The simplicity of the words belied the complexity of our experiences, encapsulating the trials, triumphs, and the unyielding hope that propelled us forward. Each line was a testament to our resilience, a reflection of the disparate paths that had led us to this moment, united in purpose and spirit.

"To Joel!" Luke's voice, suddenly booming and exuberant, cut through the night, his glass raised high in a toast that felt as much a celebration of the man as it was of the message he conveyed through his song.

"To Joel!" The response was instantaneous, a chorus of voices rising to match Luke's call. The cheer, infused with warmth and genuine affection, rippled through the air, a sonic wave that seemed to carry far beyond the confines of our immediate surroundings into the quiet distance. It was a powerful, unifying moment, the kind that leaves an indelible mark on the soul, a reminder of the strength found in shared experiences and mutual respect.

As the echoes of our cheers blended with the night, I felt a surge of gratitude for this community, for the individuals who had become more than just fellow settlers—they were family. In this spontaneous celebration, amidst the laughter and raised glasses, I recognised the profound truth in Joel's lyrics. Our story, still unfolding, was one of shared glory, of battles fought not just for survival but for the right to forge new worlds from the ashes of the old.

❖

"It's fun, isn't it?" Luke's voice broke through my reverie as he casually dropped his log into the dust beside me, claiming it as his seat. His gaze, directed towards Joel and Glenda's impromptu concert, held a mixture of admiration and contemplation. "They make a beautiful duo. Perhaps I should bring you a piano?" His suggestion, playful yet sincere, sparked a fleeting desire within me, an ache for the touch of ivory keys and the creative outlet they represented.

Ignoring the whimsical thought of actually receiving a piano in this place, I took another swig from the Vodka Cruiser, the fruity alcohol offering a temporary respite from the weight of my thoughts. "I miss my kids," I said bluntly, the words spilling out with the alcohol's blunt honesty.

"I know you do," Luke replied, his voice carrying a note of empathy as he sipped his glass of wine, the crimson liquid a stark contrast to my neon drink.

The conversation took a turn towards the pragmatic as I leaned forward, retrieving Kain's wallet from my back pocket. "He doesn't have much money. Please don't waste it," I cautioned, the concern for our precarious financial state momentarily overshadowing the night's lighter moments.

Luke rolled his eyes at my warning, a gesture that did little to assuage my worries. "Luke, I'm serious. We're screwed if you run out of funds." The harsh reality of our situation, underscored by the risk of dwindling resources, loomed large in my mind.

"You know, being stuck at the Drop Zone will be a good thing for you." Luke's cryptic comment caught me off guard, prompting a wary stare from me. *What the heck was he planning now?*

"You're good with strategy," he continued, his voice dropping to a whisper as he leaned in, his words meant for my ears alone. "I need you to do some strategy work for me."

"What sort of strategy?" The question was out before I could temper my curiosity, my gaze sharpening as I tried to gauge Luke's intentions.

"The secret sort," he whispered, the words tinged with an intrigue that both alarmed and excited me. "I'll talk to you tomorrow," Luke said, his departure marked by a light tap on my shoulder, leaving a trail of questions in his wake.

As he walked off, the alarm bells in my head clashed with a burgeoning sense of exhilaration. Secret strategy work. The concept was laden with risks, yet it ignited a spark within me, a reminder of the complexities and covert operations that had once been part of my life. *Secret strategy*, I repeated to myself, the words weaving through my thoughts like a promise of action, of purpose beyond the daily grind of survival. Despite the dangers it implied, I couldn't deny the rush of anticipation it brought, the thrill of being involved in something that required more than just physical endurance, but mental acuity and strategic finesse. *I like the sound of that.*

4338.209

(28 July 2018)

CRIES IN THE DARKNESS

1338.209.1

Lois's low growl, a sound laced with unease, jerked me from the fringes of sleep where the warmth of the dwindling campfire had lulled me into a light doze. My eyes snapped open, immediately seeking out the source of her distress.

"Lois, what is it?" I hissed, my voice barely above a whisper, tension knotting in my stomach. The night, devoid of stars, seemed to press in around us with an ominous weight.

Luke, roused from his own rest by the commotion, turned to face the gathering wind, an uneasy shadow flickering across his features. "The wind is picking up. Do you think it's another dust storm?" His question, laden with a weary resignation, mirrored my own concerns.

"I hope not," I murmured, my gaze fixed on Lois as I crouched beside her. Grasping her collar, I tried to glean some clue from the direction of her stare, but the night offered no answers, just an impenetrable darkness that seemed to thicken with our apprehension.

"I think something's out there," Kain's voice, a whisper threaded with tension, cut through the uneasy silence. His movement, cautious and deliberate, placed him between Luke and me, a protective stance that did little to ease the growing sense of dread.

The air around us seemed to thrum with anticipation, a silent prelude to an unknown threat. Our collective gaze, wide-eyed and searching, was drawn inexorably towards the void beyond the campfire's reach, where shadows merged with the blackness of the night. Waiting.

Suddenly, Lois's bark shattered the tense quiet, a sharp, commanding sound that sent a jolt of adrenaline coursing through me. Her ferocity, unexpected and startling, tightened the coil of nerves in my gut, a visceral response to the perceived danger lurking just beyond our sight.

"What's going on?" Glenda's voice, tinged with concern, emerged from the darkness behind us. Her approach, quick and purposeful, added another layer of urgency to the situation. "Why is Lois barking?"

"We don't know," I managed, my hand moving almost instinctively to soothe Lois, stroking her fur in a futile attempt to calm the growing agitation that rippled through her body.

"Probably just the wind picking up the dust," Luke ventured, his voice betraying a hint of hope that the disturbance was nothing more than a natural occurrence. Yet, as he spoke, a gust of wind whipped around us, sending a veil of dust swirling into the air, a bitter foretaste of what might be coming.

I closed my eyes reflexively as the first wave of dust assaulted us, fine particles pelting my face like a myriad of tiny darts. *Not this shit again!* The familiar frustration, a mix of resignation and annoyance, surged within me, a silent curse against the relentless elements we faced.

"We'd better get inside the tents," Luke's shout, barely audible over the gust of wind, spurred us into action. The moment's hesitation dissipated as the reality of our situation set in—the need for shelter, for safety from the capricious wrath of nature, became paramount.

"Come, Lois," Glenda's voice, firm yet laced with concern, attempted to pierce the dog's focus. But Lois, her body taut with alertness, growled again, her gaze locked onto the unseen threat lurking within the veil of darkness that enveloped us.

"Duke! Get back here!" The urgency in Jamie's voice was palpable as he burst from his tent, his movements hurried and slightly frantic as he tried to reclaim control over Duke, who, caught in the grip of some instinctual need, had dashed out of the tent.

As the initial wave of dust settled, I rubbed at my eyes vigorously, the irritation of the fine grains a minor but immediate concern amidst the escalating tension. Blinking rapidly, I sought relief and clarity in equal measure.

"Shit! We're surrounded!" Kain's exclamation, edged with a hint of panic, drew my attention. He inched closer to the fire, seeking its dubious safety as if its light could ward off whatever threat lay beyond.

Surrounded? The word echoed ominously in my mind as I squinted into the darkness, testing the effectiveness of my efforts to clear my vision.

The question from Karen, emerging from the final tent with a voice tinged with panic, "What's going on?" demanded an explanation we were all grappling to understand.

Just as my sight began to return to me, I turned towards Karen, intending to offer some semblance of reassurance. "I think it's just a dust—" My attempt at explanation was cut short.

Kain gasped, a sound that drew my gaze back to the desert's expanse. In that moment, the faint glow of the Portal's bright, rainbow colours flickered across the dunes, an ephemeral dance of light that was as beautiful as it was baffling. And then, just as quickly as it had appeared, it vanished, swallowed once more by the night.

"Is that Luke?" Karen's confusion added to the mounting questions.

"I'm right here," Luke's response, his voice faltering, underscored the surreal nature of what we had just witnessed.

A shiver ran through me, the chill of fear mingled with awe. *Then who the hell is it?*

"Duke, stop barking!" Jamie's command cut sharply through the night, his voice strained with urgency. But his plea was drowned out by Lois's renewed growling, a deep, ominous sound that seemed to resonate with the growing unease around us.

Then, without warning, a chilling scream shattered the silence, a sound so terrifying and out of place that it sent a visceral wave of fear rippling through the camp. The primal part of my brain, the part governed by instinct rather than reason, tensed for action.

"Lois!" Glenda's scream was a mix of panic and desperation as Lois, propelled by some unknown instinct, bolted into the darkness. My reaction was immediate and thoughtless; I lunged forward in a futile attempt to catch her, my fingers grasping at nothing but air.

Driven by a surge of adrenaline and an acute sense of responsibility, I took off after Lois, my feet pounding against the cold, unforgiving ground. The night around me was a blur of motion, the wind howling in my ears as it whipped against my skin, each gust feeling like countless needles pricking my flesh.

The first hill, a mere obstacle in the path of my frenzied pursuit, came and went with surprising ease, my legs carrying me with a speed and agility I hadn't known I possessed. It was not until I crested the second hill that reality caught up with me—the ground suddenly giving way beneath my feet, sending me tumbling down the slope in a chaotic slide. Sand and dust invaded my clothing, filling every space, every crease, making my skin itch and burn.

"Glenda!" My shout, half-filled with concern, half with disorientation, was met with the sound of her grunting—evidence that she too was battling the treacherous terrain.

"Are you..." My voice trailed off as another scream pierced the night, this one followed by a brief but intense explosion of colour across the sky. The spectacle was mesmerising yet fleeting, disappearing as quickly as it had appeared and plunging everything back into an oppressive darkness.

The darkness was so complete, so suffocating, that for a moment, I felt as though I was being swallowed whole by it. My breaths came in short, panicked gasps, as if the blackness itself was tangible, pressing in on me from all sides. I struggled to find my bearings, my head spinning not just from the fall but from the sheer disorientation of being lost in an endless night.

My arm jerked back instinctively, the sudden contact in the pitch darkness setting off a flare of panic in my already heightened state. "It's me," Glenda's voice, a familiar anchor in the chaos, steadied my racing heart as she grasped my arm again, this time with a reassuring firmness. The unexpected glow from her other hand cut through the darkness, a beacon of light in the form of a phone.

"Where the hell did you get that?" The question burst from me, my surprise overtaking my concern for a moment. Glenda, to my knowledge, had been as disconnected from modern conveniences as the rest of us since arriving in Clivilius. The sight of a phone in this setting was as jarring as it was inexplicable.

"I found it face down in the dust, over there, near the Portal," she explained, her words quick, her grip on my arm unyielding. The mention of the Portal, coupled with the discovery of the phone, knotted my stomach with a mix of curiosity and dread.

With Glenda's assistance, I found my footing, standing upright just in time to witness the Portal's giant screen come alive with vibrant colours. It was a spectacle that demanded attention, yet offered no solace in the surreal turn our night had taken.

"Everyone okay?" Luke's voice, arriving from the shadows, brought a temporary relief.

"I think so," I managed to respond, my attempt to catch Glenda's eye failing in the enveloping darkness. The realisation that visibility depended entirely on direct light was disconcerting, adding a layer of isolation to our already precarious situation.

"Good. I'm going in," Luke declared with a resolve that left no room for debate. His statement, as sudden as it was decisive, left me momentarily speechless. Before I could formulate a question or a protest, he was gone, swallowed by the night and the mesmerising display of the Portal.

"Lois! Stay!" Glenda's command to the dog, firm and authoritative, snapped me back to the immediate concerns. She released my arm, her attention now fully on Lois, ensuring the dog's obedience in the midst of unfolding uncertainties.

"Whoa!" Kain's yell, a jolt of alarm in the enveloping darkness, snapped my focus back to the immediate danger. His voice, though near, seemed to come from a place shrouded in an impenetrable blackness that my eyes couldn't pierce.

Lois, ever vigilant, responded with a renewed growl, her body tense and ready. "She's baring teeth," Glenda's voice, tinged with a mix of surprise and concern, informed me of Lois's unprecedented behaviour. The protective instinct in the dog was something I'd seen before, but never to this extent.

"Shit!" The expletive burst from me as another gust of wind, laden with dust, assaulted us. I raised an arm in a futile attempt to shield my face, the gritty particles stinging my eyes and skin.

Then, cutting through the howl of the wind, came Kain's scream—a sound so filled with pain and terror that it rooted me to the spot. My heart hammered against my ribcage, fear spreading through me like wildfire. *What the fuck!* The thought was an echo of my own disbelief and horror.

The beam from the phone in Glenda's hand became our only source of light, flickering erratically across the ground and sky as she waved it around, desperately trying to locate Kain. "Kain!" she called, her voice a mix of fear and urgency. But there was no response, only the howling wind and the oppressive darkness that seemed to swallow her calls.

The taste of bile burned at the back of my throat, a physical manifestation of the terror that gripped me. Memories of our first night in Clivilius surged forward, unwelcome and terrifying in their intensity. I fought to push them back, to regain some semblance of control over my fear.

"Where are you, Kain?" The words choked out of me, a plea into the darkness that felt eerily reminiscent of another night, another name—*Rose!* The parallel was unnerving, a haunting reminder of past fears that had never truly left me.

Am I going as crazy now as I was then? The question spun in my head, a dizzying mix of doubt and fear. The lines between reality and nightmare seemed to blur, leaving me adrift in a sea of uncertainty. The tangible fear, the physical discomfort of the dust, and the psychological torment of not knowing Kain's fate combined to create a situation that felt all too real, yet surreal in its torture. The struggle to discern reality from the shadows of past traumas and present fears left me questioning everything, including my own sanity.

"I see tracks," Glenda's voice pierced through the tumultuous backdrop of the wind, offering a glimmer of hope. "Lois found him!" The relief that washed over me was palpable, a brief respite from the gnawing fear that had taken root in my chest. *We've got him!* Yet, almost immediately, my relief was tempered by a spike of anxiety. The urgency of the situation demanded clarity, and despite the dread that tightened its grip around my heart, I found myself voicing the question that loomed in my mind. "Is he alive?"

"Yes, but his leg is wounded. Come help me move him," Glenda's call came back, a mix of urgency and command that spurred me into action. The panic that had flavoured her earlier cries had now morphed into a focused determination, a testament to her resilience.

"My leg!" Kain's scream, a raw expression of pain, spurred me forward, my feet finding strength despite the swirling dust and the ever-increasing ferocity of the wind.

As I reached Glenda and Kain, the reality of the situation struck me with full force. "I think it's bleeding," Kain managed between sobs, the fear and pain in his voice cutting through me.

"It is," Glenda confirmed, the phone's light casting an unforgiving glow on the injury. The sight that greeted me—a deep gash oozing blood across Kain's thigh—sent a jolt of shock through my system. The severity of the wound was alarming.

Glenda's gaze met mine, her eyes alight with a fierce determination that seemed to anchor me amidst the storm. "We have to move him out of this dust storm," she declared, her voice brooking no argument.

After a moment's hesitation, where the weight of the decision pressed heavily upon me, I nodded in agreement. "You hold the light, I'll help him," I offered, the plan forming amidst the turmoil of thoughts racing through my mind.

"Try not to let him put pressure on the leg," Glenda instructed, her tone steady and authoritative. The practicality of her advice grounded me, offering a semblance of control over the situation.

"Okay. We can take shelter at the Drop Zone for now," I suggested, the words laced with a hint of uncertainty. The idea of exposing ourselves to the open, especially in our current vulnerable state, was daunting. Yet, the immediate need to seek refuge and address Kain's injury overshadowed the risks.

The truth of our predicament was chilling. Kain's leg bore a severe wound, the cause of which was shrouded in mystery, and here we were, caught in a dust storm, far from the safety and resources of our camp. The reality that we were navigating not just a physical landscape fraught with dangers, but also an unknown that had left one of our own injured, filled me with a deep-seated fear. As we prepared to move Kain, the gravity of our situation was inescapable, a stark reminder of the precariousness of our survival in this unforgiving world.

"We're going to stand," I declared to Kain, mustering as much confidence as I could into my voice. With a firm grip behind his shoulders, I helped him to his feet, his weight leaning heavily against me. Together, we embarked on the precarious journey toward the Drop Zone, each step a testament to our collective determination, yet shadowed by an uncertainty that fate might yet turn against us.

As we moved, the Portal's giant screen cut through the darkness, a brief beacon in the night, its illumination lending a surreal quality to our surroundings. Then, Luke's voice reached us. "Paul!" he called out, his voice cutting through the wind and darkness.

"We're almost at the Drop Zone," I shouted back, my voice straining against the storm, hoping my words reached him over the shifting sands.

"I need to check the house. I'll be back soon," Luke's yell carried a sense of urgency, a mission of his own that left me with more questions than answers. My heart sank as the darkness reclaimed us, the brief interlude of light from the Portal fading as quickly as it had appeared. *If Luke hadn't gone home the first time, where did he go?* The question echoed in my mind, its answer deferred by the immediate needs of our precarious situation.

"Do you think we're safe here?" Kain's question, voiced amidst the shelter of the larger shed boxes, reflected the vulnerability we all felt. We had positioned ourselves to afford Kain some comfort, his wounded leg stretched out carefully in front of him.

"Lois hasn't growled once since we found you," I offered, clinging to the hope that the dog's calm demeanour was a reliable indicator of our safety. The reassurance I tried to provide was as much for my own sake as it was for Kain's, a way to anchor myself to a semblance of security amidst the tumultuous night.

"As soon as the wind calms, we need to get back to camp. Kain's leg needs care," Glenda's voice, ever practical, brought our focus back to the immediate.

"Of course," I concurred, the weight of responsibility settling heavily on my shoulders. As I leaned back against a box, the cold, hard surface offered little in the way of comfort. Yet, it provided a momentary respite, allowing me to gather my thoughts. My eyes continued their vigilant sweep of the landscape, searching for any hint of movement, any sign of danger that might emerge from the darkness.

❖

As the relentless wind began to ease, the unfortunate reality of our situation became even more palpable. Kain's soft, pained sounds filled the temporary lull. At Glenda's behest, I had surrendered my shirt, watching as she deftly wrapped it around Kain's leg. The fabric, now a makeshift bandage, was an attempt to stem the flow of blood and shield the wound from the invasive dust that had become a constant adversary in our struggle for survival.

Despite the urgency of tending to Kain, my vigilance remained unwavering. My gaze continuously swept the perimeter, the darkness a canvas for my deepest fears and uncertainties. Yet, involuntarily, my eyes gravitated towards where I imagined the Portal to be. Each time the darkness remained unbroken by its light, a silent knot of worry tightened in my chest. The absence of Luke, each minute stretching longer than the last without any sign of his return, cast a shadow over the flickering hope that he would emerge unscathed from whatever venture had called him away.

The effort to rein in my spiralling thoughts felt Herculean. The quiet, the dark, and the waiting merged into a torturous cycle, feeding into the loop of dread and apprehension that threatened to overwhelm me. Each scenario my mind conjured was bleaker than the last, a relentless parade of what-ifs that no amount of rationalisation seemed capable of dispelling.

The weight of leadership, the responsibility for the safety and well-being of our group, felt heavier in these moments of uncertainty. Luke's absence, Kain's injury, and the precarious shelter we had found within the Drop Zone—each element compounded the sense of being on the edge of a precipice, one wrong step away from calamity.

"I mean you no harm," the declaration sliced through the silence, a woman's voice emerging from the darkness like a beacon of uncertainty. My entire being tensed, every sense heightened in anticipation of what was to come.

In a moment of desperation, we had buried the phone in the sand, a futile attempt to cloak our presence from unseen threats. But necessity demanded its unearthing, and as Glenda retrieved it, the phone's light once again pierced the darkness, casting long, ominous shadows around us. The beam settled on a young woman standing a few meters away, her form outlined starkly against the light, a figure both daunting and surreal in our beleaguered state.

"Shit!" The whisper escaped Kain, a sentiment that echoed my own internal alarm. My gaze locked onto the sharp arrow in the woman's grasp, its sinister appearance compounded by the dark substance that adorned its length. Blood, I surmised, a tangible proof of violence that did little to ease the pounding of my heart.

"Follow me," she commanded, her voice cutting through the tension. The directive, simple yet loaded with unknown implications, left us frozen in a moment of indecision.

Glenda's grip on my arm tightened, her fingers a vice that spoke volumes of her fear and protectiveness. As the woman ventured a step closer, Glenda's voice broke out, "Stay back!" The warning was sharp, a clear boundary set against the encroaching stranger.

"Keep your voices down," the woman hissed back, the urgency in her voice belied by the calm surrender of her dropping the arrow and raising her hands. "It's not safe. We have to go. Now."

The gravity of her words, coupled with the dire circumstances we found ourselves in, forced a rapid reassessment of our situation. The immediate fear of the unknown, represented by this armed stranger, clashed with the instinctual understanding that our current refuge offered little in the way of long-term safety. Her insistence on silence and swift action, though alarming, carried an undercurrent of genuine concern—a paradox that left me wrestling with confusion and a grudging sense of urgency.

In the dim light, Glenda's face was just a shadow, her expression lost to the darkness as the phone's beam remained fixed on the stranger before us. My voice, when it finally emerged, was laced with apprehension, betraying my inner turmoil. "Where are we going?" The question felt both necessary and futile, a feeble attempt to grasp at some semblance of control in a situation that was rapidly spiralling beyond my understanding.

"To your camp," the woman's response was straightforward, yet it did little to ease the knot of anxiety tightening in my stomach. Her assertion, intended to be reassuring, instead sowed seeds of doubt. *How did she know of our camp? And why lead us there?*

"I don't think we should trust her," I whispered to Glenda, my gaze shifting between her and the woman. Kain's soft cries of pain underscored my fears, painting a vivid picture in my mind of the arrow's potential role in his injury. Lois's low growl, a sound so fraught with warning, seemed to echo my own trepidation. *Don't trust this woman*, the thought reverberated through my mind, a silent mantra amidst the growing tension.

Then, cutting through the night, came another growl—deeper, more menacing than Lois's warnings. The sound sent a shiver down my spine, its origin hidden within the shroud of night that enveloped us.

"There's something else out there," Glenda hissed, her voice a mixture of fear and determination as she briefly redirected the light towards the source of Lois's attention. The brief glimpse into the darkness revealed nothing but the unsettling realisation that we were not alone.

Which is more dangerous, the woman or the growl? The question haunted me, a dilemma of trust and survival that offered no clear answers. My heart raced, pounding against my chest with a ferocity that mirrored the chaotic thoughts swirling in my mind.

As Glenda turned the light back, the woman's movements caught us off guard. She was now crouching in front of us. "Shit!" The exclamation burst from both Glenda and me, a shared response to the suddenness of her approach.

"My name is Charity. You can trust me," she asserted, her grip on my arm firm, as if to underline her sincerity. The introduction, meant to offer assurance, only intensified the turmoil swirling within me. Yet, her urgency was palpable, a clear indication that whatever lay in the darkness was far more menacing than the unknowns she represented.

Lois's growl, more pronounced now, filled the air, her teeth bared.

"Come on," I urged Glenda, my voice a mix of determination and desperation. I hoisted myself up, pulling Glenda along with me. "If this woman wanted to kill us, she would have done it already."

"Or feed us to the creature," Glenda countered under her breath, her resistance sending a cold shiver down my spine. Yet, our dire situation left us with little room for debate.

"Quickly now," Charity pressed, her tone brooking no delay. It was a command, one that spoke of imminent danger and the necessity of swift action.

With resignation and a shared sense of urgency, Glenda and I supported Kain between us, lifting him to his feet with care. The collective effort to move, to follow Charity's lead, was a testament to our human instinct to cling to any chance of survival, however slim.

"Give me your light," Charity requested, her hand outstretched towards Glenda. The moment hung in the balance, the exchange of the light a symbolic gesture of trust in the face of uncertainty.

I watched, my throat tight, as Glenda handed over the light. The action, simple yet profound, marked a turning point, a leap of faith into the unknown guided by a stranger named Charity.

"Stay close," Charity instructed, her voice a beacon in the enveloping darkness. "And keep up." Her directive left no room for hesitation. In that moment, the path forward was clear, albeit shrouded in mystery and shadowed by the threat that lurked just beyond the reach of the light.

❖

The journey back to camp, under the guidance of Charity, felt like traversing through a different realm. The wind, once a howling adversary, had lulled into a gentle whisper by the time we approached the familiar terrain. The sight of our camp, marked by the soft, flickering glow of firesticks, offered a semblance of safety, a beacon in the enveloping darkness that had been our constant companion.

"Who is the camp leader?" Charity's question pierced the quiet as we made our way into the illuminated circle. It was a direct inquiry, demanding a clear response.

"I am," I stated, the weight of responsibility settling firmly on my shoulders once again. Her directness merited an equal measure of candour from me.

"We need to talk. You and I," she insisted, her tone leaving no room for argument. It was a conversation she deemed crucial, perhaps as critical as the journey that had led us to this moment.

My concern for Kain, however, overshadowed the urgency in her voice. "We need to see to Kain's wounded leg first," I countered, my priorities clear. Kain's well-being was immediate, tangible, a responsibility that couldn't be postponed.

Charity's reaction was unexpected. Stopping in her tracks, she squatted before us, her actions deliberate as she examined Kain's injury. Her assessment, "It's barely a scratch. He'll live," contradicted the evidence before my eyes. The makeshift bandage, soaked with blood, told a story of pain and vulnerability, not the minimalism she suggested.

Flabbergasted, I found myself at a loss. The visible trail of blood, illuminated by the campfire's glow, was undeniable. "I'd hardly call that..." My objection was cut short by her sudden gesture, her finger pressed against my lips in a silencing motion.

"Shh," she hushed, her eyes scanning our surroundings with a nervous intensity. The gesture, intimate and commanding, halted my words, filling the space between us with a tension that was both confusing and alarming. Her caution suggested unseen dangers, secrets lurking within the shadows of our camp, amplifying the mystery that surrounded her arrival and intentions.

Chris's swift approach, prompted by Glenda's signal, offered a much-needed respite as he took over supporting Kain. The relief that washed over me was instantaneous, my muscles thanking me for the break from the strain. However, that brief moment of relief was quickly usurped by the urgent grip of Charity's hand on my arm, pulling me aside with a purpose that brooked no delay. "The problem is still out there," she whispered, her breath warm against my ear, reigniting a flicker of fear just as it had begun to ebb.

"Problem?" I echoed, the word hanging between us, laden with implications that sent a shiver down my spine. The calm that had momentarily settled over me shattered, replaced by a renewed sense of alarm.

As Glenda and Chris disappeared with Kain towards the medical tent, Charity led me away, deepening the distance between us and the rest of the group. The sight that greeted us halted me in my tracks—a black panther-like creature, its life ebbing away into the dust, illuminated by the campfire's glow. "What the fuck is that?" The question escaped me before I could restrain it, my voice betraying the turmoil of fear and disbelief churning within.

"A shadow panther," Charity answered, her calm in stark contrast to my distress. "Likely not the one that scratched your friend, though." Her choice of words, 'scratched,' seemed almost trivial in the face of the lethal danger represented by the creature's still form.

"Are there more of these beasts out there? Will they attack the camp again?" The questions poured out, each one laced with an acute awareness of the precariousness of our safety.

"No. We are safe, for now. The light from the fires and the blood of this shadow panther should be enough to keep any more of them away from the camp," Charity explained, her assurance underpinned by a confidence that I desperately wanted to believe.

"How can you be certain?" The skepticism in my voice was reflexive, a natural response to the surreal turn our situation had taken.

"They won't come near the camp if they can smell the blood of one of their own. And their eyes are sensitive to the light. As soon as the sun begins to rise, our safety is guaranteed," she elaborated, her knowledge of these creatures and their behaviours offering a glimmer of hope amidst the night's brutality.

With a heavy exhale, I allowed myself to feel a semblance of relief, clinging to the promise of safety that dawn would bring.

"We have a bigger problem," Charity's words, underscored by the earnest look in her eyes, illuminated by the flickering light of a nearby firestick, gave my shoulders an involuntary sudder. Her expression, a mixture of concern and seriousness, marked a stark departure from the calm composure she had maintained up until now. The emotional weight of her gaze hinted at the gravity of what she was about to reveal.

"Duke wasn't killed by..." Her voice trailed off, and instinctively, my grip found her forearm, seeking not just her attention but perhaps a sliver of hope that the dire implications of her words were somehow a misunderstanding.

"Duke is dead?" The question tore from me, a desperate plea for clarification, my eyes searching hers for any sign that I had indeed misheard. Her confirmation, a simple "Yes," cut through me, a sharp pain that was both physical and emotional.

The tears came unbidden, a testament to the bond lost, the grief for Duke manifesting swiftly. My gaze fell to the lifeless form of the shadow panther at our feet, anger boiling within. "Fucking beast," I spat out, the words laced with a venom fuelled by grief and the need for something, anything, to blame.

"No," Charity's voice, firmer now, her hand clasping mine, drew my attention back to her. "Duke wasn't attacked by a shadow panther." Her clarification, rather than offering solace, plunged me into deeper confusion and fear.

"Then what?" The whisper barely escaped me, each word heavy with the dread of what her answer might reveal. The emotional turmoil within threatened to engulf me, a storm of grief, confusion, and now, a growing sense of foreboding.

"It appears that you have a Portal pirate stalking your camp." The term 'Portal pirate' hung in the air, a concept so foreign yet terrifyingly significant in its implications.

"A... a what?" My response was a stammer, a reflection of a mind grappling with too much, too fast. The notion of a Portal pirate, a threat I couldn't begin to comprehend, added layers to an already complex and dangerous reality we were navigating.

"A Portal pirate," Charity reiterated, her voice steady, impressing upon me the seriousness of this new threat. "And these bastards are far more dangerous than any shadow panther." Her words, meant to convey the urgency and danger of our situation, succeeded only in amplifying the fear and helplessness that had taken root within me.

My grip on her arm, a physical manifestation of my attempt to hold onto something certain in a world that had just become even more uncertain, tightened. Her revelation, far from providing answers, had opened a Pandora's box of questions and fears. The term 'Portal pirate' echoed ominously, a harbinger of challenges far greater than we had faced thus far. The reality that our camp, our makeshift sanctuary, was now the hunting ground of shadow panthers and an entity even more malevolent, was a like a tidal wave engulfing my entire being. "Shit!"

.

UNEXPECTED FATES

1338.209.2

"Did you sleep at all?" Charity asked me as I approached her.

We stood together, observers of dawn's early light, the firesticks casting a warm glow that battled the cool shadows of the night. "I think I dozed a couple of times, but nothing substantial. Did you?" I asked, turning towards her, seeking some common ground in our shared vigil.

"No. A Chewbathian Hunter sleeps very little." Her statement was matter-of-fact, yet it opened a door to a world I knew nothing about.

"Chewbathian Hunter?" I echoed, my curiosity piqued. The fatigue that clung to my bones momentarily forgotten in the wake of her revelation.

"That's what I am," Charity affirmed, her tone devoid of any pretence. "I am a Hunter and I hail from Chewbathia." Her blunt admission was a beacon in the night, illuminating paths of understanding that I hadn't known existed.

I searched my mind for any reference to Chewbathia, but found none. "I'm guessing that's not a place on Earth?" The question felt naïve the moment it left my lips, but her story was a puzzle I was desperately trying to piece together.

"No. I was born in Clivilius. I've never known Earth." Her words were a tapestry of complexity, each thread a story of its own, woven into the fabric of her identity.

"But you speak English?" I probed further, intrigued by the fluency with which she navigated the language.

"Yes. Chewbathia's founding Guardians hailed from a place they called Scotland. Four of the five Guardians were sisters." Her explanation offered a glimpse into a history that was as fascinating as it was foreign.

"Oh, from the same family?" I asked, seeking clarification, my mind racing to understand the bonds that tied these Guardians together.

Charity gave me a look that suggested the question was more obvious than I had intended. "Is there any other way to be sisters?" Her response, simple yet profound, hinted at the differences in our worlds, our understandings.

The religious context of 'sisters' flickered through my mind, a potential point of confusion in our dialogue. But realising that such nuances might only complicate the conversation, I opted for simplicity. "I guess not," I conceded, recognising the vastness of the cultural divide between us. "And the fifth Guardian?" My curiosity was unabated, each answer Charity provided only serving to deepen the mystery of her origins and the world she spoke of.

Charity's narrative unfolded like a tapestry from another time, each word painting a picture of a world both fascinating and foreboding. "His name was William Brodie. He was an Edinburgh city councillor but also had a secret life as a housebreaker," she explained, her voice steady, recounting the tale with a reverence that hinted at the depth of its importance to her people. "The eldest of the sisters, Elspeth Stewart, only nineteen at the time, had been in love with him. She was the first Guardian, and it was she that enlisted the help of Brodie and his small band of double-life thieves to provide New Edinburgh with supplies."

"How long ago was this?" My curiosity was piqued, the historian in me fascinated by the intertwining of Earth's past with the lore of another world.

"Elspeth became a Guardian in the year you would call seventeen-sixty-two." The precision of the date took me aback, the realisation that this connection spanned centuries adding layers to the mystery enveloping Charity and her origins.

The acknowledgment of our shared history, albeit from vastly different perspectives, stirred a complex blend of emotions within me. It was a revelation that humans had not only survived but thrived in this harsh landscape, albeit with challenges that seemed to transcend the ordinary. The existence of shadow panthers and Hunters, elements of a world that sounded as savage as it was ancient, left me grappling with a mix of fear and fascination. "And how does Chewbathia fit into it?" I asked, eager to understand more about the world Charity called home.

"New Edinburgh quickly flourished and the sisters set out on an ambitious campaign to conquer the vast desert lands. Chewbathia is the military hub of the main city. I belong to an elite branch and was trained from a young age in the arts of war." Her explanation offered a glimpse into a society structured around survival and conflict, a stark contrast to the life I had known on Earth.

"War?" I echoed.

"Yes. Clivilius has been at war for millennia." The weight of her words settled heavily upon me, the scope of their struggle stretching beyond the confines of my imagination.

My astonishment was palpable, the reality of Clivilius' warfare hanging between us like a dense fog, waiting to be dispersed by Charity's explanation. However, before she could illuminate the dark corners of my understanding, Luke's sudden arrival shifted the dynamic of our conversation dramatically.

As Luke's sudden presence filled the space beside me, his breaths heavy and his stance defensive, the tension between familiarity and the unknown thickened. "Who the fuck are you?" he demanded, his glare fixed on Charity with an intensity that matched his physical exertion. His reliance on my shoulder for support did little to mask the suspicion and protectiveness that radiated off him.

"Luke!" The rebuke slipped from me instinctively, a futile attempt to inject some semblance of decorum into the rapidly escalating situation. Despite the shock of Charity's revelations, Luke's blunt approach felt like an unnecessary jab in the delicate fabric of our newfound understanding.

"I'm Charity," she responded, her voice a calm counter to Luke's brusqueness, embodying a patience that seemed almost inhuman under the circumstances.

"What... where did..." Luke's confusion was palpable, his words tripping over each other as he struggled to grasp the sudden turn of events. Charity's self-identification as a Chewbathian Hunter seemed to hang in the air between them, an alien concept that neither of us had been prepared to encounter.

"I was born here, in Clivilius," Charity added.

"That explains the Warrior Princess outfit then," Luke quipped, his attempt at humour a thin veil over his bewilderment. "But... How...?"

Despite Luke's lack of finesse, I remained silent, a spectator to the unfolding drama. His directness, abrasive though it may have been, cut through the haze of my own hesitation, demanding answers to questions that hung heavily in my own mind.

"I've been tracking the pack of shadow panthers for a few days now. They're experts at finding new settlements," Charity explained, her focus shifting back to the immediate threat that had brought her into our lives.

"So, they really were here last night, then?" Luke's question, seeking confirmation, hinted at a return to a more rational, if not entirely composed, state of mind.

"Yes," Charity confirmed.

"Charity killed one of them," I found my voice, pointing towards the shadow panther's corpse that lay as silent testimony to her claim.

As we approached the fallen creature, the daylight revealed its true form, a gruesome contrast to the terrifying entity we had encountered under the veil of night. Luke's casual interaction with it, nudging its cold, stiff head, belied the gravity of our situation. "It looks so different during the day," he remarked, a note of detachment in his voice that I couldn't quite fathom.

My heart raced as I processed his familiarity with the creature. "You've seen one?" The question sprung from me, a mixture of surprise and burgeoning fear colouring my tone.

"Yeah," Luke admitted, his voice tight, betraying a tension that hadn't been apparent a moment ago.

Charity, quick on the draw, voiced the question that was burning through my mind. "What happened?"

"I think it followed Beatrix back through the Portal last night," Luke's admission sent a chill down my spine. The implications of his statement were both terrifying and bewildering.

"Shit," the curse slipped from me involuntarily, a reflex to the unfolding horror. But before I could delve deeper into my thoughts, Charity's abrupt expletive cut through the air, halting me. Her pacing, a physical manifestation of her anxiety, mirrored the turmoil that churned within me.

My mind, however, clung to a sliver of the conversation that needed further exploration. "So, that was Beatrix who screamed last night?" The pieces of the puzzle were slowly aligning, yet each revelation brought with it a new set of questions, a deeper layer of complexity.

"Yeah," Luke confirmed. "Beatrix is a Guardian now." The simplicity of his statement did little to ease the knot of worry forming in my stomach.

"Like you... and Cody?" My query was an attempt to understand, to find some footing in the rapidly shifting landscape.

"Yes." Luke's affirmation was both a balm and a blade, a confirmation of unity and yet a harbinger of unknown challenges to come.

Charity's silent stare at Luke spoke volumes, her earlier nervous energy giving way to a focused attention that demanded answers.

"How?" The word was barely a whisper from my lips, a plea for understanding.

"I'm not completely sure how she became a Guardian. She's still in shock." Luke's admission, his frustration palpable, underscored the severity of our predicament.

"Shock?" The repetition was involuntary, a reflection of my struggle to comprehend the full scope of what had transpired.

Luke's foot nudged the shadow panther as his words left his mouth angrily. "Because the bloody beast fucking attacked her, that's why."

"Back on Earth?" Charity's question, once she had regained her composure, sought to clarify the origin of the attack, to understand the bridge between worlds that had been so violently crossed.

"Yes!" Luke's exclamation was a sharp puncture in the silence that followed, a confirmation of our worst fears realised.

"Are you certain it was a shadow panther that attacked her?" Charity pressed.

"Yes. I'm certain," Luke's affirmation was a finality, a closing of the circle that left us standing on the precipice of a new and daunting reality.

The tension between Luke and Charity was palpable, a thick cloud of unresolved emotions and unspoken words that seemed to suffocate the air around us. I couldn't bear it any longer, the weight of grief and conflict pressing down on me with an intensity that threatened to crush my spirit. *There's too much tension. Too much loss. I don't want to do it.* The thought echoed through my mind, a silent plea for reprieve from the relentless tide of sorrow.

"What have you not told me yet?" Luke's question, vulnerable and laden with a sense of impending heartache, cut through the turmoil within me. His voice, faltering under the weight of unshed tears, demanded my attention, compelled me to face the unbearable truth that lay between us.

I bit my lower lip, fighting against the tremble that sought to betray the turmoil churning within. *No, I really don't want to do this*, I lamented internally, a wave of sorrow washing over me at the thought of the words that would soon pass my lips. Yet, as I met Luke's gaze, seeing the raw emotion that shimmered in his eyes, I knew there was no escaping the cruel reality that had to be acknowledged.

With a resolve born of necessity rather than strength, I took his trembling hands in mine. "Duke's dead," I stated, the words heavy with finality, a grim statement to the loss that would forever mark this moment.

Luke's reaction was a mirror to the pain that enveloped my heart. "Where is he?" he murmured, the words barely a whisper, reflecting the shock that gripped him.

"Jamie is with him. They're behind the tents," I replied, my voice a soft echo, my grip on his arm an attempt to offer solace in the face of an insurmountable loss.

The moment Luke pulled away, a surge of helplessness washed over me as I watched him storm through the camp, his steps heavy with grief and denial. He paused at the end of the last tent, a figure poised on the brink of despair.

My heart ached for my brother as I envisioned the scene awaiting his discovery—Jamie, a silent sentinel of sorrow by the riverbank, the finality of Duke's absence a cruel reality that we would all have to confront. I could only watch Luke for a moment before the sight became too much to bear, the echo of our shared loss a wound too fresh to face.

"I need to do another perimeter sweep," Charity announced, her voice a distant sound against the backdrop of my grief. Her departure, though necessary, left me feeling even more isolated in my sorrow.

With no direction left but forward, I found my feet leading me towards the Portal, a path tread not out of purpose but a need to distance myself from the immediate pain. Each step was a testament to the burden we bore, a family fractured by loss and a future shrouded in uncertainty.

❖

"Beatrix?" The surprise in my voice was unmistakable as I spotted her, an almost surreal figure against the backdrop of the barren landscape, barefoot and laboriously dragging a bright red kayak. The incongruity of the scene struck me profoundly, a stark contrast to the desolation that surrounded us.

As Beatrix halted and turned towards me, a multitude of questions raced through my mind, each vying for precedence. Yet, as I approached her, the urgency to understand her intentions with the kayak dissipated, replaced by a concern that cut deeper. The visible gashes marking her arms and legs, the torn fabric of her red dress—each told a story of ordeal, of survival against odds that I could only begin to imagine.

"You look like shit," the words escaped me before I could temper them with the tact the situation warranted. It was an observation made without malice, yet it hung between us, a blunt acknowledgment of the trials she had evidently endured.

"Like you look any better," Beatrix countered, her retort sharp yet softened by a half-smile that quickly morphed into a stern pout. Her resilience, even in the face of apparent exhaustion and injury, was both startling and admirable.

I gulped, chagrined by my own lack of sensitivity. "Here, let me take that," I offered, reaching for the kayak. Beatrix's acquiescence, silent and without resistance, spoke volumes of her current state. As we made our way back towards the camp, the myriad questions that had been swirling in my mind began to crystallise, each demanding attention.

"Luke brought you in?" The query was almost reflexive, a grasp for some understanding of how Beatrix had come to be here, in such a state, with such an unlikely companion as a kayak. Yet, even as I voiced it, I recognised the redundancy of the question, the answer already known to me.

"No," Beatrix's response was succinct.

"From Cody?" I ventured after several minutes, the question emerging from the chaos of my thoughts like a lifeline.

"No," Beatrix's response was terse, her lack of enthusiasm doing little to quell the storm of curiosity within me.

"Oh... then who?" The words slipped out, driven by an insatiable need for answers despite the mental plea to cease my inquiries. The introduction of shadow panthers, a Chewbathian Hunter, Portal pirates, and now the veiled mention of additional Guardians had left me grappling with a reality far removed from anything I had ever known. *I don't understand how any of this is possible. None of this makes any...*

"What do you know about Cody?" Beatrix's question cut through my internal monologue, redirecting the conversation with an agility that left me momentarily off balance.

"Nothing, really," I admitted, the puzzle of Cody's identity adding another layer of complexity to the unfolding mystery. "Luke mentioned the name when Joel arrived, but I haven't..."

"Joel? Jamie's son, Joel?" Beatrix interjected, her interruption laden with surprise and a hint of recognition.

"Yeah. You knew?" I asked, surprised that Luke would have told Beatrix that Jamie had a son before he had told me.

"Joel is here?" Her reaction, a mixture of disbelief and concern, suggested a depth to the story that I was only beginning to uncover. "I thought Luke wasn't going to bring him here."

"He didn't. Apparently," I responded, my mind racing to connect the dots between Joel's unexpected presence and the events that had led to our current predicament. "We think he came down the river."

"Did Luke say what happened to him?" Beatrix's question, laced with genuine concern, pulled me back from the brink of my own spiralling thoughts. The worry etched into her features reminded me of the bizarreness of Joel's situation, a narrative thread fraught with danger and mystery.

"He told us about the blood and the truck, but Glenda stitched his throat and he seems to be making a remarkable recovery." My words felt hollow, an oversimplified summary of events that had shaken the very foundation of our camp.

"Glenda? And Joel's alive?" The questions tumbled out from Beatrix, each one a testament to her shock and the rapid reassessment of the situation she was being forced to make.

"Yeah," I responded, somewhat reassured by the fact that Joel's resilience had become a point of light in the darkness that had enveloped us. "And Glenda is the camp's doctor." I added

"Can I see him?"

"I'm sure you'll see him soon enough."

The silence that enveloped us again as we continued our trek back to camp was heavy, filled with unspoken questions and fears. My pace slowed, the weight of reality pressing down on me as the dread of what awaited us at camp began to overshadow all else.

"A... a shadow panther?" The question erupted from me, a desperate attempt to grasp the threads of understanding that seemed to slip further away with each passing moment.

"Huh?"

"Your dress and cuts. Were they from a shadow panther?" The words felt clumsy, inadequate to describe the complexity of the horrors we faced.

Beatrix's blank stare was unsettling, sending a chill through me that was more than just the cold air of the desert morning. *Was Luke wrong? Had something else attacked Beatrix? A Portal pirate maybe? Like the one that killed...* The thought trailed off, too painful, too laden with implications to fully explore.

"A panther-like creature?" I pressed, desperate for clarity, for any piece of information that could help us navigate the perilous unknown.

"Yeah," Beatrix's soft admission was a confirmation, yet it offered little in the way of comfort or understanding.

"It was you who screamed last night, wasn't it?" The question hung between us, heavy with implications.

"I guess," Beatrix's nonchalant shrug belied the depth of trauma such an encounter must have entailed.

As tears that threatened to overwhelm me, I wiped them away, attempting to regain some semblance of composure, Beatrix's voice cut through the heavy air. "Everything okay here?" Her gaze, sharp and scanning, reflected a concern that went beyond mere curiosity.

I sighed, the weight of the world seemingly on my shoulders. *There's no point in hiding it*, I conceded internally, the truth of our circumstances too significant to mask any longer. "We had an incident here last..." My voice trailed off, the words hanging between us.

Beatrix's reaction to the scene that unfolded as we crested the final hill was immediate—her gasp, a sharp intake of breath that mirrored my own sense of shock and despair. Luke's passing, his eyes alight with a tempest of fury and grief, offered no greetings, no explanations. He moved past us as if driven by a force beyond his control, a man on the brink, consumed by his own tumultuous emotions.

The pain etched in Luke's eyes was a mirror to my own, a reflection of the shared agony that bound us in this moment. I knew then that there was nothing to be done, no words of comfort or gestures of support that could ease the burden of his sorrow. The decision to let him go, to not chase after him or attempt to intervene, was one borne of understanding—a recognition of the depth of his grief and the need to process it in his own way.

"Where's Jamie?" Beatrix's question pulled me back from the edge of my own reflections, her voice tinged with urgency. Her hand tugged at my arm, a physical plea for answers.

"Probably still in the river behind the tents," I responded, the softness of my voice belying the turmoil within. It was the last place I had seen Jamie, a solitary figure consumed by his own vigil, a silent guardian to the memory of what had been lost.

As Beatrix continued on, her determination to confront the reality that awaited us undimmed, I found myself rooted to the spot, unable to accompany her further. My hand, white-knuckled from the grip on the kayak, was a physical manifestation of the internal struggle I faced—the desire to support my friends, to face the aftermath together, against the overwhelming urge to retreat, to find solace in isolation.

CHAOS

1338.209.3

Dragging the red kayak across the dusty camp, I sought solace in the physical exertion, a welcome distraction from the turmoil that had enveloped our little community. The idea of actually using the kayak on the river appealed to me as a much-needed escape, a brief respite from the complex web of emotions and events that had defined recent days. *I'd much rather be testing this out on the river*, the thought crossed my mind once again, as I set the kayak down, envisioning the serene glide through water, the rhythmic dip of paddles, the quiet enveloping me.

I considered the kayak's size, my hands gauging the space within. *I reckon I'd fit in there perfectly*, the thought brought a momentary smile to my face, a fleeting sense of playfulness in an otherwise abnormal situation.

A quick scan of the camp confirmed my solitude. Emboldened by the absence of onlookers, I made my decision. With a mixture of determination and a desire for a momentary escape, I positioned myself beside the kayak, hands gripping its sides before stepping in. The initial wobble as I settled down reminded me of the unstable ground beneath, yet the sensation of sitting within the kayak brought an unexpected comfort. "This is nice," I murmured to myself, allowing the fantasy of being on the water to wash over me, eyes closed, the breeze caressing my face as if to affirm my temporary retreat from reality.

Lacking actual paddles did little to deter my imagination, which eagerly filled in the gaps. My hands lifted, mimicking the motions of rowing, the kayak and I moving in harmony across the imagined waters. *Go faster, harder,* the internal encouragement spurred me on, my body engaging in the make-believe with a zeal that momentarily lifted the heaviness that had settled around my heart.

The illusion of speeding against the current, the imagined spray of water cooling my face, provided a brief but potent dose of escapism. Emboldened, I shifted to my knees, seeking to amplify the experience, the movement less graceful than I had envisioned, nearly causing me to lose my balance.

Paddling faster than the current, small bursts of spray spritzed across my face as I paddled harder.

"Watch out for the Gorwal!" Charity's voice, laced with jest, broke through the tranquility of my imagined river adventure. Her warning came too late; the kayak rocked violently beneath me, jolting me back to the harsh reality of Clivilius. In an instant, I found myself capsizing, the dramatic overturn sending me sprawling into the unforgiving dust. The taste of grit filled my mouth, and as I coughed it out, the sound of Charity's laughter echoed in the distance, a reminder of the moment's absurdity.

Red-faced and disoriented, I scanned my surroundings, catching just a fleeting glimpse of Charity as she vanished around the corner of the last tent in the row. The embarrassment of the situation washed over me, mingled with a faint sense of amusement at the unexpected turn of events. With a heavy sigh, I picked myself up, dusting off the indignity along with the layers of dirt that clung to me. The kayak, now a vessel of my downfall, was set upright once more, the dust settling at its bottom a testament to my folly.

Playtime is over, the thought echoed in my mind, a sobering reminder of the stark realities that awaited me beyond the brief respite of my imagination. The weight of our situation, the looming threats, and the unresolved tensions within the camp pressed heavily upon me as I made my way toward where Charity had disappeared.

As I rounded the corner of the final tent, the sight that greeted me was one of sombre reflection. Charity stood by the river, engaged in conversation with Beatrix and Jamie. The heaviness in my heart grew as I approached, the sight of Jamie still clutching Duke tight a visceral reminder of the loss we had all suffered. The churn in my stomach mirrored the turmoil of emotions that gripped me—grief for Duke, concern for Joel, and a pervasive sense of uncertainty about what lay ahead.

As I edged closer, the snippets of conversation I caught were enough to send a chill through me. Beatrix's question, filled with a mix of fear and disbelief, hung heavily in the air. "Do you think somebody in the camp killed Duke?" Her voice, though meant to be a whisper, carried the weight of our collective anxiety and suspicion.

"Nobody that you know," Charity's response was cryptic, hinting at a complexity to our situation that we were only just beginning to unravel.

What do you mean?" The question from Beatrix and Jamie, voiced together, underscored the growing unease. "There's someone here that we don't know?" Jamie added.

"A Portal pirate," I found myself interjecting, stepping forward to join the conversation. The words felt heavy on my tongue, the revelation of this new threat a burden I had reluctantly agreed to bear. This knowledge, shared with me by Charity, had placed an invisible weight upon my shoulders—the responsibility of guarding this secret while assessing the potential danger it posed to our community.

"What the actual fuck?" Jamie's reaction was a mirror to the shock and confusion we all felt, his eyes wide with disbelief as he processed the implications of my words.

Charity elaborated on the nature of our unseen adversary. "He's likely lost and has been separated from his partner. Some danger must have befallen one of them before they could execute the location registration. They're always in pairs. Never work alone." Her explanation, while informative, did little to assuage the growing fear. "Cunning and violent bastards when they're together, but alone, they can be brute savages. Their instinct for hunting and survival runs deep."

Swallowing a deep sigh, a reaction I desperately wanted to unleash in response to Charity's harrowing insights, I steered our conversation back to a subject that, while still grave, felt more immediate and tangible. "Charity managed to kill one of the beasts last night. It's at the camp if you want to see it."

Jamie's reaction was swift and definitive, a fierce shake of his head indicating his refusal to entertain the thought. Yet, driven by a strange compulsion to share, I pressed on, the words tumbling out with an odd mix of excitement and dread. "She wounded another, and it appears, somehow, that a third shadow panther managed to follow Beatrix through the Portal to Earth." The gravity of this information, the implications of such a creature loose on Earth, seemed momentarily lost on me, caught up as I was in the narrative unfolding.

Jamie's attention snapped to me, a flicker of hope in his eyes that was as surprising as it was misplaced.

Regret washed over me instantly, a bitter realisation that I had ventured into territory best left unexplored. *I should have known better than to bring that up*, I admonished myself silently, feeling the weight of my insensitivity.

"It doesn't change anything for you," Charity's voice cut through the tension, her words a blunt reminder of the stark reality Jamie faced. Her hand on his shoulder was a gesture of comfort, yet the message she delivered was anything but soothing. "You'll never leave Clivilius alive."

Seizing upon a thread of hope, however misguided, I interjected, "But I think Duke can. You could have Luke take him to be buried on Earth?"

"Fuck no!" Jamie's response was a torrent of anger, the injustice of the suggestion igniting a fire within him. "It's not fair on Henri. Duke belongs here now. We'll find a suitable place to bury him here, today." His words were a declaration, a fierce refusal to entertain the notion of parting with Duke in such a manner.

My efforts to navigate the conversation, to offer some form of consolation or solution, had only served to exacerbate the pain and division among us. With a silent nod, I acknowledged Jamie's decision, the futility of my intervention becoming painfully clear.

"That's not possible to bury him," Charity's words cut through the heavy air with a finality that left me grappling for a response. *What now?* The question echoed within me, a silent wish for Charity's silence in the face of Jamie's palpable grief.

Yet, Charity seemed oblivious to the turmoil her words had incited, pressing on with a rationale that, while logical, felt like a cold splash of reality on our mourning. "You have no walls, no protection. Burying him will only attract creatures much worse than shadow panthers and Portal pirates."

I give up, I conceded inwardly, the weight of her logic undeniable yet unwelcome. "What then?" I asked, my voice barely a whisper, bracing for the answer I feared would come.

"You'll need to cremate his body." The suggestion, though pragmatic, felt like a betrayal, a final severance of Duke's physical connection to this world that none of us were prepared to face.

I knew I shouldn't have asked! The thought was a torment, a prelude to Jamie's vehement reaction. "Like fuck we will!"

His outcry, fierce and desperate, was a raw expression of his refusal to accept Charity's suggestion.

"Don't worry, Duke. I won't let them destroy any trace that you ever existed." Jamie's tender whisper to the lifeless form he held was a heartbreaking affirmation of his promise, a vow to preserve Duke's memory against all odds.

"Jamie," I ventured, my own voice laden with empathy for his loss, "we don't have a lot of options here." The attempt to bridge understanding, to offer solace amidst the harsh dictates of our survival, felt like navigating a minefield of emotion and resistance.

"No," Jamie's defiance was a wall, impenetrable and resolute. "We're not burning Duke." His words, a declaration of his stance, left no room for compromise, his determination to protect Duke's memory an immovable force.

In a gesture of desperation, I spread my arms wide, encompassing the vast, unforgiving landscape that had become our home, our prison. The gesture was an appeal to reason, to the blunt reality of our situation that offered little in the way of easy choices.

Beatrix and Charity, each adding their voices to the tumultuous debate, created a cacophony of dissent and desperation. The discussion, now a battleground of conflicting emotions and survival instincts, underscored the complexity of our plight. In this desolate expanse, under the shadow of threats both known and unknown, the debate over Duke's final rest was more than a disagreement; it was a microcosm of our struggle to maintain our humanity, to honour our bonds, in a world that demanded unceasing vigilance and adaptation.

Glenda's voice, edged with panic, sliced through the tense atmosphere. "Has anyone seen Joel this morning?" The concern in her voice was palpable, a sharp contrast to the heated debate that had just been consuming us. My body tensed, a reflexive reaction to the sudden shift in concern, as I scrambled mentally to recall any sighting of Joel since dawn.

"I've been with Jamie since I arrived," Beatrix's response, while immediate, offered no reassurance.

A sense of unease settled over me as I searched my own memories, coming up empty. "I've not seen him at all this morning," I admitted, a knot of worry forming in my stomach. The assumption that Joel was simply resting, safe within the confines of his tent, suddenly seemed naïve. "I just assumed he was still resting in his tent. Is he not there?"

Glenda's negative response, her head shake a silent harbinger of fear, sent a chill down my spine. The realisation that Joel was missing, truly missing, turned the morning's tension into a pressing emergency.

The situation escalated as Jamie, overwhelmed by the compounded stress of Duke's loss and now Joel's disappearance, collapsed.

"Jamie!" Our voices merged in a chorus of alarm as we converged to assist him, the urgency of the moment temporarily binding our frayed edges.

Kneeling beside Jamie, Glenda's swift assessment spoke to her competence and calm in the face of crisis. Her directive to me, "Gather everyone to the campfire," was a clear command, pulling me from the shock-induced paralysis that had momentarily taken hold.

With a nod, I acted on Glenda's instruction, my body responding with a readiness that belied the turmoil within. The quick pivot and stride back to the campfire were automatic, driven by the need to unite our group in the face of this new crisis.

❖

"That thing is still hideous," I couldn't help but comment loudly as my gaze drifted back to the shadow panther's corpse lying ominously beside the campfire. The reminder of last night's terror seemed even more grotesque in the light of day.

"And it's beginning to stink revoltingly already," Karen's voice pulled me away from the grim sight, her expression a mix of disgust and apprehension as she emerged from her tent. "I've never smelt something so deathly before." Her words hung in the air, a testament to the unsettling presence of death that had invaded our sanctuary.

My brow furrowed in thought. *What does death smell like?* The question lingered in my mind, uninvited. Duke's passing hadn't brought with it an overwhelming stench, or perhaps my senses had been too numbed by grief to notice.

"Are you okay, Paul?" Karen's concern broke through my reverie, her cautious approach signalling a genuine worry for my well-being.

I shook off the distracting thoughts, chiding myself internally. *Focus, Paul!* The urgency of our current situation demanded my full attention. "Have you seen Joel this morning?" I redirected, bypassing Karen's inquiry about my state. Our missing companion's whereabouts were of paramount importance.

Karen paused, her fingers tracing lines of thought across her forehead as she dredged her memory for any sign of Joel. "No," she admitted after a moment. "I don't think I've seen him since we were all at the campfire last night." Her confirmation, while expected, did little to ease the growing knot of worry in my stomach.

"That's what I feared... and Chris and Kain?" I probed further, their absence at the campsite adding another layer of concern to the already tense atmosphere.

"They're at the lagoon." Karen's response caught me off guard, a surge of surprise and apprehension washing over me. *Surely, they know the risks?*

"Chris is helping to clean Kain's wounded leg. Glenda thinks the water may actually speed up the healing process," Karen elaborated, offering a rationale that did little to quell my concern for their safety.

"That doesn't surprise me," I acknowledged, my thoughts drifting back to a painful yet revealing moment by the river with Glenda. Her unconventional methods, though often met with skepticism, had proven effective more than once. "Regardless, can you go and bring them back to camp, please Karen." My request was firm, a reflection of the importance I placed on regrouping as we faced the uncertainty of Joel's disappearance and the ominous threat that still loomed over us.

"What? Now?" Karen's incredulity was palpable, her reaction a mirror to the sudden urgency I had imposed. The timing, given Kain's condition and the myriad of challenges we were already facing, seemed less than ideal to her.

"Yes, now." My response was firm, underscored by a sense of immediacy that couldn't be ignored, despite the ongoing concerns with Kain's leg and the broader safety of our camp.

"But Kain's leg..." Karen began, her protest highlighting the practical challenges of pulling everyone away from their current tasks.

"I'll make it brief, I promise." The assurance was as much for her as it was for me, a verbal commitment to expedite the process in light of the pressing matters at hand.

Karen's head tilted, her silence loaded with unspoken questions. *Make what brief?* The underlying query was clear, even if unvoiced, reflecting her struggle to understand the rationale behind my urgent request.

"We need to do a final headcount," I explained, attempting to project a confidence I was far from feeling. The act of rolling back my shoulders and standing tall was as much an effort to convince myself as it was to reassure Karen.

"Why?" Her confusion was evident, the sudden shift in priorities seemingly coming from nowhere.

"Joel appears to be missing." The words hung heavy between us, the gravity of the situation slowly dawning on Karen.

Eyes widening as the realisation fully sunk in, Karen nodded, her initial resistance giving way to a shared sense of urgency. Without further delay, she quickly left for the lagoon, her strides purposeful as she moved to carry out the instruction.

I continued watching her until she vanished beyond the first dusty hill, a silent sentinel wrestling with a mixture of worry and resolve. The weight of responsibility pressed heavily upon my shoulders, the task of ensuring everyone's safety a daunting challenge amidst the unpredictable dangers of Clivilius. In that moment, as Karen disappeared from view, the solitude of my position was acutely felt—a lone figure tasked with rallying our small band of survivors, each step forward a testament to the hope that somehow, we would navigate through the perils that lay in wait and emerge together, unbroken.

❖

A mumbled voice abruptly halted my internal debate, causing me to spin around. "Ahh, Beatrix!" Relief momentarily lifted the weight off my shoulders as I spotted her making her way through the camp, her slow shuffle kicking up small clouds of ochre dust.

"What do you want?" Her voice was gruff, laden with the exhaustion that seemed to permeate our camp.

"I've sent Karen to the lagoon to fetch Chris and Kain. Hopefully, Joel found his way there, too. You've still not seen him?" My question was tinged with hope, albeit faint, clinging to the possibility that Joel had simply wandered off and found refuge with our other campmates.

"No," Beatrix's terse response dashed that hope.

A wave of frustration washed over me, my annoyance not directed at Beatrix but at myself. *Injuries, death and now a missing person... and it's barely been a few days!* The thought was a harsh indictment of our current state, a reflection of the myriad challenges we faced in Clivilius, each day seeming to unfold with a new crisis.

"Which tent is Jamie's?" Beatrix's inquiry momentarily diverted my train of thought. "He needs clean clothes." Her practical concern was a grounding force, pulling me back from the edge of despair.

"Follow me," I responded, motioning towards Jamie's tent, grateful for the distraction from my own spiralling thoughts.

As we approached the tent, I held back the front flap for Beatrix, a simple gesture of courtesy that felt disproportionately significant in the moment.

"Impressive," Beatrix's voice softened as she took in the interior of the tent, her initial observation cut short by my interjection.

"They're ten-man tents," I explained, almost mechanically. "Almost military grade." The description was factual, a straightforward statement that belied the complexity of emotions I felt. Offering this piece of information, though trivial in the grand scheme of things, was an attempt to anchor myself to something concrete, a detail that was unchanging in a world where everything else seemed to be in constant flux.

A loud grunt, incongruous with the sombre mood of the tent, drew our attention downwards to Henri. The small, chubby dog sat there, his gaze lifting forlornly to meet ours, a picture of dejection that tugged at my heartstrings.

"He looks so sad," the words escaped me in a whisper, my squat beside Henri an instinctive response to his apparent melancholy.

"He's hungry," Beatrix's scoff cut through the quiet, her tone a mix of amusement and realism. "Don't mistake that resting bitch face for sadness. I've seen that gluttonous look in his eyes many times." Her interpretation of Henri's expression, so different from my own, was a reminder of how easily human emotions could be projected onto animals.

Henri's yapping, a sound filled with impatience and perhaps a hint of indignation, followed by the swishing of his fox-like tail across the tent floor, seemed to underscore Beatrix's assessment. The dog's behaviour, so characteristically petulant, brought a faint smile to my lips despite the weight of recent events.

"Come on, Henri," I urged, standing up and moving towards the collection of bags stored along the wall of the right wing of the tent, intent on finding something to satiate his hunger.

"I'll feed him," Beatrix quickly took charge, her brisk movement towards the pair of empty food bowls drawing Henri's eager attention.

Rummaging through the bags, I found an unopened tin of dog food. "Here, catch," I called out to Beatrix, tossing it towards her with a flick of my wrist.

Beatrix caught the tin, pausing only briefly to read the label before Henri's impatient yapping urged her to haste. The sound of the pull-ring breaking the seal of the can released a strong beef and gravy aroma into the tent, a smell so surprisingly appealing that it momentarily distracted me from the pangs of my own hunger.

"That almost smells good," I chuckled, a hand unconsciously rubbing my stomach as it reminded me of my own neglected need for sustenance.

Henri's loud snort, whether in agreement or impatience, was a sound so thoroughly grounded in the present, a reminder of life's simpler needs.

"Hey, Beatrix!" My voice echoed slightly in the spacious tent as I beckoned her from the left wing—the designated sleeping quarters—curiosity piqued by something unusual I had stumbled upon.

Wandering over with a hint of reluctance, Beatrix's inquiry was laced with skepticism. "What am I looking at?" she asked, her gaze following mine to the ground.

Crouched beside the mattress, my index finger hovered over the canvas floor, pointing out several small droplets that seemed out of place. "Does this look like blood to you?" The question felt more serious than speculative, the implications of my discovery not yet fully understood.

Beatrix squatted beside me, the stench of the empty food tin momentarily forgotten as she scrutinised the droplets. "I guess it could be," she conceded, her uncertainty mirroring my own.

Disappointment washed over me, not so much at the ambiguity of her response but at the missed opportunity for clarity. "I would have thought you'd be able to give a more certain answer given how much blood you've seen recently," I remarked, a comment I regretted almost as soon as it left my lips.

Her eyes rolled in response, a clear sign of her annoyance as she disregarded my comment and moved toward the suitcases and bags, dismissing the conversation entirely.

Realising the insensitivity of my words, I hurried to apologise. "I'm sorry, Beatrix. I didn't mean it like that."

"It's fine," Beatrix snapped back, her terseness indicating anything but.

Just drop it now, Paul, I admonished myself silently. Acknowledging the need to let the matter rest, I was silently thankful that the exchange hadn't spiralled into a full-blown argument. The thought of how differently this might have unfolded with Claire stung with a pang of regret for the friction that often characterised our interactions.

Turning my focus back to the suspicious droplets by the mattress, the gravity of our situation settled heavily upon me. "I think Joel's in real trouble. We're just not equipped to survive out here." The words were heavy with resignation, a sobering acknowledgment of our precarious existence in Clivilius.

Beatrix's head snapped up as she turned in my direction. "There's a bunch of camping gear and related shit piled in Luke's living room."

"Really?" The surprise in my voice was genuine, a spark of hope ignited by the prospect of additional resources.

"It's where that kayak came from," she reminded me, tying the pieces together in my mind. "I think some of it may have got a bit damaged during the shadow panther attack last night, but I can bring you everything that's there anyway."

My enthusiasm was palpable. "That'd be great," I responded, feeling a renewed sense of purpose. The responsibility of leadership felt less burdensome with each potential solution that presented itself. "We'll sort that out once we've decided what to do about Joel."

"And Duke," Beatrix interjected.

The mention of Duke instantly dampened my spirits. "It's really sad that we can't give Duke a proper burial," I admitted, the weight of our situation settling back upon my shoulders.

Beatrix's silence as she collected a handful of clothes was punctuated by her parting words at the archway, "Jamie won't let you cremate him." Her brisk exit left me in a momentary lull of introspection. *Is Beatrix mad at me?* The question lingered, unanswered, as I debated the undercurrents of tension that had woven themselves into our interactions.

Compelled to address the issue head-on, I followed her out of the tent. "Charity is right, Beatrix," I began, stepping into the open air, the tent flap falling closed behind me. The assertion was my attempt to bridge the gap, to find a middle ground in our differing views on handling Duke's remains.

"You take charge of it then," Beatrix's response, sharp and dismissive, was a clear challenge to my leadership. Her abrupt departure, a swift turn on her heels and a brisk walk away, left me standing in the aftermath of our exchange, pondering the complexities of leading a group through such unprecedented circumstances.

Glenda's quizzical look caught me off guard as she suddenly materialised a few feet away. In my head, I couldn't help but silently question her sudden appearance, though outwardly, I remained composed. *Where the heck did you come from?* The thought lingered, unanswered, as we both turned our attention to the more pressing matter at hand.

"The dog needs to be cremated," Charity declared firmly from beside the campfire. Her movements were deliberate, cleaning her bloodied blade on a leather tassel of her skirt before sheathing it with an air of finality that left no room for dispute.

My gaze shifted between Charity and Glenda, the former's statement hanging heavily in the air. *I'm not going to be the one to argue with the woman with a bloodied knife,* my eyes silently communicated to Glenda, hoping she'd pick up on my reluctance to challenge Charity's assertion directly.

Fortunately, the tension was broken by the approach of familiar figures in the distance. "Look, it's Karen and Chris returning with Kain," I announced, grateful for the distraction. Their progress towards us was slow, yet there was a palpable sense of relief at their safe return.

"And Lois," Glenda's tone softened noticeably as she crouched to welcome the bounding dog, her actions a brief respite from the earlier tension.

As Karen, Chris, and Kain finally closed the distance, their camaraderie was evident. Kain's announcement, "The feeling has returned in my uninjured leg," caught me by surprise. *Had it ever been gone?* I wondered, my brow arching in response.

"Well, that's a relief," Glenda responded, as she stood back up. Her inquiry about his other leg was both professional and filled with genuine concern.

"Seems to be quite the miracle," Karen added as they came to a stop near the campfire.

Crouching in front of Kain, Glenda's focus was entirely on the wound as she carefully examined it. The sight sparked a train of thought that had been lingering in the back of my mind. *Jamie, Joel, Kain, and myself. That's four of us now that have had rather miraculous wound recoveries,* I mused silently. The healing properties of the water in Clivilius were something akin to a marvel, yet a sombre realisation followed closely. *So, why couldn't the waters help Duke? Are animals excluded?* The question hung heavily, a shadow of doubt amidst the glimmers of hope we'd found in our strange new world.

As Glenda rose to her feet, her professional demeanour never wavered. "You'll still need to give it plenty of rest," she advised Kain, her tone a blend of authority and concern.

"We can make you some crutches," Chris offered, his suggestion born out of a genuine desire to help. He shifted his weight to better support Kain, whose arm was draped across Chris's shoulders.

"Forget making crutches," Karen interjected with a huff, her voice cutting through the air. "Just get Luke to bring us some real ones." Her practicality, often blunt, was in this moment a beacon of common sense, pointing us towards a more straightforward solution.

"That's a much better idea..." Glenda's voice trailed off, echoing the solution that had crystallised in my mind. But before she could finish her thought, her attention shifted, prompting me to follow her gaze. My eyes landed on Beatrix and Jamie as they reappeared from behind the tents. Jamie was cradling a small bundle in his arms, a sight that tugged at my heartstrings, the weight of recent events pressing down on me. Yet, amidst the turmoil, a reminder of my role within this group whispered encouragement. *You are their leader.*

Straightening my back as a physical manifestation of my resolve, I addressed Jamie, my voice betraying the emotional turmoil I sought to conceal. "Jamie," I began, only to be interrupted by a cough as my voice cracked under the strain. "I know things are a bit painful right now, but we need to know when you last saw Joel."

Jamie's abrupt stop and the ensuing silence that enveloped us were palpable. My heart raced as I waited for his response, the silence stretching into an almost tangible barrier between us. When Jamie finally spoke, revealing the last time he saw Joel was just before the shadow panther attack, a chill ran down my spine. The implications of his words were clear, yet the uncertainty of Joel's fate lingered like a dense fog.

"And when you returned?" The question hung heavily in the air, my hesitation giving way to a forced steadiness as I sought to uncover the truth. Jamie's subsequent expression, a mix of resignation and sorrow, accompanied by a simple shrug, spoke volumes. Words failed him, but his message was clear.

"Then it's settled," Glenda declared, her voice cutting through the tension, her posture one of nervous determination. "Joel is missing." Her statement, though stark, was a necessary acknowledgment of our predicament.

I gulped, feeling the weight of events crash into me like a wave. *This is all really happening,* I realised, the acknowledgment hitting me with a palpable force that seemed to compress the air around my chest.

Charity, with a presence that commanded attention, stepped forward. Her voice was not just confident but imbued with a strength that seemed to anchor us. "I am certain Joel has been taken by the Portal pirate. I will hunt him down and bring Joel back." The mention of the Portal pirate, a shadowy figure that had loomed over us since Joel's disappearance, sent a shiver down my spine. *Not this bloody Portal pirate again,* I thought despairingly. As if the shadow panthers weren't a sufficient testament to our nightmarish reality.

"I'm coming with you," Jamie blurted out, his voice cutting through the tension with a raw determination that caught me off guard.

Charity's nod was solemn. "Prepare your things. We leave immediately." The decisiveness in her tone left no room for doubt or hesitation.

The terror that flickered in Jamie's eyes, however, revealed the conflict raging within him. His gaze dropped to Duke, the bundle in his arms, a silent testament to the grief that was consuming him.

Charity, understanding the stakes, closed the distance between them with a few purposeful strides. Lifting Jamie's chin gently but firmly, she locked eyes with him. "If you want any chance of finding Joel alive, we must leave immediately." Her words, though spoken with a steely resolve, carried an undercurrent of empathy that underscored the urgency of our situation.

I bit my lower lip, wrestling with the urge to step in, to offer some form of solace, yet knowing deep down that this was a moment for Jamie to confront on his own terms.

"I need to say farewell to Duke first," Jamie's voice broke, the words barely more than a whisper, yet they reverberated with a profound sadness that seemed to echo the collective heartache of our group.

Charity's gaze never wavered, her eyes holding Jamie's with an intensity that was almost palpable. "Life is full of decisions and consequences, Jamie," she said, her voice steady and devoid of warmth. "You need to make a choice: Joel or Duke." The starkness of her words, the ultimatum she presented, was a harsh reminder of the brutal truths we were all grappling with.

That moment, witnessing Jamie's heartbreak and the unbearable decision he faced, shattered the last vestiges of my resolve. I closed my eyes, desperately trying to escape the scene unfolding before me. Yet, the darkness offered no refuge; instead, it conjured a haunting question that echoed through the depths of my soul. *Charlie or your children? Or worse, Mack or Rose?* The thought was a blade, slicing through the fragile barrier I had erected to protect myself from the reality of our existence in Clivilius.

Forced to confront the tormenting prospect of such impossible choices, my eyes flew open, seeking escape from the prison of my thoughts. The sight that greeted me—Jamie, with a silent nod, entrusting Duke to Beatrix—was a poignant reminder of the sacrifices we were all being compelled to make. Beatrix's gentle hands taking Duke from

Jamie was a tableau of sorrow and resignation that gripped my heart with a merciless ferocity.

"Duke knows you love him, Jamie. He won't ever forget that," Beatrix's voice broke through the heavy air, laden with tears that mirrored the grief etched deep within all of us.

Jamie's final act of love, a kiss placed on Duke's shrouded form, accompanied by his whispered apology, was a testament to the depth of his anguish. "I'm so sorry, Duke," he murmured, a farewell laced with regret and love.

I won't make that choice! I silently railed against the inevitability of such decisions. The thought of Mack and Rose, safely ensconced on Earth, was a balm to my battered spirit, a reminder of why I endured, why I fought so hard to maintain my humanity in this unforgiving world.

Jamie's resolve, as he announced his intention to prepare for the journey, was a stark contrast to the turmoil that had just unfolded. "I'll grab my things," he declared, his voice steadier than I would have thought possible.

But the quiet whisper of Clivilius, insidious and unyielding, challenged my defiance. *But you already have made the choice,* it murmured, a reminder that the decisions we faced here were not confined to the immediate or the physical. They were battles fought within the recesses of our hearts and minds, each choice a reflection of the sacrifices we were willing to make for those we loved.

Jamie's sudden halt and the glance he cast over his shoulder were laden with an emotion that words could scarcely convey. "Take good care of Henri for me," his voice carried a mixture of hope and resignation, a final plea before embarking on a perilous quest.

I stepped forward, feeling a surge of protective resolve as I scooped the full-bellied dog into my arms. "We'll keep him safe, Jamie. You have my word." My assurance was more than a promise; it was a vow, a commitment that transcended the current crisis.

Jamie's departure, with Charity at his side, marked a moment of silent solidarity among us. Their figures, moving towards the tent, symbolised not just a mission to retrieve our lost friend but also the sacrifices we were all prepared to make for one another.

The voice in my head, however, refused to grant me peace, probing the depths of my fears and uncertainties with relentless precision. *Where are your children now?* It echoed, a haunting reminder of the choices I had made—choices that felt increasingly like gambles with stakes too high to comprehend.

My frustration mounted, the internal debate raging within me. I pulled Henri closer, seeking comfort in the warmth of his presence. The physical act of holding him, feeling his heartbeat against mine, was a temporary balm for the turmoil that churned inside.

They can't survive here, I countered the voice's insinuations, clinging to the belief that I had made the right decision for Mack and Rose. The conviction that Clivilius was no place for them was unwavering, a pillar of my resolve amidst the storm of doubts.

Are you certain they can survive on Earth? The question struck with the precision of an arrow, piercing the armour of certainty I had clad myself in. The world I had left behind was far from perfect, fraught with its own dangers and uncertainties. The realisation that safety was a relative term, that the challenges awaiting us on either side of the Portal were merely different facets of the same struggle for survival, was both sobering and terrifying.

"Clivilius!" The sound of Glenda's scream pierced the air, the intensity of her emotion grounding her to her knees as she pounded the earth beneath her in a display of raw, unfiltered distress.

What the hell's going on? The question echoed through my mind, a tumult of confusion and concern as my gaze locked onto the doctor, her actions painting a picture of torment I couldn't immediately understand.

As Glenda raised her head, her eyes, wide with a mixture of shock and revelation, caught mine. The transformation in her expression was startling—a mixture of pain and elation that seemed almost too intense to be contained within a single moment.

Taking a cautious step forward, I ventured, "Glenda, are you alright?" The concern in my voice was genuine, the bizarre turn of events leaving me grappling for understanding.

The wild flame that ignited behind Glenda's eyes was unsettling, her gaze fixed on me with an intensity that felt almost otherworldly. The grin that slowly spread across her face was equally disconcerting, morphing her features into a mask of eerie jubilation that seemed to consume her entire visage.

Eyeing Glenda with a mix of worry and bewilderment, I couldn't help but wonder about the nature of her distress. *Was this a medical emergency, or something even more inexplicable?* In Clivilius, the line between reality and the unimaginable was perpetually blurred, leaving room for endless possibilities.

"My father is alive!" The declaration burst from Glenda with a force that seemed to propel her physically, her hands reaching skyward as if in celebration of some miraculous revelation.

Gobsmacked, I could only stare, trying to process the sudden shift from despair to triumph. Glenda's trance-like state, her eyes unseeing yet filled with an indescribable fervour, left me at a loss. Even Chris' attempt to capture her attention, his hand waving futilely in front of her unresponsive gaze, did nothing to break her from her reverie.

Out of the corner of my eye, a flicker of movement snagged my attention away from the unfolding drama with Glenda. "Where the hell is she going?" I muttered under my breath, a mix of confusion and frustration colouring my tone. Beatrix, with Duke cradled in her arms, seemed to be meandering away from the camp's centre of gravity—away from us. "Beatrix, where are you going?" My voice carried across the distance, aimed at her retreating figure.

"Home!" The word exploded back at me, Beatrix's shout slicing through the air with a decisiveness that left me momentarily speechless.

"What? Now? What do you mean?" My confusion escalated into a shout, my attempt to bridge the physical and emotional distance between us abruptly interrupted by Kain's sudden declaration.

"I'm going with Beatrix," Kain announced, his determination breaking through the physical constraints of his injury as he clumsily disengaged from Karen's support, only to stumble to the ground.

"You need to rest," Karen's voice was a blend of concern and command, her stance firm despite Kain's defiance.

"I need crutches," Kain shot back, his frustration manifesting in a physical push against Karen's attempts to aid him.

Meanwhile, Chris's efforts to rouse Glenda from her shock —or whatever trance had seized her—were relentless but fruitless. "Glenda... Glenda," he repeated, a mantra of concern.

Amidst the chaos, Lois, ever the loyal companion, rose on her hind legs, pressing her front paws against me as if seeking to anchor the moment. Her bark, followed by a playful nudge of Henri's back paws, added another layer of complexity to the scene.

"Lois, down!" I commanded, struggling to maintain my grip on Henri, who squirmed restlessly in my arms. The challenge of managing the dogs mirrored the larger turmoil enveloping our group.

Turning my gaze back to Beatrix, I caught sight of her figure scaling the first dune, her progress relentless. The sight of her, so determined, so singular in her purpose, struck a chord within me. The camp, our makeshift sanctuary, was unraveling at the seams, each of us pulled in different directions by our fears, hopes, and the instinctual drive to find safety, to protect those we cared for.

"Oh my God!" The words slipped out in a hiss as I struggled to manage the turmoil unfolding around me. Closing my eyes for a brief moment, I lifted Henri away from Lois, whose playful antics felt wildly out of place amidst the unfolding mayhem. My mind was a battlefield, thoughts and worries clashing in a relentless storm. *With Joel missing, suspected foul play, Jamie imminently departing to hunt a Portal pirate, Beatrix and Duke heading toward the Portal, Karen and Kain arguing, and Chris unable to wake Glenda from her hypnotic state,* I cataloged the pandemonium that had engulfed our camp. *This camp has descended into utter chaos! Can it possibly get any worse?*

In that moment of overwhelming despair, the piercing voice of Clivilius cut through the tumult of my thoughts, bringing with it an intense burning in my chest—a physical manifestation of the emotional and psychological strain I was under. *Be brave, Paul. Now, more than ever, your people need their strong leader.*